INDIAN HILL 2: CONQUEST

Mark Tufo

Dedications: To my wife, you make all of this happen. Without you, my muse, I would have REAMS of nice clean unused white paper!

To Katherine Coynor, whose tireless work and super human eye for detail has helped to make this book as good as I can get it.

A special thank you to Lauren Dietz whose beautiful picture graces most chapter headers.

As always to the brave men and women of the United States Military, Thank you all for your sacrifice to our Great Nation.

Table Of Contents

Characters:

Michael Talbot - Captain UEMC
Drababan - Genogerian champion
Beth MacAvoy - Mike's girlfriend before his capture
Sgt O'Bannon - Helped Deb and Beth
Deborah Carody - Mike's lover on the alien vessel
Paul Ginson - Mike's best friend and leader of the resistance.
Maj Frank Salazar - Good friend of Paul, second in command
ISC Kuvlar - Interim commander of the Julipion
Sub-Commander Tuvok - second in command on ship
Sub-Commander Krulak - replaced by Tuvok
Julipion - Scout Mother-ship
Devastators - Mutated Genogerian soldiers
Max - 11 year old that helps Beth
Sammie - youth driver
Sgt/Lt Tracy Yarborough - Led mission to save Mike
Boady 'Pegged' - Hunting Beth
Dennis - Best friend of Mike and Paul, Captain UEMC
Spindler - Mike and Paul's old High School principal
Supreme Commander Vallezt - Kidnap victim of Mike
Capt. Moiraine - Spy in Paul's encampment
Urlack - Progerian-Genogerian hybrid
Iserwan Durenge - Progerian Fighter pilot
Eastern Seaboard Commanders:
HQ - Devastator Commander - Turval
S/W of Boston - Ground Commander Chofla
Ground Sub-Commander Ruthgar

N/W of Boston - Ground Commander Pantherd
Ground Sub-Commander Brocklle

And So It Ends...

CHAPTER ONE – Mike Journal Entry 1

Two weeks, two fucking weeks I spent in a hyperbolic chamber as the aliens did their medicinal magic on my shattered teeth, broken jaw, ribs, nose, left orbital socket, detached retina and a slight break in my shin. So the fucker had broken my leg when I took out his airway. Son of a bitch that he is—I mean was.

"I've learned a new term from your race, Mr. Talbot...tenacious."

My head swiveled to see from which area the voice came from. My gaze rested on a small speaker box set in the left side of my now semi-permanent home.

"It's me, Mike." The small metal box issued forth, as if that were enough explanation. I had thought about answering but the mere thought of moving my jaw made me think twice. I had no desire to revisit that pain.

"It is I, your doctor (he said it like I would remember him), and you can talk. You're jaw is almost completely healed. I must say that you hu-mans truly are a resilient species. Although not quite as hardy as the Progerians or even the Genogerians, yet you still seem to bounce back quickly from damage."

"I'm glad that I can be of service, Doc," I said sarcastically and not much above a whisper. The doc might be right, but I wanted to be sure the parts moved well and without much pain before I started doing any operatic arias.

"You truly are a unique species, both delicate and strong at the same time. A small instrument inserted in the right spot can stop your heart in a moment but yet you can survive having nearly every bone broken in your body. You talk about you're loathing of violence and warfare, yet it pervades every aspect of your culture, your entire civilization is predicated on warfare. You talk of equality of all humankind while you step on the necks of those below you. Your art, your music, your spirituality have almost no rivals among the known universe, but the vast majority of your kind would trade it all away for individual gain. You are altruistic to a fault, while self-preservation reigns supreme."

"Are you done with the semantics lesson, Doc? I'm still not feeling all that well."

"Right, right...well, that's not really what I wanted to discuss anyway. I was just musing. I am writing my report for the home world. They will be very curious about your species and we should have some record of it."

The implication was unsettling. The doc hadn't talked about it, but there it was out in the open. They wanted a record of us before we became extinct. "Doc, get to the point, or you're going to be talking while I'm sleeping." I had no desire to humor this being. Sure, he was one of the few that had been something sort of decent, but when it really came down to it, it had only been for his personal gain. It's great to know that greed could travel the star systems, as well.

"Yes, I just wanted to let you know that I bet everything that I had won on your previous bouts on this last fight. And at twenty-six to one odds, I came away with more drakkar than my offsprings' offspring could spend. I will be able to, as you hu-mans call it, 'retire'."

"Wow, Doc, I can't tell you how happy for you I am."

"Why thank you, Mike. Coming from you, that is actually great news."

"Whatever, Doc. But what does that do for me?"

"Do for you? Why nothing, hu-man. I came here only to let you know that you have bettered my life. Unfortunately for you, your time will be up in another week or so."

I sat up so fast, I was rewarded with a solid thunking of my head on the top of the chamber.

"I'm guessing by your reaction that you have no idea what I'm talking about."

"Oh, I know what you mean. I just didn't think that it would be that quick."

"If it's any consolation, I'm not betting any money on Drababan, either. He should be able to kill you in under ten seconds, but I've watched you far too many times to believe you are as far an underdog at which the odds-makers have you. Which is actually at two hundred fifty to one."

"Wow, that close?" From the silence through the box I knew the doctor was still trying to process my words. He probably thought I misunderstood what he had said.

"Well, okay…" he muttered. "I will let you sleep now. The healing medicines work much better when the patient sleeps. It has to do with the relaxation of the endocrine system."

I heard the intercom system shut down and then the lights in the chamber dimmed as if in response to the doctor's words. Hell, what did I know, that was probably exactly what happened. As much as I tried to fight sleep, I needed to think about how I was going to get out of this situation; consciousness eluded me. My dreams were filled with despair—sorrow and an aching that went deep down into the recesses of my brain. Even if by some small miracle I survived the ordeal, I would be a broken man, a shell of the person that I had the potential to become. Soon even self-pity faded away.

I washed up on a beach of golden sand and the

brilliant red of a sunset. It had been Heaven, of that I was sure upon waking many hours later. But why was I being shown that, was it in preparation for my soon-to-be earthly departure? There was no way I rated a spot in nirvana, though, I had done things for which there was no absolution; why was God tormenting me this way? Was he showing me what my loss of humanity had lost me in the afterworld? Had my brief pathetic stay in life cost me my afterlife? Or was he showing me there was still hope for my soul?

I wept for hours upon waking, even as my glimpse of Heaven began to fade from my waking. There was still hope; I came away with that, if nothing else.

CHAPTER TWO

Beth had traipsed through the woods the majority of the night; it was fear that drove her. Not fear of the woods, although that did unsettle her some. It was the fear of what was behind, glimpses of the Sergeant's bloated body haunted her every move. That, and the man's head she had so neatly dissolved; add to that the fact that she missed Deborah. The girls had become fast friends in their mutual shared agony.

Beth couldn't take it anymore; she stumbled toward a fallen tree and slouched down, her ass making a solid thud as she wept into her hands. Hunger, pain, and despair took over. Beth sobbed until she felt certain she had completely wrung out her soul, and then she cried some more. Afterward she slept, a soulless, dead sleep, no dreams permeated her mind for if they had they most assuredly would have been dark and oh so regrettably unforgettable. She awoke sometime after midnight, the sky was black—but not as dark as her soul, she figured. However, what disturbed her was the silence, or better yet, the absence of sound.

The woods were deathly silent, nothing stirred. But there was something out there, she couldn't see it, she couldn't smell it but she knew it was out there all the same. *A deer maybe?* Even in her fantasy world she knew that wasn't the case. Deer don't make the woods go quiet. Only hunters have that effect; and with that revelation, she was now wide awake and wide-eyed. Fear didn't so much creep as it leapt into her heart. She turned her head slowly from side to side trying in vain to catch some sort of sighting of whatever was in the forest with her.

Was it the sergeant? Was his purplish blue body trying to find her and take her with him? That was insane, wasn't it? Wasn't an alien invasion two years ago considered to be an insane thought? Beth hunkered down trying to make herself as small as possible.

Crack. Something off to her left had broken a fallen branch. Her heart raced as she blindly reached out trying to grab onto anything that could be used as some semblance of a weapon. Nothing happened for ages, for eternities, whatever it was had sensed its blunder and was trying to establish if its quarry had been alerted. If the quarry had been Beth, she most assuredly had been warned, but prior warning in no way implied preparation.

"Stupid, stupid, stupid," she said softly as she pounded her head. "Why didn't I take the gun?"

That small error now took on a much greater magnitude. Something or someone was close and so far Beth had only been able to secure a handful of moss as a potential bludgeon. The crack had been close enough, but whatever was stumbling through the woods was heading in her general direction. Beth pulled her legs in close and hugged them for all they were worth. She considered running, though she knew she would be running blind and there was still the possibility that the thing out there might pass her by, but with every agonizingly slow second her hope of just that diminished.

Closer.

It approached slowly as if unsure of its location, closer all the same. Beth held her breath, whatever it was, was only feet away. She could hear it breathing, if it was a meat-eating animal, she had only a few minutes of precious life left.

There it was. It muttered a semi-silent curse. It wasn't an animal in the traditional sense, but it was a meat-eater and it was looking for her. Was it the Sergeant—was he really coming for her?

"Fuck," she heard again.

It didn't sound like the Sergeant. Who was it? And why were they out here in the middle of nowhere looking for her? Was it one of the raiders? Had someone seen her handiwork? Or was it her handiwork himself coming to seek some sort of revenge? When she was sure that he would literally fall over her feet, he moved on. She heard him walk through the woods and now that her senses were peaked he sounded like a bull in a china shop. Beth finally let her breath out, thankful for one of the few times in her life that she hadn't taken a bath in the last couple of days. Her hammering chest slowly quieted as the footfalls from her pursuer grew fainter.

"Oh, Deb, where are you?" she wept. "Mike, I need you!"

CHAPTER THREE

It had been weeks since the mother ship or for that matter any of the fighter ships had so much as blinked and Paul could not help but wonder if this was the calm before the storm. Civilization for the most part had crumbled, sure there was a viable resistance set up across the globe, but could it stand up against any sort of onslaught? Paul thought not. The best mankind could hope for was to die free. It wasn't how he had planned his life, but then he figured that it really wasn't how any of them had.

"Well, better get on with it," he said out loud.

"Sir?"

"Oh, I'm sorry, Corporal," Paul said as his addled thoughts converted back to the more streamlined and simplified of the military life. "What is it, Corporal Addison?"

"Sir, the civilians are beginning to grow restless. A growing minority of them want to go topside, they're sick of living like rats, tucked away and hidden."

"Better to be hidden, living like a rat, than shot down like a dog."

"Sir, nothing has happened for over two weeks. Maybe the worst of it is over."

"I take it, Corporal, that you are part of this growing minority?" The corporal did not respond. "Do you truly believe that our 'friends' up in the sky, after so thoroughly kicking our mightiest militaries' collective asses in a matter of days, have since decided that maybe this planet isn't worth the effort after all?"

The corporal struggled for a second. Paul couldn't completely blame him; they had all lost most of their loved ones and wanted to now try to get on with some semblance of normality.

"No, sir, I don't. But what are they waiting for?"

"Well, that's the million dollar question, isn't it? Maybe they're busy prepping their ground troops, maybe they're waiting for reinforcements, maybe they're just toying with us like a cat with a mouse. Maybe they just want to completely crush our spirits when they have our greatest champion slaughtered at the hands of their champion live as it is broadcast around the globe on the Alien Sports Network. Fuck, Corporal, I don't know, but if so much as one person attempts to go topside without explicit orders to do so, I want them detained and if they resist I want them shot. I will not have our last bastion compromised because some in our group want to go smell daisies! Do you understand, Corporal?"

"Sir, yes, sir!" The corporal snapped to attention, saluted, and about-faced to tell his girlfriend that they're topside picnic was going to have to be postponed for a while.

"Frank, I know you were listening—can you believe this shit?"

"Sir, I can. Every day the aliens do nothing, the more restless our charges get. I almost wish they'd attack so we could direct our energy somewhere."

"How go the preparations for the fight site?"

"On schedule, Paul, maybe a little ahead. I think our French friends feel a little guilt for how quickly they were willing to give Mike up."

"Good. Whatever leverage we can use on our froggy friends to make sure they get the job done right is fine with me. What have the new models listed the possibility of a successful raid at, Frank?"

"Not good, Paul. Even with our changes in tactics we're really only looking at a one in four chance in pulling this off."

"Well, let's just hope this is the fourth chance and not any of the other three."

"I'm in agreement. Oh...and one more thing, Paul." The major turned and said as he was headed out the door. Paul nodded for him to continue. "Our stores are down to two months even with rationing."

"One way or the other, Frank, I don't think we're going to need the full two months." The major nodded as he put his cover back on and headed to the civilian sectors to quell any sort of uprising that might have been rearing its ugly head.

Is any of this worth it? Paul could feel his deepest doubts surfacing. He felt powerless to stop them. Even he thought they should have the chance to breath in fresh air one last time. Throw a baseball under a beautiful blue sky once more. Hear the laughter of children as they played on a swing set. Wasn't that their right?

NO! Paul forced it down.

He knew he hadn't taken their rights away, the invaders had. He just felt that he was the last stop-gap to prevent any further loss of whatever rights they may have left. Letting them go would be tantamount to mass murder, sure not by his hands, but he would shoulder the blame all the same. While there was any semblance of hope, he would hold onto it as long as possible. To let go of the tiger's tail now would be to admit defeat, and if Mike could keep going on after all he had been through, then dammit, so could he. He would not be bested; not by the aliens, not by fate or destiny, and definitely not Mike.

"Even through all this mess." Paul laughed. "It comes down to a competition with Mike. I won't lose to him, to see that smug look of satisfaction on his face as he sees me in defeat, I would rather die at the hands of the aliens." And somewhere in the deep recesses of his mind, he knew that he would get his chance.

CHAPTER FOUR -- Mike Journal Entry 2

"How are you doing, Miike?"

I was aroused from my sleep by a butchering of my name. Was it friend or foe? My memory seemed to have taken an indirect hit during my bouts, but as the layers of unconsciousness peeled away, I was able to place a name with the face hovering over me.

"Drababani?" I'm sure I returned the butchering almost as well as my visitor.

"Close, hu-man, it is pronounced 'Dra-ba-ban'. How are your wounds?"

I had not the resolve or the strength for the barbs I felt like issuing. Or lies for that matter. My next and most likely last combatant probably knew my condition far better than I. "I still hurt, Drababan. And I feel as weak as a new born lamb."

"I do not feel pity for you, hu-man. You have proved your might over and over again. And you have fought honorably. I will feel something that Genogerians seldom do. I think that your hu-man term is regret—regret that I will have to exterminate the life force that is within you. If all of your kind battled like you, we may have moved on to a much easier confrontation."

"Confrontation? Is that what you're calling it? It was wholesale slaughter. You took us completely by surprise and have done your best to exterminate what is left." I knew what I was about to say was a lie, but if I could make this brute just stop to think for even a second it was worth it. "And you'll see what my kind can do when our backs are to the wall."

"To the wall? I do not understand, hu-man."

"It means, you fucking ape, that we're not through yet. We'll make you pay for what you've done!" It was false bravado, but it was still somehow cathartic.

"Miike, I did not come here to elevate your vital signs, I came as one warrior to honor another warrior."

"Drababan, I am not a warrior, I'm just some scared kid whose world has been turned upside down. I was cornered and I did what I could for myself. But at what cost? I have lost my soul, Drababan. I traded my life for my soul."

"Ah, that is something I do understand, the Progerians do not believe in what you call a soul but the Genogerians in secret have always believed in Cravaratar."

"Cravaratar?"

"That would be equivalent to your...religion, I think is the word you use."

"You're spiritual? I find that hard to believe." Drababan seemed unperturbed at my comment.

"There are a few of us left that hold on to the old ways, although penalty of death for practicing our rites has greatly reduced our numbers."

Recognition dawned. "Is that how you became a gladiator?"

"Gladiator? Ah yes, I was the leader of a small group of worshippers when soldiers stormed my home. They killed all that were present save me. I was forced to become amusement for the masses."

"So have you sold your Cravaratar for your life?"

"Perhaps I have, hu-man. I truly had never thought of it in that manner. I do what I do now for my honor."

"Do you have family, Drababan? Do you mind if I

call you, Dee?"

"No, I would not mate for fear of what would happen to my family should it ever be found out that I had not let go of my previous beliefs."

"Have you ever thought of just stopping?" I asked

"Stopping?"

"Fighting, I mean…not believing."

He nodded imperceptibly, "I have not, Miike, for what would there be left for me? To stop would be suicide, and suicide opposes everything that the Cravaratar stands for."

"Maybe we have more in common than you think, Dee. How long have you been a warrior?" I asked, more for the sake of conversation than a true desire to know.

He might be the enemy and more than likely my killer, but somehow it was more comforting having him right in front of me than elsewhere, you know the old saying keep your friends close and your…well you know the rest. But there was something else about Dee he was for a lack of a better term, a religious being. He believed in a higher entity than himself, and he tried even under the circumstances to live to that standard. He didn't realize like me that we were both failing miserably.

"Ten years," he answered, breaking my thoughts.

"Ten years?" *How have you not gone insane?* I shouted to myself.

"One hundred twenty-eight lives I have sent to a better place."

"Is that how you get to sleep at night, with the belief that you have bettered your victims' lives?"

"These fights, Miike, are going to happen whether I am involved or not. I am not the crazed killer your Durgan was. Was it not advantageous to all life that you defeated him? How many of your species' women did you save? I do what I do because this is my lot in life. I have mourned for the majority of combatants I have felled, but some were equivalent to that monster you defeated and for them I feel nothing except sadness for their souls which will spend all of eternity in Drespenden."

It didn't take a rocket scientist to figure Drespenden was his version of Hell. Damn, a theologian would have a field day studying this species. In so many ways, our existence mirrored theirs. Life was life no matter what the form.

"You are truly an enigma, Dee."

He cocked his head in the universal gesture for 'Huh?'.

"You are by far one of the most spiritual beings I have encountered in mine or your civilization, yet you are a supreme killing machine, maybe I meant dichotomy. I don't know, Dee. You come to me as a friend to see how I am doing, but in less than a week you will be trying to kill me."

"Not trying, Miike."

He said it with such conviction, how could I not believe him? I was his next victim and I believed it with all my heart, as did he.

"I will mourn for you, Miike, as I have not mourned for anyone else I have faced in the arena, but the outcome will still be the same. You are an honorable being, you are a spiritual being, whether you believe it or not. You are an intelligent being, but you will be the one hundred twenty-ninth name I will write on my tibujarar."

"Tibu—what?"

"Tibujarar. It is a sort of journal, warriors use to keep record of those they have met and defeated in battle. It is an honor to be entered into a tibujarar. It is a sign of respect."

"Too bad I won't be around to take part in the festivities."

Dee looked at me with which could only be described as a blank look. How could they be so far up the evolutionary scale and not know what sarcasm was? *Man, too bad they hadn't attacked Boston first, they wouldn't have made it any farther*, I quipped silently.

"Is something humorous, Miike?"

"The whole fucking thing is kind of humorous, Dee. First, I got a date with the hottest girl in college, who actually liked me. Then we go to this hippy concert, which really isn't my thing, then I get picked up by aliens, which is rather humorous in its own right. But then, Dee, it gets really hilarious. The girl I start having true feelings for becomes a prize and I have to fight for her, but not in the traditional way. No, you see, I have to at the same time not only preserve my life and the lives of my charges but kill other humans, and not because they are my enemies but merely because they have the unfortunate circumstance of being in the fighting arena with me. So I win some fights, kill some people, fear the worst and begin to fall in love with another woman, not because I'm truly in love, but I am afraid for my own mortality and the false comfort of another is still better than no comfort at all. In the meantime, a full scale invasion is being planned against my home and everything that I know, love and cherish is threatened. And when all seems darkest, a light shines at the end of the tunnel and I am in one fell stroke able to save myself and my 'harem' as it were.

"So when I finally get to touch down to my home, I realize that my mother has died and my father is on the verge of coming apart because of her death and my disappearance. My best friend has set up some sort of militant camp in the mountains of Colorado.

"I go to see him because I am trying to get away from one woman who loves me for all the wrong reasons and one who loathes me for what I have done and become, I go seeking out my friend. I am treated like the returning Helen of Troy, my presence is suspect, I am an outsider on my own planet. How is that possible? My friend proceeds to shoot me in the back no less and sends me to France. Who does that? Isn't there a more hospitable place I could have gone? Say like the Sahara?

"Then I come to find out I am no more wanted in that country than I was in my own. The French can't wait to give me up. But what can you expect, they've been giving up now for close to a hundred years, it must be something inherent in them. So then I find myself back on board the USS Planet Earth Destroyer to fight the man voted most likely to be a sociopath in his high school yearbook. By some grace of God, I side-step death to be faced with the ultimate weapon of death—you, my friend. So you see, I either find humor in the whole thing or I crawl into a corner and await the inevitable."

"My friend?"

I couldn't help but smile. Apparently, Dee had 'tuned out' my entire diatribe except for two words, which I more intoned as another witticism than of anything regarding substantiated meaning. Shit, maybe sarcasm was finally going to work in my favor for once rather than something that was going to lead to trouble like my mother always said.

"Sure, my friend," I said. "You're the closest thing to it here. You talk to me without the pretense of gain. I know that you are here to gather more information for your tibujarar, but I also know that you, like me, are an outsider, you can never 'fit in' to your own society, whether it be from your masters or your own people. You are an outcast for what you believe in and now for what you do. Sure you may be revered and awed by those who you claim to know, but they are far more impressed for what you do for them, whether it is to fatten their pockets or for the thrill of your 'entertainment', it will never be for what you think you stand for or what you believe in your heart. When you die, Dee, nobody will mourn your passing. Another will take up your spot and carry forth your torch of destruction. Dee pondered this for a moment and abruptly stood.

"We will talk more of this matter later," he said gruffly. He turned to walk out of my room.

"Well, you had better make it soon, Dee, I don't think

I have that much time."

With what appeared to be a glint in his eye (was I imagining it?) he answered, "Perhaps." And with that he left me to think as I no doubt left him the same way.

CHAPTER FIVE

Beth slept fitfully at best, the slightest sound waking her. But with the approaching light of day, she could not sit in the open no matter how much her fear was rooting her to that space.

"Get up, Beth."

Trying a verbal approach to motivation, she knew staying put was tantamount to suicide. Eventually whoever was tailing her would discover they had passed her up in the night and begin backtracking methodically. But moving also had its own inherent dangers. What if she moved up on her attacker while he was sleeping? She didn't feel like she would be much of a match for anyone over the age of ten. Tired, hungry, scared, and alone, she felt she would more than likely just give up rather than face another confrontation. Now she knew what Mike meant when he had told her that he had just wanted to give up. But he hadn't, he had faced all sorts of horrible odds and still plodded on.

"Oh, God. Where are you, Mike?" she cried. But the crying did more to steel her resolve than to melt it away.

I will go on if for no other reason than to see him just one more time—to tell him I'm sorry, that I'm sorry for so many things, she thought. *And if that bastard in the woods comes for me, I'll rip his throat out.*

Even she didn't believe the last part, but it sounded a lot better than, 'I'll grovel at his feet for mercy.' Beth walked for what seemed like hours, in somewhat of a straight line, but the New England scrub brush was doing its best to keep her off course.

I've got to get to a road, I'll die long before I get to Walpole at this pace. And this she knew to be the truth. She knew after her last disastrous encounter, she would have to be doubly careful, she didn't even have the sergeant any more for protection. And with the physicality of a punch to the stomach she bent over from the pain, the pain of loss, the pain of loneliness, the pain of it all.

Beth, like everyone else, was having great difficulty assimilating all the events that had happened in the recent past. She had grown up on the far slope of the bell curve, her family was affluent, she wanted for naught as a youngster. And although personally, she knew she was attractive, she didn't wholeheartedly believe that she was the ravishing beauty that so many had labeled her as. Her whole life up to two years ago had been what many would consider a fantasy. She was head cheerleader and prom queen in her junior and senior years, boys fought over the right to date her. And she loved it, she craved the attention. And to top it off, she was only point-twenty-three percentage points from being valedictorian—beauty and brains, she was a deadly combination.

Then college started, where she felt for sure her inadequacies would start to show through. But if anything, the light that was Beth had begun to shine even brighter.

College work had come as easy to her as high school and grown men stopped to stare as she walked by. And then came Mike; he had been just one of many potential suitors. Sure, she felt something for him, but of all the men that had been vying for her attention she wasn't even sure he cracked the top five. There had been something about him that she hadn't been able to put her finger on, and she had been eager to find out what it was. So she had toyed with him to a degree trying to ascertain his secrets.

And then had come Red Rocks, an event for which

she'd been wholly unprepared for. Her head hadn't completely finished spinning when she'd tried to wrap her mind around what the games were about and what the 'combatants' had been fighting for. Although she'd known it was wrong, she couldn't help but smile a little at the fact that all the men had been fighting over her. It had been nothing conscious, but still, there it was. Even aliens were able to ascertain that her beauty was above those of her peers and had placed her at the center of attention for their 'games'.

True, she had been shielded from participating in the brutality, but she had borne witness that had been the whole spectacle. It wasn't until she began to track the progress of Durgan that a deep unsettling fear began to worm its way into her very being. This wasn't a game. This was real; real people were dying and she would be among them if that monster had his way. He was an animal, no doubt about it, and he would not place her on the pedestal with which she had become accustomed to her whole life.

And then there was Mike. She finally began to understand what he was hiding from her, it was an uncontrollable rage which could be unleashed with sudden and savage fury. She felt that he had a little devil trapped inside which he could set free when the events warranted it. He scared her to the depths of her soul,

How could anyone contain such a force inside and be able to control it? They couldn't, she deemed, eventually it would be set loose on some unsuspecting unlucky individual. She hadn't then been able to see the big picture as she could now. She had been a fool, a narrow-minded fool. He had not done anything on that ship for himself, his main concern had always been her safety and that of the women he had come to obtain. Why had she been such an idiot?

With a single-minded determination, she headed out onto the fringes of the Mass Pike Highway 90. There was no traffic for miles, but someone caught witness as she broke from the trees two miles outside of Amherst.

CHAPTER SIX

Paul walked through the throngs of people huddled inside the large gathering room. He heard many grumblings as he passed, some more vocal than others, but always just low enough as to not attract too much attention. Paul had no room in his universe for complainers but he knew that something had to be done now before any type of organized rebellion formed. He meandered down to the center of the stage and the dais that been set up. He made sure to take his time making it look like he wasn't in any sort of hurry, although he thought the rapid beating of his heart would surely give him away. Paul and his men had been training to fight, not sit and wait. They weren't a reactionary force, they were the rebellion. And nothing can stall a rebellion faster than stagnation. He knew beyond a shadow of a doubt the aliens were preparing for a strike, where and when was the question. With stores rapidly depleting, rationing would only quicken the unraveling of their tenuous hold on the world as they once knew it.

Paul had finally made it to the pulpit, and his mouth went dry as powder, licking his lips now would only signify the tremors he felt

All eyes were on him, even some of the more incessant grumblings had come to a halt when they realized their leader, or captor as some antagonized, was going to 'honor' them with some prose.

"Friends…" He cleared his throat. Where this speech

was going was anyone's guess. "I come to you not only as the leader of the Earth Corps, but as a person the majority of you know to some degree. To some I am a friend, others a classmate, and to others still, some guy you may have run across on campus or at some barely remembered all-night party." There was a smattering of snickers throughout the crowd. "But first and foremost, I come to you as a human being on planet Earth, thrust into the position of an endangered species. Don't be fooled by the calm and quiet, all is not well top side. Society as any of us knew it has been completely obliterated, even though the aliens have not landed and begun their assault yet." Paul made sure to leave no doubt that this would happen. "Man has turned against his fellow man, there is no altruism out there, it is literally every man for himself right now. There is no safe place to begin again, as I have heard some of you express. The aliens, for whatever reason, are waiting to begin their assault. My council believes this will occur right after Mike fights their champion."

"Next week?" someone cried out. Everyone's attention was now rapt. Paul had set the hook, the tricky part now was reeling them in.

"How will we stop them?"

"Is this place safe?"

Sobbing could be heard throughout the throng.

"People, please, this is the safest place on the planet. Will it be safe enough? I don't know. What will we do? We'll fight! We'll either win by sheer tenacity or we will die valiantly and with honor!"

There was more than one "OOOHHH RAAAAHH!!" Thank God for bluster.

"This I promise you—we will not go quietly scampering into the dark. We will stand and make them pay dearly for every precious inch of our home…all of our homes, all of our kinsmen and family and loved ones who have died. They will pay for it with the blood of their countrymen and of their loved ones. They will rue the day they ever viewed our planet.

"These coming days will forever be immortalized in song and story and poem on both our sides. This I swear to you today, as God as my witness, these aliens will leave our planet and they will leave not nearly as in good shape as they arrived. They will learn that humanity can be an unkind host!"

With the end of Paul's speech, he thrust his fist into the air amidst the shouting and cheering erupting all around him. Paul walked straight out the chamber as the crowd parted clapping him on the shoulder and cheering wildly.

"Great speech, Paul," Major Salazar said from the entryway he was leaning on.

"I think I bought us another week," Paul replied as he walked briskly past.

CHAPTER SEVEN

"Supreme Commander Kuvlar, I really think that we should wait until the battle cruiser arrives," Tuvok said with some hesitancy.

Sub-commander Tuvok had been studying the languages of Earth and right now he felt like using one of its more commonly used clichés. He felt he was stuck between a rock and a hard place. It was one thing to openly disagree with your commander, even if he was only the interim commander; that could still get you killed, though. But it was quite another to launch a campaign against a planet without proper provisions and lose, that could get your family killed and you imprisoned for life. Neither had its plusses.

"Sub-commander, do you really want to orbit around this swamp hole for another two to three years?"

"Sir, the hu-mans have proved they are not willing to just lie down and die. They are a resilient species."

"They are nothing more than high monkeys, Sub-commander. Really your cowardice is beginning to shine through."

The sub-commander couldn't help it. he growled a low savage warning. The commander merely laughed at his underling's discontent.

"We have crushed their armies, reduced their societies to empty shells of what they used to be. In a few years when our reinforcements get here, there'd be nothing left for them to do. They would show up and the glory and prestige would be theirs. I will not let that happen. I will claim this victory myself."

"Sir, we are a scout ship. It is our duty to find conquerable planets and call in the battle cruisers. That is what we do."

"Did—that is what we did! Sub-commander, I didn't get this job by being timid and weak."

"You got this job because you allowed our commander to be kidnapped."

Now it was the commander's turn to snarl. "Be careful, Sub-commander," he more growled than spoke. "You are walking a fine line. If I remember correctly, it was your team that scanned the Earth vessel and deemed it safe. These hu-mans are weak-minded, weak-spirited and weak-bodied. When we send our first wave of Devastator troops down, they will be more than willing to lie down and die, as you say."

The sub-commander didn't really believe that but he wasn't sure how far he should push his stance. "Sir, I'm not saying we can't take this planet, but we just don't have the troops to cover enough ground. With only ten million devastators and a couple of thousand ships operational, we won't be able to suppress any true fighting."

"When I succeed in taking this planet before the battle cruiser arrives I will be sure to let our emperor know of your temerity."

"And will you also tell him of my opposition should the alternate happen?"

Had the commander been capable of expressing his anger in the flushing of his facial features he most assuredly would have been the blood red color of a sun on the eve of a great storm.

"Sub-commander, prepare the troops for the launch the day after the hu-man champion is killed. We'll give them a little time to grieve their loss."

The sub-commander wasn't quite so sure of *that*

outcome either, but he had pressed his luck far enough, and he still valued his life to not go any farther.

CHAPTER EIGHT – Mike Journal Entry 3

With mortality dangling in front of your face, one begins to scan over some of the lowlights and highlights of one's life. And with my impending fight and the boredom of my enclosure I had plenty of time. At twenty, I was feeling greatly cheated, a life cut short, so many wrongs un-righted, so many deeds undone. So much life unlived. Sure I was being a little dramatic, but I figured that at this point I had earned it.

One of the biggest things I couldn't seem to hurdle was the semi-hidden hostility that my mother and I had shared. From the age of five on I had felt it; I was her burden. She no more wanted me than a dog wanted fleas, she often referred to me as her mistake, not quite Dr. Spock-ish. Her way of dealing with me was to either ground me to my room or leave me alone altogether. If I was to live longer, I was probably going to spend a lot of money on therapy. There were times that I wanted to ask her to let me be adopted by another family, I never got the nerve, now I wished I had.

Beth was another matter I had hoped to resolve before my untimely demise. The way she had looked at me when we had finally made it home after our escape was an image that still haunted my dreams, when I had them. The pity, the disgust, the love—all co-mingled on her ethereal face. She had crushed my heart as effectively as if she had cut it out with a spoon and stepped on it in the dirt, while it was still beating. I don't know that she had loved me or ever truly would have; she was light years ahead of me in the relationship game. I was like a high school basketball player walking on to a pro court. To her I was probably just the flavor of the month; no it had to have been more than that, didn't it?

How could I possibly justify the injustices I had committed if it wasn't for love? But did love qualify as a justifiable accounting of my crimes? There were times when the two of us had been alone that I could feel that racing of her heart, the flush of her face, the glow of her skin, the twinkle in her eyes; those were all clues to love, weren't they? And even if it wasn't quite love, then it most assuredly would have developed into it. But not now, not ever—she reviled me for what I had become. I was the monster in the closet, under the bed—hell I was an amalgamation of every monster from every Brothers Grimm tale to her. If I was such a monster, how could I possibly feel the way I do?

And then there was Debbie, a girl who had loved me with all her heart, something I was not capable of reciprocating. I knew deep down that she was dead; her ghostly appearance at the French Hospital could have only meant one thing. I would most assuredly burn in hell for my treatment of her as I would for any and all of the crimes I had committed thus far.

"I have to get out of this chamber! I'm going stir crazy. I'll think myself to death long before Drababan seals the deal."

I had briefly pondered the thought of kicking the glass out by my feet, but I was as of yet still uncertain to the status of my broken shin, or ribs for that matter. Movement like that could cause me to blackout or worse. I placed my hands on the glass by my face to shield my consternation, after a brief pause a sharp hiss broke the silence. I thought a new 'guest' had arrived. It was merely the change in air pressure as the 'glass' dissolved underneath my touch.

Had I known it was that easy to get out, I would have done it...what...days ago? Naw, probably minutes ago. No, the healing capabilities this machine had were far too important to my well-being to have discarded it that long ago. Self-preservation was still a far stronger drive than pity. I cautiously began to exhume myself from the confines of the chamber and surprisingly, I was greeted with very little pain. There was some twanging in my side from the broken rib, but almost everything else was devoid of pain, even my jaw. I wasn't sure if the chamber had been masking my more basic needs, but the moment my feet touched the floor I was famished. Broken jaw be damned, I wanted to eat. My departure from the chamber must have tripped some signal, because an attendant showed up almost immediately. Sure, he had two armed escorts with him, but he was an attendant none the less.

"Food," was all I said.

He didn't look chatty anyway. He quickly turned to leave, the guards stayed a little longer. To me, it seemed they were contemplating how much trouble they would get into if the captive was 'shot trying to escape'. I couldn't say I blamed them. I would have wanted to exact a little revenge on the person who had killed my brothers-in-arms. I wasn't truly a military man, but I knew enough to know that soldiers don't fight for their God or their country or their commander, they fight for their friends, they fight for the safety of the man beside them. Their fingers scratched on the outside of their trigger guards and, for a brief moment, I thought that sweet release was within my grasp. But, as if by an invisible gesture, they both turned and left. Apparently the punishment they would receive was more unsavory than killing the man that was responsible for the deaths of their kinsmen. They knew in less than a week that Drababan would finish what they wanted to do anyway.

I nearly collapsed when they left, the tension seemed

to be the only thing that was keeping me up. My heart had finally stopped hammering by the time the food arrived. I was able to brush away the anxiety like so many leaves on a long forgotten picnic table when the smell wafted up towards me.

"It's cow," I muttered to myself as I greedily shoveled the mystery meat into my mouth. Pondering on the meat's origin would have most assuredly led to the decline of my salivary moment, and I was only in the mood to quell my seemingly insatiable appetite, not think.

"Ah, Miike, it is good to see you up and eating," Drababan said with what could have only been considered a smile.

I had been so busy stuffing my face I had not heard him enter. The range of emotions he brought out in me were staggering, we were both captives in another's game, on opposite ends of the spectrum.

"Drababan," I said, perhaps a little too excitedly. "Sit down share some of this food with me." What was I doing? Could I have been that lonely?

What I considered to be a slight frown creased his maw. It was tough to distinguish on such an alien face, but I had been around their kind long enough to pick up on some of their more subtle facial tics. Perhaps it was their leathery skin or their need not to, that they just didn't possess the range of expressions like humans did, but they still were there.

"Ah, Miike, I would like to 'break bread with you' as your kind says, but it is my time of fasting."

I looked up at him with what could only be considered a look of questioning. "A religious fasting, Drababan?"

"Yes, it is my people's time of Chakaratyne. It was during this time many millennia ago that our savior Gropytheon was crucified and then reborn."

I almost choked on what I could only describe as a

hybrid between a pumpkin and a watermelon. Thank God it was soft, because it would have most definitely lodged in my throat.

"It's your Easter?" I gurgled as the soft melon-type substance made its way down.

"I am somewhat familiar with your earth history, and while Chakaratyne is similar it also varies greatly."

"It sounds a lot similar to me."

"Perhaps. But nonetheless, I still cannot sit down with you to enjoy your meal. It seems you have everything well in hand, anyway."

I sheepishly looked down at the mess I had made. It looked like a kid had gotten loose in a candy store and had proceeded to 'go to town' as some would say.

Drababan seemed to have noticed my discomfort. "Do not be ashamed of the way you have eaten your meal, making a mess is a show of high respect for the cook who prepared it.

I laughed, thankfully I had not been chewing at the time or I would have been rewarded with nearly choking again.

"You amaze me, Drababan. You talk about how you have been persecuted for your beliefs, but yet you still practice them right under the enemies' nose."

"Quite." He turned and walked out with as much warning as when he had entered. I sat and pondered the conversation for a few moments but the tug of my belly still had not been quenched, I proceeded back to the task at hand.

CHAPTER NINE

"You know that eventually we're going to have to abandon this place," Paul said more longingly than he probably intended. The memories he and his friends had built on 'the hill' a seeming lifetime ago weighed heavy on his soul.

"Paul, what are you talking about?" Frank responded, trying to lighten the somber mood radiating from Paul in all directions. "This is all we have, unless you pulled some other sort of miracle out of your hat."

"No, there are no more miracles." Paul looked up from his desk at the hand that held the soothing liquid in it. "Shit," he said without much conviction, holding up his glass to catch the light. "Growing up, I hated the taste of this crap. Now it's the only thing that gives me some semblance of peace of mind."

Frank wanted to add that he didn't feel Paul was grown up just yet, but even he didn't see the humor in his thought. He doubted very much that Paul would.

"What's got your goat, Paul? You've been like this for days. Sure, you're hiding it well from the men, but I know you far too well."

Paul stopped gazing at his drink to look over at his major. Frank did not welcome the scrutiny.

"They'll find this place."

Frank's spine tingled; he knew implicitly who 'they' were.

"How can you be so sure? This place isn't on any map in the world. And we have security ratcheted up so tight I don't think a rabbit could break perimeter without half the base knowing about it." But his words had little effect on Paul. Frank began to doubt himself even as he tried to bolster up Paul.

"After Mike's fight, they'll land." Frank began to question him, but Paul merely shook his head to tell Frank that he wasn't through yet.

"I've been thinking about this, Frank, just let me run with it. They first come cruising into our galaxy with their running lights off, seems to me they wanted to get a lay of the land, so to speak. See where our technology was at and if we were any serious sort of threat. When they figured they were the big kid on the block, they just came on down and snagged a few thousand people, for what? Entertainment, sure, but then what? Food. They were like the old pirates landing on an island and replenishing their stores. We do a last ditch effort to mess up their plans, it bought us time no doubt, but more than likely it just stirred up the nest. They worked day and night to get that ship repaired, and I'm sure that they had only one purpose in mind and that was revenge. How dare we try to defy them! Sure we stung them a bit when they came down, but at what cost one thousand to one? More like ten thousand to one." As Paul slammed his drink down, Frank inadvertently jumped, he hoped Paul didn't notice.

"They plan this huge television event so that we can watch our Earth champion get crushed by their gladiatorial champion. So then, when we are at our lowest, they'll hit. You know the old adage, kick 'em while they're down. Frank, that's exactly what they're going to do. My guess is we'll have ground troops here within the next two weeks. I can't imagine they have enough troops or weaponry on board that ship to take the whole planet, so they'll copy the Nazis."

"Sir?" Frank asked raptly.

"They'll turn people against people. They'll tell some that if they pledge obedience that they won't eat them or something like that. People will drop their weapons and line up to be the first to save themselves. Kids will turn in parents, brothers will rat out brothers just to save their own hide. This place will be compromised within days. To save themselves, they'll doom us all."

"Paul, do you really believe that will happen," Frank said as he poured himself a stiff one.

"Who knows, I'm probably just drunk."

But Frank didn't believe that and neither did Paul.

CHAPTER TEN

Beth ached, mind, soul, and most assuredly body. She dared not stop to check her blistering sore feet. Taking off her shoes now would be foolhardy to say the least and more than likely she would not be able to put them back on once the swelling began. And what would be the purpose it wasn't like she had any first aid supplies to soothe the pain. And something else was nagging her too, the roadway was eerily quiet. She had once retreated into the woods when a phantom sound pervaded her ear drums, but no one came—neither sinner nor saint—but her subconscious was in overdrive. She could not shake the feeling that she was being followed, she had been through too much to doubt what her mind was trying to tell her. But what could she do, she had no weapons and she didn't have the strength to outrun…what? A ghost? The man from the woods? What!

"Who the fuck is out there!" she screamed. Dreading and wishing for a response at the same time. She turned back to begin her journey anew. And there it was.

"Shhhh!" came the veiled whisper. Beth would have shot out of her shoes if it wasn't for the fact that they were molded to her feet like sausages stuffed in casing.

"Who…who is that?" she quivered.

"Lady, shut up!" the screamed whisper came again.

"What?" She felt paralyzed. The desire to flee was there, but the body was not willing. She wanted to scream but what was the point, she was caught as effectively as a fish in a net.

"Come here," the voice said semi-frantically.

As she scanned the woods, she was able to see a small arm motioning her onwards. Like a moth to a flame she was powerless, she hesitantly moved toward her doom.

"Faster, lady, or he's going to see you." The voice was near hysterics.

Beth understood that fear, even if she had no clue as to what was going on. She half hobbled, half shuffled toward the diminutive figure. He wasn't the man from the outpost, this was a boy—probably not much older than ten or eleven from the size of him.

"Come on," he said urgently.

She had no sooner reached the boy when he pulled her arm down and, the fight spilled out of her. With relief flooding through her, her whole body dropped into a heap.

"Who—" she tried to ask.

The boy was having none of it. He clamped his hand over her mouth with a strength that belied his size. And this is it she thought, he tricked me and now it's done. Fear and surrender overwhelmed her. She hated herself for being so weak.

The boy held up one finger to his mouth and with the hand that was previously cupped over her mouth he pointed to the roadway. Less than fifty yards away, a fatigue covered behemoth of a man seemingly appeared from nowhere out of the woods on the opposite side of the highway almost directly across from their position. He was heavily armed.

God, he has to be strong just to be carrying all the weaponry he had, she thought.

"Where are you, bitch!" he yelled. "I know you're close, I can smell your fear!"

And she didn't think he was lying. Her pupils dilated, her chest heaved, sweat poured out of her. The boy crouched even lower into the forest floor. She followed suit. The man crossed the westbound lanes and stood motionless in the divider for what seemed an eternity.

"You can't hide forever, bitch! I know you have no food and I know you have no weapons. I found the gun you killed my brother with! I'll never stop hunting you! If you come out now, I promise to make your death sort of fast!"

At twenty-five yards, Beth could see the rage that possessed him. He quaked with the force of it. She was almost tempted to take him up on his offer, better to get it over with now than to keep up this cat-and-mouse charade.

He began to cross the southbound lanes almost on a direct route to their hiding spot. Fifty feet...forty-five...forty. Beth thought her heart might just crash through her ribs at any moment. And then he stopped, his gaze swiveled farther up the road. He grunted as he set out on a slow trot, a pace that Beth felt she couldn't match right now if she was at full tilt

"Johnnie, head toward Fort One," her small savior said into thin air.

"Huh?" Beth mustered, her senses still in hyper-drive, the cascading adrenaline rush was beginning to subside and her limbs felt like stone. Heavy motionless stone. Exhaustion washed over her. It was then that Beth heard the tinny response.

"Roger, that Max," the voice responded, a little out of breath but not panicky.

"What's going on here?" Her curiosity began to pique now that the initial threat had been averted.

"Well, first things first, lady. Let's get back to Fort One. And then I'll tell you what's going on." Max was doing his best John Wayne impression. Beth wanted to laugh, but she didn't want to hurt his feelings. He had saved her life— who was she to question him?

"Alright, Max? That's your name?" The boy nodded. "Didn't you tell your friend to meet us there?"

"That's right," he answered, doing his best to not be annoyed by the grown-up's lack of understanding.

"So won't that man follow him there?" she asked, having no desire to run into her adversary again, especially now that she had seen him, he had been much less scary before that.

"He'll try, I'm sure," the boy said as he turned to head deeper into the forest. "Davy Crockett himself couldn't follow Johnnie the way he's going. And if he somehow did stumble upon Fort One, he'd be in for a couple of nasty surprises."

"This just gets better and better," Beth snorted and shook her head before being swallowed up by the woods.

To Beth it seemed like they had walked for hours, the best she could do was to keep putting one foot in front of the other. She watched her feet because she didn't trust her balance; one bad footfall and she knew she'd end up on her ass, and being this exhausted, she'd probably just start kicking and screaming on the ground like a five year old. She didn't want to give Max that satisfaction. It didn't look like he much cared about grown-ups as it was.

'What's his story?' she wondered. It was then that she placed her foot in a stream for the second time. "How many times am I going to get my feet wet?" she grumbled. "Hey, this stream looks the same," she said more than a little exasperated. She finally lifted her head and looked from side to side. It was difficult to tell where she was but she would've sworn they had passed that old twisted oak tree an hour ago.

She caught up to Max and a little more forcefully than she meant to, grabbed his arm and jerked him to a halt. He glared at her with hate-filled eyes, eyes that had seen probably more than their fair share of death and cruelty; likely more death in his short life span than seasoned mercenaries had their whole career, but sadness and fear were not part of the equation for the mercs.

"You grab me like that again, lady, and I'll leave you here. I'll leave you for him," he said with all the prepubescent menace he could muster. The words may have sounded funny coming out of such a small figure, but she in no way doubted he would do just as he said he would.

"I'm-I'm sorry," she stammered, loosening her grip on his shoulder. I just think we're going in circles, is all. Are we lost?" She let go, the offending hand falling uselessly by her side.

"We are and we're not."

Beth could only stare at the boy. Confusion wrinkled her brow.

"We are going in a circle and no we're not lost. God, you're pretty thick for a grown-up." Max could tell his words had hurt the lady, but right now he wasn't quite sure he cared. "Listen, lady, that guy looked like he was military which probably means he has some survival and tracking skills. I am not going to give him any opportunity whatsoever to find us, and if he does, I want to make sure we have ample time to prepare for our guest." He flashed her a humorless, big, gap-toothed grin "Are you satisfied?" And without waiting for her response, he turned and started heading back deeper into the woods. At least that was the direction she figured he was heading.

"Um...okay," she answered, he was already out of earshot. She stumbled after him to catch up, wet shoes and all.

It was another forty-five minutes until they reached Fort One, but to a miserable, cold, wet, and exhausted Beth, it seemed like three times that, for all her discomfort she made sure not to display anything to her diminutive surly guide. Max began to make a series of arm gestures of which Beth could make no sense. They looked nothing like the hand signals on her dad's old war films which he used to like to watch on cold Saturday afternoons. Beth didn't much care for those movies, but the thought of being able to curl up with her father for the day and garner the majority of his attention made it all worthwhile. A stab of nostalgia panged her. She was able, with some difficulty, to push it aside. She just didn't have the strength to sustain such a strong emotion.

Cautiously, Max moved forward, gesturing her to follow him, at least that's what it looked like. When she tried to move quickly enough to walk side by side with him, he quickly put his hand up to stop her.

"What the hell, Max, you just told me to follow you," she said, exasperated.

"Lady, you have at least two rifles pointing at you. If you make any kind of threatening move, they'll open fire." Beth halted the second she heard 'rifle'. "I'm going to walk in slowly. You follow me about ten feet behind."

Beth stood stock still, not yet knowing whether she should leave this twisted Neverland or continue on down the rabbit hole. Just then, a small breeze rippled through the barren tree tops, the cold cut through her ill-prepared clothing. Her mind made up, the rabbit hole suddenly seemed inviting.

Beth walked slowly, hands held high for all to see. She had no desire to find out how accurate a kid could be with a rifle, if in fact it was a child. She had not heard Max say anything about the inhabitants of his sanctuary. She just assumed, there was the boy who had diverted her stalker and Max. She couldn't imagine any sane parent letting their kids out unescorted these days. As she neared the opening of a large culvert, she saw as many as three youngsters make their presence known, each one standing to garner a cleaner shot if need be. When Max reached the mouth of the opening, he must have given the signal for the all clear. The three guards melted back into their stations, they looked young, but Beth didn't think they'd hesitate a moment if the threat was real.

"Come on, lady, you stand out there any longer and they might just use you for target practice."

Max snorted when Beth jumped and headed briskly into the corrugated steel opening. Max had to dip his head a little, Beth was uncomfortably stooped over, the strain on her back was unbearable. Just when she thought her mild claustrophobia and lower back pain might get the better of her, the culvert pipe ended and opened up into what could only be described as a child's slice of heaven. Toys and stuffed animals of all shapes and sizes were scattered about; *Star Wars* posters, *Hulk* flashlights, *Spider-Man* action figures were everywhere and in stark direct contrast to the wall of small fire arms lining the far side.

"What is this place?" Beth nearly stammered.

"It's Fort One, of course," Max answered smugly, letting his new guest soak it in.

"But what exactly is it?" Beth asked, looking for clarification. The room was vast for something underground, possibly fifty yards to the far wall and twenty-five yards from side to side. Bunk beds and air mattresses where pushed up against the wall to her immediate right. She looked closer and noticed some of the beds were occupied with kids that may have been previously sleeping but were now staring raptly at her.

Beth's attention snapped back as Max began to answer her. "Our best guess is that it is some sort of pump house for the Quabbin reservoir. There are other rooms back there." He pointed to a door past the 'armory'. "Mostly they are filled with machinery. We sometimes use them as offices when we don't want some of the younger kids to hear what we're talking about. We don't want to scare them any more than they already are."

"Where are their...yours...all of your parents?"

Max seemed to show the first real display of emotion with Beth's words, but he did his best to dismiss it with a wave of his hand.

"Most of us here are orphans—well, I guess all of us are now," Max said a little lower. "Wait—let me start over. Us original twelve were in an orphanage when the aliens attacked. We made it through that part fine. It was what happened afterwards that made us no longer wards of the state. Our orphanage was attacked by a huge gang of militia wannabes looking for food. They killed our headmistress and any adult that stood in their way, some of the older kids they took, for the most part they left us kids alone, and I mean all alone." Beth's heart stung with pain for the kids, not only had they started life with a shitty hand, God had decided that wasn't enough and took even those cards away.

"Lady, don't look so butt hurt," Max laughed.

"Does it show that bad?" Beth said as she wiped the precursor to a tear away.

"Lady, your face is droopier than Little T's stuffed bulldog," Max said as he pointed to a small child sitting in the upper bunk. As Beth turned to see the little boy, he immediately pulled his Superman blanket over his head.

Max stood on his tip toes to whisper in Beth's ear. "He's still a little scared, his dad went to work one day and never came home, his mom… well, she ran into the same gang of thugs we did, and it wasn't pretty. If we hadn't come along a couple of days later, he would've starved to death over his mom's body."

Beth wanted to run over to the little boy and cradle him in her arms and tell him everything would be alright. Max, sensing her motives, grabbed her hand.

"Don't—he hasn't let anyone touch him since we found him. He eats, plays with whatever toy he wants and sleeps, that's about it. We figure he'll come around eventually."

"How old is he?" Beth asked as Little T pulled the blanket back a little to expose one eye.

"Probably four, but he hasn't told us. Pretty much everyone here has the same kind of story."

"How many of you are there?"

"Well, of me?" Max said pointing to his chest. "Just the one." He flashed a brilliant smile. Beth couldn't help but perk up a little. "All of us, including you now, there's twenty-seven."

"Twenty-seven! How do you feed everyone? What do you eat?"

"For a while, we lived off the highway gas station a couple a miles up the road, we cleaned that thing out in a couple of days, we had more Devil Dogs and Ring Dings and potato chips than we knew what to do with. But I've got to tell you, I'm probably the only eleven-year-old that can't stand junk food anymore. My headmistress would have been so proud, I used to steal cookies from the pantry whenever I could, I got my hand slapped more than once. But Mrs. Herron was a really nice old lady. She always made that place feel like my home. She died protecting me."

"Max, I'm so sorry," Beth said as she stroked the little boys arm.

He shrugged, "It's over now. Now we look out for ourselves, all of us here are each other's family and for the most part it works."

"What do you do for food now that the junk food is gone?"

"Trust me, lady, it's not gone. We just don't want to eat it anymore." He grimaced as he grabbed his belly; just the mere thought of another Twinkie did that to him now.

Realizing that he had not answered her question, Max stated simply, "We trade."

"Trade what and with who?"

"You sure do ask a lot of questions for a grown-up, most of you guys could care less what a kid is up to."

"Well, for one thing, Max, I'm not like most grown-ups and another thing, I don't think that I'm all that old."

Max laughed. "Yeah, I guess you're not nearly as old as Mrs. Herron."

"Thanks, I guess," Beth said sardonically. "So really, who do you trade with?"

"There are these people out in Worcester, mostly decent folk just trying to get by. There are a couple of jerks in their group, but they leave us alone...at least since they tried to follow us a few months back."

"What happened?" Beth said, trepidation flowing into her voice. The thought of these kids being stalked like she was, scared the hell out of her.

"We shot one of the guys in the ass and they turned tail and rode away so fast I almost peed myself laughing."

"That's terrible!" Beth shrieked, "You shot someone?"

"It ain't that bad. It was only a pellet gun, the only thing that got hurt on him was his pride...and his ass, I guess," Max said a little loudly, daring Beth to reprimand him for his use of cuss words. Beth said nothing, though, she figured the kid had long ago earned the right to use swear words whenever he saw fit. "Besides, if he had kept following us, he would have gotten a lot worse."

"What did he want?"

"He wanted to know where we were located, I guess, and where our stash was."

"Your stash?" she asked.

Max stood up without a word and motioned Beth to follow him to one of the doors opposite the armory. Beth walked in and nearly froze upon gazing inside. The room was nearly as big as the room she had just left and was crammed with case upon case of different liquors, vodkas, rums, tequilas, beers, everything. It was an alcoholic's nirvana. "Where the hell did you get all this?" Beth turned to look at Max who had a huge grin spread across his face.

"Well, when the shi—*stuff* really started to go down, we had first gone up into New Hampshire. A bunch of us figured for some stupid reason that New Hampshire was probably safe." Max's face dropped a little. "Lost my best friend in New Hampshire," Max said, apparently unwilling to elaborate anymore on that subject. "Anyway, while we were leaving, one of the kids, Sammie, spotted one of those 'no goody' stores on the highway."

"'No goody'? Oh, 'no duty' stores."

"Yeah, whatever. Do you want to hear my story?"

"Yes, sorry," Beth said as she did her best to shield a smile.

"Anyway, we trade in the pickup truck we've got and Sammie gets one of those big tractor trailer trucks, we spent almost a whole day stuffing that thing with everything we could fit in it."

"Sammie drove the truck?" Beth asked.

"He's almost sixteen," Max answered defiantly.

"And so how did you find this place?" Beth said, motioning her arm across the expansive room.

"That's a whole 'nother story, lady, and don't be bringing it up to Sammie." Max looked at her until she answered.

"I promise," Beth answered.

"His big brother, who worked for the parks department or something, used to bring him here and do all sorts of awful stuff to him."

"His big brother? How awful."

"Not like his real big brother, but like one of those organizations."

"Oh Big Brothers, Big Sisters. How horrible."

"Yeah, he doesn't talk about it much. He got his revenge though. The creep was hiding out here when we took over."

Again Beth waited for him to elaborate but no new information was forthcoming. Beth figured she knew how that story would play out anyway.

"So about once a month, Sammie and a couple of other kids pack up a car we have and head down to Worcester, we trade this stuff for food. Good food like hamburgers and hot dogs and sometimes even deer if their hunters have been lucky. They tried to follow us once and once they tried to make a bad deal with us once. But when we didn't show up for our scheduled monthly runs, I guess they knew better than to screw with us. It's gone pretty smooth since then."

"Max, you are just a wonder. Not only are you surviving, you kids seem to be thriving."

"Yeah, I like that, it sort of rhymes. We have no choice, we have to do it lady, it's for the little ones," Max said.

CHAPTER ELEVEN

I felt healthy but I found myself just staring off and pondering not only my fate but that of the planet that housed all that I loved. I finally decided to get up off my ass and do something about it. I asked for and received a treadmill and some weight lifting machines. I did my best to not try and wonder where they had been confiscated from. I could allay my fears a little with the knowledge that more than likely they didn't come out of any homeowner's house.

They were top-notch machines, most likely confiscated from a Bally or a Twenty-four Hour Fitness Center. I didn't think there'd be too many people at the gym these days anyway. Trying to find ways to feed yourself would definitely take precedence over muscle-building.

I lifted weights with a vengeance, but even that was undone by my single-mindedness on the treadmill. I ran three half marathons that final week. I was possibly going to die soon, but I wouldn't be winded when it happened. That earned a laugh.

I was starting to get desensitized to the whole fiasco, I knew in my soul I couldn't beat Drababan one on one, he was the prototypical fighting machine. He was huge, he was skilled, he was faster than me, and possibly smarter. And he had faith, something I had lost somewhere down my long and winding road. I had no desire to make it easy on him, I wasn't reveling in self-pity, I just knew the outcome. Oh, hell yeah, I was still going to try, but if I had any money I would have put it on him. The treadmill was my solace; it kept me sane, or at least a near proximity to sanity. When I was on it, everything melted away—Beth, Deb, Paul, Indian Hill, my family—they couldn't keep up with me when I ran. Drababan was going to win, but I was determined to make sure that I was honored higher than any other warrior he had ever encountered. That's what I was training like a demon for.

"Drababan, come on in," I answered effortlessly as my odometer turned to eight miles.

"I do not wish to intrude on your workout routine, Miike," Drababan answered almost sheepishly. Yeah a wolf in sheep's clothing maybe.

"What brings you here at this late time?" At least I thought it was late.

"Your recovery seems to be going exceedingly well."

"Did you really come to see how my training is going?" I said, looking into his eyes for the true meaning of his surprise arrival.

He glanced to the far wall first and then looked me straight in the eye. "Tomorrow is the day."

I pulled the safety clip out of the treadmill and it came to a halt "Tomorrow, huh?" I answered as best I could between the rapid beats of my heart. I knew the outcome; but that in no way meant I was looking forward to it.

He glanced away again. He mystified the shit out of me.

"What's the matter, Drababan? It almost looks like you care."

"Miike, we must fight to your death tomorrow."

"Drababan, don't sugarcoat it." I didn't even wait to see if he would understand what I had just said.

"You, hu-man, are the closest thing that I have to a friend on this ship."

If I hadn't been holding on to the side rails of the treadmill I probably would have fallen over. That, and the fact we were talking about my imminent death, I suppose.

"Friend?" I answered, but I guess that wasn't so far out of the realm, we had talked for hours about our home worlds and growing up and the battles, I had at times forgot that this eight foot behemoth was my adversary. "Yeah, I guess the same goes for me too, Drababan. I hadn't really thought about it before, but you're definitely the closest thing that I have to a friend here, too." How much that really meant in the greater scope of things, I wasn't sure, but I wasn't displeased when he came around.

"I hope that your fight is a valiant one, I would greatly like to place you atop of those that I honor."

Hell, now he was a mind reader. "I've got a surprise or two lined up for you my friend."

Drababan stood straighter with my loose use of the word 'friend', he took it much more literally than it was intended, but if it made him hesitate five-tenths of a second longer than normal before he skewered me, that would give me time for one last vision, and it would most likely be Beth.

"I hope that you take solace in the fact that you will at least die on home soil," Drababan told me.

"What?"

"Have you not been told? The fight is to take place on your planet."

"Are you kidding me?" I asked. Drababan frowned, I'm pretty sure. I should know better, a comedian would easily starve to death on his home world. "Death is death, Drababan, I take no solace wherever it happens, but it will be nice to see my home one final time."

He nodded his head and stepped out.

CHAPTER TWELVE

"Is everything ready?" Paul asked, never looking up from his desk.

"Yes," Major Salazar answered.

Paul placed his pen down and looked Frank straight in the eye. "It had damned well better be."

Frank saluted, turned and walked out.

CHAPTER THIRTEEN – Mike Journal Entry 4

The trip to Earth went a lot smoother than my last venture. Drababan and I sat on opposite sides of the transport ship. I was completely focused on my opponent; he seemed to be rapt in his meditation. Except for the shifting and bustling about of the fifty or so Devastator troops, the journey was exceedingly quiet.

Drababan had told me that the invasion of Earth would start the day after his defeat of me. I sat dumbfounded as I looked over at the troops who knew that this was their last easy day of duty. Tomorrow they would begin to earn their keep with a full onslaught on my home world. They were confident, but they weren't stupid; you don't take over a planet without casualties, and each one would fight to the death to protect his comrade while also praying to whatever comforted them to make sure they weren't the one to have their life ended.

Drababan gazed in my direction, but he had the glazed-over look of someone on quality tranquilizers. His eyes reminded me of my own on some nights at school. I involuntarily snorted a small laugh. If anyone—including Drababan—noticed, no one reacted. Drababan was deep in his private thoughts, he most likely wouldn't even know if I tried to kill him now. There was a thought. I could end this thing before it even started. Although I knew the fifty or so troops would have something to say about that.

We landed with little fanfare. I don't know what I was expecting, a welcome committee perhaps or maybe a rescue party—now wouldn't that have been a surprise. Half of the guard detail exited the shuttle first, followed by Drababan, myself, and then the rest of the Devastator troops. We had been deposited in the same place I had been picked up. Ground Zero; France.

The shuttle took off the moment the last troops' feet hit terra firma, but it didn't go far—and why, I was to learn soon. It hovered about a thousand feet over our heads, most likely to guard against any insurgents, but also to be able to broadcast the proceedings, and another surprise that it bestowed upon us.

Almost instantly, the giant crater began to take a new shape, blurred at first. The effect was dizzying. I gazed about and could not get a fix on anything, but as the image became clearer, I was at once awed and terrified. The image became that of the old coliseum in Rome, it was amazing but unlike the changes that took place on the ship this was more of the hologram type. This was clearly only an overlay of the land with which we stood. It was very disconcerting, what appeared to be the solid ground of the stadium did not take into account the actual pock marked land which we actually stood on. If I looked hard enough, I could see the real ground beneath the illusion, but I was not going to have the luxury of being able to concentrate on the ground I was stepping on, Drababan would make certain of that. He would have the same handicap. Somehow, I did not think he cared.

The guards took up a perimeter defensive position around our newly formed battlefield. The game was drawing near. I took in a great draught of air, hoping upon hope that this wouldn't be the last time, but who was I kidding? Drababan turned and walked a short distance and picked up a shield and sword, what I had thought were just more props were in fact the weapons of choice for the event.

Where had they come from? I wondered. I didn't see any of the guards carrying the stuff, but it wasn't like I had been scoping them out too much. Most of the trip down I had sat with my head down, deep in thought of what was about to happen. Not knowing what else to do, I walked over to my sword and shield. Damn, they felt heavy. Maybe this was a good thing. I was tired of fighting, tired of trying to save others, tired of trying to justify all the things I had done thus far. I honestly hoped at that point that there was no Heaven. I did not want to have to explain myself at the Pearly Gates, if that was indeed the direction in which I was heading. The devil, though, I'm sure he had a special wing already set up for me. No, it was much better to think that once Drababan laid the killing blow I would just fade out to black.

And then I nearly dropped my shield as a voice thundered from above, "Warriors—let the games begin!"

"Fuck," I said as I walked toward Drababan.

CHAPTER FOURTEEN

The colonel watched the descent of the transport ship. He turned and spoke. "I take it everything is in place, Sergeant."

"Yes, sir," the sergeant answered calmly. For what was about to happen she showed no emotion whatsoever. She was the poster child for the professional soldier: calm, cool and collected, no matter that her heart said differently.

"Alright, Sergeant, when I give the order, I want you to hit the switch. Within five seconds of that switch, I want all of your men outside," he yelled, even though in the confined space, a whisper would have been sufficient, that and the fact that this drill had been run a thousand times before. "Look alive, folks, this time it's for keeps. And we'll have a worldwide audience, so no screw ups!"

"Oooh-raaah!" was the unabashed reply.

"Oooh-raaah!" the colonel echoed.

Now he knew that the intel was correct. The aliens had let it be known far and wide that the fight would take place on earth, but they had not disclosed the exact whereabouts. At least five different spots around the planet were being monitored after increased flybys of transport and gunships. That could mean absolutely nothing, his targets could have been fighting on the top of the Himalayan mountains for all he truly knew. At least that was the case until he saw the ring of alien troops.

CHAPTER FIFTEEN – Mike Journal Entry 5

Drababan shook his head ever so slightly as he saw me head toward him. No, matter how concerned he was with actually killing me, he would do it, I was sure. What was the point of running? Drababan shook off his distaste for the event and approached me warily but steadily. I stumbled a few times on the uneven terrain, Drababan, for all his bulk, may as well have been floating. He never faltered, and even more disconcerting, he never once took his reptilian eyes off of me.

As I closed in, I saw no good reason to stall. I swung first, my blow easily deflected off of Dee's shield. He countered and nearly took my head off in one fell swoop.

Well so much for hesitation on his side. I tucked and rolled by, swinging my sword and catching his shin-guard. I think it momentarily stunned him that I actually made contact. He pulled his leg back. Either way, he was in no position to counterstrike. Good thing, too, because a small mound had halted my progress much sooner than I anticipated. Drababan recovered quickly, but so did I, and with some effort I was able to deflect his incoming blow as I did my best to regain my footing.

"You fight well, Miike. I had prayed to Gropytheon that it would be so."

"Um, thanks? I guess?" How the hell does one answer

that when you're fighting for your very existence? He said it so matter-of-factly; like we were shooting hoops or playing darts, not trying to survive. "You too."

"Coming from you, Miike, that truly is a compliment."

Are you kidding me? Could this be any more surreal? He dipped his head slightly, I lunged, missing badly and catching sight of Dee's blade swinging down on my sword arm. I was sent sprawling in the dirt; my arm was on fire but miraculously still attached. He had hit me with the flat part of the sword. It had been no mistake, he was toying with me.

"That will be the only quarter I will allow you, Miike."

I stood up, not daring to touch my arm which felt as if it were broken. It was already beginning to bruise and swell. Well that answered that he wasn't toying with me, he was honoring me, but at that point what was the difference.

"Drababan," I answered, "if I get the same opportunity I will not yield."

He understood what I meant and nodded. "You will not get the chance."

He wasn't cocky; just sure. I circled him slowly, flexing my arm about, I could not afford to have it stiffen up if I ever got the chance to wield it. Drababan charged—God he was fast—my mind raced. I had watched all of his fights. He had done this maneuver no fewer than ten times; six times he had dodged to the right at the last moment and lashed out with whatever weapon he had, three times he had dodged to the left and crossed his weapon across his body to yield the same deadly results. Once he had just completely bowled his opponent over, skewering him like so much chicken on a spit.

I had no choice. I had to play the odds, even if they were sixty/forty. If I miscalculated, this would be over quick. As Drababan's pivot foot set and he squared to the right, I dodged to the left and tucked down, sticking my sword out, hoping it would find purchase. My sword struck his breastplate, sending seismic shivers through my forearm and into my spine. I nearly dropped it and then I felt something yielding.

Drababan had run past my assault, my sword slipped off of his breastplate armor and found the soft spot on his side. It wasn't a terribly deep wound, it surely wasn't life threatening, but Drababan stopped and turned toward me. He dropped his shield and ran his hand over the glistening wound, putting his hand up. A surge of hope leapt through me as I watched blood drip off his fingers.

He howled in what I can only take for rage. There was nothing in his flat eyes except murder. He headed toward me with no other intention than ending my life. My victory was seemingly short-lived.

The ground leapt underfoot. Drababan, in all his glory, was thrown like a puppet into the air. I, for the most part, didn't move as I was already in a crouch. I had put out my hands to brace myself as dirt and stone rained down all around and on me.

Small arms fire erupted everywhere. I was so disoriented at first that I didn't understand as I watched Devastator troops drop like dominoes. And then it dawned on me; this was the rescue I had hoped beyond hope would happen.

I was frozen. Clouds of dust made vision difficult, and my sense of balance was still reeling from the shockwave, if I stood and tried to run, I would most likely look like a drunk having one too many at happy hour. And I still had no clue from which way the rescuers were coming. How was I going to get out of there anyway?

The ship above us may have only been a troop transport, but it sported more powerful weapons than anything dreamed of on my planet. The transport swooped down and began to make itself known. I heard screams of agony and death as plasma-cannons rained down destruction.

Guards and camouflage fitted troops fell alike, no one was immune to the strafing fire. It seemed their troops' lives were of less value than stopping the rescue, and through it all Drababan began to rise. If he was awed by the whole scene, he showed little. Murderous intent still blazed hot in his eyes.

I didn't know for sure which way to run, but away from Drababan seemed like a good idea. I rose and dropped everything, heading in full sprint away from Dee and closer to what sounded like M-16s. One benefit of the transport ship coming down was the illusion of the coliseum was broken, I could once again see the ground I was trying to traverse; it was of little help. I could *feel* Drababan's heavy footfalls behind me. He would catch me long before I got to any sort of safety.

So fucking close! And there she was, a combat Marine, aiming an M-16 directly at me. *Why the fuck is she trying to shoot me?* I thought as I felt the heat of the bullets pass my left ear. I heard the grunt no more than three feet behind me as Drababan took at least three rounds in the shoulder. The shots seemed to be about as effectual as a bee stings. He slowed for a heartbeat, letting me gain a few precious steps, but he would not be so careless again. He would chase me down and use me to block the soldiers' line of site. I redoubled my efforts—thank God for the treadmill—I had been at an all-out sprint for three hundred yards and I still had another three hundred to go.

I was feeling the burn in my lungs, but it was amazing what self-preservation can do for you. Even while running I was contemplating strategy. I could see the Marine desperately seeking some sort of firing angle on Drababan. Should I drop and give her a clear shot? But if she missed, he would be on top of me in a second or two at the most. I figured she had great training; but how comfortable was I with putting my life in someone else's hands?

The decision was made for me as another sweeping cannon blow torched the ground all around the Marine. I watched in horror as her body was flung back almost ten feet—was that a hole beyond her? A hole! There was a tunnel in the side of the crater! So that's what the explosion was for…and also our means of escape. Whoever thought of this was fucking brilliant. And like a flash, there it was. Paul had thought of this, surprise was always a tactic he liked to employ when we had played Risk, and this was the *coup de grâce* of all surprises.

Fifty more yards. A twice-wounded Drababan had made up still more ground, I could feel the earth vibrate from his stride. I wasn't going to make it. I felt the tip of his sword on my shoulder blade. I immediately dropped and tucked, Drababan put one foot into my thankfully protected rib cage and then went sprawling. My ruse worked, but now he was between me and my destination.

He rose in an instant, almost faster than me, and I had known the hastily laid plan. Somewhere along his fall he had lost the sword, but that was of little concern, he could break my neck with a flick of his arm. He stood tall, blood oozing from his side and shoulder and snout, but none of it mattered to him. He was the Terminator and I was his target—nothing else mattered.

The gun battle still raged on as more Marines poured from the mouth of the tunnel, the numbers were nearly equal, but the surprise had been gained by the Marines. More Devastator troops lay still, but it was beginning to even up as the aliens' superior air power began to take over.

The more time I stood there with my thumb up my ass, the more people were going to die. I would make my move, live or die I was going to make my move. I charged Drababan, screaming with primal rage. I wasn't going to go around him, I had made up my mind to go through him. I ran into a stone wall with all my might and he didn't budge.

The ground beneath me disappeared. Drababan had picked me up like so much trash. And here it was; he was going to snap me in two like a toothpick. And then we were moving...fast. Drababan was running for all he was worth.

"What the fuck are you doing?" I screamed above the din.

"Freedom, hu-man. Shut up!" Drababan answered, more blood dribbled from his mouth.

The world was darker and quieter. We were through the mouth of the tunnel. Drababan didn't stop even as we passed what looked like a colonel laying down suppressing fire. Astonishment blazed on his face for a millisecond as he recovered and barked orders for his Marines to disengage from the heated battle.

As we retreated farther into the depths, the screams became softer until the world almost shattered. I would learn later that the transport ship had blown the escape route shut, sealing the fate of seven more Marines. Twenty had given their lives for me. On one level, I knew that was their job; but it didn't soften the blow much...if at all. The transport had blown holes in a good portion of the city looking for me, but it had retreated, in need of many repairs as the local militia had begun to open fire with handheld surface-to-air missiles. In all, thirty-eight alien troopers had fallen before the transport swooped down to pick up the survivors and make its hasty departure.

Drababan had finally stopped running and my bumpy ride had mercifully come to a conclusion. The tunnel had opened up into an underground train station, barren except for the burnt-out husk of a derailed engine car. Beer bottles and junk food wrappers littered the enclosure and the smell of urine was exceedingly strong. I was home and I couldn't have been happier. Drababan walked a few paces and slouched his great bulk against one of the cement pillars. In my joy to be free I had forgotten how truly wounded he had been.

"Drababan?" I asked as I approached him.

"Step away from the prisoner, Mr. Talbot."

I wheeled to see ten or so Marines enter the station

cautiously, all of their weapons were trained on Drababan's sagging body.

"Wait," I said trying to put myself between them and their target. "You don't understand."

"I understand all I need to right now, Mr. Talbot. I lost twenty good Marines out there today saving your ass, and I'll be damned if I go and let you get killed now."

"He's hurt, Colonel, surely you can see he's no threat at the moment. And while I do gratefully acknowledge the sacrifice you and your men made, Drababan also had a part in my getting here."

"Do you not remember him trying to kill you?" one of the Marines closest shouted. "That motherfucker is the enemy. We should be making shoes out of him!" As he approached, his finger squeezing ever so slightly, hoping that Drababan would make some sort of move. Drababan merely looked on as the drama unfolded. It seemed that he couldn't care less.

"You're sure he isn't going to kill you or anyone else for that matter?" a shorter figure asked as she pushed her way to the front.

It was the woman who had saved my life twice, even covered in dirt, blood, and a camouflage uniform it was easy to see that she was a beauty. The other Marines towered over her, but she commanded respect as she approached. They lowered their weapons, but never too far from the ready.

"Sergeant," I said when I noticed her insignia and my tongue worked, "he's injured, and yes I know he—I mean, they—are the enemy, but he was as much a prisoner as I was. He was forced into that battle just like I was and I think that you can all tell that he's done with that now. I'm asking you all to please put your weapons down and help him." And, as if on cue, Drababan coughed and blood flew from his snout.

"Grubner," the sergeant ordered, "get over there and do what you can for him. Baker, Fields, you cover him. If that thing so much as flinches, I want a belt"

Grubner didn't flinch when the order came his way. I've got to hand it to those medics, they think nothing of their personal safety when it comes to the wellbeing of others. Baker and Fields, however, didn't seem nearly as confident. I approached Drababan with Grubner, after all he was human, he had to have some fear for his safety; getting shot was one thing, getting eaten was entirely another. He nodded to me as we got on either side of Drababan.

"Drababan, this man is going to help you," I said, fearful that it already may have been too late.

"I would welcome that, Tal-bot." He fell into unconsciousness.

CHAPTER SIXTEEN

Indian Hill was abuzz, everybody had been crammed around the twenty or thirty televisions that were stationed throughout the complex. Everyone had seen what had transpired, but no one knew what had happened. Paul had kept the raid very tight to the vest in case there was a spy amongst them or, at the least, a sympathizer. *Pretty much the same thing*, Paul figured. One definition let that person sleep easier at night.

Paul had yet to hear from the Marine raiders and he was apprehensive as hell. He didn't know how anyone could have survived the barrage the transport laid down, but if anyone could, Paul was confident it would be Mike. The guy was just about unstoppable. Whatever doubts Mike might harbor about his skills, Paul knew he would be the key to any type of successful resistance.

The price had been high to save him, but the payout would most assuredly be higher. Paul heard from the Marines almost ten hours later. The message was sent over a ham radio with a taped message. There was no doubt in his mind the aliens would be scanning the globe for any and all transmissions, so it would be a lot safer for the senders to put the message on tape and have it go off at a safe time when they could put as much distance between themselves and the radio.

Four minutes after Paul received the message, the bunker that had contained the sending radio had been destroyed.

"The packages are in hand—will deliver on schedule."

"Packages?" Paul muttered. "That has got to be an enunciation error." But Paul knew better, the Marines wouldn't have said the plural if they hadn't meant it. What it meant he would find out soon enough he figured.

"Hey, Paul, at least you won't have to stop any riots tonight," Frank said, leaning against the doorframe leading into Paul's office, a drink in each hand.

"Double fisting it tonight?" Paul asked speculatively.

"No, not at the moment," Frank answered. "I thought you might want to join me in a celebratory toast."

Paul had to ponder for a moment, but the feeling of utter relief was flooding through him, "Actually, that sounds pretty good," Paul said as he stood up to receive the proffered drink.

CHAPTER SEVENTEEN

"So when is the next Worcester run?" Beth asked as she finished off her supper of canned apple pie and something that resembled meat—of what variety she didn't dare ask.

Max looked at her a little curiously, "Why?" he asked cautiously.

"I would like a ride," Beth answered.

"Lady, it's not exactly a trip to the mall," Max said, doing his best to impress the seriousness of the situation.

"It's not that at all, Max. I'm trying to get somewhere. I've been here for three days. There's someone I'm trying to get back to."

In more ways than one, she thought.

"Lady, there is no 'home' anymore," he said. "There's just here."

"Max, I know you won't understand, but I need to. There's some wrongs I need to right," she said, having a hard time believing that she had to explain herself to an eleven-year-old. "There's a place I know that might be safe."

"You're gonna leave this place for some other place that *might* be safe?" he stressed.

She could see his logic, but her determination remained "Max, can I get a ride or not?"

Max understood the tables were turned. Here was an adult asking for his permission, even at his tender age he could understand the irony of it.

"What about the little ones?"

Beth stared at him, not understanding.

"They need a mother," he said, trying his best to put on a brave front, but Beth could've sworn that he turned his head to wipe an eye that wasn't quite as dry as it previously was.

"Mother? Me? Max, I barely know them…and I'm far from a mother."

"But…but you're the closest thing we…they have here."

Beth's stomach turned. She had not even really thought about what the children needed. Could she really leave them there all alone? But they were doing much better than she had been, if not for them her ticket would have already been punched.

"Come with me," she answered.

"I can't leave the little ones. Who would take care of them?" Max's lip trembled, he was done being grown-up, he wanted more than anything to have all of his responsibilities stripped away.

"No, all of you," Beth said.

Max's eyes lit up and then went out. "How? We'd never all fit in the car, or even the pickup truck if you drove it."

Beth's heart was sinking. "What about the semi that you used to haul the liquor here?"

"We had to ditch that a few miles up the road in a rest stop. It was just too big to hide."

"Is it still there?" she asked, hoping beyond hope.

"It's still there, but somebody torched it about two weeks ago."

"Max, I've got to go. If you can't all come with me, I will get transportation for you when I get to where I'm going," Beth said.

Max didn't answer. He didn't so much as say a word. Beth figured that her words were ringing hollow.

"Max, if you don't let me catch a ride, I'll just go back out and start walking."

Now Max did look up, but his words shocked her. "I can't let you do that."

"What? Are you telling me I can't leave? Am I a prisoner?"

"Whoa, wait, lady."

"And stop calling me 'lady', my name is Beth," she spat.

"Okay-okay, Beth," he said tentatively. "I can't let you walk. You-know-who is still out there."

Beth's anger evaporated. She knew who Max was referring to.

"Are you sure?" she said softly, convinced if she talked too loudly he would somehow hear her and finish the job he had set out to do.

"Yeah, Johnny and a couple of the others have been keeping an eye on him. He keeps going back to the place where I found you, trying to pick up your trail, I guess."

Beth shivered. "Why doesn't he just go home?" Beth more said to herself.

"So you see, I can't let you walk, and if you're that determined to leave," Max said scornfully, "then you can get a ride. But only to Worcester—Sammie doesn't like driving any farther than that."

"Oh, thank you, Max," Beth said as she kissed his cheek. Max blushed.

"Lad…I mean, Beth, Worcester isn't any better than the rest of the world right now."

And without going any further, Beth knew what he meant. "Just have him get me to the city limits and I'll stay to the tree line on the highway."

"Are you sure, Beth? It's been kinda nice having you around here," Max said, hopefully.

"Max, it has been great to be here and I don't know how I'll ever repay you for what you've done for me, but this is something important, something I should have taken care of a lifetime ago. And I will send help as soon as I get there."

"If you get there," Max mumbled, hoping she didn't see the tear that was once again beginning to well up.

CHAPTER EIGHTEEN

"We should have just left him to die after the Durgan fight," the interim Supreme Commander sneered.

His second-in-command did his best to hide his contempt for the commander, but barely. "It seems that your plan to show the hu-mans how weak and pathetic they are has backfired, your supremeness." He bowed.

But the Interim Supreme Commander was far too angry at Talbot to even begin to notice the insolence that had dripped from his second-in-command's words.

"Sub-Commander, I want you to launch everything that we have! Now!" he shouted.

"As you wish," the sub-commander stated as he bowed again and turned to leave.

He couldn't wait to get back to his quarters to note in his officers log, this latest slip up from the Interim Supreme Commander. Once he showed this to the Council of Wisdom, the Interim Commander would be tried and executed and he would become a Supreme Commander himself, and not of some ratty-ass discovery ship, but for a full-blown battle cruiser. He nearly growled in anticipation, but while he was still under the thumb of that incompetent fool, he would do his best to make sure that his head stayed rested firmly on his neck.

The alien fighters and heavy bombers launched within minutes of the order. They had already been on a high alert status. Even with the unaided eye, people knew trouble was coming, like a giant meteor shower the ships lit up the night sky. Those who could, sought shelter underground. Some took up refuge in school buildings and town halls—the more prudent (or at least more realistic) took up sanctuary at their local churches.

The attack was furious, swift, global and devastating. What little infrastructure had remained from the previous attack was now completely obliterated. The alien bombers were completely foreign to anything the Earth had been exposed to previously. They didn't so much as drop bombs as they let go of an energy ball roughly fifteen feet in diameter from the underbelly of the vessel about five hundred feet from the ground.

It stopped and exploded, the effect was not unlike that of a giant soap bubble on the ground. When it burst roughly twenty seconds after forming, everything from skyscrapers to blades of grass were sucked up into the vortex caused by the collapsing bubble, a mile across by almost half that length high of material was crushed into matter no bigger than a London double-decker bus.

What mathematicians that were still alive tried every calculation they could to figure out how it was even possible. Bubble bombs were dropped on every major metropolitan area on the planet. The effects were devastating and instantaneous. Hundreds of millions died in what the aliens called a *war*, whereas humanity saw it as an extinction event.

The few thousand jets that were able to be mustered and flown did some damage but not enough to stop the carnage. Two days after the bombings ceased, the ground troops began to land. Right as people thought the worst was over, as the old adage goes, they hadn't seen anything yet. Devastator troops didn't distinguish between combatants and civilians, or domestic animals for that matter. They shot at everything that moved.

Indian Hill suffered no damage in those first few days of the occupation. But Boston twelve miles to the northeast was for the most part a memory now. That was something even diehard Yankees fans would not have ever wished. All communications had ceased from the once major metropolitan area because there was no one or nothing to deliver a message.

The aliens set up one of their major headquarters a little south of Boston in Dedham. Resistance was brief and for the most part futile. People did harbor some hope when they realized their weapons could inflict damage but that was briefly lived when the return fire started. Scouting reports and shortwave communications made the reality even more disconcerting than what many had only imagined as being the worst case scenario. The only major city left standing on the Eastern Seaboard of the United States was Washington D.C., and that more as a political maneuver than an oversight. The aliens, it seemed, wanted the carnage to stop almost as much as humanity did, but for far more sinister reasons, at the rate people were dying it would become increasingly difficult to be able to harvest them as a valuable resource.

The president acquiesced, there was no choice, he either surrendered or watched what little was left of his country crumble, there would be no third term for him even if it was allowable under the current Constitution.

The aliens mustered their biggest forces in what was once the hub of the free world, every American monument was torn down. Every flag replaced and every remaining person was interred in make-shift holding areas. Many died in the first few days of captivity, most because of shock and hopelessness. Many more would wish that they had gone out that way rather than endure the horrors that were still to be bestowed.

CHAPTER NINETEEN

Beth walked slowly with Max as he led her out of the woods and to the rendezvous point with Sammie and the car. From time to time they stopped as they listened for Johnny's signal that the way was all clear. Johnny was scouting ahead to make sure no one, especially her pursuer was anywhere in the vicinity.

"Surely by now he has to be gone from here?" Beth asked, concerned they were taking too long to get out of the woods and that she would have to begin her journey in Worcester in the burgeoning darkness.

"Probably," Max answered. "Do you really want to take that chance though?" He stopped to look up at her to gauge her reaction.

She shivered. "No. Perhaps you're right."

"Perhaps?" he muttered, shaking his head.

"Max, stop," a hushed voice said over the walkie-talkie.

Beth's blood turned to ice.

"I hear something over in Cobbler's Field," came the tinny voice. "Let me check it out."

Beth didn't move for fear that she would divulge her location even though she was a good hundred and fifty to two hundred yards away from the other walkie-talkie's owner.

"Be careful, Johnnie," Max replied, not really believing they were in any imminent danger. "Probably just a deer. Maybe we'll be able to send a hunting party out to get it."

The shots caught both of them by surprise. Beth nearly dragged Max down to the ground with her.

"Johnnie! Johnnie! Are you all right!?" he screamed into the radio.

Beth desperately wanted Max to be quiet and come down to the ground with her. But her voice failed her.

"Johnnie!" he screamed again.

Beth's adrenaline kicked in—she grabbed Max by the shin and pulled him over. He tried to kick her away as she grabbed the radio with one hand and covered his mouth with the other, using her body weight to silence his struggles.

"Is that you, bitch?" came the malevolent voice over the walkie-talkie, sounding far more insidious through the circuitry. "Come on, one or two more screams for poor little Johnnie and I'll have you. What is it, bitch, you too high and mighty to do your own handiwork? You have to send little kids out to do it for you?"

"Oh, Johnnie," Max wailed, muffled through Beth's fingers. Beth was shaking from a combination of fear and rage.

Max had finally squirmed loose from Beth's death grip.

"Come on," he said, grabbing at Beth's hand. "We've got to get out of here. This is the only path from where… from where Johnnie was." Max tried his best to keep from crying. "If we stay here, he'll find us."

That got Beth moving. "Where are we going?" Max led her off the path and into the thickets.

"We'll take a shortcut to where the car is."

"Is it safe?"

"It's safer than staying here," Max said without ever turning to look at her. Both walked crouched over, expecting at any moment to come face to face with their pursuer. The radio crackled to life.

"You're really starting to piss me off. Why don't you

just come out and get this over with?" The man stated, almost matter-of-factly.

"Why don't you just die?" Beth replied with as much hatred as she could muster, before she shut the radio off.

"That's the spirit," the man shouted far too close for comfort.

Beth and Max moved towards the sound of the man's voice, though she wished they were moving away from him. Max quietly explained that he was directly in the way of where they wanted to go and that they would have to go around him. The plan was going well until they heard a scream.

"Johnnie!" Max said in a loud whisper.

"Hey, I've got some company. You should come and visit," the man shouted.

"Oh, my God!" Beth cried.

"He's got Johnnie, what do we do?" Max pleaded. Fear sweat dripping from his brow.

Beth knew what she must do, though she didn't want to. She began to move in the direction of Johnnie's whimpers which were becoming clearer and clearer. Max caught up to her and grabbed her hand.

"You can't, he'll kill you both," he said, looking into her eyes.

"I can't let him have him," she answered. "What kind of person would that make me? You have to stay here, Max. I couldn't live with myself if something happened to you. I'm the reason Johnnie is in danger, I can't just leave."

Max was torn, his best friend was in mortal danger and one of the only grow-ups he liked was about to put herself in the same situation.

"Max, whatever happens, promise you won't follow me," Beth said as she knelt down to look him eye to eye. Max didn't answer. She shook him a little fiercer than she meant to. "Promise me, Max!" she begged.

Grudgingly, he answered, "I promise," his lip

quivering.

Beth walked closer toward her boogeyman, occasionally looking over her shoulder to make sure that Max was honoring his promise. But he had left, running in the opposite direction. Beth was saddened, but not completely without understanding. She didn't want to hear herself get shot, either. Beth was approaching the edge of the woods, and the clearing up ahead, Cobbler's Field, she assumed. And twenty-five yards from where she stood was her pursuer, with the quaking form of Johnnie at his feet.

"You let him go and I'll come out!" Beth yelled, the words were hers, but she didn't feel like it was her talking. Her legs were like lead, her heart raced, her mind was going a mile a minute.

"You come out and I'll let him go!" he responded. Even from here she could see his yellow stained grin. Beth hesitated. "I've got no use for the boy. You show yourself and he's free to go. What choice do you really have?" He smiled again. He knew he had her, and if he pressed he could have the both of them. "Now!" he shouted. "Or my good disposition might change, I'd hate to accidently put a bullet in his leg."

Johnnie whined. Beth came out of the small copse of woods; her legs moved, but not of her own volition. The man's smile got even bigger. His camouflage clothes torn in many places and two weeks of growth on his face made the man look that much more menacing than she could have imagined. With Beth's emergence from the woods, the man's attention was completely drawn away from Johnnie.

"Johnnie, run!" Beth yelled.

"Yeah, Johnnie, run," the man echoed, never taking his eyes off of Beth.

Johnnie seemed to be frozen. "Get out of here, Johnnie, FUCKING run!" Beth screamed.

The expletive seemed to have broken through the ice. Johnnie slowly rose and looked warily at the man and imploringly at Beth before he ran away as fast as his legs could take him.

"Damn, you're fine," the man said as he rubbed his forehead with the barrel of his gun. "It's such a damn waste to just kill you." He leered at her. Beth felt violated merely from his stare. "Maybe I'll have a little fun with you first. Hell, maybe I'll keep you as a pet for a while." Beth involuntarily convulsed, she had hoped that the end would come swiftly, not as some extended nightmare. "But then, I did see what you did to my brother, you'd kill me the moment you had an opportunity."

"I would," Beth said as she stopped ten yards away. She figured if she could get him mad enough, or at least a little concerned that she would kill him, he'd just finish her off. At least that way she knew Max and the others would give her a proper burial.

"Put the gun down," came Sammie's voice.

"What the fuck is this!" the man yelled, swiveling to his left where the voice came from.

"Put the gun down or I'll shoot," the boy said, his voice cracking a little from the stress.

"Yeah, alright. I'll put the gun down 'cause some squeaky-voiced teen told me to," the man laughed.

The boy gave a warning shot, the noise was deafening, birds flew from trees, dirt spewed up from the foot of the man. His cracked grin fell away.

"Listen, mister, at this range and with a scope, I can put a bullet in your belly button," Sammie yelled.

"Hold on, kid," the man said as he turned toward the woods. "I've got no beef with you, I just came for the girl."

"You can't have her," he replied.

"She killed my brother!" he yelled, rage and anguish etched on his face. "She has to pay!"

"Mister, if you don't put the gun down, I'm going to gut shoot you and leave you for the crows," Sammie answered.

The man was shaking with rage as he bent to put the gun down and his hands halfway up.

"This isn't over!" he yelled. "Not by a long shot. First, I'm gonna track this bitch down again and I'm gonna take my sweet ass time carving her up like a Christmas goose. Then I'm going to find your little hide-out and kill every one of you little fucks!" he screamed. Spittle flew from his mouth as he over enunciated each word.

"Beth, come on," the boy said, his voice cracking even worse this time.

Beth started to move toward Sammie. "Shoot him!" she shouted. Not caring in the least that this would be killing in cold blood. "Shoot him!" Beth yelled as she got closer to the woods.

"I've never shot a man," came the trepid response.

Oh God, why did he say that out loud? Beth moaned inwardly.

The tree next to Beth's head exploded in a shower of bark and sap. Sammie's rifle answered in return, the noise was deafening. Beth's heart was hammering as she dove into the woods. But there were no more shots, when the smoke cleared, the man was gone.

"Let's go!" the boy said, grabbing Beth's arm as she was absently picking the tree bark from her hair. Beth couldn't hear him but from his gestures and rapid mouth movement she could tell that he wanted to go, and fast.

Being deaf is very tranquil, Beth noted. As she was slowly extracted from her shock and good fortune, she realized her good luck could be very short lived if she didn't get a move on. Beth's equilibrium was also on the fritz—more than once she caught her shoulder on a tree. Slowly, but surely, she was able to run a little straighter and began to hear her own labored breathing.

"How much farther?" she said a little too loudly.

"Beth, I'm right here," the boy answered.

"Sorry," she answered sheepishly, again too loudly.

"Just come on and shut up!" he hissed.

Beth couldn't be sure, but she would have sworn he was swearing at her.

When Beth thought she might be at the limit of her sprinting ability, the woods finally thinned out, and not more than thirty yards ahead stood, the most beautiful sight she had seen in ages; a 1970s mint green Buick Skylark, battered and bruised as it was, still represented everything she could hope for, escape from the mad man behind them and another step forward into the waiting arms of Mike. She would have wept if she had the breath.

Beth circled around to the passenger side and got in, the boy's door shut only a split second before hers.

Beth's hearing had almost come back in full as the rear windshield shattered. Glass fragments peppered everything.

"Fuck!" the boy yelled as he tried to put the car in gear.

The man was no more than twenty yards behind the car and closing fast.

"Hurry!" she screamed as she turned to look back at her pursuer. His face contorted in rage. "Fucking Hurry!" she screamed, she could make out the whites of his eyes.

Sammie got the car in gear and gunned the 350hp engine. Pebbles shot up from the rear of the car, assaulting the man, Beth noted with some satisfaction. His gun roared again as the front windshield exploded out. The car began to veer wildly to the left, Beth grabbed the wheel instinctively, narrowly missing a pine tree.

"Sammie? What are you doing?" Beth asked as she kept steering, the car picking up speed.

Sammie looked over at her, his eyes glassy.

"You've been shot! Sammie, take your foot off the gas or we're going to crash." He couldn't understand her or he was unable to comply, either way Beth knew they were in immediate danger. She didn't have time to see where the man was but she figured they had put enough distance between them so she could do something. She pulled Sammie toward her as hard as she could until she was sure his foot had left contact with the accelerator, and trying her best not to lean on his wound, she contorted over until she was able to put her foot on the brake. Sammie grunted as he smashed forward into the gear shift.

The man, noting his good fortune, was once again running full speed to the now idle car. Sammie seemed to be made of stone as Beth grabbed him by his jacket and tried to force him over into the passenger seat. She had moved him halfway over into the bench seat, before she hazarded a look at her pursuer. She would never have enough time to get out and run around to the driver's side. Apologizing as she went, Beth crawled over the now lifeless form of Sammie. Part of the steering wheel disintegrated as Beth slid into the driver's seat, the shot had missed her by no more than three inches, and he had done that while he was at a full sprint. Beth jammed her foot on the accelerator, the car burped, lurched, and shot forward like a rocket. She didn't hear another shot.

"Sammie, hold on!"

She reached over to check for any signs of life. His chest was rising, but it was labored. He'd never make it an hour to Worcester, but where else was there? Beth jetted out of the woods and onto the Mass Pike with a thump. She didn't know what kind of speed the car could handle, but she was determined to find out.

CHAPTER TWENTY – Mike Journal Entry 6

The ride on the Zodiac, considering what was going on around us, for the most part, was uneventful. The night was moonless and should have been dark enough for the covert mission for which we were involved, except for the fact that the French landscape was blazing like a bonfire gone completely out of control. Drababan and I sat in the middle of the small boat as it zoomed toward the rendezvous point. Drababan slipped in and out of consciousness, the paramedic wasn't sure if he had helped or made matters worse by extracting the bullets from Drababan. But Drababan was still alive and so the proof was in the pudding, so to speak.

The Marines stayed professional throughout the ride, but I could tell they felt the tradeoff for their comrades was seemingly not worth the payout. I had to agree. Twenty Marines had died. France, and most likely the world, were ablaze. I couldn't help but feel responsible.

"Fuck, I just wanted to see Widespread Panic," I muttered.

"Did you say something?" the female sergeant said. The blaze of the fires made her eyes even more electrifying.

"Uh, no. Just...ahhh..." I stuttered.

"Yeah, right," she said as she turned back around to keep her vigil.

"Dee, you still with us?" I asked Drababan, since it

didn't seem like anybody else wanted to talk to me.

"Hu-man, leave me be. I must rest," Drababan answered.

That got the Marines' attention as they all turned to see their 'guest' was indeed still alive. Everyone assessing the threat Drababan might yet still impose on them or their fellow Marine.

I knew what was coming, but it still surprised the hell out of me. The black gleaming hull rose huge out of the ocean not ten yards from our location. The bow broke through the churning ocean water. Moments later, a small detachment of sailors appeared on the hull, looking nervous. They did not appear to like being so exposed. They worked quickly, throwing rope ladders over the side.

"Drababan," I said as I nudged him in the side. He looked up at me and then to the submarine and then his eyes gazed on the rope ladder. "Will you be able…"

"I am not quite dead yet, Talbot," he answered. "I should be able to muster enough strength to scale that contraption.

Five of the Marines boarded quickly, sensing the danger being in the open presented. I climbed up next as the Marines set up a perimeter on the sub to guard against any imminent danger. The sailors glanced around nervously as Drababan grunted through his slow ascent, making them even more nervous. He was imposing even if he was half dead.

"I didn't think he'd be so big," one of the sailors stammered.

"Holy shit," another said, startled as Drababan's hand and then face broke over the top.

I stooped to grab an arm and help him over. It was tough to tell, but he seemed to appreciate the gesture, whether or not I really helped pull his five hundred pound frame up was still in doubt. He shuffled to the side while the rest of our rescue team made its way on board.

Sergeant Yarborough was the last and began to issue orders. "Hennessey, Brooks, get our *guests* down below and secured."

"Ay-ay, Sergeant," came the replies.

Secured? I thought, wondering if we would be held in the brig. My question was soon answered as we were ushered below. No, sooner had we made contact with the floor when the sub made preparations for a dive. Drababan and the rest of us headed towards the sick bay. The sub's doctor did a quick scan of me with some handheld sonic device. When he seemed happy with the results he let me get back up.

"Clean now. He's all yours sergeant." He smiled and turned away.

"I want you two to stand guard on the alien," Sergeant Yarborough ordered Hennessey and Brooks. "I will send replacements as soon as everything is settled and then I want you down in the debriefing room at 2200. Is that understood?" She didn't wait for their reply. "I don't want him so much as fluffing his pillow without one of you covering him." And then she turned to me. "Let's go."

She looked weary, bone weary, sort of the way I felt. Drababan didn't look like he was going to be any trouble. The bed creaked and groaned as he plopped his frame down into it. Even though his legs were hanging over by two feet, he appeared to be sleeping before his head hit the unfluffed pillow.

"You, with me." She said as she pointed.

"Where are we going?" I asked, too tired to be tactful.

"The ship's commander wants to see you and then he'll decide," she replied.

We weren't twenty feet from sick bay, when the shockwave hit, Sergeant Yarborough slammed into me as I cushioned her fall when I hit the wall nearest me. I winced in pain.

"What the hell was that?" I said as I stood up, rubbing the side where my almost healed fractured ribs were, now throbbing in protest. Sergeant Yarborough collected herself and refused my hand to help her up. "Whatever," I said as I went back to caressing my injured innards.

The sailor who had been escorting us after the initial shock answered. "The aliens, somehow they see us as soon as we break surface. Luckily, we learned their targeting systems are for shit once we get to below a hundred feet. We don't know why that is, but they take pot shots anyway. We've lost a few subs, but nothing like the wholesale destruction on the surface units. They'll take a couple of more tries, but where they think we are is not where we really are. At least we can hope those aren't the same points." As if to reiterate the sailor's words, the next shockwave hit, but with nothing of the force the first had. My pulse was finally coming back down.

Sergeant Yarborough kept on walking as the seaman stopped and knocked on the Commander's door. "Sir, Captain Talbot is here."

It had been so long since I had been addressed that way, I was slightly taken aback.

"Show him in, yeoman," he replied. "And could you please ask the chef to send up some coffee? Thank you." Without waiting for an answer, I entered the fairly spacious—for a sub—compartment. The majority of the room was taken up with models of all subs from its earliest conception, to the latest super boomer models.

"My son," the Commander said as he noticed where my gaze rested. "I suppose it's his way of showing appreciation for what I do while I'm away. And probably the only way he feels connected to me on my long absences," he said as his chiseled features dropped a little, no doubt at the thought of being away from his family.

"Where is he, sir? If you don't mind my asking," I said

"Safe, for now. I sent him and his mother back to her home, in a small province outside of Alberta. The aliens have thus far only been targeting larger metropolitan areas." He left the rest unanswered. We both knew relatively soon, 'safe' would not be a word used casually.

"Sit-sit, Captain," the Commander said as he motioned to a small leather chair off to the side. I gratefully accepted. I was dog-tired and sore to say the least.

"I've been reading your bio since we started on this mission," he started.

I have a bio? But I let him continue.

"Pretty impressive stuff, I might add. Too bad the Navy didn't get a hold of you first, I would have commissioned you myself."

"With all due respect, sir, my father was a Marine, I don't think he would have approved."

"Quite," he mused.

"Sir, I only did what I had to do. Everyone keeps thinking I'm some sort of hero. But a hero makes a conscious decision and strikes out to do just that against overwhelming odds. I did what I did because I had no choices."

"That's where you're wrong, Michael," the commander stated. "A true hero does not set out to become a hero, those are usually the idiots that get themselves or their troops killed. You sacrificed of yourself for the wellbeing of others against odds no one would touch. So yes that qualifies you as a hero in my book and a lot of other books."

"Not everyone's books, sir, not by a long shot."

He looked over quizzically at me, but I didn't feel the need or the desire to elaborate. The yeoman returned with two cups of coffee and hastily retreated, probably to the sick bay to get another look at Drababan.

"And so what is the relationship between you and the alien?" the commander asked.

"Drababan," I interjected.

The commander's pleasantries stopped with me, he wasn't quite ready to start referring to the enemy by name. He was waiting for my response, I think anything less than a kinship to Drababan might have his head on the executioner's block tomorrow.

"Sir," I started and hesitated. "I guess he's sort of my friend."

This startled the commander, his tongue and the roof of his mouth took the brunt of the splashing hot liquid as he placed his coffee mug down. "Sir, we talked for hours while I was captive on that ship. About everything—our home worlds, religion, friends."

"Talking about such matters does not make one friends," the commander added.

"Sir, he saved my life," I threw in on Drababan's defense.

"Yes, there is that. I was briefed on the matter and still I have my doubts.""

"Sir, he was as much a prisoner on that ship as I was, and when he had the opportunity to escape, he took it and me with him," I said.

"Would he have killed you?" the commander asked.

No need to hesitate this time. "Without a doubt."

The commander raised his eyebrows.

"Yeah, well, there is that," I said dejectedly.

The yeoman who had previously brought us coffee burst into the commander's quarters. "Sir—sir! The alien is awake and he's tearing stuff up." The yeoman didn't wait for a response. The commander and I tried to keep up with him.

I heard the din long before I got there, four Marines were at the door, M-16s at the ready, and about a dozen or so sailors were behind them trying to get a better look. I barged my way through the sailors but that same tactic wasn't going to work with the Marines. Sergeant Yarborough barred my way with her weapon.

"And where do you think you're going, mister?"

I was through with this crap, she had been treating me like a punished third grader for the last time.

"Listen, Sergeant I am a captain in the United States

Marines and if I want to go into that room, I damned well will," I barked. Well orders, were orders even if she didn't like them.

"Stand down, men," she ordered.

I walked in. Drababan was against the far wall, his snarl making him look the meanest croc that ever walked the planet.

"Drababan," I said with my hands chest high. "What's going on? What's the matter?"

"You tell these hu-mans," he spat, "if they don't stop poking me with their needles I'm going to start launching fireballs through my nose!" Everyone at the door took a step back. I unfortunately kept approaching.

"Can you do that?" I asked softly.

"No, but I knew it would scare the hell out of them," he snorted.

I almost broke down laughing. At least some of the aliens had a sense of humor.

"Damn, Drababan, I almost lost it," I said still approaching. "Are you alright?"

"I'm fine, Talbot, but every time I try to go into deep meditation, these little scurrying fur balls keep *taking my blood*," he yelled the final part for dramatic effect, was my guess. I again had to suppress a smile.

"Drababan, if I get them to stop," I said as I turned to look at the doctors who seemed a little depressed about not being able to do any more lab work on their new favorite project, "will you go lie down?"

"And I'll want him restrained" Sergeant Yarborough added.

"Sergeant!" I snapped. "Don't you have some boots to polish?" Her eyes shot lasers at me as she turned and pushed her way through the growing throng of spectators. "All of you!" I yelled. "If you are not essential personnel, go back to your business." The crowd began to reluctantly disperse.

Commander Denton stepped forward through the crowd. "Captain, would I be considered 'essential personnel'?" he asked.

I had to hand it to the commander, he didn't hesitate for a millisecond as he approached Drababan. No, matter what the commander was feeling, it didn't show.

"Drababan, is it? I would appreciate it greatly if you would no longer attempt to dismantle my ship, rivet by rivet."

I looked up at Dee, I couldn't tell whether he wanted to eat Denton or salute him. And then the tension was finally broken as Dee acquiesced.

"Yes, sir," Drababan responded. "I will not dismantle your ship, rivet by rivet."

The commander seemed appeased with that answer, I personally thought that left a lot of room for maneuverability.

CHAPTER TWENTY-ONE

Sammie died halfway to Worcester, his breath rattled once and then he was still. Beth had pulled over five minutes earlier, realizing he had taken a turn for the worst. She had placed his head on her lap and caressed his face hoping his last few moments on Earth would be gentle. He never regained consciousness which Beth guessed made him better off. She placed his body in the back seat and covered him up with a spare blanket. She hoped to properly bury him when they reached Walpole and Mike. She let out a small cry.

"Now's not the time, Beth. Gotta keep moving," she said to herself.

Sixty…fifty…forty…thirty—Beth's car was rapidly losing speed.

"I guess that's what happens when you run out of gas," Beth said as she slammed her hands down on the steering wheel. "Isn't there some sort of patron saint of fuel stops?" she asked the heavens.

Beth had finally left the desolate Mass Pike and had started south on Interstate 495, and due to its vast emptiness made the Pike look like Times Square on New Year's, in comparison. The smell of smoke was everywhere and it was acrid. *This was no forest fire*, she surmised.

"Shit!" she whispered vehemently as the car came to a complete stop. Two miles outside of Natick, she began her trek anew on foot. This time she grabbed the gun.

"I'm sorry." she said into the back window. "I'll get

someone here to give you a proper burial." That was two promises she had made to come back, she desperately yearned to be able to keep them, but she didn't like the odds.

CHAPTER TWENTY-TWO

The absence of traffic on the highway worked to his advantage. Boady was his given name but 'Pegged' was how he was known to everyone outside of his family, because his anger was always at full-throttle.

He had no idea where the bitch that killed his brother was going. After he had 'borrowed' a motorcycle, he headed due east, not knowing if he was losing or gaining ground on her. And then his luck changed. A fine mist of dust, which was making driving a bike a little more difficult, was also leaving him a trail to follow almost as good as the Yellow Brick Road. Two miles before, The Bitch had exited the highway; she was leaving telltale tire marks in the dust.

Pegged could only reason that God was on his side, how else could it be possible she had left clues to her destination moments before she left the Mass Pike. Ten minutes after he turned off the highway, he spotted the car on the side of the road. He ditched the bike and headed into the woods so he could come up on the car quietly. He was quivering with excitement, he hoped beyond hope she was sleeping and he would be her last waking image. He couldn't have imagined it any better than that.

He might be nicknamed Pegged, but he wasn't crazy. He knew there was at least one gun in that car, and he'd be even more damned if he let her get off a lucky shot that would end his 'crusade'.

For ten minutes he had laid in the trees watching the

car. Having not seen any movement, he crept closer in the standard military advancement technique—arm over arm and pushing along with his legs like some malformed crab. If she had been lying in wait, he would be a goner by the time he reached the door. But what would she be lying in wait for? There was no reason in the world for her to think she hadn't completely and utterly lost him once and for all. What she didn't realize was that God was on his side and he wanted her dead even more than Pegged.

He stopped to revel for a moment and then continued on once again, realizing where he was and what he was doing. He rapidly closed in on the car, not liking the feeling of being completely exposed. He slowly peered up and over the lip of the window and saw the blanket. He almost wanted to clap for joy at his good fortune. He stood up slowly and quickly opened the car door, making sure to firmly press the barrel of his gun against her head. It didn't work out quite as he had planned. She didn't wake up screaming and begging for mercy. She didn't move at all. Maddened, he yanked the blanket off to reveal a completely blue, young, dead boy, who wouldn't be getting any older…at least not on this plane of existence.

"Fuck!" he screamed, and then his frustration turned to fruition as he spotted Beth's footsteps heading off onto the roadway.

"Thank you, Jesus!" he said as he started off on a slow trot.

CHAPTER TWENTY-THREE

"Colonel Ginson, we have reports coming in of alien ground troops making their way into Dedham."

Major Salazar tried his best to act nonchalant about the news when the private had finished, but Paul knew better. Frank had nearly spilled his drink all over the front of his uniform, had the private not been so fixated on the report he also would have noticed.

"Thank you, Private. Let me know if you hear any reports of their movements." Paul was as matter-of-fact as possible, taking into consideration his pounding heart.

"Aye-aye, sir!" The private said a little too enthusiastically. Paul wondered if he would sound that thrilled when the aliens were marching down Main Street in Walpole. Probably not, Paul reasoned.

"Damn, I really wish they had positioned themselves north of Boston, not south," Paul said as he turned to Frank.

"Well, we knew this day was coming, Paul. What difference does it matter where they are?" Frank asked.

"You're right, Frank, just having them that close is a little unsettling," Paul responded. "It will, however, make raids a lot more logistically easy."

"Speaking of which, when should we begin?" Frank asked.

"I'd really like to have Mike back here first, but I'm concerned the three or four days we wait for him will give the aliens that much more time to make a foothold."

Frank looked at him sideways.

"Okay…a stranglehold," Paul retorted. "I'd like to have an assault slated for tonight. I don't want a full-on engagement yet, I would like to have something set up to test their strength and tactics. I don't want to commit fully to something when I don't have a complete understanding of what we are up against."

"Understood, sir. I can have Charlie Team fully operational and equipped by 1600 tonight," Frank said.

"That's Dennis' team, right?" Paul asked.

"Is there a problem, Paul?" Paul shook his head. "Since his team almost lost the grocery store, he has been working them non-stop to get them prepared for this invasion. His team is the most physically fit and well trained platoon we have," Frank added.

"Old allegiances die hard, Frank, it's difficult to send a friend out into what truly amounts to an unknown quantity," Paul replied.

"I understand, Paul, and that's why I want to send the best, anything less could be disastrous."

"Get it done, Frank," Paul said as he sat down at his table and began writing into his log. This was Frank's cue to dismiss himself. Paul still surprised the hell out of Frank at times, but this was one mannerism Frank had down cold.

"Dennis, can I come in?" Frank said as he knocked on the pole that held up Dennis' tarp.

"Yeah, come on in, Frank." Dennis sat up on his bed putting down the old copy of *Sports Illustrated*.

"*Sports Illustrated*?" Frank asked.

"Yeah, it's kind of nice to catch up on them. Had a subscription for three years and never really read any of them. And now I know how everything turned out," Dennis answered with a wry smile. "What brings you down to this end of the barracks, Major? I know this isn't a social call or you would have brought down some beers with you."

"Right now, Dennis, I'd love to have a beer with

you," Frank responded.

"This sounds serious, should I be taking notes?" Dennis asked, half-jokingly.

"It is serious," Frank said as Dennis scooted on to the edge of the bed. "As you already know, the aliens have landed and have begun to set up station in Dedham. Colonel Gin…Paul wants to assess troop strength, weaponry, and tactics."

"And he needs guinea pigs to find this out?" Dennis answered.

"It's a recon mission, Dennis. We have got to find out what we are up against and your men have proved themselves to be a well-trained unit," Frank said. "This isn't a full on engagement, Paul just wants you to gather as much intel as possible and get your asses back here."

"Frank, you don't have to explain yourself to me, I knew what I was getting into the day I started working for Paul," Dennis answered. "This is why I have been pushing my men so hard—I wouldn't have it any other way. I couldn't live with myself if another unit went out there in my stead and got cut to ribbons. Since the store incident…" Dennis began looking up at Frank, whose expression didn't change in the least, "…I've been chomping at the bit to prove I've got the right stuff to get us out of this jam." Frank's expression did change this time, luckily, though, Dennis wasn't looking.

If he considers this merely a jam, I'd hate to think what a real mess constitutes, Frank thought.

"And I just want to get out there and pull my weight. Paul runs the show here, Mike has been through more than any of us combined, and I sit here and read old magazines. I can't friggin' take it anymore—what am I going to tell my grandkids when they ask about the Rebellion! Oh yeah, kiddies," Dennis said with his best old man voice. "I watched some of the biggest heroes of our time take on the invasion force and kick their asses. Me? What did I do? Well, I learned the '83 Swimsuit Edition was arguably the best of all time. Come on, Frank, you know I have to do this thing. I'm honor bound."

Frank could understand him completely. It was difficult to be surrounded by greatness and only be mediocre.

"Be ready by 1600. I'll have the beer on ice when you get back."

"Always a pleasure," Dennis answered as he moved off of his cot and out the makeshift tent to round up his men for the briefing.

Frank stood there a few moments longer, wondering if he had just spoken his last words to a man he now considered one of his friends.

CHAPTER TWENTY-FOUR – Mike Journal

Entry 7

We were making excellent time across 'the pond' as they liked to call it, and I couldn't have been happier. Number one, to get back to Indian Hill; and two, to get out of the friggin' tin can. I never considered myself a claustrophobic but the sub was making a strong case for it. I relished the thought of getting hope back, of being able to stand up and fight the true enemy for once. I was done just trying to survive, it was time to make them 'just try to survive.' I can't say I was completely confident we could pull it off, but I'd rather die trying than not.

Three days into the trip and I was going stir crazy, I had had enough time to teach Drababan, who was recovering nicely, how to play chess. And after our third game he beat me, from there on, it was a fifty /fifty struggle. His mastery of strategy left me hoping he was more the exception than the rule. If his brethren could adapt this fast, what little fight we had left was not going to make much of an intergalactic splash.

"Ah, Miike, I must say I most enjoy this game of chess. It is much like our game of..." he stopped to use the alien word, which sounded like a bunch of grunts and snarls, but not quite as difficult."

"You'll have to teach me, er...that game (I wasn't

going to even begin trying to mimic his words) when we have a chance."

That would be nice, his eyes said, but both of us knew the chances of that were pretty slim. It was tough to tell his meaning as I was too busy backpedaling from his aggressive, queen's pawn opening.

"Captain?" I looked up to see Sergeant Yarborough framed against the door jamb. "May I have a word with you?"

This was a new development, this was the first time I had seen her use any type of military dictum with me. It was far too disconcerting for my likes.

"Sure, Sergeant, go ahead."

"It's lieutenant now, sir. I've been field promoted." She pointed to the gold bar pinned on her lapel. "And I would like to speak with you alone," she responded as she looked over at Drababan.

I got up off of Drababan's bed. "Congratulations," I told her and then I turned to Drababan. "Sorry, Dee, it looks like we'll have to finish this one another time."

"No, matter," he answered. "It was mate in fifteen moves anyway."

I looked down at him, his snout pulled back in a sneer, which I now knew was his equivalent of a smile, and I believed him.

"Maybe the next game I'll show you will be Monopoly," I said as I strode toward the door.

Drababan was still trying to grasp this new word as I headed out of sick bay with the lieutenant in quick tow.

My quarters weren't that far away, and compared to what the rest of the crew was sleeping in, it was the Taj Mahal. My room consisted of a couch cushion, a desk, and a chair roughly the size of those uni-desks we all remember so well from grade school. Still, I wasn't complaining. It was infinitely better than any of my alien quarters or the crew bunks, if that's what you wanted to call them. Those men had to get out of their beds if they wanted to roll over into a different position. It was a phenomenon some seamen carried throughout their wholes lives much to the chagrin of their significant others. Even in a spacious king-size bed, those old salts would get up out of bed, invariably disturbing their spouses and then getting back in as if they were still packed like playing cards.

I sat down on my cot. I didn't know if that was proper military bearing or not, but the last two years of my life had taken their toll and whenever I saw a chance to take a respite I did so. Lieutenant Yarborough didn't seem to mind.

"Sir," she began.

Well this was getting interesting, I thought.

"I came here today to apologize for my behavior the other day, and if you wish to press charges for insubordination against me I will secure myself to the brig."

"This place is big enough for a brig?" I asked

Her wonderfully gray-green eyes enlarged for no more than a split second. Did she really think I'd press charges?

"Lieutenant, relax—I mean, at ease. I have no intention whatsoever of pressing charges." Her body relaxed slightly. She probably wasn't even aware of it, but after so many fights my senses were a lot more in tune with the nuances of the human body. "Listen, Lieutenant, I know what you're going through. I've also lost a lot of people I was responsible for—you keep second-guessing yourself whether there was something you could have done to save them, let me tell you, Lieutenant. You couldn't help—it was their time to die. And I'm not gonna give you any bullshit about it being a good day to die, because any day you die just plain sucks. If you want to ask me if your mission was worth it, I'll tell you flat out, no. I wouldn't sacrifice that many for one on any given day, no matter who that man was. I'll guarantee you one thing, Lieutenant…I will make the aliens pay ten-fold for what they did to your team, I promise that."

"Thank you, Captain," Lieutenant Yarborough said as she turned to leave.

"Lieutenant, one more thing," I said hurriedly.

"What's that, Captain?" she answered, never fully turning to look at me, I thought she might have had a tear in her eye.

"What time do you eat around here?"

"0600," came her quick reply.

"Would you mind if I joined you?" I asked with an edge of nervousness in my voice.

"Officers always eat together, sir," she answered.

Not exactly the response I was looking for, but it was a start.

"Anything else, sir?"

"I meant what I said, Lieutenant."

"I know you did, Captain," she answered as she leveled her gaze on me. Yep, my heart definitely stopped. Luckily, she left fast or I would have looked mighty stupid having a heart attack at my ripe old age.

CHAPTER TWENTY-FIVE

Beth sobbed for the first mile she trudged through the ash that was Boston. She cried for Deb, for her family, for Boston, for herself, but most of all she cried for the sheer hopelessness of it all. Who was she kidding? What was finding Mike now going to mean even if he was still alive? He couldn't right all the wrongs no matter how hard he tried. But, she reasoned, she could make it right with him somehow and that counted for something. She was a good twenty miles from where she wanted to be, and she was scared. But she had a purpose, and with luck, she would be in Mike's arms within the next two days. The thought spurred her on.

***

Cut the bitch's head cut clean off.

The thought spurred him on. The Bitch's footprints were getting much more defined, with each passing minute, he was making great gains. At the pace he was moving, he figured to have her in sight within the next hour. And let her see him—what did he care—what was she going to do, shoot him? He laughed, crazily. Where was she going to go? He hadn't seen a car since the journey began, he didn't see any reason to believe that that was going to change anytime soon. Besides, God was on his side—what could go wrong?

CHAPTER TWENTY-SIX

Dennis was primed and ready; as were his men. The distance to Dedham was only eight miles as the crow flew. Unfortunately, Dennis knew they would not be taking the crow's route. He and his men had twelve bristle-laden miles to trek, and they only had a couple of hours to do it in, if they were going to be able to complete their mission and get back undetected, it would be tight and he had no illusions of this being easy, it would be extremely dangerous, because the times were inherently dangerous. The time for pondering was over; the time for action had come. Physically and mentally he felt he was up to the task. Dennis' men were chomping at the bit to finally get into some action, the majority of them were either prior military or still technically in their respective services until their fighting forces were forcibly disbanded. Most had a personal grudge to bear. Dennis had to rein them in more than once during the mission briefing, telling them it was a recon mission and nothing more. This was not the time or place to make a stand, soon but not yet.

"Alright, everyone pack enough supplies for two nights and tape up your magazine cartridges I don't want any extraneous noise. We leave in ten," Dennis said as he picked up his papers and headed to his own quarters, hopefully, he thought to himself, not for the last time. But something was different. He couldn't quite put his finger on it, something just wasn't quite right. "Nerves," he muttered as he moved on.

Paul was nowhere in sight as Dennis and his men moved out. He didn't expect him to be, but he had hoped

"Good luck, my friend," Paul said as he watched Dennis' men slide into the edge of the woods some hundred fifty yards away.

"He'll be fine, Paul," Frank said as he came out on Paul's side.

"What are you doing here?" Paul asked as he turned to look at Frank.

"Same thing you are," Frank answered. Both men turned to look where Dennis' men had slipped into the twilight, no longer in sight.

Dennis surged with pride as he turned to look back at his home for the last few months and saw Paul and Frank standing at the exit way.

***

It was close to ten o'clock when Dennis finally got his men into position. His heart pounded as he looked upon the scene below him, an unfriendly alien race had beach headed on planet Earth. And they weren't wasting any time setting up. As fast as air ships could land, workers were unloading them. Dennis wasn't entirely sure what the offloaded containers held, but any army relied heavily on weaponry, ammunition, and food.

Dennis began to formulate a plan to disrupt the supply chain, but he was under strict orders—this mission was a recon mission only. He reasoned that, by the time he got the intel back to HQ, they would have effectively landed unhindered and would have a stable base from which to launch their occupation. Dennis was pondering a few well-placed rockets when one of his men came crawling up.

"Sir, one of our scouts has reported that we have visitors." Dennis' heart skipped into overdrive. A few rockets was one thing, but he wasn't sure if he was quite ready for full on contact just yet.

The corporal pointed to a place about three hundred yards off to their immediate left, a small sloping grass embankment. Dennis grabbed his night vision goggles to see a dozen armed men slowly crawling directly into the alien encampment.

"What the hell are they doing?" Dennis said more to himself. "They're going to get themselves killed and more importantly, they're going to give our position away." Dennis took off his hat to rub his head. "Corporal, tell the men to get ready to move."

"Out or in, sir?" the corporal asked.

"I haven't decided that yet. Just tell them to be ready. Stupid friggin' rednecks with shotguns are going to get us in a world of hurt in a matter of minutes."

Dennis could see it in his corporal's eyes. He knew the man was scared, but he would do what he was told and what his training had taught him, but the fact still remained he had no desire to see what waited on the other side tonight. Dennis's second in command, Gunnery Sergeant Hayes, a short stocky man who could probably beat one of the aliens in an arm wrestling competition, made his way over.

"I just heard, sir. What are your plans?" he asked.

"Don't have any at the moment—this wasn't in the contingency handbook. What are your thoughts?" Dennis asked, knowing full well the answer still lied with him no matter what the gunny offered.

"Well, sir, my first disposition is to let those yahoos get what's coming to them and tactfully pull our men back before this place lights up like a Christmas tree."

"But?" Dennis prodded.

"But, sir, they're doing exactly what I want to do. Maybe not in the exact way I'd go about it, but they're going to go and exact a little revenge for all the shit those bastards have done to us in the last two years and I'd like to be there to get my own little piece of that."

"Gunny, get the men into proper firing lanes, I don't want to fully engage the enemy but I would like to give those 'yahoos' as you call them some sort of fighting chance should they began to volley off some shots."

The Gunny began to move off to issue orders. "One more thing, Gunny, if we start to take fire from any of those airships I want a hasty retreat no matter what those men down there are into, have I made myself clear?"

"Like mud," the Gunny answered with a gleam in his eye.

The gunny came back three minutes later. "All set, sir. And one more thing, sir," the Gunny said as he checked his magazine and made sure his safety was off.

"Yes," Dennis replied.

"I'd like to take out that big ugly one on top of the unloading ramp, and I told Lance Corporal Carver to put an RPG round in that landed ship right after I do it."

Dennis found it hard to smile, but he found a way as he also checked his magazine and took his weapon off safety. "Get it done."

The gunny was looking at the potential battlefield through his night vision goggles when he sighed audibly.

"What's the matter, Gunny?" Dennis asked with a little concern in his voice.

"You're about to find out, sir," the gunny answered hastily, as a whoosh passed near to their location, followed quickly by a loud explosion.

"What the hell? Who the hell gave that order?" Dennis yelled.

"Ah, sir, apparently our friends down there had the same thought in mind. They took out the guard on the loading ramp." The implications were clear, Corporal Carver had seen the big alien go down and loosed his RPG as instructed. It was probably as big a shock to the invading men as it was to the aliens.

The aliens didn't panic as one might assume from the

surprise attack, the ones that were still in fighting capacity immediately took defensive postures and proceeded as best they could to ascertain where the threat had originated. What they didn't know was the insurgents were already amongst them. Dennis had to appreciate the thoroughness with which the men down on the landing site were taking care of business. To him, they weren't so much yahoos as they were commandos. Alien guards were falling wherever the men went, but running room was quickly evaporating as more and more of the enemy became aware that the threat was in their midst. Dennis watched as the alien noose began to tighten around the men.

"Gunny, do you see how the ring of aliens is beginning to constrict?" Dennis said.

"I see it, sir," the gunny answered.

"I want you to get your men to concentrate fire on the northeast side. I want a gaping hole on the same side where the men made their initial intrusion."

"Understood, sir."

In a matter of seconds, all hell broke loose on the alien defensive ring. Huge Genogerians were cut to pieces as lead reigned down from above.

"It's good to see they can die," the gunny said as he paused a moment to reload his M-16.

Dennis didn't answer as he watched the confusion of the commandos turn to understanding as they began to make their way through the carnage being laid out in front of them.

"Sir, we have incoming!" the gunny yelled above the din.

Dennis looked up. "Three o'clock, sir." Dennis cocked his head to see three gunships bearing down on his men.

"How long until those men down there clear the enemy lines?" Dennis asked, never taking his eyes off of the gunships.

"If they get a move on, about a minute, sir," the

gunny answered, fully understanding.

"Well, Gunny, if my calculations are correct, we've got about thirty seconds until those ships figure out our exact position. And once that happens, well, you get the picture. Order the men out now."

"Sir, you understand that's a death sentence for the men down there?"

"Gunny, it's the nine of them or the forty of us. We need to live this night out to fight another time. Go get moving. Have Lance Corporal Carver drop one more RPG before he withdraws."

Within seconds, all of Dennis' men had melted into the woods. Lance Corporal Carver was quick to follow after blowing up what appeared to be a small arms depot.

Dennis watched his men withdraw with a smile of satisfaction on his face. He understood they by no means won the war, but they did bloody their opponents' nose and that was well worth a slap on the back. Dennis reloaded his magazine and got back to the campaign. The aliens had begun to regroup with the loss of firepower from the ridge. Dennis decided to alter their perception slightly as he set his M-16 to fully automatic.

"Fuck the three round burst!" he screamed.

Genogerians began to fall in heaps as Dennis' rifle became hot to the touch. He knew what he was doing was equivalent to suicide but it was really just a matter of numbers, his one life in exchange for the nine that had almost made it out of the kill zone. Before Dennis could reload his weapon he heard small arms fire off to his right, he turned to look and noticed his gunnery sergeant had moved to a small knoll twenty-five feet away and was resuming fire while Dennis reloaded.

"I thought I told you to get the men out of here!" Dennis screamed above the roar of the SAW machine gun the gunny was firing.

"I did get the men out of here," the gunny yelled with

a large smile across his face, never taking his finger off of the trigger as he spoke.

The Genogerians had finally figured the real threat was coming from above, blue beams of weapon discharge rocketed all around Dennis and his Gunnery Sergeant. Dennis wasn't quite done berating his second in command, he figured that could wait for later, though, if later ever came. The gunships silently screamed by, had they not been tearing up chunks of the ground with their huge plasma discharges their passing would have gone completely unnoticed. The muzzle discharge from the gunny's machine gun muzzle discharge was equivalent to a lighthouse for wayward ships. The second gunship lined him up and came within inches of cutting him cleanly in half.

"Shit, that was close!" the gunny laughed. He didn't even stop to wipe the clods of sod that had peppered his body.

"Gunny! Stop firing and get the hell out of here! They have your location!" Dennis yelled above the roar and destruction of the third gunship. The gunny never even looked up. The first few discharges were right on course, the gunny had seconds to live and seemed unconcerned that the end was nigh. The shots were ten feet from where the gunny lay when Dennis heard the tell-tale *'pfft'* of Lance Corporal Carver's RPG. The gunship couldn't have been more than fifty feet over Dennis' head when the round hit it. The round ripped through the side of the gunship, the explosion blew Dennis and the Gunny farther into the ground, hot metal rained down all around them, momentum carried the ship a couple of hundred yards past them.

Dennis was deaf, all was quiet, even as he watched bullets being fired from the Gunny's weapon. *Did he ever stop?* Dennis wondered. As he stared down at the alien encampment, the blue phaser blasts had slowed, but he knew they would pick up shortly. The most distressing thing to Dennis was he couldn't hear his heart hammering in his chest and that unnerved him.

Dennis ran for his gunnery sergeant. And believing he was screaming at the top of his lungs, Dennis was ordering him to get his gear and get moving. The two remaining gunships were circling back and Dennis had the distinct feeling they would not miss again. Dennis was beginning to believe he was mute as well as deaf until realization dawned on him, the gunny was as stone deaf as he was. Dennis grabbed the gunny's vest up by his shoulder and yanked as the entire world lit up in a vision of blue death.

CHAPTER TWENTY-SEVEN – Mike Journal Entry 8

The sub ride was quiet for the most part. I found every excuse I could to spend time with Lieutenant Yarborough and it seemed to me she didn't mind so much. Aside from the occasional glance I caught her stealing at me, nothing significant happened. I wish it had, but nothing ever materialized, at least not on the voyage. I assuaged my feelings, knowing that if I so much as touched her side the crew would most likely know before I could put my hand back in my pocket. I figured she had to know that too, and hopefully that was why what I considered to be a blossoming relationship didn't happen. Who knew—maybe it was all just happening in my mind. I could tell in a millisecond how and when a man was going to attack, but I couldn't for the life of me figure out even the minutest thoughts of a woman. I was pondering this very question when I heard the commander summon me to the bridge, in not as steady of a voice as he would have liked. I quickly put on my military attire and headed straight for him. I didn't like what I saw, the commander had just turned from the periscope and his ashen face belied all the truth I needed to know.

"Mike, you might want to see this," he said, stepping away from the scope.

I had hoped to lighten the mood, it didn't work.

"From the looks of you, sir. I'm not so sure." He didn't answer.

I placed my hands upon the imaging handles and stared into the scope. For the life of me I couldn't figure out what I was looking at. I turned the handle to try bringing into focus the object the commander had wanted me to see. My view was obscured by what looked like gray ash and smoke.

"Commander, I don't understand. What am I looking at?" I asked, concern starting to well up in my breast.

He never turned to me, his face buried in his hands. All the men on the bridge were working diligently even as they watched their commander. In all the years they had been under his command, I could imagine they had never remembered him being so distressed.

"Look beyond the ash, Mike," he managed to say.

I attempted to focus on the foreground as best I could. The auto-focus kept distorting the image, and finally the computer compensated for what I was trying to gaze at. The first thing I noticed was the painted gas tower I had marveled at as a youngster. But this was different, only about half of it was there, and that was significantly more than the rest of the structures that had been my home for the past two decades.

Boston the land was still there, but nothing else remained over a story or so high. Anybody who had lived or worked in the city was now part of the debris that had rained down. I couldn't pull my gaze away, the sheer enormity of it threatened to overwhelm me. I felt that if I let go of the imaging handles I would fall to the floor in a heap. My stomach convulsed, my eyesight narrowed to pinpoints, the end had come. All I had known or ever would know was gone. Lieutenant Yarborough came up on my right side and grabbed my arm. I would have swatted her away if I didn't think it would disturb my tumultuous hold on reality as I knew it.

"Captain," she said. I barely looked at her, I looked through her. "Captain, please come with me," she asked. She took hold of my forearm and led me.

My legs moved on instinct rather than any willful volition. Somehow she got me back to my quarters.

"What happened?" I mumbled

"Shh," was her answer.

Grief threatened to overwhelm all that I was, my very being was in harm's way. And then a ray of sunshine struck my lips. Lieutenant Yarborough, Tracy, kissed me. From somewhere deep inside, I was able to recognize this fundamental part of humanity, I crawled back from the abyss. For the next couple of hours I wasn't able to forget my grief but I was able to compartmentalize it. The love we made shook me to the core and more than likely saved my humanity. Her love was a rock that I tied myself to, the turbulent storm threatened to unmoor me, but she fought valiantly to keep me with her. When I finally planted my seed in her, I was beyond grief, I was beyond happiness, I had nothing left to give. The stroke of her hand on my face was my last conscious thought. I gave myself over to the void. Blackness enveloped not only my eyes but my heart and my soul.

"Sleep," she whispered.

I would have, but I was afraid of the nightmares that my psyche might conjure up. I went much deeper; a place to where no thoughts or feelings could touch me.

CHAPTER TWENTY-EIGHT

"Sir, the men from Dennis' platoon have just returned," Frank said.

"Why the long face?" Paul asked, wanting to know, but dreading the answer.

"They lost two men," Frank answered flatly.

"What!" Paul exploded. "They were on a recon mission!"

"I haven't completely debriefed the men, Paul, but there were other factors involved," Frank answered in a calmness that was in direct contrast to Paul's outburst.

Paul could tell by Frank's demeanor this was not all the news that was to be delivered.

"Frank, now tell me what you really want to say," Paul said as he turned his back to sit down.

"Paul, Dennis and his Gunny are the two that are missing." Frank's words hit Paul as hard as any sucker punch could.

"Frank, get the men some food and set up a debriefing in fifteen minutes and keep them away from the rest of the population for now," Paul said hurriedly before the reality of the pain set in.

"Yes, sir." Frank departed.

Tears threatened to stream down his face as he looked back on his relationship with a friend who had been there through thin and increasingly thick. His loyalty had never wavered as Paul had demanded more and more from him.

Paul smiled as he reflected back on the first time he and Mike had brought Dennis up on top of the supermarket and his sheer amazement when Paul had produced an icy cold beer from the refrigeration unit. They had sat up there all day in the warm spring-like sun talking about girls and baseball. How they had ribbed him for being a dreaded Yankees fan, especially in the heart of Red Sox nation. They had touched briefly on their dreams of the future.

Paul couldn't remember any of their dreams involving battling aliens for their very existence. He thought of their first tentative steps onto Indian Hill. The exploration in all of their minds and the hill itself. Even when Paul and Mike had gone on to bigger and better things in college, Dennis always let them know that he was still back in Walpole, and he would be there whenever they needed him. That wasn't any more evident than when Mike had disappeared, Dennis had flown out on the next available plane, with considerable hardship to his finances.

"I will miss you and your friendship," Paul muttered.

He got up to go into his private restroom—he couldn't let his men see him in that state, it would do no good to let them know he valued any one of them over another, even if he did. Hell, he sacrificed a capitol city and put dozens of his elite forces in direct harm's way to save Mike. He knew Hell had a special place reserved for him, but Hell would have to wait a little while longer while he finished up there. Paul washed his face and straightened up his uniform as he headed for the debriefing room.

CHAPTER TWENTY-NINE

Beth rummaged around in the small pack she was carrying. She made a make-shift mask out of an old t-shirt. It wasn't perfect, but it kept the majority of dust out of her mouth and nose. As she tied the shirt around her neck she glanced down at the straight line of footprints she had been leaving. She didn't know why, but it disturbed her. It wasn't so much that she was walking in the remnants of what used to be Boston, it was something else. She just couldn't put her finger on it. And then the thought wormed its ugly head into her consciousness; she might as well be leaving a flare in the sky for anybody to follow. But not just anybody. Could he still be following her? She trembled with the mere thought of it. What were her options? The woods? Route 495 was lined with thick woods, he would know she wasn't veering off into the woods, she basically had to follow the line of the highway or her going would be a lot tougher and slower. Then what anyway? He would just wait for her to emerge and get to her when she was even more tired.

She pulled the shirt over her face and began again, this time at a slow and steady jog. *He might catch up eventually*, she thought, *but he was going to have to pay heavily to do so.*

***

Two hours later, Pegged was standing exactly where

Beth had stopped to put on her mask. He looked at her footprints as she had turned to look back at where she had come from. The prints leading away were considerably more spaced apart than the ones leading to the spot he now occupied. Somehow, she knew. That enticed him.

Good, he thought, *she knows I'm coming for her.* She has to rest some time. Pegged trudged on, having never been known for his running abilities. He never second-guessed his decision to ditch his ride. She was on foot, so, as a true hunter, he felt he should be too.

***

Beth kept up her pace for three miles according to the highway markers, but now she rethought the wisdom of her decision. She was tired, thirsty and as soon as the cramps went away she knew she would be ravenous. She found some solace in the fact she was able to run for three miles. It had been a long time since she had done so; *probably a few days before she went to the concert*, she figured. One thing was certain; she wasn't going to be able to run anymore, besides the fatigue factor, the fine dust raining down would choke her lungs. She again looked back the way she had come, fear inched its way up her spine. She didn't know how she knew, but she knew the boogieman was coming. And then a plan began to formulate.

Beth walked another quarter mile to a curve in the road that would hide her exit from the highway. She found a brief respite from the cloying dust under the trees, all was unnervingly quiet as she entered, almost like a church at High Mass. It was as if the forest knew something was going to happen and was waiting patiently for the outcome. Beth backtracked into the woods almost to the position she had originally come up with her idea. If the madman came no closer to the woods than her own footprints, she figured the shot to be about fifty yards. *That was nothing for a marksman,* she reasoned. But then, she was no marksman.

Who knows? she thought. *Maybe it's all just an over-active imagination that makes me think I'm being followed and I could actually get a little rest.*

She had no sooner started to doze off, her head listing to the left, when something made her sit up with a start. Beth's heart hammered. *He* was standing where she had stopped, looking around, sometimes into the woods, his eyes scanned over her exact location. She held her breath, *He can't see me.* She hoped. Beth wondered with true concern how much longer her labored heart could keep up its pace.

***

Pegged knew something was up. He just didn't know what it was. For years, his mind had been clouded with drugs and alcohol, and only since the beginning of the end had his instincts begun to become clearer, his senses heightened. Without a doubt in his mind, he knew his quarry had done something to try to change the outcome that he had foreseen. He saw the girl's footsteps heading in her same southerly direction, but the curve in the road did not go unnoticed and the fact that she had stopped running.

Perfect place to set up an ambush, he reasoned. Was his prey able to bite back? He had been on enough hunting trips with his father to know that even the most skittish animal, when cornered, would turn and fight for everything it was worth. And she might not yet be cornered, but he could tell from her running that she was beginning to feel desperate.

He could smell the fear; he knew she would not be able to keep her jogging pace up, especially in the dust. No, she had laid a trap, a crude one perhaps, but a trap nonetheless. Pegged squatted as if to tie his shoe, but in reality he was making a smaller target of himself. He scanned the woods closest to him, knowing that was where she would have to set up if she wanted to take a shot. He tried unsuccessfully to look over as nonchalantly as possible. Anger and revenge spurred him on, but he wasn't a fool—those traits alone wouldn't save him from a bullet. He got up slowly and exposed his profile, doing his best acting job of pondering his next move.

Beth slowly moved around the tree she had been leaning against, sweat pouring in her eyes. She brought the rifle up. It seemed simultaneously to weigh a hundred pounds and nothing at all.

He could feel his time running out. Action was called for, but of what nature he had not yet discovered. It was a good fifty or sixty yards away from where he stood to get to the dip in the green belt that separated south and north bound lanes. That would afford him some measure of cover. Even though he was probably in the best shape of his life, that would still give his prey a good seven or eight seconds of his completely exposed back.

"It might be a crude trap," he muttered. "But she snared me by the short hairs. Fuckin' bitch."

In the unearthly silence that was route 495, Pegged heard the telltale click of a safety being disengaged. He bolted to his left for all he was worth as the sharp report of high caliber rifle fired.

CHAPTER THIRTY – Mike Journal Entry 9

The trip in the Zodiac boat was a blur. I can remember the swell of the waves and the spray of the ocean on my face but little else. I tried in vain not to look at what remained of Boston off to my right, but I was drawn to it like a moth to a flame, or better yet, a rubbernecker on a busy highway to an accident.

This was no accident—not some huge nuclear meltdown—this was a deliberate act, an atrocity committed by an enemy that I had already resolved to fight with everything that I had. What else could I vow but that? The conviction left me empty, knowing that I could not do more than promise the complete destruction of an alien race or more likely my own death.

I got out of the boat and took what I now knew was my last look at my beloved city. The commander's accursed periscope could not truly prepare me for the devastation that was wrought there. I wished I'd never seen it and then I could live my life in plausible deniability.

Well, I reasoned, *those one-and-a-half million Bostonians would have died no matter what I believed.* It wasn't to say it wouldn't have happened anyway, but I was, at that moment, the sole reason that two major metropolitan areas had been destroyed. I hadn't pulled the trigger, but I had definitely shown them where to shoot, and because of that, millions of my fellow human beings had perished.

If I was ever given the chance to exact my revenge, I would have to take my own life afterward, knowing full well that I would not be able to bear the burden of the guilt, but to end my life now, pre-fulfillment was to cheapen the worth of those who had died for me. No, for now I would have to drag the guilt around until such a time when I could hoist it onto my shoulders and let it smother me under its oppressive weight.

The march to Walpole was surprisingly peaceful as a new wave of determination washed over me. I couldn't see how anyone or anything could stand in my way. Drababan walked up alongside.

"Hello, Miike," he semi-hissed.

The suddenness with which he came upon me startled me out of my new-found resolve. I knew it was not Drababan's fault any more than it was truly mine, but that did little to ease the prejudice that welled up inside of me when I saw him. I bit back the words that threatened to tear from my mouth; the taste was pure bile. It was a long moment until I was able to come up with something more appropriate than 'Fuck you and all of your kind'.

"Tonight is a good night for a march," he added.

I looked at him out of the corner of my eye, I had been around the aliens for close on two years and I still had not a clue what they were really thinking. But I had the distinct feeling this alien from millions of light years away was attempting to do something very human. He was trying to draw me out of my obvious distress. I however didn't know whether I wanted to thank him or shoot him.

Instead I answered, "Yeah, not too bad."

"How long until we reach this Indian Hill?" he asked.

"At this pace, Drababan, we should reach there sometime midday tomorrow."

"Will the hu-mans there be more receptive to my presence than they were on the sub?"

I thought carefully before answering. "Actually, Dee, probably less. Most of those folks at the Hill are civilians, uprooted from their lives, losing almost everything and everyone they know to your masters." God, I would have sworn he was frowning as he looked down at me; maybe it was just a trick of the moonlight. "Whereas the men and women on the sub are military, and they knew the inherent dangers they were exposed to when they signed up."

"I will just have to prove my honor to them."

I know Drababan wanted the conversation to continue, but small talk was not what I had on my mind. I sped up my pace to pull away from him. Again he surprised me, he understood the gesture and actually slowed his pace to increase the distance between us.

CHAPTER THIRTY-ONE
Eastern Seaboard Ground Occupation – Location Southwest of Boston

"Sir, we have lost thirty-eight Genogerian shock troopers and at least a quarter of our allocated supplies."

"The Genogerians can be replaced, the supplies however are going to be a little more difficult," the commander answered.

"Sir, we have captured one of the soldiers that was in on the assault," the alien sub-officer added.

"Excellent. I was hoping for a late night meal," the commander snarled. "Get as much information out of him as you can, then bring him to me."

"At your command," the sub officer answered as he slammed his fist to his breastplate armor.

CHAPTER THIRTY-TWO

Dennis had been blown more than twenty-five feet away from the explosion created by the gunships. Only pure dumb luck had saved his ass and he knew it. He had landed squarely in the middle of a huge briar patch.

The gunny had not been so lucky. His travels through the air had been much shorter and he had landed well clear of the thorny plants and onto a small outcropping of exposed bedrock.

Dennis more felt the patrol coming than heard anything, his hearing had not returned yet, if it ever would. Dennis rolled off his back, careful not to move too fast in case something was broken or out of alignment somehow. What Dennis saw both elated and scared the living shit out of him. The gunny was alive and about fifteen feet directly ahead. He could see the gunny's chest rising and falling. And the thing that would give even the hardest soldier nightmares for life was the six Genogerian soldiers fifty feet away and coming fast. The sheer size of the monsters made Dennis shudder involuntarily, add to that the bright red body armor they wore and the superior firepower they carried, Dennis could do little more than stare in horror. The gunny only had moments before they were on him.

Dennis felt around for his M-16, hoping to take down as many of them as he could before being overrun. It wasn't anywhere within reach, he moved as fast as his battered and bruised body would let him, searching for his rifle. The soldiers now stood over the gunny. Dennis could do little more than watch as the closest soldier picked up his second in command with one hand and thrust his near lifeless body over his head.

The primeval guttural sounds that emanated from the soldier's snout was almost as upsetting as the rest of the situation. Dennis' hand somehow came in contact with his weapon as his eyes were still on the scene before him. The gunny was being tossed like a rag doll through the air from soldier to soldier. The sheer agony in the eyes of him told Dennis, bones were breaking even without his being able to hear them snap.

On the fifth toss, the soldier stepped aside and let the Gunny land with a shattering thud almost exactly where the explosion had deposited him. Dennis had lifted his rifle and was taking aim at the nearest shock trooper when he caught the gunny's eye. He couldn't hear a thing he said, but the imperceptible shake of his head and mouthing of the word 'no' couldn't have been any clearer.

Dennis shook with rage and frustration. The gunny knew if Dennis fired his M-16, it was as good as a death sentence. Dennis knew it too; but at this point that seemed trivial. Tears streamed down Dennis' face as the soldier that had let the Gunny drop picked him up by the foot and headed off to their encampment. Dennis didn't move as his targets got considerably smaller and then finally vanished over a low rise in the terrain.

Dennis didn't move for the better part of an hour, shock was setting in. With slow deliberation he got his body moving knowing that stagnation meant death and that would be no way to avenge his fallen comrades. That last look on the gunny's face would be something Dennis would take to the grave.

CHAPTER THIRTY-THREE – Mike Journal
Entry 10

Tracy was next to attempt to bridge the gulf that was widening between me and everything around me. Unlike Dee, I heard her footfalls as she closed the gap, although I think she wanted me to. She didn't say a word as she grasped my hand. The touch, the human contact, the simplicity and beauty of the act eased my soul. We didn't say anything, we didn't have to. I silently thanked her.

After a few more hours the colonel found what appeared to at one time have been upscale apartments on the outskirts of Roslindale, the looted and burned property would never again grace the pages of good housekeeping, but it would do for the night. And then Dee did what I thought wasn't even possible; he made a joke.

"I wonder what kind of amenities they have here."

Two of the Marines bringing up the rear, looked in shock at Drababan. I couldn't take it, I burst out laughing. Drababan kept right on walking as if that was the most normal thing to say. I shook my head in a vain attempt to stop my gut churning laughter. Tracy kept walking a small smile spreading across her face.

Well fuck, if we have nothing else, we can still laugh.

CHAPTER THIRTY-FOUR

The high-pitched whine of the .30-30 caliber bullet ripped Pegged's right ear off even as his momentum spun him to the ground. He was right, if he had hesitated even a millisecond longer she would have blown his head clean off. As it was, he could feel the blood running down his neck. If he didn't get moving, she would put one in his ass for all his troubles.

For the first time since this mad little dance started, Pegged questioned why he had undertaken the adventure. Sure it was his snot-nosed little brother she had killed, but they had never been that particularly close. The little fuck was always ratting him out whether he committed the act or not. He definitely couldn't turn back now, though. Oh no, he couldn't do that. If not for his brother, then she was going to pay for his ear. He crawled to the median, wondering why the fatal hammer blow had not happened.

"Oh, my God!" Beth shouted. "I hit him! I really hit him!"

Her joy was short-lived as she watched him put his hand to his now earless right side. She could see the menace in his eyes even from a distance. He turned from her and began to crawl toward the grass. Beth chambered another round in the bolt-action rifle. She tried to calm herself as she sighted in on the only target available to her, his ass.

"It would serve him right," she said to no one in particular. "It might not kill him, but it sure as hell isn't going to make him any better."

Beth slowly eased her finger back on the trigger. Frustration roared through her. The trigger pulled the firing pin back and struck the projectile with an audible smack. Nothing happened.

"Misfire!" she screamed in a rage.

She pulled the trigger two more times before enough of her senses returned to think the problem out. She pulled the bolt back to displace the unoffending bullet. As she brought the rifle back to bear, he was gone. She screamed.

"Fuck!"

A piece of bark mere inches from her face shattered, long before Beth could process that her prey was shooting back. Beth dove for the ground, as a second bullet whizzed over her head like an errant hornet.

"I bet that was pretty close!" the taunting voice yelled.

"Closer than you think," Beth muttered.

Beth was too frightened to rise up and take a shot. She was more afraid that her rifle would prove its inadequacies than she was of missing her quarry.

"What's a matter, girlie, did the sight of blood make you lose your stomach…or did you really think that you could kill me?" Pegged was afraid, she had damn near done what his mother had tried to do twenty-seven years ago when she found out she was going to be a teenage mother.

Beth had had enough. His taunting on top of all the shit he had put her through the last few days was coming to a head.

Screw him. He wants to play head games I'm all for it.

"Hey, fuckhead!" she yelled, doing her best to keep any shakiness out of her voice lest she give herself away. "I just wanted to keep you alive a little longer. I want to be close enough to see your eyes when I finally kill you!"

That struck him harder than thunder. He hadn't been

ready for that and could only pull out a stock retort. "Yeah, right!" But they both knew he lacked any true conviction behind the words.

"About fucking time someone besides me is scared shitless," Beth said to herself as she crawled deeper into the woods.

She had nothing to fear for now, it was a good long while before he found the nerve to get his legs up from under him. If she came straight out of the woods at him, he wasn't sure that he would have been able to do much more than wait for the inevitable.

That's one tough bitch, he thought as he wrapped a makeshift bandage around his head, the side throbbing with every heartbeat. If he didn't stop the bleeding soon, the girl wasn't going to get her wish of watching him die. He shuddered as he tightened the bandage. He would have turned around if he thought he could catch up with his friends, but he was positive they had already moved on to new hunting grounds.

For better or worse, he was stuck on this path. One of them was going to die…and soon. He just wasn't as sure of the outcome as he had been even fifteen minutes ago.

CHAPTER THIRTY-FIVE – Mike Journal Entry 11

As we entered into our luxury accommodations for the evening, a light rain began to fall. By the time we made it up to the third floor it was coming down in sheets. I found comfort in the steady drumming of the water on the roof. It brought me back to my childhood days when it was pouring and I would stay in the house on a cold fall day and read a good sci-fi novel. Who knew, though. If I thought I was someday going to live a sci-fi book, I might not have liked those far off exotic places nearly as much. A few of the soldiers came back a few moments later as I stood looking out the window, lost in my own thoughts.

"Captain." One of them saluted. I half turned, still not completely back from where I was journeying. "The building is empty and secure."

"Alright, Sergeant, I want you to rotate some guards, and make sure the men get some rest. That might be in short supply soon."

The sergeant turned to go and issue the orders.

"One more thing, Sergeant."

"Yes, sir?" he asked.

"No, lights. Not even flashlights unless they have red-lens suppressors on them. There is something amiss here. I don't quite know what it is. This place may not be the chateau Deville, but it's dry so why there isn't anybody staying here is tickling something in the back of my head. If I wasn't so friggin' tired, I think I'd move on."

I could tell by the sergeant's expression he thought I might be a little crazy. To his credit he didn't voice his opinion.

"I'll take care of it, sir." The Sergeant snapped a salute and turned on his heel.

Tracy came to my room wrapped in nothing more than a towel.

"Well, at least the water works, if not the water heater," she said with a small smile.

I turned from the rain-soaked sliding door. She was a sight for any eyes. The water dripping from her red hair on to her almost exposed breasts was more than I could take. Our slow love-making mixing with the charged ozone in the air made every touch electrified. I slept the sleep of the spent, but it was short-lived. The sound of a man screaming had me out of bed and rifle in hand in under three seconds. I was butt ass naked, but I didn't even notice. I saw Drababan coming from the end of the darkened hallway, the colonel was in his arms as he literally squeezed the life out of him, I could hear his bones snap as Drababan approached.

"Dee, what the fuck are you doing?!" I screamed. "And where the fuck did you get red body armor from?"

My body may have been able to react instantly but my mind was having great difficulty coming up to speed. Dee dropped the now lifeless body of my commanding officer as he began to raise his shock rifle. Realization came in a flash, I opened fire as I watched my round fly helplessly off the armor. I raised the muzzle and sent multiple rounds downrange, I watched as the Genogerian's head exploded in a spray of crimson and gristle.

By now, everyone was awake and ready, I pulled my magazine out and went to reload when I realized that unless I had an extra magazine shoved up my ass it wasn't going to happen. Nobody paid any attention to my clothing or lack thereof, our number had just been reduced by one and the threat that had not been assessed was still very much imminent. Tracy came out of the door, her pistol at the ready just as what remained of our enemy hit the floor. Dee came running up the hallway from behind the dead shock trooper. He would have joined him if I hadn't jumped in the middle of the hallway. It was then as I stood in front of God and everyone that my nakedness started to become an issue, especially since I was in a halt position, legs apart, arms over my head and outstretched—it didn't leave much to the imagination. Still it was worth it, I had saved my friend. But had I? How the fuck had they found us? We hadn't seen so much as a patrol as we marched there and then hours after we stop, they find us? I was about to ask Dee this, but his roar cut me off.

"Get into defensive positions, there are about twelve of them and they're right behind me!" He shouted as he bent to pick up the fallen snouter's rifle. A moment of apprehension sliced through me like a winter wind, the rifle was at my side, but at that distance I wouldn't miss. Dee caught the gesture but said nothing as he ran past me and into my room.

"You heard him, get some cover!" I yelled. "Aw fuck, I don't want to die with my clothes off, that's embarrassing," I said to myself.

"Not from where I'm standing," Tracy added. God, I loved that girl! We were about to enter into a firefight and she was making jokes.

The first shock trooper rounded the corner, the now familiar blue streaks lighting up the hallway as he fired blindly. Tracy threw me a fresh mag as I dove for the floor. She steadied her rifle against the doorframe as her shots found their mark. The second trooper had begun to round the corner and jumped back after he saw his two fallen comrades.

"Hu-mans!" came the inhuman voice. "Throw down your weapons and we will not kill you here."

They really weren't all that good at diplomacy, he made it abundantly clear that while they may not kill us here, they most definitely were going to kill us.

"Ummm, no!" I shouted as I motioned for Tracy to get me a grenade.

She might be an excellent shot, but she had a terrible throwing arm. The grenade nearly bounced off my skull as she tossed it at me. I rolled out of the way and placed my hand out and caught the explosive before it hit the ground.

"Nice toss," I said.

She shrugged her shoulders and mouthed 'Sorry.'

My hand throbbed from being driven into the ground from the heavy weapon. Thank the heavens she hadn't aimed for my crotch, it would have been hours before I felt like a man again. I pulled the pin and overhead-lobbed the grenade down the hallway, but tonight my aim was about as good as Tracy's. The grenade hit a light on the ceiling almost directly over the first snouter I had killed.

"Fire in the hole!" I yelled as I got up, grabbed Tracy, and dove into the room.

The explosion rocked the building like a hurricane force wind, for a moment the world lit up like a Walt Disney parade. And then everything was unsettlingly quiet. It wouldn't stop the snouters, it would, however, give them pause for their next plan of attack, and I believed that would involve reinforcements.

"Get dressed," I whispered to Tracy. "We're going to have to get out of here in a hurry."

"Dee, watch the door." He had been looking out the window, presumably for the reinforcements that were on the way.

I hurriedly began to dress almost as fast as I had taken them off.

"It's me they followed," Dee said, never turning from

his post at the door.

"Huh?" I said, half falling while trying to put my socks on.

"I've been traced," he said with a touch of melancholy.

"How can you be sure?" I asked with my t-shirt half over my face.

"They didn't just stumble across us, Mike. They were looking. If I hadn't been outside doing my prayer ritual, they would have killed us or captured us all. When you leave you will have to leave me here."

I paused, pulling up my pants. I must have looked somewhat foolish arguing with an alien with my pants halfway up my legs.

"Not a fucking chance, Dee."

"They will find your Indian Hill if you take me."

He was right and we both knew it.

"Fuck! How long until reinforcements, Dee?"

"I do not yet know how strong their landing invasion is, but my guess is not more than ten minutes."

"Can we cut the tracer out of you in the next five minutes?" I asked futilely.

"Possibly, if we knew where it was," he answered.

"Yeah, that does present a problem."

Tracy came back in the room fully clothed carrying a radio. She turned the volume all the way up. The noise was almost as disturbing as the dozen or so armed snouters.

"Any chance you could tell me what you're doing?" I shouted.

"Infestation removal."

My eyebrows furrowed. I thought maybe she had lost her mind. She then proceeded to sweep the irritating device across Drababan's body. The pitch changed dramatically every time she got anywhere near his right thigh.

"I think I found our snitch," she said as she shut off the radio. She pulled a large knife out of a sheath tied to her ankle.

"Shit, we got company," I said as I watched two troop transports land across the street from our apartment complex. Troops began to stream out.

"Mike, you need to leave before it's too late."

Who was he kidding? I thought. It was already too late.

"Sergeant!" I yelled as I ran to the doorway.

"Sir!" came the reply from two rooms down.

"Have someone light up one of those transports—we need to buy some time so we can get good and gone."

"Done!" came the reply.

"Tracy, grab your gear we're getting out of here."

"What about Drababan?" she asked.

I didn't answer her as I spoke directly to Drababan.

"We'll take out who we can. Good luck, my friend."

"Do not worry yourself about me, Miike. You are doing the right thing."

"Yeah, well just because I'm doing the right thing doesn't make it feel right. Keep the radio, Dee. If you make it out of here, I will contact you tomorrow on channel three."

If I thought the grenade had produced a bright light, I was wholly unprepared for the effects of the rocket launcher, the troop transport and a good third of its troops had now found their way to whatever heaven they believed in.

"That's our cue, Lieutenant. Let's go." I stopped to hug Dee on our way out. "Good luck, my friend."

"Don't believe in luck," he answered as he hefted the large rifle.

"Well, good luck anyway, you big lizard."

"As opposed to you, monkey man."

I grasped his arm, "I'll talk to you tomorrow."

"Gropytheon be willing," he responded.

CHAPTER THIRTY-SIX

Dennis' hearing came back minutely. The first thing he noticed was the beating of his heart, laboring with the effort as he put as much distance between himself and the aliens new outpost. The image of the dying gunny was still fresh in his mind. He had just crossed the Dedham-Norwood line when he felt more than heard a rumbling from his chest. At first he was perplexed as to its origin, he was reminded of the huge earth movers that had helped shape the new Indian Hill.

That's it, he thought *to himself, machinery.* Instinctually, Dennis dove farther into the cover of the surrounding woods, moments before three huge troop transports hovered by. They were not the same as the flying transports, but they were very similar. The front was low and steeply sloped to the cockpit, the turbines that kept the machine afloat bent the trees back, so much so that Dennis feared they might snap in two and expose him.

Dennis did not by any stretch of the imagination like that they were going in the same direction he was. Had the aliens not killed the gunny? But somehow got him to reveal where the Hill was?

"Oh, God, no!" he screamed.

Dennis went farther into the woods in an attempt to pick up the railroad track and the express route to Indian Hill. He began to run for all he was worth.

CHAPTER THIRTY-SEVEN
Eastern Seaboard Ground Occupation –
Southwest of Boston

The ground troop commander came out of his command module in time to see the guards tossing about what looked to be a human, or at least what remained of him.

"Sub Ground Troop Commander!" he yelled. "I thought when you said we had captured a prisoner that you meant a *live* one."

The sub ground commander walked out of the module, hoping that his over-zealous guards hadn't taken matters into their own hands. He was visibly relieved when he noted that it was not the prisoner that he had spoken of.

"No, sir, that is not the hu-man that I spoke of. The guards must have found a dead mammal. And decided to make sport of it."

"Well, make sure they don't do too much damage, the flesh will still make a good meal."

"Yes, sir."

"And bring me the live hu-man. He has much to answer for."

The sub ground commander motioned over two of his guards looming above a quivering mass of humanity. Snot and dirt and blood covered the man from head to toe. One of the guards grabbed the man by the hair and yanked him up. The man shrieked a high-pitched cry.

"He is somehow even more repulsive than the rest,"

the ground commander stated. "Give him to the Genogerians when I'm done questioning him."

The sub ground commander merely nodded.

The man shrieked again as he was thrust to the ground in front of the ground commander.

"Please," the man begged. With his hands interlaced and an expression of true horror upon his face. "Please don't eat me, they forced me to come here. I didn't even have a weapon."

"That seems to be true, Ground Commander," the sub added. "The guards found him cowering in the woods a full fifty yards from the firefight." The man was nodding vehemently in agreement with every word the sub-commander stated.

"Kill him," the ground commander stated as he began to turn away. "The shrivata (weasel) turns my stomach."

"Wait, I have information," the man-thing groveled.

"What kind of information could you possibly possess that would make me want to not kill you?" the ground commander snorted and kept heading into his node.

"I know where there are more humans—many more!" the man wailed.

"Get him cleaned up." The ground commander motioned to the guards, "He disgusts me in his present state. And, hu-man, if what you tell me isn't worth the water they pour on you, I will have my guards strip you piece by ragged piece of your flesh while you are alive."

The man shivered, but his eyes still betrayed a glint. A small smile flashed across his eyes.

Bennett, once again you have saved your own ass, he thought. *These things might be brutes, but I've been able to manipulate brutes all my life, it doesn't matter to me if I betray my people, what have they ever done for me?*

CHAPTER THIRTY-EIGHT – Mike Journal Entry 12

I pushed the troops hard to put as much distance between us and the attackers. We had been able to slip out the back of the apartment building before the aliens could close their net. The added confusion of the exploding transport aided in our escape. But I'm sure the distress was visible in my face.

"He'll make it out, Mike," Tracy said when we stopped to catch our breath, but it had sounded false to me and probably to her as well. Even from a half mile away, the explosion nearly ripped us all off our feet. The sky lit up like a summer day, blindness shaded my eyes almost as quickly as the shadow that crept over my heart. If we had felt the explosion from that distance how could anything have survived at the epicenter? I turned and continued moving to put more distance from the new killing fields. I had lost another near to my heart. It was another notch in my ever growing list of people I would eventually avenge.

"Fuck," I whispered and pushed my pace a little quicker.

The squad quickened with me. The aliens were sure to send more raiding parties out to check for survivors and nobody including myself wanted to be present when they showed. And now with the colonel gone I had to add the burden of command, this night had started off great and gone downhill fast.

***

Drababan watched as his friend and the rest of the humans escaped through the rear exit. His heart swelled when he realized they would make it. After living his life in solitude for so many years, he had believed he could never develop feelings for any others. His soul felt good.

Reality sunk in as he heard the activity in the front begin to reorganize after the transport had exploded. The Genogerians were more cautious in their approach, but approach they did. Drababan for the first time in a long time decided he was not quite ready to die, but he also knew that, having tasted freedom again, he would never go back to life on the Progerian ship.

He worked fast with a knowledge that was outlawed, but one in which he learned just in case of an eventuality along those lines. Although what was happening now was well beyond anything in his wildest dreams, he had merely hoped for some sabotage, but this would do just fine. The alien rifle began to whine at an ear piercing shriek the moment Drababan put it back together. He began to sit to say his prayers as the rifle's crescendo steadily grew.

A small thought popped into Drababan's head and it changed everything, his eyes flew open. "Gropytheon and possibly Michael's God wishes me to live!" he yelled. "They have shown me the way!"

The rifle began to vibrate, the oscillations were becoming quicker and quicker. Dee could praise his God later, for now it was time to make a hasty retreat. He bounded down the steps, five at a time, knocking one startled trooper unconscious long before he had been able to raise his weapon. Dee ran straight through two more troopers as he smashed through the rear exit. The first one knocked over got up on one knee and sighted in. He pulled the trigger the same instant the sun landed, or so his senses told him.

The shot went wide right; another was not forthcoming. Drababan was hurtled through space like a stone from a slingshot. What passed for a smile among his race spread from ear to ear.

"It is as his God has promised," he tried to say, but the wind ripped the words from his mouth. Drababan landed with an impact that would have made a small meteor jealous, consciousness nearly slipped from his grasp.

"Move or die," he muttered. "Move or die." He pushed himself off the wet turf. "So much like home," he mused and grabbed tufts of the wet sod between his claws.

Dee shakily got to his feet and never looked back as he managed a staggering walk away from the devastation of the feedback exploded rifle, now wishing that he had remembered to grab the radio before escaping.

CHAPTER THIRTY-NINE

Beth moved a quarter mile through the woods, always traveling south, but the going was slow and she was becoming fatigued quickly. Lack of sleep, food, water, and the constant stress of pursuit were taking their toll. If she didn't find help soon, she would not be able to make good on her threat to Pegged.

She wanted to get back on the highway as soon as possible, but somehow instinctually knew that only death waited there. She had to break through the woods and find a neighborhood where she could take refuge for the night, the thought of a tall glass of ice cold water spurred her on.

***

Pegged knew that Beth had gone farther into the woods, but he was not of the mind to follow her in there in case she had set another trap. He slowly trod along the highway, confident that she would have to come out eventually and then the chase would begin again in earnest.

Thirst scorched his throat and hunger gnawed at his stomach, but hatred spurred him on. He was confident that he could ride the hate out until the end.

CHAPTER FORTY

Frank was at the observation room when he noticed the three enemy transports pull into the super market parking lot.

"Oh shit," was all he could manage as he slammed his cup of coffee down on the desk in front of him. He depressed the silent alarm and all the lights in the complex went to a red glow.

Paul was in the room almost before Frank had the chance to pull his hand off of the alarm. His face drawn, his skin a little pale, although in the present light it was difficult to tell.

"Something must have gone wrong with the scouting party," Frank stated, never looking away from the screen as dozens of well-armed troops began streaming from the cargo holds of the transports. "Either the gunny or Dennis have given our whereabouts away," Frank said, running his hand through his hair.

"No, it's not that," Paul stated. "It's something different."

"How can you be so sure?" Frank asked. "Dennis and the gunny don't come back, but the enemy does."

"If Dennis or the gunny had been tortured enough to finally give our position away, why would they give them that point of attack? If they had been broken they would have gave up everything. No, this is something different. Look how they're standing around waiting for direction—they know we're around here, but they don't exactly know where."

Frank wasn't so sure, but now was not the time to argue. They were here and they weren't going to leave without some convincing.

"Should I send some troops out to greet them?" Frank asked.

"No," Paul answered flatly.

"No? If they breach The Hill, we'll be like fish in a barrel," Frank answered with a little too much vehemence.

"No, Frank," Paul said as he finally pulled his gaze from the screens and looked Frank dead in the eye. "They don't know exactly where we are. They may or may not wait for us to show ourselves. You can bet that if we engage them in a firefight, we'll have half the alien nation down here for a tailgating party."

"We can't just sit here waiting for them to decide the next course of action," Frank stated, understanding Paul's words but not liking them any more now that he understood.

"We'll let them sit for a while, let them stew in their own juices for a bit," Paul said as he walked away.

"I'm sitting here stewing in my own damn juices," Frank said to Paul's back.

CHAPTER FORTY-ONE

"Well, I guess ice is out of the question," Beth said as she stepped through the shattered door and into the lightless kitchen of a quaint Victorian style house, now reduced in grandeur by graffiti stating this was the end.

Pretty prophetic, Beth thought.

Her heart picked up a beat or two as she noticed the kitchen sink and the still existent faucet although the majority of the cabinets and a good portion of the countertop were gone. She felt her heart might break if she lifted the handle and nothing happened. She was almost ready to resign herself to the luck that had been following her for the last couple of years of her life. So sure she was of a dry rattle coming from the hidden piping that she began to turn back to the door, not ready to have another disappointment heaped on her plate.

Thirst won out, she half-ran, half-leaped to the faucet, fearful that it might be some kind of illusion like in the old desert war movies that her father used to watch. A pang of remorse crossed through her midriff; more likely it was the beginnings of dehydration.

She lifted the handle—nothing happened…and then, like an awakening monster, she heard creaks and pinging from below and then cool, cool water came out; although no color of water she had ever seen. She shrieked as the blood-red water spewed forth from the faucet. Beth couldn't help but picture a reservoir full of dead bodies releasing the last drops of their life's blood into the now tainted water supply.

Slowly, but surely, the water began to clear up. Beth's heart, in proportion, began to slow when she realized it had only been rust churned up from the bottom of unused pipes. Beth bent her head under the spigot and drank heavily from the near clear water. The metallic taste somehow comforting as the cool liquid coursed down her throat and spread its goodness into her stomach. The water was almost a shock to her body which had been getting used to a steady diet of dust.

When she had her fill, Beth stood up, water sloshing in her belly, and turned the faucet off. It looked like she had spilled more on the floor than she had drank. Now Beth was ready to investigate her surroundings. Her thirst slaked, the edge of her hunger dulled for a moment from the mineral rich water. Rifle raised, safety off, and hopefully live ammunition in the chamber, Beth stepped over the dismantled cabinet into the living room and into a nightmare.

CHAPTER FORTY-TWO – Mike Journal Entry 13

"Damn it," I whispered, as I put my binoculars down. I hadn't really needed them to see what was going on. It was more by habit after crossing into Walpole. I had decided we should stick to backstreets and cut through yards as opposed to waltzing down Main Street.

It panged me more than I cared to admit that not one barking dog or irate neighbor came out to yell at us for tearing up their azaleas. But even if anybody had been watching us from their darkened windows, nobody wanted to give a heavily armed column the slightest bit of lip. Danger was all around, whether from an invading alien race or bands of marauders desperate to keep themselves alive in the dark days. And 911 wasn't an option; there was no one on the other end of the line to pick up even if the phone lines still worked. Occasionally, we would see a half-starved, near feral dog slink away from our advance, but nothing more.

"They can't all be dead," I said to Tracy.

"They're not. I've seen a few window shades rustle as we go by," she answered. "You can't blame them, they have no idea which side of the line we fall on. Right now everyone looks like the enemy." Echoing my thoughts.

"Great minds think alike. Unfortunately," I answered.

She looked at me to gauge what exactly my response

meant, then shrugged her shoulders and moved up the column to give some additional orders to our point man. Who knows, maybe she was telling him to be less mean-looking so some old lady might come out and offer us some lemonade.

When we finally arrived at the street I grew up on, I couldn't help but feel like the returning prodigal son. It wasn't justified, but I felt it all the same. And then my already rock bottom heart dug a little deeper. My house was gone, not so much as a wall stood, it was just gone.

In the twilight, it was difficult to tell what had happened, whether my neighbors who felt I had brought this upon them needed to strike out at something that belonged to me or the aliens had made sure I could never go home again I couldn't tell. I walked over to the devastation with steely determination, lucky for me that my emotions did not make it to the forefront or I would have begun to cry like an infant. Tracy kept the unit moving past as I was rooted to the spot, maybe for some much needed privacy or to give me incentive to get my ass moving.

"What's done is done," I said, sadness in every syllable. In a few moments I had caught up to the rear guard.

"That your house, sir?" a soldier asked, condolence in his tone.

"Not any more, Private." I tried my best to not show how much it had rattled me. I didn't stay with him for what he was sure to say next, I was positive it would be some sort of apology that I had no desire to hear.

My street ended in a cul-de-sac that abutted Cobb's pond, which was directly across from the S&S parking lot. In the winter, the pond froze over and became our personal skating rink—the Bruins would be proud—but in the summer, it was a haven for nesting mosquitoes. They were a blight, but nothing like what I had just seen through my binoculars.

"How many?" Tracy whispered as she crawled to my position.

"At least fifty from what I can see, but I can't tell if any more of them are behind the store or in it for that matter," I answered.

"Has The Hill been compromised?" she asked, fear creeping around the edges of her question. She knew as well as I did that if Indian Hill was gone, we would become a roving band of marauders with no base and no supplies.

"No, they wouldn't have gone so quietly. But it scares the living shit out of me that they're this close, this quick. Something or someone gave us up. But if they knew the true strength of the hill and its armaments they would have sent ten times the amount of soldiers they've got here now." Truth was in my words but also hope, I wasn't a hundred percent sure of what I said but I would have been willing to bet on it.

"Do we skirt around and come in from the back?" Her words surprised me until I realized that she had probably seen the schematic of Indian Hill and would know as well as anyone its many exits and entries.

"No," I answered matter-of-factly. Even if I thought that my plan didn't involve some folly, I was ready to exact some small amount of revenge for the hole that had once been 2 Cobb Terrace. "This is what I want you to tell the men."

I picked up the binoculars as I laid the plan out for her. Guns would be blazing soon, but for now I was content to shoot my wrath through the curved optics I was staring through.

***

Dennis' breaths came in short ragged little bursts as he hunched over to catch his wind. He didn't see how he could possibly beat the aliens to the Hill, but he would die before he gave up trying. He had been in the throes of his fourth big attempt to gulp air when he heard small arms fire erupt about a half mile from his location.

It starts, he thought as he quaffed down his fifth breath and began his final run into the fray.

***

"Colonel, you'd better get in here!" Frank said, talking into the intercom system. Paul entered the observation post before Frank could release the talk button.

"Who sent men out there!?" Paul screamed as he heard the tinny sound of assault weapons firing over the monitor speakers.

"I can only guess the firing is coming from across the street. I can't see them with our camera angles, but that is where the aliens seem to be sheltering themselves from," Frank answered. "They're not ours, sir, the compound is in complete lockdown."

"Whoever is firing caught them by surprise and they know what the hell they're doing," Paul said smugly as alien after alien fell to the ground, unsure of which way to direct their fire. The bullets seemed to be coming from all directions at once. Death reigned from all around. When the aliens had finally coalesced enough to get orders and return fire, the attackers ceased.

"They're playing Indian," Paul quipped.

"What?" Frank asked looking up from the monitor.

"Hit and run, Frank. They laid down as much devastation as they could and they most likely melted back into the woods behind Cobb's Pond."

"Who the hell is it, sir?" Frank asked incredulously.

"Oh, I think you know," Paul answered, a huge smile spreading across his face. "I'm going to catch some shut eye."

"Now?" Frank asked, barely able to suppress his curiosity.

"Wake me in about an hour. I'm sure the aliens will be sufficiently lulled into thinking the attack is over by then."

"What the hell is going on out there?" Frank asked, grabbing the monitor by both hands, wishing he could peer around the edges of the image he was viewing.

CHAPTER FORTY-THREE

Tracy shuddered as she watched the place they had just moments before evacuated, light up like a Christmas tree, albeit a blue one.

The noise was deafening even from their perch three hundred yards away, the blue rays ripped through every piece of vegetation they encountered. Cobb's Pond hissed when a misplaced round struck, illuminating the pond up from underneath for a brief moment.

"That'll give the fish something to talk about," I said, sitting down next to Tracy after taking stock of our munitions and health; *unfortunately*, I pondered, *in that order*. I wasn't quite yet done exacting my revenge on the cold-blooded bastards and if I ran out of rounds early, I was almost willing to use my knife. I was not quite that insane *yet*.

We watched as a half dozen advance guards slowly approached what they presumed to be our final resting place.

"Sir, do you want to take them out?" Corporal Hawthorne asked.

"No, that would just give our position away," I said, handing him my binoculars. "Look over at the parking lot, their leader in the blue armor, that's just what he's waiting for. As soon as we start firing, he'll probably call in an airstrike. No, we'll just lay low, let them think they either evaporated us or we took off because of their superior numbers. Why don't you get a little shut eye, it's gonna be a long night."

"Yes, sir," the corporal answered, never fully taking his eyes off the snouters as they probed the area we had fired from.

Having not found anything but a few remnants of cloth, the guards began to head back to the relative safety of their makeshift defensive positions in the parking lot. Not more than a minute after the guards left three heavily armed alien fighters flew almost directly over our hiding spot. Next time we would have to hit and run a lot quicker, the fighters would be on alert now for any type of insurgence. That, and I was sure that after the dozen or so snouters we killed, reinforcements would be on their way shortly. While those around me began to doze, I couldn't keep my eyes off the enemy. As each peaceful minute went by, I could watch them visibly begin to relax. It was in their posture and the lax way they held their weapons, scanning the entire area. And why shouldn't they, they had superior numbers, superior weapons and complete control of the sky. Every visible sign of relaxation in them only agitated me that much more.

"Well, fuck them," I said as I grabbed a small satchel and skulked back from whence we had come.

Nobody noticed my departure or if they did they may have noticed my maniacal gaze and decided it was better to not say anything. The going was slow, I might have been half-crazed, but I knew enough to stay low. Their commander, at least, was still vigilant and on a consistent basis picked up what I figured was their version of binoculars and scanned the area for any tell-tale signs of impending violence. For my better and his worse he never saw me coming.

***

Frank went to Paul's quarters and was truly surprised that Paul had indeed grabbed some shut eye. Paul had just sat up and was rubbing the cob webs out of his eyes.

"It's been about an hour, Paul," Frank said, needlessly realizing that this was the reason Paul had risen.

Paul never looked up as he began to lace up his boots. "Frank, get me ten men."

Frank was slightly taken back. "For what reason, Paul?" Although he already knew the answer.

Paul finished lacing up his right boot and looked up. "I'm going to bring him back here."

"Paul, I don't think you should go. I'll get the men and I'll lead them back here."

"Frank, he's right outside our door, I'm going to get him," Paul answered, not leaving Frank any room for maneuverability.

Frank realized any further argument wouldn't lead to anything favorable answered, "Fine, but I'm coming with you."

"You've got five minutes, meet me by the west exit," Paul said, bending back over to get the left boot done.

Four minutes later, ten heavily armed men and Frank came to the exit. Paul had been there at least three minutes waiting. Frank wondered if he had run to get there, but if he had he wasn't breathing heavily.

"Did the major brief you?" Paul asked the assembled men. A few, Paul knew, had been battle tested, but a few of the others had the wide-eyed stare of those who were about to come face to face with their worst fears.

As one they answered. Some more vehemently than others. "Yes, sir!" the cry rang off the walls.

"Good, this is just a simple extraction, if, however, something should go wrong, do not, I repeat do *not* come back here. Is that understood?" Paul looked at each and every man to make sure this was clear. "Head back to the pump house and stay low until someone comes to get you. There's at least a week's worth of water and MREs." There was a soft moan from the men. Paul knew their pain; MREs could sustain life, but that was about it as far as taste went, and the pump house, although a safe haven was cold and dank.

Paul clapped Frank on the shoulder, "All right, let's move. We've got a hero to go and save."

The men moved silently through the exit. All of the parts on their gear that could make even the slightest whisper had long ago been taped up with electrical adhesive.

***

I slipped through the storm drain that went completely under Main Street, careful to make sure the bag I carried didn't get wet, not that it would have mattered, but it seemed like the right thing to do at the time. The rage that had flowed through my veins and sent me on this mission began to ebb ever so slightly to the point where I asked myself what the fuck I was doing.

"Well, too late now," I answered. "I must be losing it. I'm starting to answer the voices in my head."

The going was difficult through the flow pipe. It didn't measure more than three feet across and even that estimate was a gracious one considering all the debris that had accumulated over the years. And the smell of death was not something I had been prepared for, even though I had smelled it enough over the last two years to become more than acquainted with that acrid metallic odor. The pipe wasn't pitch black, but it was getting close. The thought of smacking into a body right now was not on my top ten list of things to do.

Even though I had more to worry about from the living than the dead. The smell increased the farther I crawled in until I knew without a doubt—like a great horror novel—the dead lay smack dab in the middle where the least amount of light was. I pulled my shirt up over my nose in a vain attempt to block out the worst of it. It didn't work. Claustrophobia, not my worst phobia but it was steadily climbing up the ladder, a panic began to well up from depths unknown. To make matters worse, dust and debris began to rain down on me as the ground above the pipe began to vibrate.

Earthquake in Walpole? It was long moments before I realized it was heavy troop transports traveling on the road I was underneath. Was the body a sign? Was it a hint from a merciful God to stop now and turn back?

No! God isn't merciful and he's not vengeful. He's worse; much, much worse, he's apathetic. Kicked back like a fat man drinking a beer on a Sunday afternoon, feet propped up and watching the games begin.

That wasn't fair, though, at least not entirely. I had looked to God more than once during my ordeal and like a crutch he had on some occasions propped me up. God hates whiners, he helps those who help themselves. I believed that wholly.

I moved forward with a new determination, just as my hand sunk up to the elbow in what I was one hundred percent sure wasn't a two foot deep pool of jelly, more like jellified human remains. I gagged on small pieces of my lunch as it made a return visit. I pulled my arm back through the cavity. I had just punctured through something's soft innards. With an audible plop, my hand came free. I wrestled for a long time with a scream caught in my throat, I had a realization that my voice would come through on the other side as if amplified from a megaphone, and any resultant shot taken down the pipe would almost certainly hit me, unless I dove for cover and that pretty much meant diving on the body.

"Yeah that's no good," I said softly. With my stomach under some semblance of control I pushed it as far away from me as I could and did my best to put as much distance between me and it as was possible.

"Oh, fuck!" I yelled as I felt something pull on my belt.

Visions of a demonic clown rising up and biting out my throat spurred me on. But the hand on my belt wasn't letting go. I expected the other hand to wrap its cold jelly-laced fingers around my neck; my vision began to pinpoint. I had to get that hand off my belt, it was dragging me down, both literally and figuratively. I began to thrash and kick at the entity but my foot couldn't find any solid purchase, like a gelatinous mass, my foot would only sink in and come back out followed by the putrid stench of the decayed. I hoped beyond hope that one of my kicks didn't end up in the creature's mouth I kept kicking. Nothing happened, nothing got bitten off, nothing came any closer, and nothing let go of my belt.

Reason tried desperately to reassert itself. Fouled water and sweat covered me from head to toe. The adrenaline shakes wracked my body. I pushed through some tangled up branches but still the dead clung as if holding onto me would bring them back to life. Panic would not allow me the fortitude to turn and face my adversary, flight was my only choice, but no matter the advances I made, it stayed one step behind.

Unconsciousness would have been welcome and it was a very viable option as my heart labored under the stress. I had to take my chances with what was behind me if I ever wanted to take my chances with what was in front of me. I turned my head to the left to see what it was that I would have to pry from my belt. Stark, bony fingers had latched on to my knife. Panic welled, not only was it trying to kill me, but it was going to use my own knife! I was repulsed at the thought of touching the fingers, but instinct won over and I grabbed them anyway. They weren't hard, in fact they were soft like cloth. The pinpricking of my vision began to subside, my hammering heart slowed to something closer to a hamster rather than a humming bird.

A small jewel dangled from the rope looped around my knife sheath. I pulled up to unloop the tangle and up from under the putrid water, the head of an enormous dog popped up, sprawling me on my back. The eyeless muzzle stared at me without an ounce of malice in it. It was only a dog that had been long dead and entombed in this underwater grave. I wanted to vomit but the thought of my undigested lunch floating around with me repulsed me more than the half decayed dog ever could. I pulled his collar over my knife sheath and pushed him away as far as possible.

"So much for keeping the satchel dry," I mumbled.

The Genogerians would have to go a long way to make me more scared than I had just been. It was possible, I admitted, but I didn't think I would have enough reserves in the adrenaline tank for it to happen. I was feeling washed out, the dog had literally taken a lot of fight out of me, but I sure as shit wasn't going back that way. 'Onward Christian Soldier,' I began humming.

***

Tracy awoke with a start, her soldier instincts telling her instantly something was wrong.

"Where's Mike?" she asked Flaherty, the sentry on duty.

"He went to relieve himself, Lieutenant," he answered, never taking his gaze off the enemy encampment. Tracy couldn't determine if it was because he was being diligent, or because he couldn't actually believe what he was seeing—like rubbernecking a roadside crash on a clogged highway.

"How long ago was that?" she asked, trying to keep calm even as she knew she had reason for apprehension.

"I'm…I'm not sure?" Flaherty said, finally pulling his eyes off the enemy encampment.

"What do you mean you're not so sure, Corporal?" Tracy flared, making sure he knew who he was talking to.

"Uh, Lieutenant, it didn't seem like that long ago, but now that I'm thinking about it, it's been about fifteen minutes."

"Get the men up!" Tracy ordered. "And give me those binoculars before you go. I'll deal with you later."

Flaherty swallowed hard. He knew Lieutenant Yarborough. She could be much more formidable than anything the aliens threw at them. "Yes, ma'am," he said hastily, retreating to where the rest of the squad had gone to get some rest.

Tracy scanned every possible entryway into the enemy stronghold and almost missed him as he climbed up a small embankment and into a small copse of woods not twenty feet from the nearest alien sentry. She noticed also with increasing alarm that he hadn't come out of the ditch and into the trees completely unnoticed. The alien commander was even now grabbing some of his guards and directing them toward where Mike had stopped. He had his back up against a tree, not facing the parking lot, completely unaware of his impending doom. He seemed to be doing something in his lap, but her view was cut off by a small mulberry bush.

"This is no time to be messing with your fly. Get up," she hissed through her teeth.

Dozens of more enemy troops were patrolling all around the parking lot. If she laid down cover fire she thought she could wipe out half of them before they realized what was happening. She watched Mike as he stood up, the guards had closed to ten feet and still he seemed oblivious. Weapons raised, the element of surprise and superior numbers, and still they approached hesitantly.

"At least the bastards are scared of us," Tracy voiced, but that would be small solace if she were to watch the man she thought she was falling in love with die in the next few moments. She watched Mike swivel away from the tree, his arm moving upward in an arc, surprise etched in his features as he realized how close the enemy had got to him.

"The C4," she whispered, "that's what he was messing around with in his lap."

The guards were momentarily frozen as they watched the small green bag just clear their bone ridged heads. But in milliseconds they trained their weapons back on Mike and in a few more milliseconds he would be dead because his rifle was still leaning up against the tree where he had left it. Tracy involuntarily shuddered as the first volley of shots was fired, the surprise never left Mike's face as the two nearest guards fell in a heap, lethal wounds erupting blood, like small volcanoes. Mike saw his chance and dove for cover grabbing his rifle as he did so as more small arms fire flared. Blue laser shots whipped through trees in the area that Mike had just vacated.

Tracy watched in semi-horror, not fully understanding what was happening. Some crazy bastard was running like a madman right at the guards, they had been surprised for the moment but they were quickly adapting to the new threat. Several of the guards pinioned and began to fire at the man that was screaming obscenities, most of which Tracy was sure she had never heard before. Mike's rescuer would have been cut in two, but Mike had recovered and was on one knee laying down savage deadly fire on the guards that were nearest. The crossfire had them addled, the one that had seemed to be leading them was dead and no new orders were being issued, survival instinct reared and the guards broke for cover as the hail of bullets began to wither their numbers. Reinforcements were having a difficult time getting to the skirmish because of the ones retreating.

Tracy could still see this was a losing struggle. Nearly twenty of the big brutes were with a leader and headed straight for the man she would later learn was Dennis. Brave, dumb Dennis. Dennis had dropped to one knee and was futilely attempting to put a full magazine into his rifle. The guards were almost past their makeshift defenses and would have him in their sights when, without warning, the earth moved. The blast sent death and debris everywhere. No one within fifty feet survived the blast. Mike underestimating the power of the explosives was saved only by blind luck as the tree he was hiding behind took the majority of the energy released. The bark from the bottom of the tree to halfway up was sheared off. Dennis was luckily out of the main part of the blast zone but was still unceremoniously deposited on his ass from the concussion.

Who knows, maybe it'll knock a little sense into his head—what the hell was he thinking? I owe that man a kiss, Tracy thought.

And it was pretty much the same thought Mike had, without the kiss, well maybe the kiss too. A crater ten feet deep formed in the asphalt and dirt of the parking lot, small rocks rained down, what was left of the soldiers were being quickly disposed of as Tracy saw from the north side of the parking lot what looked like a small band of Marines doing mop-up duty. There was no more fight left in the Genogerians, but Tracy knew this would be a short-lived victory if she didn't get her squad out of there now.

"Sergeant!" she yelled, more so because she was afraid that after the blast she had gone deaf, she was relieved when he answered her and she heard him just fine.

"Ma'am!" he answered, possibly a little too loud.

"Must be having the same thoughts I am."

"Ma'am?"

"Get the men. Let's get the hell out of here."

"Yes, sir, I mean, ma'am."

In an instant, they were on the move; caution in their movements, speed on their minds.

CHAPTER FORTY-FOUR
Eastern Seaboard Ground Occupation – Location southwest of Boston - Dedham
Ground Commander Chofla and Ground Sub-Commander Ruthgar

"Sir, one of our fighters has reported a battle in the town the hu-mans call Walpole," the underling said, more than a little exasperated at being the bearer of bad news.

The underling didn't like this savage backward little planet. Nothing good had come out of it so far, it just didn't seem to be worth the effort when there were so many less inhabited planets scattered throughout the universe. And the multi-colored, ugly-looking puny hu-mans. They were like feral fahquar (dog-like animals) on his home planet, not too bright or too big, but they could pack one hell of a bite if provoked.

"How many of the hu-mans have been killed and captured?" Chofla asked, not even pondering any other outcome.

"Sir, the fighter couldn't be sure."

"Well, if his radio was broken, why didn't he just land and ascertain the situation himself?" the ground commander still not understanding the flow of the conversation.

"Sir," the underling gulped, "there wasn't a safe place to land his ship."

Recognition finally began to ignite in the

commander's soulless eyes.

"Ruthgar, what exactly do you mean?"

"Sir, the entire detachment plus the reinforcements, from what the pilot could tell, were completely wiped out."

"That's impossible—there had to be over one hundred front-line Genos there!" the commander yelled.

Ruthgar backed up. "A hundred and twenty-five, sir."

Pure savagery echoed in every mannerism of the commander. "Could the pilot estimate how many of the humans had perished?" he asked with a menacing snarl.

"He couldn't see any, sir, but..." he answered before Chofla could explode, "They aren't quite as primitive as we thought, they may have taken their dead with them."

"Perhaps," answered the ground commander, but even this notion did not calm the savage beast within. How could he possibly call the mother ship and tell them of this new devastation? Simple. He smiled. He wouldn't."

"Sir?"

"Get the majority of the troops loaded up, they're moving out."

Ruthgar hoped beyond hope that he meant off the stinking little insignificant planet, but he knew better. He could smell the bloodlust scent gland from the ground commander from across the room.

"May I ask where, sir?" Even though the answer was a foregone conclusion.

"To Walpole, Ruthgar. Where else?" Chofla smiled now that he had a plan in mind.

"Home would be nice," Ruthgar responded softly. Anything less than total commitment would be construed as weakness and weakness generally got you killed.

"Communicate with Ground Commander Pantherd, I will require more of his troops as well." Chofla said as he ushered Ruthgar out of his make-shift office.

CHAPTER FORTY-FIVE

Paul's men had made quick work of what was left of the alien detachment. Paul noted with interest that when their commander fell the rest of the survivors had become a disorganized mass, barely mustering a defense. He wasn't sure if it was fallout from the concussion of the explosion or something even more significant. Paul strode quickly to where Mike and Dennis were hugging and exchanging greetings. Paul could only hope their reunion would be so cordial.

"Hello, Mike," Paul said as he approached, still a good fifteen feet away.

Mike turned from his embrace with Dennis. Paul couldn't be sure but he would have sworn he saw a glimmer of malice flash across Mike's face and in an instant it was gone. The coolness however in Mike's voice was not.

"Hello, Paul," came the flat reply.

Paul had closed the remaining gap physically, but now he had to try to bridge the gap in their relationship. Nothing truly inspiring came to mind.

"Took you long enough," Paul said.

"Well, I got a little lost. I took a left hand turn and ended up in France," Mike added.

Paul could not tell if this was a jibe or a joke, Mike's face belied nothing.

"Good to see you, man," Mike said as he pulled Paul close into a bear hug. Paul reciprocated, a visible release of tension exiting his body.

"I guess I owe you both, you really saved my skin today." Mike beamed.

"That makes us even, Mike," Dennis said solemnly. "I'll never forget the day you pulled us out of that car, even if I wasn't awake."

Paul nodded in agreement. Paul in his elation to see Mike had almost forgotten that Dennis had been missing in action. "Shit, Dennis, I thought you were dead," Paul said, turning toward him.

"It was close, Paul. They got the gunny, used him like a hacky sack," Dennis said, forgetting his earlier elation in a matter of a heartbeat. Grief threatened to overwhelm him as he placed his hand over his face.

"Let's go back to the Hill, Dennis. We'll get those wounds checked over," Paul said, placing his arm around Dennis' shoulder.

"Paul, I'll be right in, I'm going to go get my squad," Mike said.

Paul acknowledged him with a nod of his head.

Frank was walking over after issuing orders to his men. He welcomed Dennis back, a huge smile spread across his face to see his friend returned from the dead and safe and sound; his earlier morose replaced with joy. So fixated on the scene in front of him, Frank never saw the three Genogerians coming through the broken glass pane windows in the front of the store. Rifles firing, Frank was shot repeatedly, a small smile forever frozen on his face even as his insides oozed out of the foot and a half long gash across his back.

Dennis was first to attack and bring his weapon to bear, the short staccato sound of the M-16 breaking through the eerie silence as Frank fell to his knees. Mike wheeled, rifle at the ready as the nearest of the insurgents dropped in a heap. Multiple rifles now took up the call to arms, at least a hundred or so rounds had found their mark. The second shock troop to die was split down the middle like an over ripe banana, his comrade close behind in death. The damage had been done, though.

Paul ran to Frank's crumpled body hoping beyond hope he would still be alive. If Frank had any final words they would be forever lost, he lay still, the smile of seeing his friend still upon his face. Paul wanted to weep, Dennis fell to his knees and did; the events of the last ten hours finally taking their toll. Mike knew better than to try to console either man, both would grieve in their own way. Mike turned, his barrel still smoldering, and headed off to get his Marines before the inevitable happened and the Genogerians returned.

Time was of the essence.

***

Tracy and the troops were even now making their way across Main Street and coming into the mouth of the parking lot. They had taken defensive positions when the firing had erupted and were now seeing what the din was about now that it was once again quiet. Mike walked over to meet them, his rifle slung over his shoulder. Weariness set in now that they had made it back, what came next surprised him more than anything had in a long while. Tracy came up and punched him square in the jaw, staggering Mike.

"What the fuck do you think you're doing?" she yelled.

The Marines around her stopped, mouths hanging open. Even those closest to Frank stopped to stare at the new development. Mike would have answered, but he feared she may have shattered all the work the alien hyper-chamber had corrected, that and the fact he was still in shock from the blow.

"Are you trying to get yourself killed!? Is that what you want? You don't have that right anymore!" she spat at him.

Mike still had not managed a viable defense. And if

he didn't react soon she would finish what the Genogerians started.

"The right?" Pathetic but still words, the effect was instantaneous and it did not have the desired effect he was looking for. Tracy became enraged. Her steel gray eyes almost smoldering.

"The right!" she reiterated. "I'll let you know when you can die. You've taken my heart and I'm not in any rush to get it back," she said as she punched him mercifully on the shoulder this time, but it was by no stretch of the imagination a pulled punch. Mike knew he would suffer some bruising.

"I love you, Mike, like I've loved no other. Maybe it's because of how crazy the world has gotten and how many loved ones I have already lost. I can't take losing someone else I care for. I won't let it happen again. Never again."

She finally broke down, tears streaming from her eyes, ineffectual blows now hitting his arms. Mike grabbed her and pulled her close, partly to keep her from hitting him but mostly to just reassure her that he was in fact alive and well. There was something about the woman he couldn't quite put his finger on. He wasn't sure if he was quite in love with her yet, but he was rapidly approaching it and just because she reached there first did in no way diminish what he felt for her. If anything, it only strengthened it.

The squad streamed around them, attempting to give them some semblance of privacy. Besides, they wanted to see if they could get their hands on some of the alien weaponry strewn throughout the parking lot before the rest of the detachment already there took everything. Relationships were cool and all, but that didn't compare to the shock rifles.

Tracy's sobs subsided somewhat, her face buried in Mike's chest. He lifted her face so that she was looking at him.

"You've never looked more beautiful," Mike said as he kissed her, and for the briefest of moments, everything around them dissolved; the chaos, the carnage, the stink of death—replaced with the wonder and need of a new love. Mike's heart ached with the thought of what he had put her through.

"I promise I will never do anything that stupid again," Mike said, fully meaning it. But nevertheless, as time would point out, he was lying through his teeth.

CHAPTER FORTY-SIX

Beth nearly swooned when she looked into the living room, a small family of three had been strung upside down. Multiple deep cut wounds crisscrossed all of their bodies so their entrails were left dangling to the floor. It looked like some version of a piñata from Hell; grimaces of pain and suffering were forever etched upon their now taut mouths.

The youngest appeared to be no older than nine or ten, of which sex was impossible to tell. Though they were all nude, the mutilation was so severe as to make identification impossible. Beth struggled to hold on to the precious water she had just drank and for all appearances it looked like it was going to be a losing battle. Beth had turned and was heading for the door before she lost her precious cargo, when she heard a deep and menacing growl. It was coming from somewhere in the shadows off to her left from what appeared to be a hallway leading most likely into a study or spare bedroom. Beth figured this was probably at one time the family pet, but now it looked like the family was more dinner than companionship.

"Scruffy, want to taste some fuckin' lead?" she said as bold as possible while also trying to suppress throwing up.

She was rewarded with a growl that was considerably closer, but she was no closer to finding its location in the near darkness the shadows of the house were affording her new adversary. She wanted to back away and get out of that circle of hell, but she knew if she fell, the dog would be on her before she could pull the trigger and the rifle would be useless if it got too close. The dog growled again, almost as if it could read her thoughts.

"Well, one things for sure," she said. "You aren't a Chihuahua." The rumblings took on an echoing effect in the small antechamber.

Beth kept backing up, doing her best to not run into anything, the dog's growls becoming louder. She could hear its toenails on the tile. *But how could that be?* she wondered. That would mean the dog was no more than ten feet from her, and she still hadn't seen it. Fear started to rear itself in Beth's psyche. *Maybe it's the demon that hung this family up.* A dog was an acceptable threat right now, a spawn of Satan was not. And then her fears were instantly inflated and deflated as the dog passed through a brighter spot in the hallway. It wasn't a demon, per se, but it was by far the largest dog she had ever seen. It's massive head even with Beth's chest.

"Jesus," she let out involuntarily.

Spittle hung from its gaping maw, teeth bared in an insanely large mouth, one with which Beth was sure could take her arm off in one bite. Beth unsteadily raised her rifle. She had no intentions of becoming anyone's dinner. The dog stared at her savagely, its red-rimmed eyes locked on to her own. One was the hunter and one was the prey, but for the life of her, Beth didn't know which was which.

Beth sighted on the monster and pulled the trigger, fully expecting the loud noise in the small confines to make her head ring like the Bells of Notre Dame for at least a few hours. She heard nothing, save for the settling of the now turned-off water pipes, she'd forgotten to flip off the safety. The dog was nowhere in her sights. It leapt and slammed into her shoulders. The rifle clattered to the floor uselessly. Beth could only hope that a ripped out throat wouldn't hurt too much, her mind working in over-drive. She figured she would only be conscious for a minute or so while the dog ate her alive. She slammed to the floor with the full weight of Cerberus on her chest, white, shooting stars of pain floated through her eyesight as the air was forcefully pushed out of her body. The white stars began to turn brown as she fought valiantly to hold on to consciousness.

She most likely would have passed out if not for the extraordinary event that happened next. The dog didn't rip her throat out as she feared, but licked her from her lips all the way to her hairline. The thick saliva trail nearly finished off what the dead family in the living room started, her stomach was roiling. The thick muzzle still hung perilously close to her face. She in no way wanted to provoke the beast, but if she could somehow get herself into a more defendable position, maybe she could still get out of there.

***

The beast which she dubbed Sampson drank greedily from the empty coffee can she had filled with water. She wasn't completely comfortable with the dog, but he didn't seem now to be so intent on ripping her face off, if he ever had. A perfunctory tour of the rest of the house showed the dog had nothing to do with the carnage in the living room. Far from it. The near starving dog had not taken even the slightest bit of meat from its now deceased family.

From what Beth could tell, the dog more than likely had been locked in the laundry room when the killings had begun. The door was a thin paneled one that had been shredded in the dog's attempts to vacate the room and most likely assist in the defense of his family. Unfortunately, his freedom had come far too late, or she figured that the killer or killers would have had some serious problems to contend with when the dog unleashed his savage fury.

"You hungry, boy?" Beth said as she returned from the top floor, checking to see if there was anything that could help her during the rest of her trek. Sampson looked up and what at first Beth took to be another growl quickly turned into a floor rumbling belch. Beth sighed in quick relief.

"Let's go, boy. Let's find somewhere a little more hospitable for the night."

With uncanny understanding, the dog walked to the opening of the living room and let out a slow, mournful throaty sound and walked out the front door into the burgeoning twilight. Beth shook her head and followed. She saw some small fires off in the distance, but her trust of the majority of humanity had taken a serious hit and she planned to avoid those small outposts of 'civilization' at all costs. Anyway, it seemed Sampson was of the same ilk, he walked a few steps ahead of her but in a direction parallel to the fires, always keeping them downwind, most likely so he could tell if anyone approached. Beth was thankful for the company even if she thought only fifteen minutes ago he was going to eat her. Sampson turned every few streetlamps to make sure his new charge followed, Beth wasn't sure where he was headed but it was nice to follow for a change. After a while, Sampson stopped his tail wagging. Beth approached cautiously.

"What is it, boy?" Beth said as she approached the dog. His tail moved faster at her words, he waited for her to catch up and made a beeline for the variety store ahead. Even from this distance and in the near darkness, Beth could tell the pickings were going to be slim. Most of the empty shelves had been overturned and the windows broken out. What had been in there once was long gone.

Sampson was not deterred, he strode purposefully through the shattered door, Beth approached more deliberately with her rifle at the ready. Food debris littered the floor, the crunching of old cereal echoing eerily in the emptiness. Sampson did his best to clean the mess up. She thought she may have named him incorrectly; Hoover seemed a much more apt moniker. Beth walked through the store, hoping that possibly some edible morsel had been passed over or else she would be on the ground soon fighting Sampson for floor scraps. She walked into the back storage area. This place was worse off than the rest of the store.

She was about to walk back through the door and out into the main part of the place when a shimmer of red and yellow caught her attention, it was almost completely under a rack used for dairy products, a nearly full box of Slim Jims. Something which at one time she would have turned her nose up to but right now it took on a near mystic quality. Had she found filet mignon right now she couldn't have been more pleased.

"Sampson!" she cried. The dog slammed through the door quicker than Beth could have imagined. Eyes wild, teeth barred. Whatever trauma he had been through, he was anxious to make sure it never happened again. Beth was in awe of his reaction.

"It's nothing, boy. Come here." His face quickly relaxed and his tail began to wag as he realized there was no threat to his new pack. He trotted over, pieces of Cap'n Crunch still clinging to his snout.

"You big moosh," she said as she wiped the cereal off him. "I've got something you might like a little better."

Sampson's tail wagged even more furiously as he got his first whiff of the near meat product being unwrapped. Drool poured from his mouth. Beth was tempted to put the Slim Jim on the ground, lest the dog in his haste to eat mistakenly take her fingers off. But he waited patiently as she struggled with the wrapper. When she put her shaking hand out to his mouth, Sampson looked into her eyes as if to ask if she wanted him to have this tasty treat.

"You led me here, you should have the first bite."

Sampson gently took the offering from her hand and in one bite had the snack in his mouth. Beth couldn't be entirely sure, but she would have sworn on a Bible that he was smiling. Beth took a little more time to savor hers, but not by much. Sampson waited patiently, his front paws occasionally pattering in anticipation but he never made a threatening move. Ten minutes later and a dozen and a half Slim Jims gone they headed back to the main part of the store. Hunger not yet gone, but the edge definitely dulled. Sampson stopped first, right at the storage room door. Beth stopped too, she hadn't heard anything, but the dog's reaction froze her in her tracks.

"Are you sure you saw somebody walk in here, Jimmy?" The deep voice carried even in hushed tones.

Beth's heart began to trip over itself. *What is wrong with people?* she wondered. Sampson made as if to go out and deal with the threat. Beth gently put her hand on his massive shoulder, his muscles quivered with a surge of adrenaline. He looked up at Beth, she shook her head and mouthed the word 'no'. Sampson eased a little. Muscles not shaking, but they were taut. He would react quickly if the need arose.

Beth could tell the people in the store were trying to be stealthy but the spilled dry goods on the floor made their approach pathetically loud in the eerie quiet. She could hear the two men methodically walk up each aisle, searching. Why they were so intent on finding her was a mystery.

"Whoever you are, you need to come out," one of the voices yelled dangerously close to her hiding spot. Sampson laid his ears back, as if to make himself more aerodynamic when he sprang. "This is our store and we don't take kindly to looters!"

"Looting?" she whispered. "There's nothing in here."

Sampson turned to look at her, as if to say, 'be quiet'.

"Yeah, we won't hurt you," came the other voice.

"Yeah, right, where have I heard that before?" she mumbled.

Sampson looked at her again as if beseeching her to stay silent, even if she had said it loud enough for only the dog to hear.

"Okay, okay," she mouthed. Sampson seemed to be

happy with her answer and returned his full attention to the store room door.

"Listen, we're good people, we don't want any trouble. We just want you out of here."

Beth knew she was being stupid, but he sounded sincere. She was about to go through the door, when a voice she heard too many times before froze her in her tracks.

"You might not be looking for trouble, but it sure as hell found you," came the voice of the man that had been relentlessly tracking her for miles.

"Look, mister, we—" Beth never heard the rest of the man's plea as a gunshot roared through the store.

"Wait-wait!" came the other man's cry, but it fell on deaf ears. Another shot silenced him even before he could ask God for help.

The acrid smell of gun smoke filled the small store room. Beth feared Sampson might sneeze. But he held fast, even more leery than he had been only moments before. When the echoing from the rounds had finally dimmed, the man spoke again.

"Honey, I'm home," came the almost cheery voice, but Beth could feel the malice dripping from his words. "Are you here? Were you just picking me up a little something?"

Pegged knew in the very depths of his black soul that his quarry was in the store somewhere. He wanted to rush in and finish this off now, but there was absolutely no light inside whatsoever and she could be anywhere. And something else was troubling him; he couldn't be sure, but he didn't think she was alone. He didn't know why he thought that, but he was sure. And whoever was in there with her was dangerous. Very dangerous.

"What kind of fucking greeting is this, bitch!" he yelled in impotent rage. "I come miles and miles to see you and you don't even come to meet me at the door—pretty ungrateful if you ask me!?"

He's the devil incarnate, Beth thought. *How in God's*

name could he possibly know I'm in here? Beth didn't dare voice her concern for fear the man's hearing was somehow even better than Sampson's. Even Sampson sensed how dangerous this man could be. He didn't back down but his stance showed he was going to be more on the defensive. Beth understood his motives completely.

She jumped a little bit when Pegged startled her out of her thoughts.

"I'd love to come in and shop with you, but I think I might wait until the morning when I can see a little better."

Beth fought down panic at the thought of spending a sleepless night in a store room with no possibility of escape. Surely the sound of the gunshots would bring help, wouldn't it? No. She had to be honest with herself, it was more likely that anybody that had heard was going to barricade themselves in. Beth moved to the far wall and slid down as quietly as possible.

"I guess it's going to be a long night," she said almost inaudibly.

Sampson turned and imperceptibly nodded. He took two steps toward her, turned back around and unceremoniously plopped to the floor. His body supplied ample heat to her rapidly cooling legs. Beth almost couldn't believe it, even as it happened. Her eyes fell like a stone, she was asleep before her head hit her chest. Sampson propped his head on his front paws. He dozed, but not too deeply; nightmares of his butchered family haunted his dreams.

Beth awoke to Sampson's massive muzzle nudging her arm. Beth stood up slowly and went to the front of the storeroom to look through the glass partitions that at one time housed the dairy section. Sunlight was slowing creeping along the floor of the store and right behind it, quiet as death, was Pegged, his eyes blazed as his head swiveled from side-to-side as he tried to take everything in.

Beth held her breath as she slowly lowered herself so she wasn't quite as exposed. Sampson bristled as he watched the man come up the far aisle. Beth moved without thinking as her pursuer disappeared down another aisle. She opened the storeroom door and motioned for the dog to go through. He didn't need any further urging. Beth and Sampson moved to the opposite side of the store, Beth keeping careful to make sure she was never out in the open, her heart leapt when she came around the corner and stepped in a semi congealed pool of blood, if she hadn't had Sampson to brace against she would have fallen and landed in the gelatin-like liquid. Sampson skirted the carnage, never taking his eyes off the front of the store.

Beth contained her angst and managed to not make an uncontrolled run for freedom. She was still scared the madman had somehow noiselessly backtracked toward them and would mow her down the second she left the relative safety of the aisle. Sampson seemed to sense her trepidation and apparently was not of the same mind that the bad man was waiting. He almost casually walked to the front and stopped, waiting for Beth to follow.

Fine, apparently at least one of us knows what he's doing.

Sampson wagged his tail. Upon successfully exiting the store, Beth went to the left so as to be out of sight from the windows. She took her first big intake of air in over ten minutes and it felt good.

***

He eyed the store room door for over fifteen minutes to discern if there was any movement in there. It was impossible for anyone to be that motionless. Unless he had been spotted and she was merely waiting for him to come out in the open, which he would have to do to get to the door. But maybe she was asleep and that was why there was nothing going on. If that was the case, then he should just open the door and be done with her, but what of the other presence? Maybe they had taken shifts, there was no way they were both asleep, was there? He hated being this indecisive, this was something more the bitch was going to pay for.

Good or bad, Pegged had never truly pondered any action he did. Only after it was long over would he spare a short moment to mull over his decisions and then it was never an analytical process, it was more of a sweet remembrance.

CHAPTER FORTY-SEVEN

Dennis was sullen, looking at his rapidly cooling cup of coffee as I sat down next to him. He briefly looked up to acknowledge my presence and then stared back at his beverage as if he fully expected something magical to issue forth. I felt awkward, on one hand I was happier than a pig in shit that I was back at the Hill amongst my friends, on the other hand I knew the pain Dennis was going through, so I was attempting to reign in my jubilation.

"It's good to see you, Dennis," I said. I put an arm around his shoulder.

"It's good to see you too, Mike." Dennis finally looked over at me, instead of the steam issuing forth from his cup of coffee.

"I've got to admit, I never thought this day would come. Escaping the aliens the first time was a one-in-a-million chance. Being able to do it again pretty much seemed like an impossibility."

Dennis nodded in agreement. "We're going to die here," he added.

I nodded in agreement. "I don't see any other outcome. But it's not going to be a slaughter, Dennis. We're going to do some serious payback for all that we lost. They'll win, they'll take this Hill—hell, they'll take the planet, but it won't be something they will soon forget. They aren't super beings, they bleed and they die just like we do. They just had the advantage of surprise and superior technology. But the surprise is gone and we've got some of their technology now. And one more thing, we're way more pissed off than they are."

"You got that right." He flashed a smile for the first time in days.

"Hey, bud, any chance there's something around here a little stronger than coffee?"

"Yeah, Frank was saving a little something for when I got back from my last mission. Now's as good a time as any."

"Frank would want it that way," I said.

"You know, bud, I think you're right," Dennis said, standing up, we headed out the door of the cafeteria together.

CHAPTER FORTY-EIGHT
Eastern Seaboard Ground Occupation – Location northwest of Boston - Lawrence Area
Ground Commander Pantherd and Ground Sub-Commander Brockell

"Sir, we have lost contact with our detachment sent to the Walpole Township in tandem with Ground Commander Chofla's troops," the sub ground commander of landing party 117B said nervously. Landing parties around the globe have been attacked, sometimes viciously, but none yet have taken the damage of the Boston contingent.

"Sub Ground Commander, get in touch with the mother ship," the ground commander said, his upper lip twitching in the universal sign of nervousness among Genogerians. "Tell them we will need reinforcements—a battalion if they've got it—and have them sent to the Town Center in Walpole."

The ground commander knew the personnel around the globe were spread thin until true warships from their home planet arrived, this was more of a containment operation than of an occupation. The ground commander still didn't understand why they hadn't waited for the larger force to arrive, but he knew in the eyes of the Progerian leaders, he and his kind were expendable and the new Supreme Commander was of the mindset to show his higher-ups he was worthy of his own war vessel by taking this little planet on the outskirts of the known universe with only a heavy scout vessel. The commander knew the whole excursion was teetering on the brink of disaster, if the hu-mans had any idea how truly low in numbers the ground forces were they would rise from their holes and slaughter the Genogerians.

"And, Ground Sub Commander, tell them to hurry."

"Yes, sir," the sub ground commander said as he rushed out the door to relay the message to the communications officer.

Within six hours, close to a thousand heavily armed shock troops began to set up camp in Walpole's center. A stream of troop ships clogged the sky as they jockeyed for position to land, deposit their cargo, and head back to do it again.

CHAPTER FORTY-NINE – Mike Journal Entry 14

I had tossed back more than I planned. Dennis seemed unwilling to stop drinking to Frank's memory and I had obliged. Me, my liver, and my head were going to pay dearly.

I stumbled back to my quarters and had fallen asleep almost before my body made contact with the bed. Tracy came in a little later after assimilating her men in with the rest of the soldiers on the Hill. She knew where I had been and deeply sympathized with Dennis she would tell me so the next day as I nursed one killer hangover. Tracy took off her battle fatigues climbing as quietly into bed as possible. She snuggled up next to me and within minutes was fast asleep.

***

"Mike, want to go for a walk?" Paul said from the doorway.

I was halfway out of bed before Paul had finished his question. I quickly rubbed the cobwebs out of my eyes and reached for my boots before I realized I was still wearing them.

"Rough night?" Paul quipped.

"Yeah, I had a drink with Dennis," I answered.

"A drink?" Paul asked.

"You get the point. Where're we going?" I asked, my hangover threatening to cleave my head in two.

"Grab your rifle," Paul answered.

"Oh, that kind of walk." I suited up and was out the door in less than two minutes. It didn't hurt that I was still mostly dressed from the night before.

"What about her?" Paul said, motioning back to Tracy's still sleeping form.

"Who?" I said, still a little out of it as I turned back. "Shit, I didn't even know she was there."

"You didn't know *she* was there? You must have drank a lot." Paul laughed out loud.

"Well, you know Dennis. Let her sleep." I pulled the door shut behind me.

"What's the story with her?" Paul asked as we got away from the door.

"Not sure, my friend. After Beth pretty much told me to go fuck myself I was in a bad way. Basically, I wanted to take a break from the fairer sex."

"You weren't going gay on me were you?" Paul asked with a small smile on his face.

"If I did, I'm sure you would have been the first person to call me," I shot back.

Paul punched me in the arm and, for a small moment, we crossed over a span of time. We both felt more like the eighteen-year-old carefree kids we had been than the warriors we had been forced to become. But our smiles ran from our faces as we rounded the corner and twelve well-armed Marines awaited us.

"What exactly does this walk entail, Paul?" I asked as I tightened down my ammunition belt

CHAPTER FIFTY

Beth was a good three hundred yards away from the store when she heard the muffled sounds of gunshots. She knew without hesitation that it was her pursuer either shooting at phantoms or in frustration when he discovered she was no longer there.

***

Chills ran up and down the length of Pegged's back like currents from an electric eel after blowing gaping holes through the metal-covered storage room door with his newly acquired .45. He had expected to be shot himself as he kicked the door open, fully thinking the bitch to be lying in wait for that exact maneuver. What happened next scared him more than the thought of her waiting. That, he could have dealt with, but this took him completely by surprise. There was nobody there, and after a quick survey of the room, he was certain there was no back way out, no small windows and certainly no doors.

"What are you?" he screamed. Fine lines of insanity began to edge in on the perimeter of his mind. He began to wonder if she was ever even real, or if he had taken a deep dark plunge down a rabbit hole and was chasing a figment of his blackened mind.

But what about your ear? a disembodied voice whispered.

"Yeah, what about my ear?" he said aloud.

That didn't happen by itself, the voice answered.

"Yeah, it didn't happen by itself," he echoed as he absently reached up to touch the still-puss-oozing hole in the side of his head. If he hadn't known better, he might have thought it was his brains leaking out. That would have been infinitely better than the infection causing the putrid liquid. It would have been a much quicker and easier death.

"*Fuck!*" he bellowed.

***

Beth paused a moment, thoroughly enjoying that her pursuer was frustrated.

"Serves him right for making us stay in a closet for the night," Beth said as she reached down and scratched behind Sampson's ear.

Sampson looked up grateful for the scratch but not nearly as happy as the woman he traveled with. He could smell the disease and insanity of the man chasing them from where they were and he wanted no part of it, not in the slightest.

CHAPTER FIFTY-ONE – Mike Journal Entry 15

For forty minutes Paul, myself, and the other twelve soldiers with us, watched an alien beehive of activity in the town center. Genogerians tightly patrolled the perimeter as dozens of transport ships continually off-loaded supplies and personnel. Paul sat back down from the hedge he was looking over.

"Looks like they weren't too happy with our welcome wagon committee," Paul said wryly.

I kept looking at the spectacle before me. Although we were a couple of hundred yards from the nearest sentry it was still entirely too close. "What makes you say that?" I answered in the same tone Paul had used as I sat down with a hard thump. "There's got to be about a thousand of them and they look pissed off. I hope I'm not the reason why they were so pissed."

Paul looked over at me and had to try with great difficulty to not laugh.

"Fuckin', good one," he said.

"So what's the plan?" I asked. "You didn't bring me out here to sightsee."

"Ulterior motives? Me?" Paul said, trying to placate me. "Alright, you know me better than that. I want to launch an assault." Paul had expected me to act with trepidation or at the least with hesitation.

"When?" I responded.

"Shit, I knew I loved you for a reason."

"Must be for my insanity," I answered.

"I want to hit them after they get everything they plan on getting here, here. But before they get too settled and start to explore their surroundings."

"So by 'explore' you mean seek and destroy?"

"Yeah, that's pretty much what I mean."

"Do you really think they could find the Hill?" I asked, now showing the signs of trepidation that Paul had expected earlier. Paul knew I wasn't concerned for myself, I had someone else in mind.

"Do you really want to find out? If they stumble on the Hill, it'll get real bad, real fast."

I shivered.

"We've got to bring it to them before they have that chance. But only after their air support is gone."

"Do you think they'll have some ships available?"

"We've been monitoring their maneuvers around the globe. We can only speculate that either our air forces around the world took down more than was initially thought or that they just really didn't have all that many to begin with."

"Well, that makes sense."

"What's that?" Paul asked, curious to discover some more information about a puzzle that had been mystifying him for weeks now.

"The ship that's sending all these aliens and weaponry and supplies is not an assault ship," I answered.

"Are you fucking kidding me? All this death and destruction and that thing up there's not a battleship?" Paul asked incredulously.

"To be honest, bro, they classify it as a Heavy Scout ship."

"So that's why they haven't just pounded us into the ground," Paul said to no one in particular. "I thought they were spread too thin. But why? And how much time do we have?"

To the last question, I knew what Paul was asking without any further elaboration.

"Well, my friend, it's not like I had a direct pipeline to the Supreme Commander's war room, but I did get some information, and it comes down to power, or more exactly the pursuit of power. The new commander on that ship saw an opportunity to seize power and took it. The normal process, if there is such a thing for planetary takeover and domination, is for the scout ship to find a viable planet, radio the coordinates back home and then they wait, basically planting a flag on the planet. And my understanding is that from the time the signal is received to when the true war ships arrive is somewhere in the neighborhood of two to three years."

Paul shook his head. "So then, what we're doing here is—"

"Surviving," I answered quickly.

For the first time in a long time, Paul began to doubt their whole objective. "So no matter what we do to this little bully, his big bully brothers are coming and then will really start to dish out some whoop-ass? Is that what you're saying?"

"Listen, Paul, I'm only relaying the message. I don't like the news any more than you do, but there it is. Just because someone bigger and badder is coming down the street, doesn't mean we should just give up now. I still want to kill as many of them as I can before this thing ends."

Paul nodded in agreement. "You're right. I'm sorry. That just wasn't the news I was expecting or hoping to hear."

"I understand, bud. But it's not like I told you the Pope wasn't Catholic."

"What do you know about that?" Paul asked conspiratorially.

"How long until we attack?"

"Tomorrow morning." The men began to melt back

into the woods surrounding the town center.

***

I got back into my bunk. Tracy still sleeping, the perfect vision of an angel. Her auburn hair fanned out around her beautiful face. I stared down at her a long time, soaking in everything about her from her straight nose to the curve of her slightly thin lips, to her almost elfish ears. I didn't think I had quite crossed over to love, but I was damn close and falling fast. I was snapped out of my thoughts when Tracy spoke.

"Instead of looking, why don't you come over here and kiss me," Tracy said dreamily. We made love with a passion heretofore unbeknownst to the both of us. An hours later we lay next to each other breathless and spent.

"That was amazing," Tracy said as she half rolled over, drawing small circles with her finger in my sparse chest hair.

"Yeah, I was pretty good," I answered with a wicked smile on my lips.

Tracy teasingly punched me in the arm.

"What time do we leave tomorrow?" Tracy asked out of the blue.

I had hoped to avoid that conversation. I had planned on sneaking out before she ever woke. But the cat was out of the bag now. I wouldn't be able to dodge the issue no matter how hard I tried. How the hell had she found out?

"Five AM," I answered solemnly.

"What, no fight? I thought for sure you'd try to talk me out of it. I'm a little disappointed."

"Would it have helped?" I asked.

"No," she answered matter-of-factly. "But what's the fun in that?"

"Listen, Tracy, I would be able to concentrate a whole lot better if I knew you were back here and safe."

"Listen, Mike," she said, sitting up now. "I was a soldier long before you. I was training in Annapolis when you were playing quarters and trying to get in some freshman's skirt."

"That's not fair, Tracy, you know what I meant," I answered, true hurt in my voice. "I'm not doubting your ability to fight, I'm doubting my ability to fight when I'll be constantly watching to make sure you're alright."

"You love me, don't you," she stated, not asked.

"I think I might."

"You think?" she asked staring directly into my eyes.

"Alright, alright, I do."

"And I love you, Mike. How do you think I'll feel sitting here waiting to see if you come back or not?"

"See, I should have never opened this door, I knew I'd never win."

"And you never will," she answered with a smile. "Now go to sleep, I don't want you all bleary-eyed when we go and kick some ass."

"Do you think so?"

"Do I think what?" she asked.

"Do you really think we're going to kick some ass tomorrow?"

"Call it woman's intuition if you want to, but I feel it in my bones. This is going to be a class-A ass kicking."

I wasn't quite as confident, but the table had been set and now it was just a matter of sitting down to eat.

Tracy laid back down. "Now go to sleep, because I want to do this again tomorrow night and the night after and then, who knows, maybe the night after that."

"Yes, dear," I answered, using my best whipped dog imitation.

I could tell within scant minutes Tracy had fallen asleep, looking no more troubled than if she had to get up in the morning and let the dog out into the backyard. I had no such luck, as quietly as I could, I arose and went in search of some solace. In five minutes I found what I had been looking for. It was a large conference room that had been converted into a non-denominational chapel. God and I had for the most part been on uneasy terms, but I was going to try my best tonight to smooth that over.

"God, I know in my heart you exist, no matter what my head says. And I know you are aware of the devastation your world has come under. We need you, now more than ever. Is it right of me to only seek your help now when things are at their darkest, when for most of my adult life I have turned a cold shoulder? No, probably not. But don't you hear those who stray and then come back to the flock? I learned at least that much in Sunday school. Please, God, don't turn your back like so many of us have to you. Your children need you." I performed the Holy trinity and then rose and turned, slightly shocked to see Dennis leaning against the door frame, a half drained bottle of Southern Comfort in his hand.

"Did he hear you?" Dennis asked earnestly, with not the slightest hint of a slur.

"Look around, Dennis, do you think so?" I answered just as earnestly as I reached for the bottle Dennis had now proffered.

"Yeah, I didn't think so, either."

CHAPTER FIFTY-TWO

"Holy shit," Beth yelped joyously as she looked upon the Norwood sign, bent over at an angle most motorists would never be able to see. "One town away, Sampson," she said excitedly.

Sampson couldn't for the life of him understand why the girl was so excited about the metal object. He had sniffed it and knew without a shadow of a doubt he couldn't eat it. He would've reflected her feeling happy if it had been a steak or some corn chips—his personal favorite—that the little boy used to share with him even when the older lady half yelled at him for doing so. He wagged his tail, remembering. But it wasn't steak and it wasn't corn chips, it wasn't even those hard little crunchy things that tasted like old cardboard that his family called dog food. With little ceremony, Sampson lifted his leg and let this girl know exactly what he thought of the large metal object.

"Sampson?" she said laughing. "That's fine for now, but you sure as hell better not do that when we get to the Walpole sign."

Sampson's tail wagged as they began to move again. Hopefully in the direction of food. His belly was beginning to rumble, and he didn't like that one bit.

***

Pegged burned with a fever of hatred and death. All

reason was smoked out of him. He had become something more and less than a man. He had faculty enough to know he was losing his humanity but not enough sense to care. He didn't just want to kill the girl, he wanted to destroy her, to mash her into so fine a visceral mess that she would be undistinguishable from anything that had ever walked the planet. He had been to the history museum, he knew some extraordinarily strange creatures had once roamed the earth. He laughed, as small pieces of red-ribboned phlegm dislodged from his lungs and hung from his bottom lip. He did not rest, he did not eat, he did not drink. He knew the pace would kill him, but she would die first and in such a manner that would earn him a spot high in the realm of hell. A place that had been seemingly more real with each passing day, spurring him ever closer even when he had thought his quarry had indefatigably escaped. He was close, he could smell her as one of the strands finally broke and landed on a sign he never saw.

CHAPTER FIFTY-THREE – Mike Journal Entry 16

At three AM, five hundred Marines, soldiers and militia streamed out of various hidden exits along the eastern side of the Hill. Tracy had been put in command of her men plus a small squad, giving her a total of fifty for containment on the left side. I wasn't sure if that was a blessing or not.

I had been tasked with leading the vanguard into the heart of the enemy encampment and that was infinitely more dangerous than the flanking units, but now she would for the entire battle not be anywhere in my field of vision. If somehow her position was overrun I wouldn't even know until the planned fall back twenty-five minutes after the first volleys were launched. Paul had seen to it that Tracy would be on the outskirts of the major fighting with a small prompting from me, but now I was not sure if I liked it any more than if she was at my side.

"Mike, you there?" Paul asked as he readjusted his ammunition belt. "She'll be fine, Mike. I talked with her, she's as tough a warrior as they come."

"That obvious?" I asked.

"Dude, I'd have to be blind to not see what was going on in that head of yours, and even then I'd probably be able to feel the oppressiveness of your psyche. I need you here and now, Mike, these troops need you here and now. We're going to hit them so fast and so hard, they'll still be scrambling for cover when we head back. They'll never even get the chance to try and outflank us. You with me?"

I nodded in agreement, my unease, for the moment at least, abated.

At five AM, all of the fighters were in position. The cue to unleash hell would be the distinctive 'whoomp' as the first round of mortars made their way into the heart of the alien camp. Our soldiers had positioned themselves a mere twenty yards from the ring of Geno guards surrounding their camp. From there, it would be another long fifty yards to the fringes of their newly erected barracks. And Blackburn Hall, host of many a school dance, now converted into the command center for the insurgents.

"I want everything that moves in Blackburn Hall dead," Paul said to his sergeant.

"I just want everything dead," his sergeant answered back.

Paul nodded in agreement. "The hall first."

"Understood, General," the sergeant said as he quickly moved off to relay the info.

On another prompting from me, I had convinced Paul to up his pay grade from colonel to general.

"He's a good man. He was one of the Staff Sergeants from the Guard unit attempting to take the grocery store," Paul told me.

I grunted an acknowledgement.

"He likes to set his shoes on fire every night," Paul said, testing my alacrity.

"I'm with you, Paul. I was just checking my extra magazines."

Paul nodded, pleased to know I was beginning to hone in on what was about to happen.

At 5:42 the sun made its debut, followed closely by the launching of nearly fifty mortars. Molten death spread from the sky, explosions rocked the new day. Small arms fire blistered, the nearest guards were cut into pieces as lead flew down-field. Dazed Genogerians stumbled out of their barracks only to die where they stood. The iron rich smell of blood mingled deeply with the acrid smell of smoke.

Paul stood up. "Sergeant, now!" he shouted over the din.

The sergeant nodded. "Charge!" he bellowed, his booming voice carried over the chattering M-16s and then at once drowned out as three hundred men and women stood and screamed their fiercest battle cries, racing across the small field separating them from their objective. I noticed with satisfaction some of the aliens were so completely overwhelmed by the charge, they actually dropped the weapons they were carrying and began to retreat.

"They're fucking running!" I shouted.

Not knowing how I could have been heard over the cacophony, Paul answered as if he were sitting in his parlor watching a cribbage match, "Well, that's gotta be a first."

I just grinned as I let loose another full magazine into the backs of the enemy. But some did not run. Even with the surprise attack and the retreat of a good number of the aliens, the Hill soldiers were still outnumbered almost two to one. The distinctive blue streaks of death struck several of the soldiers around us; screams of agony were threatening to overtake the war cry. Some of the less experienced people began to hesitate as the threat of their own impending deaths loomed larger than it ever had. But as Paul streaked to the forefront, the charge was brought anew.

The human wave crashed around and through the aliens' first line of defense. Some stopped to more intimately express their feelings for the aliens. Half-dead aliens had nothing more to look forward to in this lifetime than the snarling wicked faces of their opponents as they were repeatedly shot, stabbed and sometimes bludgeoned until at last, merciful death found them. The staunchest defense the aliens could muster was around the perimeter of the

Blackburn Hall.

Paul slowed the charge down as he checked his watch, six minutes had passed since the assault began, they had four minutes to attack and fifteen to withdraw before the enemy air support arrived. Any longer than that and the ships would be able to track and kill them as they tried to get back to safety. Paul was amazed at how quickly the aliens had gotten back under control. Hundreds of them had taken up defensive positions in and around the hall protecting their superiors with everything they had.

The superior firepower of the aliens began to take its hold as more and more of the Hillians (Hill Residents for short) died. I watched in rising horror as more and more of the troops around me fell. Paul's leading unit had halted its charge and had also taken up defensive positions, a stalemate looked to be the aliens' strategy, for they did not press the attack but merely laid down suppressing fire holding us off and in place. They knew help was on the way and soon.

Another crucial minute ticked by. Paul's attackers were stuck, unable to move forward or back. If they got up and ran, they would be cut down before they could go twenty feet.

"Paul!" I yelled. "Call in more mortars!"

"We're too close!" Paul answered, his voice nearly cracking from the effort of being heard over the battle being waged.

"Just a couple of rounds, I need some distractionary cover."

Paul wasn't sure what I was up to, and he wouldn't have time to find out. If I had a plan, that would be good enough for him.

Paul shouted to his radioman even though the man was within touching distance, "Call in two mortar rounds, *now!*"

The radio operator didn't hesitate, although he knew the danger.

"This is Spearpoint One, calling Hammer. Spearpoint One calling Hammer."

"Go ahead, Spearpoint, this is Hammer."

Paul breathed a sigh of relief. He wasn't sure if they would be able to hear.

"Hammer, two volleys now. Repeat two volleys. Now!" the radioman shouted.

"Incoming!" Paul shouted, as the high-pitched whistling made itself heard.

The effect was instantaneous, alien and human alike dived for cover. Except for one. Even as the mortars were closing in, I bounded out of my hiding spot and ran for the rocket launcher that had been dropped ten feet from my position. The first owner of the weapon having been sliced to pieces by alien fire. The tube was blood-caked, but otherwise appeared undamaged. I knew I wouldn't have enough time to get back to my former, safer position before the mortars hit, so I fired, the action and thought were instantaneous.

If I'm going to die, they're coming with me.

Flicking off the safety, I fired as the first of the mortars struck, the concussion from the impact took me off my feet and drove me almost ten feet back. Light turned to gray, gray faded to black. I was conscious no more.

***

"Mike, you there? Mike?"

Black shaded to gray, gray became muted light.

"Heaven?" I asked, weakly.

"Um, not quite," Paul responded. "You saved our asses out there."

"Everything still where it's supposed to be?" I croaked.

Paul stared down at me for a second before realization dawned on him. "Ten fingers ten toes, and Tracy was here earlier, she was smiling, so I would imagine everything's where it's supposed to be."

"Yeah...good." I fell back to sleep.

***

"Fuckin' guy, hero of the day," Paul said to Dennis. "And he's worried about where his pecker is."

"Wouldn't you?" Dennis answered.

Paul laughed. "Got me on that one. Let's go grab a brew."

***

I awoke a few hours later, feeling infinitely better, which wasn't saying much. I took stock of my body and couldn't find a spot that didn't have some sort of pain, from a dull ache to mind-numbing fire.

"That was pretty stupid, what you did," Tracy said as she wiped a tear from her eye.

I tried to reach up to console her, but pain shot from the tips of my fingers down my right side. I winced.

"You know you promised me you'd never do anything stupid again. You didn't even make it forty-eight hours," she said.

"If I hadn't of done it, I wouldn't have made it. Which way was less stupid?" I asked

Tracy leaned down to hug me.

"Careful," I said. "I'm fragile."

And I meant it. I awoke a few hours later. Tracy was fast asleep in a chair she had requisitioned. She fully intended on never leaving my side again. Not only while I was recuperating, but in every battle from here on out. If I was going to keep doing the insane stunts, she was going to be there to minimize the risk.

***

Paul noticed I was awake. "Hey, buddy, came by to see how you were doing."

"Well, aside from the excruciating pain in my back and the fact I'm partially deaf in my left ear, I'd say pretty good."

"That's good news then," Paul quipped.

"Paul, I've been meaning to ask somebody, but I'm not usually up for more than a few minutes."

"Go ahead, you seem pretty lucid at the moment. It's amazing what drugs can do these days."

"Thanks, I think. What the hell happened after I got the shit blown out of me?" I asked already feeling the fringes of fatigue fighting their way in.

"Well, buddy, up until the mortars struck, you were right there with us. I still can't figure out how you didn't get shot. Those alien rounds were everywhere. It was like a blue light special out there. I mean, Mike, I really can't figure out how you didn't get blown away, you were a very viable target for a full five seconds. Hell, there were houseflies that wouldn't have lasted half that long out there." Paul scratched his head. "I can't say I saw your rocket shot hit the target, I was in the process of ducking and covering from the mortar rounds, but the effect was instantaneous—Blackburn Hall rained down all over the place."

"Could it have been a mortar round?" I asked.

"Could've been, but it wasn't. The mortar rounds landed about midway between us and the uninvited guests. Besides, I said I hadn't seen it, but I got firsthand accounts from troops who were a little farther back."

"That's good to know," I answered, sleep already tugging at the corners of my eyes.

"But, Mikey, does it matter how it got destroyed as long as it got destroyed? You once told me 'any way to good is good'."

"Yeah, Paul, it really does," I answered, seriously. "I

promised that girl over there I wouldn't do anything that needlessly put my life in danger."

"You love her, Mike?" Paul asked.

"I do, Paul, and it scares the shit out of me. It's not like this is the best of times."

"Yeah, Mike, you're right in that respect. But even so, isn't it better to have it than not?"

"I'm just so scared I could lose her before we really had a chance," I answered.

"That might also be true, Mike, but I guess I'd have to defer you back to your original quote."

"I gotcha, bud. One more thing, Paul. What kind of causalities did we take?"

"We lost a hundred sixty-seven, and we have another eighty to eighty-five injured. I know it's some steep numbers, but we estimate they lost somewhere in the neighborhood of eight hundred fifty."

I echoed what Paul was already thinking. "Those numbers are great for the amount of kills, but we can't absorb those kinds of losses. We're going to have to rethink our strategies. They recovered way too quickly from the initial attack. I thought we'd have them on the run up until the Wrentham town line."

"You and me both, Mike. But your shot, besides saving our asses, taught us something very valuable." I fought off the vestiges of sleep as valiantly as I could to hear the new development. "After you blew up the Hall, something pretty strange happened. Sure it took out a lot of the aliens around the base of it but by no means all of them. The ones that were still alive and kicking…for lack of a better term, became very hesitant…um, very unsure of themselves."

I liked the news, but I wanted to make sure all the angles were being covered. "Was it shellshock?"

"I thought that too, Mike, but even the ones farther away that weren't directly affected by the blast had the same thing happen."

"This could be huge, Paul. Cut off the head and the snake dies."

"Exactly, but it was a temporary effect. Some of our soldiers stayed just a little too long and found out with the ultimate price. Their lives."

"What do you mean?" I asked.

"Well, as soon as those damned fighters showed up, any latency in the Genogerians disappeared. They picked up right where they had left off, as if they had never stopped in the first place."

"We need to get a hold of a prisoner," I said.

Paul laughed.

My expression didn't change.

"You're not kidding? Tell me you're kidding?"

"Think about it. We need to know how to sever that connection. What if it's just a matter of jamming a radio signal?"

"I didn't even think of that. We could start routing them on every field of battle." Paul was truly excited now. As was I. "We can't send anybody just yet. They have two of their fighters parked at the town hall and they've trucked in at least a few hundred more soldiers from God knows where. And they've been having patrols fly over the whole town since the battle. I'm afraid if we send anybody out, we'll give our position away."

"That's alright. It doesn't sound like they have the resources to keep up that pace. We'll wait them out. Shouldn't be more than three or four days. By then I should be good to go."

"Whoa, wait a second. You just told me you weren't going to do anything to needlessly endanger yourself."

"I'm not, this is very needful. Now I'm going back to sleep."

"Good night, my friend," Paul said as he walked out of the room a lot happier than when he walked in. Hope had that effect.

CHAPTER FIFTY-FOUR

Beth had spotted a few of the enemy fighters from a distance, but had crossed over into Walpole without the slightest hitch. Sampson padded alongside, stopping occasionally to mark his territory, partly for the sake of the aliens and partly for the sake of the crazy man following them. Sampson had caught the scent a couple of miles back and no matter how much he tried to urge his new friend on she just wasn't having any of it. He knew she was tired and she was stopping more and more frequently even when he would muzzle her lap to make her move forward.

"I know, Sampson. I know you're excited about getting there and so am I," she said as she sat down on a large boulder looking over Bird River. "But then how would you know we're getting close? Huh, boy? You're just picking up on my excitement…is that it?" she said as she scratched behind his ears.

And whereas, he liked that sensation immensely that was not the reason he kept pushing at her. The crazy man was close, and Sampson knew it. He turned and bristled. Beth stood in alarm. Sampson began to bark and growl. White foam poured from his mouth as if on cue. Beth began to shake, trouble had caught up. Pegged emerged from the woods fifteen yards from where she sat. Even from that distance, Beth could tell her pursuer was a long way from healthy. Red angry blotches covered his face, hair had begun to fall out of his scalp in bunches, he was coated in sweat, his eyes burned red like the coals of a still hot fire. His sanity, what remained anyway, was completely shredded and in tatters, pooled around the remnants of his conscience.

"Ah, so we meet again," he said as casually as if they had bumped into each other at a mutual friend's dinner party. "I see you have a companion. No, matter it's only one extra bullet."

The dog lowered to the ground slowly inching his way toward him.

Pegged had known she had a dog with her, he had found some tracks a while back, but he was wholly unprepared for how immense the thing actually was. There were just enough wits about him to realize the danger.

"Make your little lap dog heal or I'm going to put a bullet right between his eyes!" he said with vehemence.

"Sampson, come here!" Beth said, hoping the dog would listen. She didn't see a way out, but she wasn't dead yet and neither was Sampson, so there was still a chance.

"Aptly named," Pegged said as Sampson partly did as he was told. He stopped moving…period; neither going forward or backwards.

"It's good to see you again," Pegged said, leering.

"I wish I could say the same."

He moved a few feet closer, his gaze never wavering from Beth.

"Ummm, you look good. Maybe I'll give you some before I kill you." Pegged ran his free hand over his groin.

Beth's stomach turned. She would cut her own throat before she would ever let him touch her. "I'll kill myself long before you have the chance."

"Hey, as long as you're still warm, that suits me too."

"You disgust me, you pathetic pig!" Beth shouted.

"Yeah, that's right, bitch! Keep talking dirty." He stepped a little closer.

"It's Beth, you worthless piece of shit," she said, her heart hammering in her throat.

"Well, since we're going to be all civil and introduce ourselves, my name is Pegged."

"Fitting."

He smiled. Beth was torn. Pegged was increasingly cutting the distance between himself and Sampson. She feared for the safety of the big dog but wanted the death of the *mad* dog.

Beth stalled for time. "Why have you followed me? What could I have possibly done to you to make you come across a whole state to try and kill me?"

"Bitch." His eyes flared. "You killed my brother back there in that bathroom stall."

"You don't seem like the kind of person who would care about someone enough to put yourself out like this."

"You're right. I couldn't stand the whiny little shit. But he was still family, and I have to do what's right."

"Oh great, a madman with morals and a code of honor," she chortled.

"Fuck you, bitch," Pegged said, taking another step closer, his pistol raised, the barrel of the .45 looking like a small cannon from that distance. "I'll fucking drop you right here…right now."

Beth froze, her breath caught in her throat. The world slowed as her mind raced.

Sampson had hoped the crazy man would get a little closer, but he could sense the man that had precariously been hanging on to the edge had finally slipped over. If he was to act, his only opportunity was now. Sampson bolted from a pure standstill to full speed in a fraction of a second. The only thing that gave his stealthy launch away were the rocks shooting out from his rear paws from the thrust of his powerful muscles. Pegged looked down as Sampson slammed into his lower legs, the locking of his left knee sent the bullet he had released slightly off mark. Beth felt the impact of the giant slug slam into her upper body, pain blistered throughout her as she was thrown to the ground.

The force of the bullet sending her to the ground.

Before she lost consciousness, she heard three things, the first was the snapping of a bone, the second was the sharp report of another bullet and the third—the one that struck her the deepest—was the grunt and whine of Sampson as she realized he had been the recipient of that last round.

"So this is how it ends," she said, looking up into the rapidly graying blue sky. Something flashed by on her right side but she had neither the strength nor the inclination to try to find out what it was.

Beth awoke for a few moments, blood rushing to her head. She was feeling somewhat like a sack of potatoes. She was unsure as to why, then consciousness eluded her and she blacked out once again.

CHAPTER FIFTY-FIVE – Mike Journal Entry 17

"Hey, buddy," Dennis said as he walked into the room, the now familiar bottle of Jack accompanying him. He noticed me eyeing the bottle. "Want some?"

"Nah, I already feel like a train wreck. I don't need a hangover on top of it," I answered.

"You sure? This stuff cures just about everything."

I waved my hand and Dennis nodded as he took another pull.

"Ah man...Mike, do you remember that time you, me, and Paulie came up to the Hill? That night after the Ozzy concert," Dennis said, looking off into the distance.

"In one aspect, bud, the memory of the event is crystal clear, however the details, well, they're pretty fuzzy."

"Ain't that the truth? That was probably the best overall night of my life."

I sat up in my bed, realizing that Dennis had something on his chest and this was just his preliminary way of leading into it. "You know when we got those hits of mescaline, I got to admit, I was scared shitless to take them. I know you and Paul had taken it before."

"A couple of times," I added.

"Yeah, a couple of times, and you weren't any more fucked up after than you normally are."

"Uh, thanks, I think."

"You know what I mean," Dennis said hastily.

"Only messing with you, Dennis."

"It's just that, you know we went to this awesome concert tripping our trees out and then somehow made it back to the Hill to look at the sky and talk about stuff I don't even remember ever having thought about before."

I smiled. It had been a pretty good night and hearing Dennis talk about it brought the memories to the forefront.

"I mean, we even talked about how there had to be life on other planets, just because of the sheer odds. And honestly, Mike, I think I was just agreeing with you to agree with you. I didn't honestly think there were any such things as aliens. But now, looking back, I was just being ignorant."

"Don't beat yourself up, Dennis. First off, we were blasted. I think at one point we were talking about alternate tangent realities."

"Yeah, I vaguely remember that. My point, though, Mike, is I didn't really believe in it. Hell, I didn't want to believe in it. Just the thought of it scared the shit out of me."

"Dennis, I definitely wanted to believe we weren't the only ones out in the universe, but had I known we were going to run into a species hell-bent on enslaving us and taking over our planet, I think I would have rethought my stance."

"It's not even that. It's just that the night was truly the last peaceful, serene, content night I've had."

I looked at him quizzically.

"After we left Indian Hill I went to Angela's house and stayed the night with her. I mean, there I was, had a great night with my two best friends and then spent the rest of the evening with the only girl I've ever loved. And you know we broke up a couple of months after that and then the following week, you and Paul headed out to Colorado. I was pretty eff'd up for a while, really got into some heavy drugs."

I cocked my head. "Dennis, I never knew, man. I'm sorry it went down like that."

"It wasn't your fault, Mike, and it's not like I

broadcast it, either. I guess I just wasn't ready to grow up and move on. If it hadn't of been for the project Paul put me in charge of I probably would have died sitting at the Kihei restaurant bar getting drunk."

"Den, I think we've all done some growing up we weren't quite ready for."

"I'm not done yet."

"Sorry, sorry," I said in a placating manner.

"What I'm trying to get at in a roundabout way, is…" Dennis hesitated. "If all of this shit hadn't gone down, would we have remained friends?"

"I'm not sure if I understand, bud?"

"If the Geno…whatever the fuck they're called had never come, would you and Paul have stayed in touch? Would we have stayed friends?" he asked pleadingly.

"Dennis, just because Paul and I were up at college didn't change the friendship we have. Sure, we were doing our own things, but I'll never forget the times we shared growing up. Obviously, we weren't going to see each other almost every day like we used to but, you're a friend Dennis—a best friend—you don't just discard those things when you move away, there's way too much time and effort put in to make great friendships to so easily leave one behind, so to speak.

"Can I say with absolute certainty we would have remained friends? No, I can't, but I can answer definitively that you were in my thoughts a lot while I was up at school. I was always asking myself what would Dennis be thinking if he were here now? Or, I bet Dennis would get a kick out of this. And I leaned on a lot of the memories we had shared to get me through some pretty tough times on that ship. Am I glad to see you now? You can bet your ass I am. I'm just not happy with why I am seeing you now. We've both lost a lot over these last couple of years, and to still have you and Paulie around, well…that just really helps to ease some of the pain, my brother."

Dennis crossed the room and gave me a gentle hug, a small barely noticeable tear tried to escape his eye. He quickly wiped it away.

"How 'bout those Bears?" I said to try and alleviate the seriousness of the scene.

"Thank you, Mike," Dennis said, and turned and walked out the door.

I stared after him, wondering what that was all about.

"What was that all about?" If the voice had been deeper I would have thought I had unintentionally said out loud what I was thinking. Tracy was looking out over the top of the blanket she had pulled up almost to the bridge of her nose.

"Uh, hell if I know," I answered. "But I think it probably had something to do with Frank's death. From what I understand, they were pretty good friends."

"You never get used to it."

I looked at her wonderingly.

"Loss…death, no matter how much of it goes on around you, every time it happens, it hits as hard as it did the first time."

I didn't have a rebuttal or anything to add to her statement for that matter. She had nailed it on the head. Although, what she hadn't added, I wasn't going to voice. Sure, death hadn't gotten any easier, but killing had. I shivered even as I thought it.

CHAPTER FIFTY-SIX

Beth woke screaming, mostly from the pain in her side, but definitely a good portion could be attributed to the huge green arm wrapped around her, carrying her as if she was no more than a Raggedy Ann doll. She passed out.

Sampson had more than once let his bladder go, partly from the pain, but mostly from the huge thing carrying him. He couldn't sense anything evil permeating from the animal holding him, but he couldn't sense anything good, either. The bullet hurt his hind quarters, but he would have been much happier on the ground with the searing pain than a mere two feet away from that teeth-lined snout. He wasn't happy about it and it made him piddle again.

***

My injuries must have been worse than they had told me and that was why Dennis had come in and had that conversation with me. He knew I was dying. I now knew I had died, but what the hell was Drababan doing in Heaven? Not that I regretted seeing my friend, but didn't he have his own version of Nirvana to go to?

"Hello, Drababan," I said, using my vocal cords. "Funny," I said. "I thought in Heaven we'd just project our thoughts, wouldn't be any reason for speech."

"Ah, Miike, you are a funny hu-man," Drababan roared.

"Holy shit, *this* is real!?" I said, sitting up much too quickly. Pain sluiced through me. Drababan rushed forward, the other people in the room tensed, especially me, but for a different reason.

"Whoa, hold on Dee," I said, holding my hands out. "You'll break me in half if you hug me."

"I am just so happy to see you, hu-man. Tracy has told me how foolish you were in battle."

I looked over at Tracy. She merely smiled, shrugged and looked back up at Drababan.

Then a light came on. My pulse accelerated, the monitoring machines next to the bed letting everyone know.

"Dee, what about the bug?" I asked, impending doom hanging in the shadows.

"Neutralized," Dee said smugly.

I didn't even question him. "Well, then you might as well come over here and get this done with."

Drababan approached, a teeth-showing grin spread across his face. Some of the more nervous in attendance let their fingers get ever so closer to their triggers.

"Paul," I said as I grimaced from the ministrations I was receiving from Drababan. "Could you please have your men stand down? They're making me nervous. They're just as likely to take me out as anything else. You can see Drababan isn't planning on eating me."

Drababan stood up. "Besides, he would probably taste bad."

"You're not helping," I said to Drababan. He shrugged, looking a little too much like Tracy's gesture earlier for comfort.

"Alright, alright," Paul said. "I want the clinic area cleared out, but post two guards outside the door," Paul said, acquiescing to my request, but not completely. "It's more to keep the gawkers away," he added, trying to appease me.

"He looks pretty tasty," Drababan said, pointing to one of the plumper guards to usher the men out just a little quicker. It worked superbly. Paul, however, was not amused.

"We'll talk later, Mike," Paul said as he left, making sure Drababan was not included in the statement.

"Mike, I've got guard duty in a half hour—you'll be alright?" Tracy asked.

"I'll be fine, thank you," I told her.

"I'll be back after." She leaned in for a small kiss. "I never thought I'd say this, but it's nice to see you, Drababan."

"Likewise," he said as she walked out of the room.

"How the hell did you find this place?" I asked, turning back to Drababan, who had pulled up a large couch which when he occupied it, nearly became invisible.

"I knew generally in what location this place was, and I knew it would be guarded, so I more or less let myself be found."

"How could you be sure they wouldn't just shoot you on the spot?" I asked. "I mean, they could have thought you were some sort of scout or something."

"There were a couple of things making my entrance fortuitous. First, you're unfriendly friend had passed information to the sentries that they wanted a live captive if possible, and second, I snuck around a little until I recognized one of the men in the platoon that escorted you here."

I laughed. "How the hell did you manage that? I thought we all looked alike to you."

"That may be true, but the platoon we traveled with had a red insignia patch over their left shoulder."

I laughed again.

"One more thing, Miike," Drababan said gravely. It snuffed out the rest of my merriment. "I brought in two guests, both were injured, and that probably more than anything got me in here unharmed. I'll admit when I stumbled across them, that was sort of my plan. I had no way of knowing you would want a live Genogerian or that I would run into someone I knew. One or two of your world seemed a much better bet. If they hadn't been injured, I most likely would have just taken them."

"You mean kidnap?" I asked solemnly.

"Kidnap? I do not think I know that word, but take them against their will and use them to gain entrance here, yes. I could not think of any better way. But that is not the point. Mike, one of them was what you hu-mans call a dog, a very large one from what I was told when I brought him in. The other was your Beth."

I almost choked. "What?" I sputtered.

"I did not know who she was when I first approached. She and the dog were involved in some sort of fight with a man who was chasing them, the majority of the fight was over by the time I arrived. Beth and the dog had been shot."

"What! Beth was shot? Where is she?" I asked as I started to rise.

Drababan put a big arm out across my chest to stop me. "She should be okay. Your doctors told me it was a shoulder wound, the dog's was a little more serious, but they were confident he would be alright as well."

My heart raced. *Beth…here!*

"I broke the man's neck before he could do any more damage."

"How did you know he was the one in the wrong? You yourself said you arrived late."

"You were right when you said that you hu-mans all look alike, but not this one. He was far over the edge—what we on our planet would have called 'frakenstug'. He was crazy, the fever burning through his eyes was something I will not soon forget."

I shivered thinking about what Beth had been through.

"They will be bringing her here once they are done working on her. I thought you should know."

"Does Paul know Beth is here?" I asked

"I do not think so. There was much confusion when I first entered your Hill. Most of the people wanted to shoot me on the spot, your Tracy saved me from an early demise." Drababan smiled. "She finally convinced everyone I was not trying to eat the dog and the hu-man I was carrying, but rather trying to get them help. After your doctors had taken them, your commander, Paul, met Tracy and me in the hallway as we were coming here to see you."

I could still not believe the words I was hearing. Beth was here! What was she doing here? What about Tracy? I had moved on, hadn't I? Then why was I feeling so conflicted?

"This sucks, Dee."

Drababan looked confused.

"I can't even remember the last time I even thought about Beth. I guess I figured she'd been killed in the initial invasion maybe I grieved her loss, and I'd moved on. Now I'm in…well, I've found this girl I truly care for. Beth can't be here."

"Oh I can assure you, Miike, she is here. I brought her myself."

"No, Dee, I wasn't questioning her presence…just the reality of the situation."

Drababan still looked confused. "Did I do something wrong by bringing her here?" Drababan asked in all seriousness.

"No, Dee, as crazy as this sounds, you did the right thing—the human thing. Hell, a little plastic surgery and you might even pass for one of us." I laughed.

Drababan snorted. "I do not know what this plas-tic surgery is, but I do not want to look like any of you hu-mans," Drababan said indignantly.

"Relax, Dee, I just playing with you. Besides, I don't know if they'd have a scalpel sharp enough to cut through that thick hide of yours."

Drababan rubbed his arm. "Let them try," he said

looking over his shoulder. "I will make them eat their plastic."

"I bet you would."

"Miike, I have made it here and I have told you what I feel you must know now. But I am tired and I have had very little food or water in the last seventy-two hours."

"Guards!" I yelled. They ran in rifles at the ready, expecting trouble. I was both approving and annoyed at the same time. On one hand they were ready for anything, on the other they had their weapons pointed at my friend. "Could one of you please get my large green friend here four cots, a couple of gallons of water and the biggest hunk of meat you can find?"

I had to give the man some kudos, he never even hesitated with his response.

"Cooked?" he asked.

"Rare would be splendid," Drababan noted.

"Right away." He turned and left.

Within a few minutes, Drababan had eased onto his new over-sized cot/bed, downing the first gallon of water in under two minutes. The second gallon he savored with his food. The ten pound roast looked like a sausage link in Drababan's huge hands. He bit off half of it in one smooth tear. I involuntarily shivered as I watched the damage his teeth could inflict on an enemy.

"Is that going to be enough?" I asked. "I don't want you coming over here sleepwalking and take a chunk out of me."

"I have told you before, Miike, you hu-mans are not nearly as tasty as you would like to believe."

I didn't know if he was kidding or not, and for the most part, I really didn't want to push the issue. Drababan looked over at me, bits of roast hung from his teeth. A smile pulled back to reveal even larger and sharper teeth in the back.

"Relax, Miike, I am only playing with you."

I visibly un-tensed myself.

"I decided long ago I would not eat anything that approached our state of intelligence. If you were a little dumber, I would eat you in a heartbeat."

"Thank God for algebra," I said seriously. "That's the first time I *ever* said that."

"Your cows, however, they are fantastic. I could eat them anytime. The roast has taken the edge off of my hunger, and it was the water I wanted more than anything. I would much like to sleep now and we will talk later."

"As you wish, my big green eating machine."

Drababan laid his head down and within seconds had found a state of relaxation much to his liking. I eased off my bed, not feeling quite as bad, but still moving more like a man triple my age. Slowly and deliberately, I dressed myself, much to the chagrin of the nursing staff.

"You haven't been cleared to leave, mister," shouted one of the more heavyset nurses.

If she forced the issue, I would have no choice but to comply. I frantically searched for an approach that would work against my formidable opponent. Brute force wasn't going to work and I didn't feel good enough to lay on any charm.

"Get Paul, I'm sure he'll see to it that I can check myself out," I said, hoping the name dropping approach would be my ticket to freedom. I had suddenly found my hospital bed much too confining, restlessness had taken over. My nurse looked as if she might protest the new development, but she thought better of it.

"Boys who think they are men," she said much too loudly.

Wrong button…and she had pushed it.

"What did you say?" I asked harshly as I turned back around.

Nurse Grogan must have suspected she might have crossed the line, but she didn't appear to be the type of person who ever backed down from a confrontation, and she wasn't going to with some still-wet-behind-the-ears kid like me.

"I said," she annunciated, "that you boys who think you are men don't know half of what you think you do."

"Are you done?" My eyes blazed.

Nurse Grogan actually backed up a step; something I'm sure none of her staff up to that point had ever seen. It would be great fodder for conversation for the next week.

"Um, why…yes I am," she answered meekly.

"Good, then get the fuck out of my way," I said softly enough so only she would hear even though a half dozen people had stopped what they were doing to watch the small drama unfold.

Nurse Grogan moved as fast as anyone with that kind of bulk could. I made it to the corner with perfect form. It was when I finally made it out of sight that I had to brace myself up against the wall, lest I pass out. I had to admit, the battle-axe was probably right to try to keep me in the bed.

Oh well, too late now. I go back and she'll probably piss in my Jell-O. I knew where I was going and I was determined to get there, it was just going to take a little longer than originally planned.

CHAPTER FIFTY-SEVEN

Beth awoke from surgery, disoriented and confused. For a fleeting moment she thought she was back on the alien mother ship, but then her eyes began to focus on the walls. *Bricks? There's no bricks on the alien ship.* She was trying hard to remember where she was and how she had got there. Something disconcerting stirred in the back of her mind, but she could not pull it to the forefront. Her consternation must have shown.

"Relax, relax, Beth. I'm Dr. Corren. Your surgery went quite well, no major damage and you're not even going to end up with much of scar. Now if some other hack doctor had been work—"

"Please," she interrupted. Her throat was raw from the intubation.

"Oh, I bet you would like to know where you are?" Dr. Corren finished.

Beth nodded, unwilling to strain her throat at the moment.

"Let me get you some water first."

She shot her arm out and grabbed his surgical gown. "Now. Where?" she croaked.

"Alright, alright. You're inside of the Indian Hill Nuclear Launch Silo number seventeen."

Beth let out a sigh of relief, she had finally made it. The miles of pain and anguish melted behind her like snow in mid-March.

"Dog?" she managed.

"Please, let me get you some water." Beth had a look of anguish on her face. "Fine, fine, the dog is fine. He came out of surgery an hour before you. Look," he said, pointing to what appeared to be a small bear covered in several spare blankets. "He's sleeping, I gave him a sedative. He wouldn't stop howling when he couldn't find you and I didn't want him to rip out his stitches. Scared the hell out of me, I might add. Luckily, I had a tranquilizer gun. He wouldn't let anybody near him he was so determined to track you down."

Beth smiled and put her head back down. But all her questions weren't answered yet. "How?"

"Enough. Let me get something for your throat. I know how painful it can be upon awakening."

She eased her death grip. "Thank you," she added.

In a few moments, Dr. Corren returned with some aspirin, water, and throat lozenges. Beth eyed the pills suspiciously.

"Aspirin, I assure you," Dr. Corren said, exasperated. "I will be back shortly. I have some other patients I must attend to. Let the aspirin and the lozenges work and I will answer your questions. You should also try to get some more sleep, it speeds the healing process. Your dog, if that's what he really is, won't be awake for another couple of hours. You should use that time to rest." Dr. Corren walked out the door.

Beth knew he meant well, but she had finally arrived. She was so happy, she wanted to hug herself. She was safe, Sampson was safe. Was Mike safe? He had to be. What good would her whole trek have been if he wasn't? Deborah would have died in vain; that thought both saddened and scared her.

Maybe they could have just hidden out back in Denver, together and alive. They might never have known Mike's fate but that could have been for the better. If he was dead, would she stay? She would be alone—no family, no friends, no Mike. Beth shivered uncontrollably, her earlier euphoria quickly becoming replaced with dread.

***

I looked through the window and began to shiver. Cold sweat broke out on my brow. Beth, even after surgery, looked like an angel lying on her gurney. I ached with indecision. Just rush in and hug her, or go in and tell her off. I left.

***

Beth turned to look over her shoulder, certain that someone had been watching. Moments later, the impossible happened, she fell asleep, more deeply than at any time in the last few weeks. In her dream, she was a little girl unwrapping presents. She didn't understand the relevancy of the dream but it made her feel safe and loved and maybe that's all it was supposed to do. The first box she unwrapped was a puppy. It wasn't really a puppy, it was a mini-Sampson, but when she pulled him out of the small box he began to grow to his near mythical proportions. Beth hugged him until she thought either he or she might burst from the pressure.

"It's you and me," the little dream girl Beth said aloud. The scene faded and Beth plunged deeper into sleep, her pillow still held tight to her chest.

***

Paul stopped by my quarters a few hours later to find me seated at the edge of my bed, head in hands.

Paul took one look. "Your big green friend told me when I went to your hospital room."

I did not look up.

"Have you gone to see her?" Paul asked.

"Uh…in a manner of speaking," I answered, finally looking up.

"You look like hell, Mike. Do you think you should have checked yourself out of the hospital?"

"I'm having doubts myself, but if I go back now, Nurse Grogan will have my nuts in a sling."

"Yeah, I heard about that too." Paul smiled. "That's the first I've ever heard of her backing down."

"I'd chalk one up, but I don't think I could raise my arm that high."

Paul had concern on his face, I really did have a slight greenish tinge.

"Relax, bud," I said, noticing Paul's expression. "I'm not quite ready to throw in the towel just yet. I mainly feel sick to my stomach and it's mostly nerves. Yeah I know, big bad freedom fighter taken down by a case of butterflies."

"I'm going down there now; do you want to come?" Paul asked seriously.

"Not yet, Paul. Maybe not ever. I don't think I can."

"She came here for you, Mike. Nobody else."

"Don't you think I know that? What if I go down there and I end up not being able to leave her? I don't think I could take it. I have strong feelings for Tracy. Beth is my soul, Tracy is my spirit. It's like choosing between life and existence. Paul, if I thought I could make it more than fifty feet without passing out, I would have just flat out left the Hill by now."

Paul's expression deepened and then lightened. "I don't know, man, I can't say I'm feeling all that much pain for you. You've got two beautiful women vying for your attention and willing to die for you. Pretty much sounds like a dream come true."

"The problem, though, Paul, is that unlike a dream, I can only walk the path with one of them. I don't want to do this. I would rather be out fighting than have to deal with this mind fuck."

Paul walked over to my bed and clapped me gently on the shoulder. "Come on, man, just come and say hi."

I shook my head. "Not yet, Paul. Not yet."

"I understand. Do you want me to say anything on your behalf?"

I thought hard for a moment, a hundred things passed through my mind. A thousand memories flashed. "No," I answered flatly.

"Get some sleep, bud."

"Yeah, wouldn't that be nice."

***

Paul headed out the door and down the hallway. Beth turned her head when she heard the door open.

"Paul!" she said energetically. She moved her good arm to reach toward him.

"Hold on, I don't want you undoing anything our good doctor has fixed," Paul said as he rushed to her side. Paul squeezed her hand. "Beth, it's so good to see you. How have you been?" Even as Paul was finishing the question, he saw a dark cloud pass through her eyes. He knew her story would be no more enlightening than any of the thousand or so he had heard since the epic had begun.

"I'll tell you everything, Paul, but first…"

And here it comes Paul braced.

"Is Mike here?" she asked, hope flitting across her face.

God, she was beautiful. At one time, she had looked his way with those beautiful eyes, but he had been too immature as their fledgling relationship had begun. He had messed around with one of her friends in a drunken stupor. She remained his friend, but she had lost a great measure of respect for him. Something he had strived bit by immeasurable bit to win back.

"He is," he answered, not knowing how to handle the situation.

"Is he alright?"

"In a manner of speaking."

"Paul, please don't make this like pulling teeth. I can tell by your face that something is going on."

"Please, Beth," he pleaded.

She could tell by his reaction that something was amiss, and she didn't care how uncomfortable she made him, she wanted answers.

"I asked how he was," Beth demanded.

"He's been in the infirmary for the last few days," Paul started, worry creased Beth's face. "He's fine for the most part, got banged up a bit by an explosion." Beth involuntarily gasped. "Uh, don't worry, he caused the explosion. Wait, wait, I know that doesn't make it sound better. God, Beth, the guy is fuckin' amazing. He stood up in a shit storm of a firefight, risking his life to save us all. I know I grew up with him, and I might know him better than anybody, and then he goes and does shit like that and it's like I don't know him at all."

"You love him, don't you?" she asked.

"With all my heart. He is my brother just not in name."

"Paul, I love him too," Beth stated. For some reason that stung Paul somewhere deep down. He made sure to stomp that lit match before it consumed him. "What is going on? Why hasn't he come to see me? Is he too hurt?"

"He'll come when he's ready, Beth. That's all I can really tell you. The rest is his to say." Paul segued as best he could to move on to another subject. "So when did you start traveling with a small bear?"

Beth turned toward Sampson. She knew it would be fruitless to keep pumping Paul for information, he had said his piece and it didn't look like there was any more information forthcoming.

"Paul, he is the most amazing dog I have ever met. I wholly believe he's more than just a dog, I think he's a guide of some sort. When he looks at me, I can tell there is true intelligence in his gaze. He saved my life. First, he killed the man that was chasing me and then Sampson somehow carried me here, although how he found this place is just another mystery I'll never know."

"You don't know?" Paul said rubbing his hand through his hair.

"Know what?" she asked.

"I don't doubt that your... Sampson, did you say?" Beth nodded. "I don't doubt at all that Sampson is a very intelligent dog and he did save your life. He did not, however, kill that man or carry you here."

"Is that madman dead?" Beth asked haltingly, fear creeping in around the edges.

"He's quite dead."

"Again, Paul, with the teeth-pulling thing."

"Sorry, this is just so much fun."

Beth nodded in mock agreement. "Tell me what the hell is going on or I'll get out of this bed and beat you silly with a bed pan."

"A bed pan?"

"It's all I could think of on short notice."

"Fine, fine, lord knows where those things have been, I'll tell you. Mike has made a lot of alien enemies, but he has made one friend. One that he calls Drababan."

"What, an alien is his friend?" she asked in disbelief.

"Oh, it gets much better than that. Not only is this monster his friend, it killed your pursuer and carried you and your wooly mammoth over there to safety."

"Are you kidding me?" she asked, looking into his eyes for any sign of a practical joke being played on her. "You're not, are you? This is insane. One of those creatures!" she said disdainfully. "Saved me and Sampson? Oh the universe has truly turned on its ear."

"Beth, I hear you. I wanted the thing shot the moment it walked in the door. The mere sight of it struck something so deep in me I could only label it as primordial. It's like it wasn't just a threat to my life, but to my very being. It is so against everything I have ever learned. I'm not sure if I'm around that thing for a hundred years that I'll ever be comfortable with it. But Mike, shit, he has heart-to-heart conversations with it. They laugh and joke, they've played games. It's just one more piece in the master jigsaw puzzle that is Mike." And by trying to avoid that one topic, he had brought it back full circle. An uncomfortable silence fell over their conversation.

"Um...Beth I really need to go and check on a few things. You know...the bane of leadership," Paul said limply.

Beth knew he was trying to get out of dodge before she pressed him any more. She let him off the hook. "When are you coming back? I would really like you to meet Sampson when he is up and about."

Paul was thankful, he knew his retreat was lame at best. "It'll at least be a few hours. I want to check on some of my wounded and I still have a few unanswered questions about that huge croc running around my complex. I love you, Beth, and no matter what happens I cannot tell you how truly happy I am that you made it here."

Beth thanked him before he left and sat wondering what his cryptic message about 'no matter what happens' could possibly mean.

***

"Did the doctor check you out of the clinic?" Tracy asked, coming into my quarters.

I had been dozing when she came in and for the briefest of moments, with the light shining behind Tracy's head, I had not been able to recognize who she was. Luckily, I had been too surprised to say anything or I was fairly certain 'Beth?' would have been the first thing out of my mouth. That would not have gone over well. I sat up, wiping the sleep off my face, hoping that I had successfully hidden the panic that had instantly welled up inside me. Tracy seemed none the wiser.

"Did he?" she asked again, looking, I thought, deep into my soul. "Are you alright?" she asked concerned. "You look a little flushed."

I was a horrible liar, so bad in fact that I had determined long ago to just not even bother. I had found the truth to be so much easier and if for whatever reason the truth could not be told then to just not answer at all. I had found to my amazement that if I just did not answer a question, the person asking would generally answer it themselves. I knew this time that silence was not going to get me to safety.

"Beth's here," I stated with as little inflection as possible.

"*The* Beth?" she asked incredulously. "Have you seen her?"

"Yes and no," I answered.

"What does that mean?" Tracy asked, her palms suddenly clammy.

"I walked by her room, but I didn't go in to see her."

"Why?"

"Why what? Why did I go to her room or why didn't I talk to her?"

"Both."

"Tracy, this is something I never thought I would have to deal with again. I thought she was out of my life forever."

"But she isn't. So now what?"

I could hear desperation creeping into her voice.

"I've got to at least talk to her."

"Why? You don't owe her anything," Tracy answered with true hurt in her voice.

"I don't owe her anything, she owes me…at least a simple damn thank you," I shot back, maybe with a little too much vigor.

"Do you love her?"

"I loved her as much as I love you," I answered, although in all truth it was in avoidance of an answer. I knew I was close to loving Tracy completely, and I wanted to believe that I had put Beth behind me. The fence I sat so precariously on was tall, thin and very unstable, I thought of just letting go and let the chips fall where they may.

Tracy shut the door behind her as she left, I believe wiping tears from her face.

CHAPTER FIFTY-EIGHT
Eastern Seaboard Ground Occupation – Location southwest of Boston

"We lost almost nine hundred troops in less than an hour!" Ground commander Chofla screamed. "How is this possible? We were told there was no viable opposition left."

"Apparently the information was wrong, Commander," the second-in-command said, immediately wishing the words had never come out of his snout.

Fortunately for the underling, the commander was much too involved in his own thoughts to register what his lieutenant had said. "How will I be able to explain this to the Supreme Commander? I cannot tell him of this defeat. He will have me replaced, and I will become the next warrior in the games."

Normally, the second-in-command would have relished his position, because he would be next in line to take command, but then his neck would be in the noose and these tiny, thin-skinned devils scared him deeply. They attacked out of nowhere and disappeared in the same fashion. No, it would not be wise to let his commander fail just yet; he must wait until there was a more opportune time.

"Sir, perhaps one of the prisoners has some information we could use?" he asked.

The commander turned, the frustration and fear quickly evaporated with the chance of success still in his grasp. "The prisoners? Yes, the prisoners. Bring them to me at once."

"All of them, sir?"

"Yes, all of them. We will teach them a lesson if they do not talk to us freely."

"Yes, sir," the second said, hoping one of the humans had something useful to say. He had no desire to die on this little dust speck in the middle of nowhere and he sure didn't want to become fodder for the games. He shivered at that thought as he headed across the still smoldering complex.

Thirteen people were lined up in the old mayor's office. Five men, seven women, and one child. All were more frightened now than any of them had been in their entire lives and two of the men were World War II veterans. That enemy had been savage and brutal in their own right, but at least they had been human; mostly.

The commander walked over to one of the women, tears streamed down her face. She began to say the Lord's Prayer—without a hint of hesitation he shot her. The stink of the burnt flesh hung in the air for a moment before the realization of what happened finally took hold. The remaining six women and the child began to sob. Three of the men stood stoically, realizing that if they were in the final moments of their lives they wanted to go with some measure of dignity. One of the men made a run for the door; he was cut down before he could even grasp the handle. The fifth man, having completely given up any chance at hope or dignity, loosed his bladder.

The commander knew the male child and the inferior females would have no answers. The three men who stood firm might, after some brutality, give him the information he desired, or more likely, they would die holding onto what they knew. But the weak one he would tell all without the slightest provocation.

"Guards, put them back in their pens," the commander said, relief flooded on their faces. "All except this one." The commander placed his meaty paw on the shoulder of the man who had wet himself.

And there it was again. Spindler couldn't believe it, he had squeezed blood from a stone. He had not a drop of moisture in him, yet he had relieved himself in his pants twice within the last five minutes. He wasn't proud of it, but the rapidly cooling liquid on his leg let him know he was still alive.

As the people were lead out, the commander asked Spindler if he would like some water. Spindler could think of nothing else to say, except, yes.

He gulped down the water, the searing pain in his throat immediately eased. Spindler was scared, no doubt about it, but he was also intrigued. And just enough to see how far he could get.

"More?" he asked raising his glass.

The alien leaned in, sneering. *This is it*, thought Spindler *I went too far, he's going to chew my head off.*

"Certainly," came the very distinct inhuman voice.

The burly commander waved over his under commander and in a harsh language asked for what Spindler could only assume was water.

"Hmm," Spindler muttered.

The commander turned his attention back to him. "Do you have a question, hu-man?"

"Ah, not really," Spindler said licking his lips. "Well, maybe I do." *In for a dime, in for a dollar*, he figured. "Why is it that you speak English?"

"You mean why do we lower ourselves to speak a language so far beneath us?"

"I didn't ask it that way, but if that's the way you want to answer, then yes," Spindler said nervously.

"I can speak almost every one of your Earth languages and a hundred sixty-two languages from worlds you don't even know exist. When we take over a planet, it is a sign of our superiority. Not only do we take your land and

your oceans, we take your languages. It is total domination."
From where Spindler was looking, it didn't look like
total domination. The alien encampment had been reduced to
a molten crater, if the prisoner pen hadn't been so far from
the center of the camp he would be dead too.
"What happened here?" Spindler asked in sincerity.
The base commander took it as a taunt standing up
abruptly. Spindler shrunk back in his chair. The
commander's huge arms quivered. Spindler knew just one
backhand from the mighty hand and his spine would shatter.
The commander sat back down, his rage under
control for the moment.
"I am not quite sure," he answered, almost in a
whisper. "And that's why you are here."
Spindler sat back up, realizing that at least for the
moment his life was not yet in jeopardy.
"What is it you want from me?" Spindler asked.
"It says here," the commander said, pointing to a file,
his huge hands having difficulty maneuvering through the
hole punched pages, "that you were a principal."
"Yes, that's correct." Spindler tried in vain to grasp
what significance a small town high school principal could
have to do with an alien invasion.
"Well, 'principal' means of utmost importance. A hu-
man that is of utmost importance must have information.
True?" the commander asked.
"Well, I think you may have the meaning…"
Fortuitously for Spindler, he was looking at the commander
as he began to answer, even in an alien facial expression, he
knew he wasn't giving the appropriate response. He cleared
his throat. "What I meant to say is that yes, 'principal' as a
verb means of utmost importance, as a noun it signifies that I
am the head." Of what he didn't finish.
"Then you are a leader?"
"Oh, most definitely," Spindler answered without
hesitation. It was the truth…even if it was stretched out like

salt water taffy on a hot day.

CHAPTER FIFTY-NINE
The Supreme Commander

Kuvlar was in a quandary. The battle was not going as well as planned. Yes, who would win was never in doubt, but the losses were staggering. Progerians valued material assets above all else, there were the countless broken backs of the discarded Genogerians to prove this theorem. When the battle fleet arrived, someone would have to stand tall and feel the full wrath of the Dominion; Kuvlar did not want that Progerian to be himself.

He had known the whereabouts of the Supreme Commander Vallezt since the hu-man had done him the huge favor of getting his competition out of the way. He had made a show of trying to launch a rescue, but the damage to the ship had been a perfect cover to allow the hu-mans to get away.

His secondary plan had been to send a raiding party to save their missing leader, only to have that ship fail miserably upon return, thanks to some strategic subtle sabotage that was sure to have the ship explode on its return. The Progerians and the Genogerians would mourn and Kuvlar would be the Supreme Commander without question. And there in lay the problem when the fleet arrived he would first and foremost be held responsible even though it was the dolt Vallezt that had allowed himself to be taken captive.

No, he decided, *a successful rescue was to be his salvation, but it was going to take a delicate balance of timing and cunning to stay in power.* Vallezt could easily send Kuvlar to the games merely for taking so long to launch troops to recoup their leader. Kuvlar shivered at the thought; he was a thinker, a schemer not a fighter, he wouldn't make it through one fight. He was a TRUE leader of men, always willing to let others die for his ideals.

He had at least two years most likely three before the fleet arrived, but he could not wait until that long to make a rescue. Too many things could go wrong, Vallezt could die or be killed by the hu-mans if they did not value his importance or one of their experiments did not go as planned. But to bring him back now was even more distasteful. And then the equivalent of a Progerian smile crossed his features, it was not a sight any human would draw comfort from.

Quarantine, was the one word he thought. "Yes he will be infected with some rare and exotic microorganism that could wipe out all the personnel on board. He will need to be restricted to his quarters with guards." *He will know the ruse for what it is*, Kuvlar thought. *But what will he be able to do? I will keep him in a drugged stupor the entire time until I need to drag him onto the carpet when the Battalion Commander arrives.* Kuvlar rubbed his hands together, it was an eerie mimicking of Earth's less than savory villains.

"He will very much look the part of an idiot when I release him. That many drugs for that long will have put holes through his brain."

Kuvlar walked onto the helm with a lightness in his step he had not had since he had taken command of the ship.

"Sub-Commander do we still have a lock on the Supreme Commander?" Kuvlar asked his subordinate.

Sub-commander Tuvok had been raised to this position when his superior Sub-Commander Krulak had mistakenly questioned Kuvlar's lack of commitment to launch an immediate rescue of their leader. The words had no sooner left Krulak's snout when the Interim Supreme Commander had shouted "Treason!" Krulak had not even the chance to explain his side at a tribunal, ISC Kuvlar had said war superseded normal protocols and that mutinous insubordination had to be dealt with swiftly. Krulak had died on the way to his cell when a Genogerian guard had mistaken his movement to his pocket as an act of aggression.

Krulak had died unattended in the hallway while the guard that had shot him was given two weeks of liberty for stopping an insurrection. All of this went through Tuvok's head; he had been waiting for the rescue attempt to happen, but he was not foolish enough to demand it.

"Yes sir, he has not moved since the hu-mans placed him in that present location," Tuvok said evenly, even though his heart was beating rapidly, that was as close as he dared to approach insubordination. Kuvlar seemed lost in thought or was completely ambivalent to it.

"We will launch the rescue mission as soon as the teams can be assembled. Get it done." Kuvlar said as he stared through the viewing screen and to the tiny blue jewel in the distance. He would feather his cap with that planet soon enough. Then he would command a true war ship.

Tuvok was happy to finally hear those words, life aboard a Progerian vessel was never easy, but certain commanders appreciated the efforts of their crew and others, like Kuvlar, were merely in it for the glory and were more than likely going to get their charges killed or worse, dishonored.

Twenty fighters, along with five troop transports loaded with seven hundred of the finest genetically altered Mutated Genogerians the Dominion had to offer, departed the *Julipion* less than an hour later.

Their destination: Colorado Springs, Colorado.
Cheyenne Mountain to be specific.

***

When Paul's militia had left the mountains of

Colorado for the tunnels of Walpole, minus their star player Michael Talbot, General Burkhalter had recalled his right hand man Captain Moiraine. The general had specifically sent the captain to keep an eye out for Mike and to also see what Paul's next move might be, but Paul had been cagey, the general had felt that Paul had seen through his 'plant' from the beginning and with Paul going to ground anyway, the general saw no reason to keep such a valuable asset away any longer.

Captain Moiraine was hesitant to accept any armed force on American soil that was not in the United States military, but there was something about Paul Ginson he could not put his finger on. A 'resolve' was as close to an adjective that he could get. Paul was unhindered with the bureaucracies that were keeping the rest of the military might on a leash, he envied him that as he sat holding a rapidly cooling cup of coffee. Although he still held onto a grudge, when Paul had evacuated he'd had the Captain rendered unconscious. He'd awoken the next morning in a motel in Breckenridge. Some day he hoped to pay back the courtesy. His mug shattered to the floor when he misplaced its resting spot when the giant radar screen off to his left lit up like downtown Tokyo.

"Incoming!" The radioman shouted after the fact.

Lights dimmed from white fluorescent to red. Klaxons peeled as men began to run to their battle stations. Dozens of fighters scrambled from the nearby Peterson Air Force base. In theory it looked like an underwhelming force, but Captain Moiraine knew the capabilities of their formidable opponent. If more than five of those scrambled fighters survived he would be amazed.

"They came out of nowhere!" Lieutenant McNult said.

"They have a tendency to do that." Captain Moiraine said evenly.

"Where do you think they are headed?" the LT asked. But even he knew the answer. This was one of the very last strategic hold outs AND they had in their possession one very pissed off Supreme Commander.

The captain didn't answer he looked longingly down at the smashed glass and spreading brown liquid of his coffee wishing he had something to wash down the rising panic that was threatening to well up.

"Get everyone to the armory," Captain Moiraine ordered his subordinate.

The lieutenant, turned to look at his superior officer the weight of the words not fully registering.

"Lieutenant, unless I am completely off base we are about to be breeched and in the midst of an all-out assault, would you rather die looking at your console or fighting with a weapon in your hand?"

"Sir I'd rather not die at all," the LT said, taking a big swallow.

"Poor choice of words. We need to defend ourselves, LT, or we will die. Is that clearer?"

"Sir I've only ever shot once, and that was with a nine millimeter pistol. I don't think I'm qualified."

What I wouldn't do for a squad of Marines, the captain thought.

"Lieutenant, get your ass up and issue the order for everybody able to wield a weapon to get down to the armory and do so," the captain said evenly. "And if you say one more word about it, I'll shoot you myself."

"Yes, sir."

It had taken over twenty minutes to convince everyone including the scientists to grab a firearm; in that time, the captain had wondered on the validity of his order when he already had two injuries from accidental discharges.

The air battle had gone better than expected but was still a pre-determined outcome, the Americans had adapted their tactics to the superior handling and firepower of their adversary but it was still not enough. Three F-22s limped away, four alien fighters had dropped along with two of the heavier troop laden transports. Captain Moiraine hoped that was enough. Now it would be their turn to hold on, although he already knew the outcome of that battle, as well. *Maybe if he had some Marines*, he mused, just as the first blasts above them rocked the mountain.

"We've been breached!" one of the Air Force staff sergeants said as he checked his panel.

The mountain was rumbling from the multitude of explosions. As deeply buried as Moiraine and his team were, they could not yet hear the small arms fire, but it was really only a matter of time. He walked over to the coffee machine, grabbed a Styrofoam cup and poured a lukewarm cup of Joe that gas stations would have turned their noses up at.

"Sweet ambrosia," he said as he took a sip. *Funny how good this tastes when you know it's your last one.* He pulled his wallet out and took one last look at his wife and kids who he hoped were still safely tucked away at his sister's house in upstate Montana.

As he took his final drink, he began to hear the staccato bursts of small arms fire. In less than ten minutes the aliens had taken over three quarters of the mountain. If he hadn't been there to witness it, he wouldn't have believed it.

"Lieutenant, take your weapon off of safety," the captain said.

The LT pulled his pistol close to look. "How'd you know?"

"Just a guess. It has been and honor and a privilege to share this uniform with you, gentlemen," the captain said. The room was silent. What more was there to say?

The floor bounced as heavy feet tramped down the hallway. "Mother of God." the staff sergeant sighed as the Mutated Devastator troops rounded the corner. He had not so much as fired a shot when he was liquefied.

Captain Moiraine opened fire, followed quickly by the rest of the men. Two Devastators fell as they were struck multiple times. Instead of impeding their progress this seemed to spur the rest of them on. Their goal seemed to be overwhelming by vastly superior numbers. The lieutenant fell next followed by a lab technician that had to have been pushing sixty, but looked like he had been born with a rifle in his hand. Moiraine wished he had a dozen more like him.

The captain had never seen an enemy so willing to sustain damage, his rifle barrel was threatening to burn out as he repeatedly popped out spent magazines and inserted new ones. It was down to himself and a green private. They were holding their own but ammunition was getting down into the red.

The captain felt a burning sensation as his shoulder absorbed the full brunt of an energy discharge. At first it hadn't felt much worse than placing one's tongue upon the terminals of a nine-volt battery, but as time progressed he began to lose functionality in his left arm and the pain began to increase; gradually at first, and then to the point where he could think of nothing else…at least until he was struck square in the chest.

"Margaret," he called out his wife's name as he fell to the ground.

***

Ground Frontsman Nacir strode through the wreckage of the last fortified human enclosure. "Have you found the Supreme Commander?" he asked his troops.

"Not yet, Ground Frontsman," his second in command relayed.

Nacir was angry, he had lost a fair amount of equipment and almost half his troops and still they had not secured the package. Interim Supreme Commander Krulak had been very specific in his orders: if he did not come back with the Supreme Commander, then he might as well stay on the planet…and that was unacceptable. Colonization was for colonists, he was a warrior, plain and simple.

It was two hours later and some sporadic fighting when the troops emerged with a bedraggled Supreme Commander. There was no 'thank you' or 'congratulations', only 'What took so long?'

"Blow the mountain", Nacir said as he got the Supreme Commander aboard the transport.

The Supreme Commander said nothing to those around him. He was seething with anger and considered it below his station to talk with those aboard the ship.

***

"Seize them," ISC Kuvlar said over the sound system as the transport ship came to rest inside the *Julipion*.

"What is the meaning of this?" Supreme Commander Vallezt shouted as he was roughly grabbed by two guards.

"We've been ordered to place you in quarantine. The hu-mans have introduced you to biological weaponry," the guard said.

"They have done no such thing!" Vallezt shouted. And then it dawned on him, he looked up to the launch bay control center. "Kuvlar, this is your doing. I can smell the taint from here. I will not sit idly by while you destroy everything. I have Progerians loyal to me!"

The guard on his right slid a needle into Vallezt arm. he barely had enough time to register a protest before he was sliding to the ground.

"Place him in his quarters," Kuvlar said as he turned to get back on the helm. *Fortune shines on me today*, he thought.

CHAPTER SIXTY – Mike Journal Entry 18

I found myself hungry but unwilling to go and get food, certain I would run either into Beth or Tracy. And right now that would be enough to turn off my appetite. But sitting there and contemplating wasn't going to solve my hunger problem. I was trying to remember the layout of The Hill in the hopes I could find the most obscure untraveled route to the mess hall and then I would order the quickest meal possible in hopes of getting out undetected. I was deep in thought of a grilled cheese sandwich when a soft knock sounded on my door.

Please be Dennis, I prayed to the heavens.

"Come in," I said with a small upward inflection, showing my nervousness which I hoped didn't travel through the door.

The door swung in, it wasn't Dennis. Beth strode in wearing a sky blue dress that matched her eyes. My heart alternated between stopping completely and then hammering through my chest cavity.

"Hello, Mike," Beth said, looking down more at the floor rather than at me.

Good, I thought, *she's at least as nervous as me.* Thoughts ran rapid through my head, but for whatever reason, I couldn't formulate anything into words. She was just as beautiful, if not more, than I had remembered from any of my most vivid dreams. She had toned up, I could tell from the way the dress clung to her body. Yet she also carried a deep sorrow in her eyes. Something that was not there when we last spoke.

"Debbie's dead," she said, finally looking up.

"I know," I answered flatly. "I saw her."

Beth looked surprised but did not press the issue.

"Mike, I've missed you," Beth said, tears welling up in her eyes.

I wanted to be vindictive and tell her she abandoned me, leaving me in the void to stumble and pull all the pieces together to get on with some semblance of a life. But none of those words came. I still was having great difficulty engaging the function of speech.

Beth continued. "I have nothing left in this world, Mike. Except for you." She looked hopefully into my eyes.

I wanted nothing more than to push her out of my room, but I was afraid that if I even brushed up against her I would pull her down onto my bed and never let her go again.

"You left me," I whispered. The words scraped like sand as they came out of my constricted throat.

Beth looked stung, her eyes threatening to cry. She moved a step closer. I involuntarily flinched backward on the bed. The movement didn't go unnoticed, Beth stopped.

"I need you, Mike. Now more than ever," she nearly cried.

"Why, because I'm the only one left?" I wished the moment it had left my lips that I hadn't said it. The effect was instantaneous. Beth began to sob inconsolably. I had never been able to handle a woman's crying and now was no different.

"Please, Beth, don't do that. I didn't mean it." The crying slowed but didn't stop. "Listen," I continued. "You hurt me like I've never been hurt before. It took me a long time to get over you."

Beth's tears almost doubled. "Yuh-yyyou're over

me?" she cried.

"Please...please, stop. Yes and no. I've finally stopped thinking about you every minute of every day—now it's more like every other minute."

Beth smiled a little.

"I know what I did was wrong," she said haltingly. "I guess I didn't want to believe how bad off we really were and the extreme measures we were going to have to take to survive," she said. "I've had to do some pretty terrible things myself just to get here."

To my surprise, I found myself almost against my own will rising and crossing the distance between us. In a moment, I found myself hugging her and being hugged in return by the girl who had showed me what love was and then shattered my heart into fragments. I had been able to piece some of it back together, but it would never be like the original.

Beth's sobbing began anew as she buried her head into the crook of my shoulder. I stood there holding on for dear life, my own eyes threatening to loose their water works.

***

Tracy had been on her way to Mike's room and had just turned the corner in the hallway to see a person that could only be Beth as she walked into the room—and by the looks of it, she had been invited. Tracy wavered between an all-out confrontation or quiet withdrawal. She was frozen in indecision. It wasn't until she noticed movement at the far end of the corridor that she began to move. But much to her dismay, it was away from there; she wanted nothing more than to go to her quarters and put a few well aimed slugs into her wall. Hopefully, they would find their final resting place in the picture frame she had managed to salvage that now contained Mike's likeness. She was so blinded by rage, it took her more than a moment to discover she was somehow sitting on the ground, having walked into a wall.

"Small female hu-man," the booming voice echoed in the constricted quarters. "Are you alright?" Drababan stooped over, extending his giant hand to help her up. She attempted to swat away his offer, but anything less than lethal force was not likely to move any part of Drababan.

"I'm fine!" she shouted, wincing at her outburst.

Drababan didn't seem to notice, or at least he didn't mind. "But there is water coming out of your eyes. I know that generally signifies pain in your species."

"Oh, so now you're a doctor?" Tracy knew Drababan had nothing to do with what she was feeling, but she couldn't help using him as her whipping boy.

"No, I am not a doctor, but I have studied your species' physiology enough to probably be considered as such in some of your more backward societies."

Tracy looked up at him, stunned. She was having as difficult a time as Mike when trying to figure out Drababan's wry sense of humor, if that was even what it was.

"Let me help you up, small female hu-man," Drababan repeated.

"Tracy, my name is Tracy. Not small female hu-man," she answered as Drababan nearly sent her into orbit as he pulled her to her feet. "Thank you," she mumbled.

"You certainly are welcome," he said graciously. "Have you been to Miike's?" he asked.

"You call him Mike. Why do you call everyone else around you by a description?" she nearly shouted, more so because he was so tall and she didn't know if he could hear her from where she stood.

"He has earned it," he said matter-of-factly.

Tracy knew arguing with him would be futile. In her own way she had more than earned respect for the things she had done and accomplished; why then did she feel the need to earn the ugly alien's respect? If she had the chance back in France, she would have filled his tough green hide with as many bullets as her rifle magazine could carry.

"You know that I have earned the Navy Cross?" she threw out.

More perceptive than she could have ever imagined Drababan answered back. "Why do you care what I think of you?"

More in a rage than anything Tracy let loose anew with her tears. "I DON'T CARE, YOU FUCKING OVERGROWN LIZARD! I JUST WANT YOU AND ALL YOUR KIND TO GET OFF MY FUCKING PLANET!"

Her shouting drew the attention of a lot of civilians and just as many soldiers who had been ordered to 'escort' Drababan around the base 'at a distance'.

"Ah, look what you have done now, small female human. You have brought my entourage," Drababan said, but with what seemed like a lot less humor in his voice.

Six soldiers loosely encircled Drababan, weapons not drawn yet.

"Is there a problem, Lieutenant?" the nearest one asked.

"Yeah, there's a fucking problem," she said with more control, but laced with more vehemence in her voice. "Why is this fucking lizard walking loose around this bunker?"

Tracy's fight was not with Drababan but rather his kind, he just happened to be within her range of anger.

* * *

"Because he is my friend," I said as I broke through the circle of soldiers. "Put your weapons away and leave now," I said to the sergeant closest to Tracy.

A corporal that had been on our detail coming in had come to get me when he saw the rising anger in Tracy. I was grateful that he had, this looked like it had the potential to turn disastrous.

The sergeant looked to Tracy and then back to me. "Sir, we have our orders," the sergeant replied.

"Fuck your orders!" I shot back. The sergeant visibly recoiled. "You don't take your men now and withdraw, then I'll make sure you all are skinning potatoes for the next year!"

"I'll have to tell the general about this," the sergeant said, trying his best to save face as he withdrew.

"Do you know who I am, Sergeant?" I asked with more control in my voice.

"I am well aware of who you are, sir," the sergeant said, swallowing what appeared to be a big knot in his throat.

"Then do you really think that I care if you go run off to the general about what happened here?"

The sergeant finally broke eye contact with Drababan and looked squarely at my hard features, for a moment unsure which of the two of us was at the moment more dangerous.

"Yes, sir. I mean no, sir," the sergeant stuttered, "We'll withdraw now. Men stand down, go back to your secondary positions." The crowd began to disperse as the tension drained away.

"Mike—Mike, what's going on?" Beth said as she pressed through the dissipating crowd.

She stopped short when she came up on the scene. I stood in a triangle with one of the Genogerians and with what Beth would tell me later was one of the most beautiful women she had ever seen to grace a battle dress uniform. Most women got lost in the clothes, this woman's beauty seemed to rise above her garb, she had said it with a note of jealously.

"Mike? Is everything alright?" Beth asked, skirting the Genogerian as much as was possible. But from the aura of hatred she could feel seething from Tracy, she tried her best to keep her distance there too, which in a small corridor was not an easy feat.

"Yeah, Mike," Tracy mimicked. "Is everything all right?" Her tone was marked with bitterness and barely controlled rage.

"Mike, is something going on here?" Beth spoke.

"You think?" Tracy answered, infusing as much sarcasm as the words could convey.

"Listen, I don't even know you. What could I have possibly done for you to look at me that way?" Beth asked, and then it dawned on her. *The way she looked at me, the rage that was threatening to overwhelm the woman, the hatred she directed towards her. Only one thing could make somebody that crazy. Love was the answer.* "Is she the one?" Beth asked me.

"Oh, it was nice of you to bring me up while you two were getting reacquainted!" Tracy shot out before I had a chance to reply to Beth.

"It's not…it wasn't like that," I stumbled across my words, doing my best to diffuse what could only be considered a time bomb with no discernible way to shut it off. "I was in the process of telling her about you when you were trying to get my friend shot."

I was only all too happy to see one of Paul's aide-de-camps rapidly approaching from the far end of the hallway. I knew from experience that I was only summoned this way when something big was happening and usually I dreaded finding out what it was. But at this particular point the aide looked like Gabriel himself coming to rescue me from some far worse fate than whatever was going on in the HQ.

"Does the general need me?" I asked pleadingly before the aide was more than halfway down the hall.

The aide-de-camp was an undersized man who looked more like a child in his father's uniform but his quick mind and strategic skills made him a respected man when push came to shove.

Major Whittingly knew he was called Dr. Doom behind his back because he only showed up to summon people when the shit hit the fan. So, for the most part, people—especially the officers—avoided him like the plague. To see someone willingly make eye contact and initiate conversation completely caught him off guard.

"Um, yes, Captain. The general is requesting your presence."

I cut him off in the fear that the meeting might be sometime in the future, anything less than 'now' was unacceptable, I needed to extract myself from the conversation (confrontation) as soon as possible. "Let me get my boots."

I left the two women to their own devices. Drababan stayed merely to watch the interaction. For long moments they could do nothing more than stare in the direction in which I had so rapidly retreated.

***

"Man, I was never so happy to see Dr. Doom as I was just now," I said with a smirk on my face. "He saved me from a huge—" I stopped talking when I saw the look on Paul's face. "What's going on?" I said, now all business.

"Have a seat." Paul motioned with his hand.

I was about to sit when I noticed Dennis off to the side of the office, the same grave expression written all over his face. I thought, *This doesn't look good*, but felt that to say the words would be lost on my audience. I sat silently.

"Dennis, could you please tell Mike what you saw?" Paul said without emotion, his attention now miles away.

Dennis stood up from his leaning position and walked solemnly over to the chair next to mine. He sat down with a loud 'umph'.

"Holy shit, bud. What's going on?" I asked, an unsettling unease beginning to worm its way through my innards.

Dennis answered with one word. "Ratspindler."

I was thrown aback by the name, but couldn't for the life of me get how the name could convey the attitude that was circulating around the room.

"What about him?" I asked.

"He's here," Dennis answered.

"*Here*, here? Like *this* complex?" Yes, that would suck, but the man had no authority over us anymore. Sure he had tried to make our adolescent years a living hell, but that was ancient history, something else was going on here.

"Guys, I'm not seeing the big picture. Unless he's got a nuke strapped on his back, who gives a shit. He doesn't have a backpack nuke, does he?"

"He might as well," Paul answered. Noticing that Dennis was going to involuntarily draw this out longer than necessary, Paul interjected. "Dennis had a squad out scoping their new landing party in Dedham when he caught sight of thirteen prisoners being led into their HQ." I was starting to grasp the situation, the worm in my innards was beginning to expand. It felt more like a squirrel now. "One of them was Spindler."

I stood. I didn't know what else to do. "Are you sure?" I said, looking over at Dennis.

"See for yourself," Dennis said sliding a picture over on Paul's desk that I had not noticed before. "I was three hundred yards away and I didn't even need the 'nocs to recognize him from his portrait at school. That hook nose is difficult to forget."

He looked a little thinner than he had when he left Walpole High with his tail tucked between his legs, but there was no denying who it was. Before I could ask any more questions, Dennis continued.

"Thirteen prisoners went into the HQ only eleven came out. Of the two that didn't come out, one was a woman..."

"And the other was Spindler," I finished. "Paul, Spindler knows about this place. I mean, not this place specifically, but about the silo for sure."

"I'm not wearing this expression because our old high school principal might be coming back to look for the two individuals who blew up his caddy."

"You two did that?" Dennis asked, momentarily forgetting the weight of the news in the room.

Paul and I both looked to Dennis. "We never told you about that?" Paul said.

"I always thought it was Lester from two grades ahead of us," Dennis said.

Laughter ensued for a full minute before the true business came back around.

"Alright," Paul started as he wiped a tear from his eye. "Our options are limited at best. There is obviously an entire evacuation to consider, but with the Genogerians so close, our chance of doing so successfully is greatly diminished. And even if we did escape, where would we go? We couldn't take enough provisions with us to last a month. Do we stay and do nothing hoping Spindler doesn't give them any useful information?"

I looked over at Paul, eyebrows raised.

"Yeah, I feel the same way," Paul answered. "That miserable little fuck would sell us all out in a hot minute if he thought it would buy him one more day. The last idea and probably least likely to pass a majority vote is we go all out on the offensive."

"Last I checked," Dennis threw in, "this isn't a democracy."

"No, you're right," Paul answered derisively. "But half of the Hill's population is civilian. What I would be asking is tantamount to mass suicide."

"Not so much suicide," I stated, "as Kamikaze. The Japanese used it with devastating effect in World War Two."

"So you were actually paying attention in History class," Paul quipped. "But you have to remember, it still ended up in their deaths."

"Paul, you know where I stand. Every one of those options ends in death, the only one that allows our deaths to have meaning is to make them pay dearly for their conquest," I said vehemently.

"There's another plan," Dennis stated matter-of-factly.

We both stopped and turned his way.

"Well, it's more like two of the previous plans combined."

"We're listening," Paul said.

"Alright, we go all out on the offensive with our military and we cause a big enough diversion that the civilian populace can sneak out undetected. The chances that they can get out will be a lot better."

"That's brilliant," I said as I clapped Dennis' shoulder. I had really hoped there would be a way for Beth to escape. Tracy too, but I knew there was no way I would be able to not have her engage in this final battle. Unless...

"Paul, I think that you should send some troops with the civilians, they'll need to have some sort of firepower. They would be ripe for any band of rogues unless they had some sort of guard."

"You have an idea on who you want to send?" And before I could answer, "And also do you have an idea how you're going to keep her from coming with us?"

My face fell when I realized how transparent my thoughts were.

"Relax, pal," Paul said. "I see the necessity for what you are saying, it's the implementation that is going to be tough."

"Wait, Paul," I said, holding up my hand. A new plan was almost smacking me upside the head. "I thought of another way."

"Don't let me stop you," Paul interjected after a pregnant pause.

"Assassination," I blurted out.

"What the hell are you talking about?" Dennis asked.

"I'm saying we send in a small raiding party and take Spindler out."

"You're talking about murdering another human being," Paul said shaking his head slowly from side to side.

"It's him or us, Paul. I'm not seeing the dilemma," I said heatedly.

"You wouldn't, would you?" he shot back, maybe a little too quickly.

"What the fuck are you implying, Paul? I did what I had to survive and don't go giving me that holier-than-thou shit. I know what you told Sergeant Bolito's squad to do!"

Paul stood up quickly, his chair toppled behind him. I could see the question of 'How do you know?' forming on his lips.

"Men talk, Paul. You did the exact same thing to preserve the secrecy of this base. That's all I'm saying we need to do now," I said, bringing some of the fire out of my words.

"When does it stop, Mike? How many people do we need to kill? Those people haunt my dreams."

"The burden of leadership," I told him. "The only one beating you up over your decision is yourself. Spindler needs to die, if he tells them about the silo, they'll figure it out. They might be ugly, but they aren't stupid."

Paul stooped over to right his chair. It seemed gravity itself was weighing him down. He sat before he spoke. "What's your plan?"

"Mike has a plan? This oughtta be rich," Dennis said, smiling.

So I spent the next ten to fifteen minutes laying it all out there in its naked glory. It did not look nearly as good in the open.

"You sure, Mike?" Paul asked, looking into my eyes for any sort of deception.

"Fuck, no," I told him honestly. "But it gives us a

chance."

"They're not gonna screw with you anymore if they catch you, Mike," Dennis said. "They're just gonna fry you with that blue shit."

"It's the blue shit or two women here. I'll take my chances out there," I told them, stupid male bravado making me do things that were detrimental to my health. As a male of the species I had already attracted female counterparts with my actions; what did I need to prove now?

I was relieved as I left Paul's office. I was most assuredly heading to my death and my thoughts couldn't have been any lighter. The two women I loved would be safe, for how long I didn't know, but they would be safer for longer than me and that somehow gave me an inner peace I hadn't had in long, long while.

***

Eastern Seaboard Occupation - South West of Boston.

"Ground Commander Chofla, what do you want me to do with the hu-man?" Sub-commander Ruthgar asked.

"Kill him," came the terse reply.

"Sir, what if the information he gave isn't valid?" the sub-commander asked.

"If it's valid we kill what's left of these hu-mans' resistance. If it is not..." He seemed to ponder. "Well, if it is not, then the disgusting little pink thing in there had nothing to barter his life for anyway."

"As you wish, Commander," the sub-commander said and gave a small bow.

***

"General Ginson!" the private screamed as he ran down the hall at full tilt.

Paul stopped mid-stride, he had been heading down the hallway to get some much needed coffee.

"Sir!" The private practically came to a screeching halt. Paul nearly laughed.

"Take a breath, private—what's going on?"

"Sir, Outpost One has relayed that 'Principal A' has possibly been retired. I don't know what that means, but they made sure that I repeated it word for word. Is that serious? Sir, are you okay?"

Paul's innards had nearly evacuated themselves, either Spindler was the biggest hero Earth might ever know and withheld information that cost him his life or… "Tell Major Wagner that the plan we talked about is in full effect."

"Sir? What—" the private began to ask.

"Private!" Paul shouted. The young man ceased talking and asking questions. "Do it. Do it now," Paul said with as much determination as he could without yelling.

The private knew something huge was going on but, he could not grasp the meaning. All he knew was that if Major Wagner didn't have this message in the next five minutes, he most likely would be facing a firing squad, he was halfway down the corridor before he realized he had forgotten to acknowledge the general.

"Sir!" he screamed, to no avail, the general had left the hallway almost as quickly as he had.

***

Ground Headquarters Eastern Region

"Devastator Commander Turval." Troop Leader Urlack stood in the doorway, his hulking mass nearly taking up the entire doorframe. The commander could not stand the abomination that stood before him, half Genogerian half Progerian, it was a wonder he had been let into the officer ranks. If Urlack's father had not been a high cabinet member it would've never happened. He would have died long ago in the games to one of his bigger cousins on the Geno side.

"What do you want, Urlack?" The lack of proper rank identification a definite insult.

A small snarl spread over Urlack's snout. It was something he had been working on for years, to not show that the insults got under his hide. In the early days, he had attacked his then commanding officer nearly ripping his arm off before being subdued. That stint had cost him nearly a *partring* (a Progerian year) in jail even with his father's influence. Any lesser Geno he knew would have been unceremoniously shot in the head. This commander who had gotten nearly nine hundred brave soldiers killed was not worthy of his title and if they were not in the midst of a war he would openly challenge the useless *svark* to a duel. Not a ceremonious one; no, it would be the kill or be killed variety.

"Commander," Urlack snarled, "do you want me to call in an air strike on the location that the hu-man circled on the map?"

Devastator Commander Turval almost paled his huge maw opened in a show of aggression. Urlack did not submit, which further infuriated his commander. "You will do no such thing, underling!" Turval spat. "I will not let those air dogs claim victory when I am so near to eradicating this troublesome species!"

Urlack knew his boundaries. He also knew when he stepped over them. "Eight hundred and ninety-two dead and another hundred and twenty on an emergency ship does not sound like a near victory."

Turval stood, rage emanating from features. "Abomination! I will not have you speak to me like that!" he spat. "Your mother I can understand, for wanting to procreate above her station. Your father, however, should have drowned you as a whelp!"

Urlack launched himself in the air before the mood

dampeners he had set in his mind all those years ago could even begin to take effect. Turval was a huge Progerian by any standard and had been in the military almost his entire adult life, but he quickly found himself on the losing side against an opponent nearly half again his size with an unchecked rage.

Urlack paused as the first of the stun rays impacted his body. It took eight more before he finally collapsed in a heap. Turval's bodyguards stood in amazement, the most any Geno had ever taken was four stuns and that had nearly killed him. A human couldn't take even one full charge without most of his major muscle groups shredding apart from the shock. But there was Urlack on the ground looking at them all with a ferocity that still burned in his eyes.

Turval pulled himself off the desk he had been slammed upon and walked over to Urlack. "You know, I was going to have a couple of gunships hang back and use them if the hu-mans proved to be more resilient than I think they are. But instead, just for *you*," he emphasized, "I am going to amass the largest Geno army yet on this planet and march them straight into the teeth of whatever defense these hairless apes have left and you will lead them. I will win, but it will be a costly battle with thousands upon thousands of brave Genos dying. I will be considered a legend by the time this is over. Thousands of your half-brothers will die because of your stupidity and I will be doing everyone a favor; ridding the earth of the lice that now inhabit it and reducing the numbers of our lesser brethren. That we share even some of the same genome disgusts me. When my people had the opportunity, those *partrons* ago they should have taken a lesson from the hu-mans and just eradicated your kind."

Urlack struggled to get up, his muscles still spasming from the after effect of the shock. Turval involuntarily backed up. A small victory, Urlack thought, but a victory nonetheless.

"They will sing songs about me, Urlack, when word

of this battle gets back to our home planet. I will probably become a Supreme-Commander when this is done. And all at the expense of the Genogerians!" Turval roared in laughter. "Put him in jail, unharmed. I want him to live long enough to lead his men and watch as I rise on the fallen of his kindred."

Urlack was helpless as he was dragged away from Turval's office. He was two hallways away before he couldn't hear Turval's echoing laughter. Hatred boiled over, but he tried to relax as much as possible. To fight the shock was the worst possible solution; let it course through him and out was the only way to be rid of it. He had practiced more than once, realizing that this day or at least one like it was only a matter of time for someone like him. He calmed himself even further, going as limp as was possible, his dead weight making matters difficult for the guards.

Urlack waited until the hallway was clear before he made his move—the speed in which he moved completely caught the guard to his left by surprise, he never had a chance as Urlack reached one hand behind his neck and the other around his jaw, the short quick movement was punctuated with a loud crack as the guard's neck snapped. The guard dragging Urlack's right arm found himself against the far wall before he was able to take his next breath.

One of the rear guards had just brought his stun weapon up to the ready when Urlack brought his mighty fists to bear on the somewhat sensitive snout. The guard crumpled to the floor without ever firing a shot. The second rear guard was attempting to figure out which of the three stun weapons he was carrying could be fired the quickest, or at least removed from its holster. His thoughts were completely interrupted as the first blast caught him center mass. Urlack shot him twice more for good measure. The guard against the far wall was beginning to stir when Urlack shot him in the head, effectively scrambling his thought processes for the rest of what would be a short existence.

Urlack cursed himself for what he done as he

surveyed the damage around him. He had let his emotional Geno side take over from the cold calculating Progerian side. He had no plan, all he'd done was just make damn sure he couldn't stay there. It didn't matter now that his father was a supreme ruler, Urlack would be shot on sight. But where was he going to go? The planet was as hostile an environment as he had ever stepped foot on.

In the end, he had to take the only chance available to him. He grabbed some weapons and headed for the outer perimeter, concocting a viable story as to why he needed to leave the safety area. He was no more than fifty yards from the makeshift demarcation zone when the alarm was sounded.

Well, no turning back now, he thought as he casually strolled on. The guards were focusing all their attention on the perceived hu-man threat they thought was approaching rather than the lunatic officer that was rapidly retreating from view.

CHAPTER SIXTY-ONE

Tracy waited in her quarters until she just couldn't take it anymore. Mike hadn't come at all, was he with Beth? Already? She couldn't believe he would just abandon her—could he? She wanted to go straight to his quarters but she didn't think she could take it if he wasn't alone.

She went to the cafeteria first and bought a cup of coffee, trying to make it look like she had come specifically for that and wasn't wandering around aimlessly like a lost puppy. She hated herself for having those feelings, but there they were and she couldn't do anything but deal with it. She was attempting to cool the coffee off when she spotted Mike at an intersection right outside the eatery, her heart skipped. He was clearly talking to someone, but she couldn't tell who because the person was in the other hallway. She walked as casually as she could which more resembled a speed walk. Mike never turned, he hadn't even noticed her. She was close enough to hear him now.

"I love you, too," she heard him say. Her coffee splashed to the floor as Mike turned her way.

"Oh…hey, Tracy. I was just coming to see you," Mike said with a genuine smile on his face.

That caught her off guard. She hadn't seen a genuine smile from him since she'd known him. *Did Beth give him that smile?* She was furious and confused. Confused because he honestly looked happy to see her; he didn't look like someone who had just got caught with their hand in the cookie jar.

"Who were you talking to?" She tried her best to not let the rage that threatened to overtake her show in her words.

"Huh? Oh, that was my brother." He smiled.

Her face flushed with relief. Mike stooped over to try to salvage some of her coffee, but it was to no avail.

"Come on, I'll buy you another cup. Figuratively…we don't have to pay for shit here," he answered when she looked at him strangely.

"Don't bother, I didn't really want that one," she said. Mike looked at her quizzically.

"Well, then come on I've gotta get some napkins from the counter so I can clean that mess up."

"Uh-huh," she managed to get out.

Mike finished picking up the spillage. "Come on, let's go to my quarters, I've got some things I'd like to discuss with you."

After five minutes of talking with Mike, Tracy's mood did reach the rage threshold, but not for the reason she would have guessed.

"Don't think I'm stupid, Mike!" she yelled.

Mike backed up a step, wary of her fury. "Hold on, hold on," he said, putting his hands up for emphasis and partly for defense should he need to. "I never said you were stupid."

She didn't let him finish. "Just because the orders are coming from General Ginson…" her tone getting angrier, "…this idea reeks of you!" she said, and violently thrust her finger toward his sternum. He was glad that he had the foresight to back up, he was pretty sure she put enough force in that finger to lodge it up to the first knuckle in his chest.

"Hold on," he pleaded again. "I came up with that idea, but there were a few other people at the table. Paul, I mean, the general had to pick the one that made the most sense for everyone."

Her edge didn't ebb in the slightest. "This doesn't

make the most sense for *me*!" she yelled even louder. "The heaviest resistance battle this planet may ever see and you want me to lead a legion of doomed refugees to where? To what?" she screamed.

"That's only if my initial plan fails. Tracy, you've got to take it down a notch," Mike tried.

"Don't tell me what to do," she said as Mike tried to draw her close. Partly to calm her down, but mostly to try to quiet her down. Him she could yell at, but to take away what little hope the civilians had was unacceptable. "And speaking of your 'initial plan'," she spat the words out. "What are you thinking?"

"I do what I have to, Tracy. You're an officer, you're a leader. Now is your time to lead these people to safety. I told you what is going on. If I should fail, to stay here is absolute suicide. Those 'doomed refugees' include my brother. I am putting my family in your hands."

"Don't try to turn this," she said, her posture easing. "This has nothing to do with protecting these people, it has to do with you trying to get rid of me." A small tear began to form in her eye—that pissed her off almost more than Mike.

"I'm not trying to get rid of you, Tracy. I'm trying to protect you."

"Ah, so the truth comes out." Almost making good on her threat to put her index finger through Mike's sternum. "I don't need your protecting, Mike," she said. "I'm a big girl now. I made it all this way all by myself."

"Okay, okay," he plead. "This is about me."

She looked at him waiting for him to clarify. Mike's mouth went dry as he fought to find the words to explain what he was feeling.

"Tracy, you and I both know the odds of my raid aren't good, it isn't quite a death sentence but I wouldn't put any money down on it, either." She nodded minutely. "There is no way I will be able to be an effective part of the mission if I'm constantly thinking about your safety. I need to know that if push comes to shove you will get out of here, that you will survive. That means more to me than anything else."

"Mike," Her tone softened as she watched the pain cross his face. She grabbed his face in her hands and stroked him softly. "I was a Marine before I met you, I'm a Marine now, and I want to go out a Marine. There is no way I would be an effective part of the mass exodus if I had to constantly worry about you. If you die, I die."

Mike nodded. He knew he had lost. The only way he was going to get her to leave with the civilians was in chains.

"Fuck," Mike said softly.

"I knew you'd see it my way." Tracy smiled.

For nearly an hour and half they explored each other's bodies in a tantric bliss, almost in direct contrast to the loud fight they just had, their lovemaking was quiet, part need, part desire. They held each other long after their climactic ends. They both knew this was most likely the last time and they wanted to savor it like a vintage French wine.

Tracy left an hour later. Mike had almost finished dressing when there was a knock on his door.

CHAPTER SIXTY-TWO – Mike Journal Entry
19

"Did you forget something?" I said as I opened the door. My expression froze. Beth stood in the doorway. Recognition flashed across her eyes, but she moved on as skillfully as a cat skirts water.

"Expecting someone else?" she asked sensuously.

"I—ah—hey, Beth. What brings you this way?" I asked, knowing I had done nothing wrong, but still feeling like I was guilty of something.

"I came to see you. Do you really need to ask?" she asked, looking hurt. "And what's this rumor I've been hearing that we're leaving?"

"That's classified information, Beth," I told her, shock in my voice.

"So it is true." She smiled. "Give me another chance, Mike," she pleaded.

I tried to stay stone-faced, but it was no use. I was a person who had worn my heart on my sleeve since I could crawl; changing now was not going to be an option.

"You know, Mike, people can say a lot when they say nothing at all."

I still was unable to form anything reasonably coherent. Beth reached out and grabbed my hand. I didn't resist, but I didn't help her, either. This was driving me nuts, less than five minutes ago I was holding the girl of my every dreams in my arms, the complete love I felt for Tracy couldn't even allow the thought of Beth to creep in, so why now was Beth the only thing I could think of?

"Beth, I don't want you here," I said woodenly.

Something akin to pain flitted across Beth's features. She moved past it with alarming speed. "I know that's not what you mean, Mike. I can tell by the pulse racing through your hand."

I pulled my hand back like electric current was running through it. "Mike, we were meant to be together."

My face softened. Beth pressed her attack. She was in a winner take all battle with Tracy and she was determined to win. What she wasn't taking into account was I was not the boy she had first fallen in love with. The two years of constant battle had hardened me, well maybe not my heart but definitely my psyche. One thing that I did not respond to well was attack. The fight-or-flight hardwiring was tuned to the max in me. Unfortunately, I was woefully short in the 'flight' part, My first and only instinct now when attacked was: fight. And my instinct was beginning to hum with the high voltage coursing through me. But this wasn't a traditional fight, I didn't know what my next course of action should be. I didn't want to argue or flee, but I couldn't risk being with her.

"We had something special, Mike," Beth said, moving past the doorframe.

I held my ground, if she was able to cross the line, the battle might well be over before it began.

"Beth, I can't do this now," I offered.

"If not now, when?" Beth asked, knowing full well that our time together was going to be measured in days at best, hours at worst.

"Beth, I'll never be able to repay you for the strength you gave me on that ship. You're the reason I made it through."

I was unable to finish as Beth cut in. "Stop it, Mike."
Her vehemence made me give a step. "I am not some
mystical figure who granted you some super powers!" she
screamed. "What you did, you did on your own." I was
stung, taking the wrong meaning from her words. Beth must
have seen the confusion in my eyes and explained further.
"No...no, Mike, not what you're thinking. I'm saying those
things...wait, it's coming out wrong. The determination, the
strength, the will to survive—that came from within you. If
you used me as a focus for that, I'll take credit, but
everything else was you and you alone. Nobody could have
done what you did and come out even half the man they were
when they entered, but not only did you survive, you grew.
People can feel it radiate off you, they see you and they see
hope. They see what we can all become, what we can all
overcome. If one person could take on an entire starship and
survive what are the possibilities of three thousand. Even
your big green friend—"

"Drababan," I interjected.

"Right, Drababan," she continued. "Even an alien life
form can see something different in you. Can't you forgive
me for taking longer to see what everyone else does? I knew
you before the transformation. I guess I just didn't know
what I was looking at. While everyone else was watching the
butterfly I was still looking for the caterpillar."

"Listen, I'm not so sure about the analogy, but I've
definitely changed. And at a time when I was clinging to my
sanity, you abandoned me." Beth kept eye contact as long as
she could before erupting in tears.

"Mike, I think about those last moments when we
parted," she sobbed. "If there was one thing in my life that I
could take back, that would be it. But I can't...I can't undo
what I have already done."

"And neither can I," I said, my resolve starting to
break down under what seemed a relentless onslaught of
emotions. "Beth, I contemplated suicide that day."

Beth put her hand to her mouth, shock apparent on her face.

"I've never told anybody that. After all the good men that I killed while we were up there just so I could hold you again…" I left the sentence unfinished.

"You also killed a lot of monsters," she added.

"When I realized what I had done, and had not achieved the outcome I had hoped for, I didn't see the reason in going on."

"I had no idea," Beth said.

"How could you…you left."

Beth cried anew.

I grabbed her and pulled her close. "I'm not saying that to be mean, I'm just stating a fact."

"Mike," she started, "I needed to work my mind around everything that happened. I didn't see the whole picture. You can't hold me at fault for my naivety."

"I don't, Beth. I forgave you a long time ago, but I— as of yet—have not been able to forget you. Not for lack of trying."

Beth winced. "You sound so cold."

"The calluses around my heart have hardened this last year. If they hadn't, I wouldn't be here."

Beth gasped as Drababan pushed past her and the doorframe and walked in. He didn't so much as soak up space as to redefine it. He was massive.

"Miike, I would like to talk to you."

"Hey, Dee," I said casually, pure relief coursing through my body. The tension had shattered like a clay pigeon under a hail of shotgun pellets.

In his best impression of a smile, Drababan noted Beth's presence as best as his courtesies would allow. "Hello, small hu-man female that travels with bear cub."

The smile appeared more like a snarl to Beth as she moved past me as casually as she could before answering. "The name is Beth."

Drababan merely cocked his head and summarily dismissed her.

"Miike, I would like to talk to you," Dee repeated.

I grasped Drababan's huge forearm.

"What's going on, Drababan?" I asked.

Drababan pointed toward Beth.

"Beth," she answered annoyed.

Drababan merely grunted.

"Beth," she repeated much softer, as if hoping the big brute didn't hear her and would now just ignore her completely.

Drababan stared intently at me, to Beth I think she thought that he was sizing me up for a snack. But when I answered him with an 'It's alright' she knew it was more, she saw that we were communicating by our expressions, I think Beth was astounded. Not only had I made a friend of one of the things, I was close enough to it to understand its facial expressions as minute as they may be. And what was more astounding was once Drababan had made clear he wasn't comfortable talking in front of her, he still deferred to my will. She seemed to feel a little safer all of a sudden.

"I'll come back later," Beth said looking over toward me.

I hoped I'd be gone by that time, just being in her presence threatened to pull my heart from its location in my chest. Drababan paid her no attention as she departed.

"Mike, I smell fear."

"Yeah, that's probably me," I answered in all seriousness.

"No, Miike, I smell anxiousness on you sometimes, but never fear."

"What? You can smell anxiousness? What else? Forget it, I don't want to know. Could you clarify who you are smelling the fear from?"

"That's the problem, Miike. It is coming from so many sources, and it is such a deep-rooted fear, I know that something is happening, but I barely get these silly little humans to talk to me, much less tell me what is going on."

"Not to make you feel bad, big guy, but do you think that it is just the fear when they spot your huge ass walking down the hallway?" If Drababan caught the slight he ignored it completely.

"That is part of it, as it should be," he said and I would swear he was bragging a little. "But not all of it," he added gravely. "It is the smell of the defeated. It is a desperate fear. As a commander of shock troops, I have smelled it from many different races."

"I didn't know."

"How could you? Your small hu-man noses are not as adept at smelling as ours."

"Not that, that you were a leader of men. I mean Genogerians."

"My unit was among one of the most decorated in all the galaxy," he said proudly, his chest puffing out.

"Fuck, you're huge," I said looking up to him. "What are your concerns, Dee? And please sit down, all the blood rushes out of my head when I have to look up that high."

Dee did as I asked. "You must find a way to give your people hope, Michael. Desperate people will do desperate things."

"When did you become a psychologist?" I asked him, semi-seriously. "And why do you butcher Mike but not Michael? Forget it."

"Living, sentient beings are strikingly similar when threatened, Miike."

"I think it's anything living, Dee. It's just that sentient beings have more ways to express their feelings. Even a lowly rabbit will bite in the end. It probably won't be able to gnaw through a neck or anything but it could still draw blood."

"I do not know of this *rabbit*, but I would fear anything that could chew through my neck."

I laughed. "I'm sorry, buddy," I told him. "I was referring to an old movie we used to watch. Television? The signals your ship intercepted," I clarified when Dee looked like he didn't know what I was talking about.

"You will have to show it to me someday."

"I hope we have that chance," I told him in earnest. "Now back to the infusing of hope. One of our patrols came across some truly detrimental information."

Dee closed his eyes.

"You tired, my friend?" I asked sarcastically. "Am I keeping you up? You want a pillow?"

"I know you jest with me, Michael, I am merely concentrating. I find that your fluorescent lights disrupt my ability to do that effectively."

Now he had my interest. "You know sarcasm? I thought that was lost on your kind."

Dee snorted. "Most of them, perhaps. But I have spent more time with your kind than any other, at least while they are not comatose."

"Experimentation? Are you talking experimentation? Forget I asked—I don't want to know."

"I am beginning to understand that the tone in which one utters words has much more to do with the meaning than the actual words themselves. It is a form of deception? Correct?"

"I think it's more a form of rudeness."

"Yet you do it all the time," Dee said, calling me out.

"Maybe we should move on to another topic."

"That is not sarcasm."

"Nope, that's avoidance."

"We will revisit this topic, I think."

"Yay, I can't wait," I said, clapping my hands together lightly.

Drababan opened up one large eye, even sitting he had to look down at me. "I see that we have already come back to it."

"Sorry, as a Bostonian, it's ingrained. It's as much a part of me as your green skin is to you."

"You are saying it is genetic?" he questioned.

I thought long and hard, I wanted to be as truthful as possible. "Yes…yes, it is."

"Funny, the scientists never spoke of this sarcasm gene," he said, his eye closing again.

"Can we move on?" I asked.

"I am aligning my chakras so that they might better help me to understand your words."

"Chakras?"

"That is your hu-man word for it. It is a similar concept to our sepitars, I figured you would know chakras, those are points of energy—"

"I know what chakras are, I just didn't know you did and that you would know what to do with them. Although, why wouldn't you? You are one of the most spiritual beings I have ever met."

"I am ready to accept your words," Dee told me.

I more than half expected him to pull his massive legs up in the Indian style of sitting with his hands folded in his lap. I would have had to hunt down a camera if that came to fruition.

"I'm still waiting," he said when I didn't immediately speak.

"Right. I've got a plan."

This time both of Dee's eyes opened in surprise.

"I get that a lot," I said wonderingly. I spent about ten minutes laying the whole thing out for him.

"That will not work without me," Drababan said as I wrapped up.

"I know. I could not volunteer you for something so dangerous, though, Dee. I wanted to ask you after I told you the whole thing."

"We will probably die in this attempt," Dee said, not out of fear. He had been processing the information and that was the obvious conclusion of the facts given. "We must go as soon as I have had a chance to commune with my god."

"Are you sure, Dee? I mean, you just got your freedom, and I am asking you to essentially die for a different species."

"I will fight and I will die, Michael, because I now have my freedom. There is no power on your Earth that will prevent me from giving that up. I would rather die free than any other alternative. Wouldn't you?"

"We're a lot alike," I told him.

"Except for the green skin and I am much, much stronger than you. Yes, we are very similar." He snorted again.

"You're the funniest alien I know." And I meant it.

I could hear footsteps going past my door. They had initially slowed and then picked up when they heard the raucous, human-alien laughter that ensued, a pack of in-heat cats must have been a more welcome sound, and still we roared.

***

"This was a lot funnier, when we were in my room," I said to Drababan as we got all our gear together in the long tunnel leading out to the western exit.

Dee snorted, thinking back a mere hour ago. Now he was all business. He looked a lot more intimidating now that he was out of his slave tunic and in full Genogerian shock troop regalia.

"You scare the shit out of me dressed like that," I told him honestly.

"These are merely clothes, Michael. I am the same Genogerian underneath."

"Thank you for that, Dee. That means a lot."

"Sarcasm?" he asked, trying to discern my true meaning.

"Not at all, my friend, that was genuine."

He pulled his maw back in his reasonable facsimile of a smile. It was terrifying to the uninformed and it wasn't much better to those who knew it for the gesture it was.

Dee and I were closest to the exit hatch but we were by no means alone in that large tunnel. Although I wish we had been, it would have been much better than having to say the multitude of goodbyes that I was expected to go through. It added a completeness to the event that I just wasn't willing to accept, even if on some level I knew the inevitability of it.

"I'd like to come with you," Dennis said as he grasped my hand.

"I don't even want to go with me," I told him.

"I'm serious," he said sternly.

"So am I, my friend. Another person does not increase the odds of success. Stay here and do what you can if this doesn't work."

He nodded tersely and gave me a big hug. He pushed through the crowd before the tear that threatened to fall could be witnessed.

Paul came up next.

"I feel like Dorothy in *Wizard of Oz*," I said.

"What? What are you talking about?" he asked, clearly confused.

"You know…at the end when she's saying all her goodbyes? It has such a finality to it, like she won't be back."

"Don't you say that or I'll nix this whole fucking plan, do you understand me?"

"No, you won't, but thank you for saying it. This is too important."

"You stay safe, Mike. I'll have the beer ready when you get back."

"None of that canned shit," I told him as we did our secret handshake learned so many years before.

"You got it." Paul stepped back a pace or two as Beth came up.

I looked past Beth's shoulder to see Tracy making her way over. I thought Beth better say what she wanted to say quickly or the big fight was going to happen here, not outside.

"I'll be waiting for you," she said with a longing in her eye.

"I wouldn't hold your breath if I were you," I said it more as a joke. I was hoping to ease the fear that was threatening to make my knees start knocking into each other. She took it a completely different way as she began to cry.

"I'm sorry," I said.

She threw her arms around me.

"It is a surprise to me that you hu-mans can stay hydrated with all the water you leak out of your eyes," Dee said, looking at Beth.

"Not a good time for observation," I told him quietly. Beth was squeezing so hard, I thought I might be blacking out due to lack of oxygen.

"Mike, you loved me once, can you find it in your heart to do so again?" she asked as she was so tightly pressed up against me we could have been a single entity.

Tracy made her perfect timing way up to us. She stood no more than two feet away. I watched as Paul subconsciously moved away. I placed my hands on Beth's shoulders, gently pushing her away. She resisted at first. Tears cascaded down her face.

"Beth, you're right. I did love you once, more than anything on Earth…or space for that matter, but I've met someone who not only takes my breath away, but also gives it back, what more could I ask for?" I asked, Beth looked devastated.

"You done?" Tracy asked. I wasn't sure if it was directed at Beth or myself.

"Yeah, I think so," I told her.

I was able to get Beth at arm's length, but she didn't move any farther as Tracy came closer.

"I'm pregnant," Tracy said flatly.

I fell against the close wall, grateful it was near enough or I would have gone on my ass.

"I was wondering when you were going to tell him," Drababan said.

"You knew?" I asked Dee.

"I could smell it," Dee replied as he went back to adjusting his uniform, no more troubled than if he had told me lunch was ready.

"And before you ask your next question and really make me mad, yes it's yours!" Tracy shot at me.

I closed my mouth quickly; thankful she had cut me off at the pass. I think it must be a guy self-defense mechanism

"I…I didn't know," I stammered out. Very poetic I thought.

"Was this really the best time to let him know?" Dee asked Tracy.

I literally watched as the anger began to flare in her.

Paul stepped back even more. "Bad move," he stage-whispered to Dee.

He looked down at me. "I am merely saying that we are about to embark on a dangerous mission and the odds of survival are already slim."

Beth hitched a breath and started to cry anew.

Dee continued uninterrupted. "It is imperative that Miike concentrate solely on the mission, and you have now given him news that will keep him distracted."

Tracy jabbed a finger in Dee's thigh, I don't think he even felt it. "I told him, you oversized piece of luggage, because I wanted to give him reason to come back!" she cried.

I still did not feel that I had recovered from the initial shock well enough to join back in the conversation even though it was revolving around me. My next question was almost 'How?' I'm sure that would have perfectly diffused the situation.

"Are you going to say anything at all?" Tracy asked me, unwillingly to come any closer, but threatening to head farther away if the wrong answer was issued from my lips.

Beth's sobs had diminished somewhat but they had slowed sufficiently so that she could also witness my response. The entire hallway, which was full of people, had directed all of their attention on me. I felt like an actor without a script. I was about to be judged on the merits of my actions in those next few seconds.

"I hope he doesn't have your temper," I said. I think I heard a piece of dust fall at the far end of the hallway, and then Dee let out a large guttural laugh.

"That is funny to me!" Dee roared.

He was immediately followed by the majority of people there.

Tracy was caught in confusion. I grabbed her before she could come to the wrong conclusion.

"I love you," I said, trying to whisper, but the laughter was still too loud. "I'll be back," I said into her ear.

Beth melted back into the crowd.

"You'd better be," she said, wrapping her at first stiff arms around my neck and then sufficiently loosening up and melting into my arms. "What about Beth?" she asked, pulling far enough away to see my eyes as I spoke.

"Who?" I asked, and meant it.

She gripped me tighter. It was a few minutes longer before Paul tapped me on the shoulder. I looked over to him. He was pointing to his wrist in the universal, 'We're running out of time' gesture.

The murmurings ceased as a tunnel guard began to spin the wheel on the exit hatch. I kissed Tracy and headed out into the day, Dee close behind. As the hatch closed behind us it once again blended in perfectly with the local fauna.

"Clever camouflage," Dee said.

"I don't feel as good about this as I once did. How are they not going to see through this? We both have to be on the Progerian most wanted list," I said, now unwilling to move much farther away from the Hill.

"We do not rely on visual cues like your species to recognize each other. It is pheromone based."

"Even with humans."

"Especially with humans," Dee said. "You all look alike." And then he snorted.

"This funny for you?"

"I like humor, Michael. My people should adopt more of it. We would be better for it."

"I don't know, Dee, your smiles scare the crap out of me."

"Here, I prepared a solution that will mask our scents sufficiently for us to gain entry into the compound," Dee said, handing me an old glass cleaner bottle full of a liquid that suspiciously looked like piss. I unscrewed the cover to get a better whiff.

"I don't think that would be wise," Dee said, looking at my trepidation. "It smells much worse than it looks."

"Are you sure, because it looks like piss," I told him.

"If you are referring to the waste elimination fluid, then you are correct."

"What?" I thrust the bottle back at him. "Is this your pee?" I asked, alarmed.

"It is my waste water. If that is what you are asking."

"Dee, I am not spraying myself with your waste water."

"It has been treated to mask our scents."

"I don't care if it's been treated to smell like fine cologne, it's still piss."

"It's a little waste water or these," he said pointing to his teeth.

"That's a powerful motivator, my friend." I reluctantly took the bottle back. "Where do I need to spray it?"

"Mostly on your head, neck and reproductive region."
I looked at him hard for any signs of humor. I could
not detect any.

"Are you sure? Because this is really grossing me
out," I told him.

He nodded.

"I'm not gonna even go into how much this blows," I
told him as I sprayed the top of my head—lightly, very, very
lightly.

"You are going to get us killed!" Dee shouted,
grabbing the bottle from my hands. "Stand still, Michael," he
said as he liberally sprayed me with his concoction.

I would have yelled in anger if I didn't think he'd get
some in my mouth.

"I think that's plenty!" I told him as the front of my
pants looked like I had an accident. "If I'm going to die, it's
going to be with some dignity!"

"I might have overdone it," he said smelling the air.

"What about you?" I told him, swiping the bottle
back. I was about to unleash a torrent of the stinky solution
on him.

"Already done." He smiled.

"I think you're full of shit, Dee. I think you just
wanted to spray me with your piss."

He snorted. "That would be funny, Michael, at
another time perhaps, but this needed to be done."

I still mostly doubted him and if we lived through the
day I was going to pay him back somehow.

"Let's go," I said, trying to breathe through my
mouth, I did not want to smell the strong scent emanating
from my body. "What the hell did you eat? Smells like
broccoli."

He snorted again. "It is working, you no longer smell
like Michael Talbot to me."

"How long does this last?"

"A few hours."

"Let's get moving then, because I am not getting doused again. I don't know if I'll able to take a hot enough shower to get this unclean feeling off me."

"Urine is sterile, prisoner Talbot. Let's go," he demanded.

I looked back—he was adopting his new role entirely too well.

Two hours of some hard hiking and minimal talking, we were at the doorstep of the Dedham landing zone. A hastily erected wall had been erected around the entire perimeter.

"Dee, if I wet myself, will that undo your camouflaging elixir?" I asked him as I looked over the compound.

Genogerians and some Progerians were busy scrambling around making sure their defenses were adequate for whatever the humans might have planned. I saw at least three dots up in the sky, they looked to be fighters circling, they were trying to find any threat or lend assistance in an attack.

"I would not recommend that, hu-man," Dee said, pushing me in the back. "Move," he growled.

"You keep this shit up and I'm not going to name my baby after you."

Dee snorted again. "Move and do not make me laugh again. We Genogerians are a very serious species."

The weight of the Colt .45, strapped to my leg should have been comforting, but its added heft seemed to be dragging me down. My legs were becoming wooden, and the kicker was that I had volunteered for this. Who volunteers for this kind of crap?

Some indistinct command rang out from atop a guard tower. I would imagine it was 'halt' or 'Drababan, where are you going with Michael Talbot, the escaped prisoner?' It was most likely 'halt' though, because we weren't shot on sight.

The guard motioned us forward with the wave of his rifle. Dee pushed me toward a rapidly opening gate.

"They travel a million light years in advanced spaceships, and they can't do any better than a chain link fence for a gate?" I asked Dee.

Dee pushed me in response. "Bigger and better fortifications will be up soon," he whispered. "Stay quiet now."

"I have a prisoner. I would like to put his filthy vile self into the stockade before he ruins any chance I have of eating a meal."

"You should have just eaten him," the guard said, pointing toward a small building that had no windows. It looked to be a storage shed for a mechanics garage at one time before it became a prison.

"Move!" Dee shouted, pushing me in the back.

Another guard was outside the small structure, waiting to let me in. The guard sneered at me as Dee shoved me into the darkened building. His nose wrinkled as I passed him by, but he didn't stop me to question further.

"You will need to report to the Commander," the guard said, speaking to Dee in their native language. He would explain later the exchanges.

"Not that I care too much, but don't eat that prisoner until he speaks with the Commander."

"I've already eaten, and if he tastes as bad as he smells, I don't want any."

Dee snorted a little then spun on his heel and went to find the Commander.

The room was dark but enough light was streaming in that I could tell there were others nearby.

"Sit your ass down before you step on someone," I heard someone snarl to my right.

Always the diplomat, I told him to kiss my ass. He didn't rise to the taunt. The gloom was making identification of the others impossible. Spindler had a slight build and I might be able to recognize him that way but most everyone here was on the floor wrapped up in whatever was available.

"Listen, buddy, I'm not going to tell you again, sit your ass down." The man was now literally breathing down my neck.

He was a little bigger than me and was trying to use his size to intimidate me. Did he think this was prison and he had to convince everyone he was the head bull?

I turned to face him, a small penlight lit up my face, recognition dawned on his.

He began to stammer. "I'm...I'm sorry, I—um, do you want my blanket?"

"Where's Spindler?"

"Who?"

"Go sit down."

"Yes...yes, sir. And feel free to have my blanket."

"Don't intend on staying long enough to get cold. Give me your flashlight."

The man almost dropped it in his haste to hand it over. "Spindler, I know you're here, just show yourself," I said as I started to check out every human pile. The one with the covers drawn over his face I figured to be him. I walked over, the covers literally began to quake.

"Who wants to know?" he finally said in defiance, pulling the blanket back and shielding his eyes from the intense light.

"It's Michael Talbot," the man whose flashlight I had taken answered.

I could see the wheels spinning in Spindler's head. "You destroyed my Cadillac."

"It was an accident."

"My insurance company wouldn't pay me for it. They said I had done it myself and that it was fraud. Almost went to jail because of you."

"It was a prank that got out of hand."

"Why are you here now? Not to offer an apology, I

would imagine."

"What have you told the Progerians?" I asked him flatly.

Spindler might be a sniveling little shit, but he was a smart sniveling little shit. "I've told them nothing. What could I tell them?" he asked, trying to redirect the conversation.

"You grew up in Walpole, you sat on the board of trustees. I think you could tell them a lot. Especially to save your skin."

"Have you seen what they do to their prisoners?"

"I'm well aware."

"I guess you would be."

"Spindler, what have you told them?" I asked again with a little more force.

"It's true then, isn't it? I'd heard rumors I figured it was pretty far-fetched but now here you are."

"Spindler, you've got two options. Either you escape with me or I will kill you."

Spindler scrambled back at the words, but he didn't quite cower as I had expected. "There's a third option," he said smiling.

Why the fuck I didn't just put a bullet in him at that point I'll never know.

"Guard!" he screamed. Before I could react, he yelled again. "Michael Talbot is in here and he is trying to kill me!"

The light that flooded in from the door nearly blinded me as I dropped the small flashlight and pulled the hidden pistol from my hip holster. The guard hadn't even decided to discriminate as he began to blow holes in everything that moved. I dove to the side as blue bolts whizzed by. I brought my pistol up and placed a hasty shot in the Geno's knee, the .45 round shattering his knee cap. The next round caught him in his chest plate. I could hear the air rush from his lungs from the impact, but the body armor had stopped the round. The third caught him in his open mouth, the blue bolts stopped.

I could hear more heavy footfalls running for the hut. I had to get the guard's gun. The man who had initially threatened me was closest and ran over to grab it. "They'll kill us all," he said, turning to level the gun on my chest. "Spindler, you're an asshole," the man said turning to point the gun back outside.

A shock of adrenaline coursed through my body, giving me the pins and needles sensations through my arms and hands. *Dodged another one*, I thanked a silent God.

Alien rounds peppered the building. If I was going to die, I had to make sure I had, at the very least, accomplished what I had set out to do. I turned to face Spindler, he had pulled up some supplies and was attempting to barricade himself against the oncoming onslaught.

"I don't think that'll stop them," I told him. "Or me for that matter."

"And what of it, Mr. Talbot? Will you just gun me down like a common cur? I did not realize that arsonists became murderers, but I guess somehow it is a natural progression."

I'd killed a lot of men, but this was different. I had gone on a mission; this was a planned assassination. And the taste of that was not sitting well in my stomach.

"You're right, you were a royal pain in the ass when I was a kid, and it doesn't look like that has changed much. But it's not enough to kill you." He sank farther into his hastily built fort as I removed the chaff to get at him. "You're coming with me," I told him as I ripped him onto his feet.

"Where?" he sniveled.

"I think you know where."

"The silo? I can't go to the silo, they'll kill us."

"They're going to kill us now. Would you rather have it happen now or we delay it for a little while?" I asked him.

"They're coming…and fast," the man at the door yelled.

"What's your name?" I asked the guy.

"Wamsley," he shouted over his shoulder. "Brian."

"Listen, Brian, I came in here with one of those Genos. If you see one that seems to be acting a little different, do not shoot him."

"You came in here with one of *them*?" he asked. I could see his shudder from here. "How the hell am I going to tell?"

Our shed was being rocked from the assault the guards were placing on it, I was having my doubts about Dee being able to do anything to get us out of this mess. Well at least Spindler wouldn't be able to betray the human race.

"They're setting up a perimeter," Brian shouted.

"Shut the door and get in here," I told him.

He did as I asked.

"How much have you told them?" I turned, asking Spindler.

"I had to—they would have killed me," he whined.

"I'm going to ask again, and I'd really like you to be more specific."

Spindler was eyeing the door…and my gun. I knew he was weighing his options, but for him to run out that door was suicide-by-Genogerian-gunfire.

"Why'd they stop shooting?" Brian asked, peeking out the door.

"I've got a feeling they got orders from a higher authority," I said, never taking my eyes off my old principal.

"Your friend?" Brian asked.

"No, he's too far down the chain of command. I think the Commander might have put a halt to this."

"Why?" Brian asked.

"I think Spindler may have saved our lives," I told him. "Inadvertently maybe, but he saved our lives. I think he promised them a lot of information and has yet to deliver. Am I close?" I asked Spindler.

"It's too bad you never used that brain of yours when

you were in school, Mr. Talbot," Spindler replied condescendingly.

"How much do they know? I'm not going to ask again."

Spindler licked his lips. "I'm not a complete idiot."

"That's debatable."

He continued with a slight sneer. "As soon as I gave them what they were looking for, they would have killed me. I gave them the armory location in Norwood. They know there's some sort of base nearby. I don't know how, and it's only a matter of time until someone tells them."

"We'll deal with that when the time comes, but it most certainly won't be you." He tried to shrink back down. "I'm not going to kill you." Spindler visibly relaxed. "Unless you give me reason to...but you are coming with us if we get out of here."

"Puny hu-mans, you must come out at once!" a booming voice shouted.

"At least they're polite," I said.

"There's that," Brian said. "What now?"

"Hi, everyone," I said to the group. "Besides Spindler who most definitely is coming with me if I get out of here, the rest of you are free to come along or go outside and into the waiting arms of our distinguished hosts."

An old woman and an even older man shuffled toward the door. "We're too old to play resistance fighter," the old man said as he passed me by.

A young couple with a baby also got up to go out. They never looked at me as they moved past Brian.

They had not traveled more than twenty feet from the shed when I heard the same booming authoritative voice. "None of them are him." Blue streaks blazed past as the five people were quickly dispatched.

I turned away, my heart weighed heavily with the thought that, had I not come here, they would still be alive.

Brian witnessed my reaction. "Not your fault, my

man. We were all dead before you got here. They just hadn't filled in the time yet."

There were more than a few sobs from the remaining prisoners, but no one else was heading for the exit.

"I beg to differ," Spindler chimed in. "Every single one of them would still be alive. That baby might have actually had a future, Mr. Talbot. The aliens promised us sanctuary before you killed one of their own."

"As slaves, you idiot," Brian yelled at him.

"I for one would rather be a *live* slave than a *dead* martyr," Spindler said, holding his chin high, like he was high and mighty.

"Well, I guess that's the difference between us then, isn't it?" I said coldly. "And what makes you think you're held in high enough regard to become a martyr?"

"Puny hu-mans, send out more of you!" the voice said.

"He can't be serious, is he?" Brian asked.

"Oh, I'm sure he is. They don't have much in the way of a sense of humor."

Spindler kept eyeing the door like it led to salvation and a cheeseburger.

"Go," I told him.

He was looking at me to determine if this was a trick of some sort and then actually took a step.

"But remember—" His steps faltered. "They said 'none of them are him.' They want one of us alive. Are you willing to bet your life on fifty-fifty odds? You know what happens when you assume, don't you?" Spindler did not answer.

"You get shot with blue shit!" Brian said.

"Fifty-fifty odds. You can either walk out that door and hope they don't fry your innards, or you can throw your lot in with the human race."

I didn't think Spindler liked either option much, but there really wasn't a third one coming down the pipeline.

"I'm coming with you," Spindler said in resignation, his head dropping down.

"I had a feeling you'd see it my way."

"Not sure how long our little stand-off is going to hold," Brian said. "They look to be getting very impatient."

"At college, I once protested the use of animal hide for jackets, purses, and shoes. I mean mostly it was to get into this chick's pants, but I did it all the same. I really did feel kind of bad that crocodiles were being used for boots, belts, and luggage—now I wish I had a pair of those damn boots. Two maybe," I said, thinking back longingly.

"Did it work?" Brian asked.

"Huh?" I asked "Oh, shit yeah, I mean they kept making shoes, but I got in her pants. Sure did." I laughed.

"Well, that's all that really mattered back then. What about now?" Brian asked.

"That's rather juvenile, Mr. Talbot," Spindler said.

"Wait until you really get to know me, it doesn't get much better. And stop looking at the door, you already made your choice. Brian, we're going to have to hope my friend thinks of something that gets us out of here. We hadn't really planned for this contingency. I was going to kill Spindler and then sneak out tonight."

Spindler took in a sharp breath of air.

I walked over to Brian to get a better idea of what we were dealing with. "Shit," I said, pulling my eye away from the crack. "No real chance of blasting our way through there."

"Why you?" Brian asked.

"Why me what?" I asked him back.

"Why'd they send you on this little mission?" he asked.

"I volunteered. On reflection that doesn't seem too bright now."

"Understatement, my man. Any idea how long your 'friend' might take?"

Brian fell into me as a giant explosion rocked our shed and the compound as a whole.

"It'd be safe to say now," I said as I regained my balance and opened the door a bit farther. Guards were scurrying about, looking for the new threat. Some had not left their posts, but they seemed distracted. "You ready?" I asked Brian as I shoved some more rounds into my pistol.

"Well, I do have 'to die' on my bucket list."

"I think we'll get along fabulously," I told him.

Brian took down two guards. I was able to kill one with my less than climactic weapon. I was having blue beam envy.

"Do we keep pressing the attack?" Brian asked as the guards rallied.

"Not sure if we'll get another opportunity!" I shouted over the din.

I was a few shots left of running out of bullets. I had to get one of the alien weapons before it was time to reload. Blue streaks came off to our right side and into the exposed flanks of the alien guards. They were caught in a small crossfire.

"Way to go, Dee," I said as we hid behind some pallets. I quickly shoved rounds into my firearm.

Brian kept up a withering assault. The aliens still seemed reluctant to shoot our way, but did not hesitate to shoot in the direction from where Dee's shots were ringing out.

Dee's shots were becoming less and less frequent as they began to pin him down. "We've got to help my friend."

"Did you just say 'friend'?" Brian asked.

"It's complicated."

"You will tell me later."

"I will. Promise." I stood up and was staring straight down the giant barrel of one of those stupid ray guns, but the guard didn't fire. He had me dead to rights and yet I lived. "This is going to hurt you way more than it's going to hurt me," I told the guard as I blasted him twice with my heavy rounds.

"They're not shooting!" Brian said excitedly as he kept mowing the guards down.

"I've noticed that before," I said, ducking down to reload. "They won't do much of anything without orders."

"Sucks for them!" he yelled, still blasting away. He had moved away from our hidey-hole and was heading right for the guards who looked as stunned as I felt.

They started backing up, almost falling over themselves in a rush to get away from the crazy hu-man advancing on them.

"We might be puny!" Brian shouted. "But we're not stupid!" He blazed away.

"Got you a gun!" he said, turning back toward me.

"Well, fuck this," I said, sticking the half-filled pistol back into its holster. I jumped up and ran to meet him. "In for a dime, in for a dollar," I said, almost like a prayer.

I grabbed the rifle, my heart crushing violently against my rib cage and looked up to truly get an idea of the predicament we were in. It was not an enviable position. A small wall of still functioning Genogerian guards were in front of us. They had backed up, but they were not in total retreat mode. We were also in the open with clear firing lanes from us to at least three guard towers. There had to have been at least fifty or sixty weapons pointed at us, yet we stood.

"Spindler, let's go!" I yelled. The uneasy détente did not break.

"Is it safe?" I heard him whimper.

"Sure!" I answered.

"That's kind of mean," Brian said between heavy breaths.

"Don't worry, he's kind of a dick."

Spindler came out of the shed, followed by a couple of kids who couldn't have been more than eleven or twelve, a middle aged couple, and a young woman.

"This a good idea, putting everyone out here like this?" Brian asked. He kept his rifle at the ready.

"Sure."

"That's the same answer you gave Spindler."

"I know," I said, looking around for Dee. I could hear the high-pitched whine of fighters as they streaked to our position. I looked up as death approached.

"What now?" Brian asked holding his ground.

If the fighter had serial numbers I would have been able to read them as it bore down.

"Will they fire so close to their own kind?" Brian asked.

"They give about as much a shit for the Genogerians as they do about us," I replied.

"I take it these are Genogerians then?" Brian asked, clearly confused. "What else is there?"

"There are two classes, the smaller Progerians run the show, and they're usually a different color."

"Oh, I thought he was just old. The commander I mean, I saw him the first day I got here."

The Genos were still not firing, but we might as well have had a 'drop bomb here' sign on us. The guards were backing up; they knew what was going to happen.

"We're fucked," I said just as vapor trails came from left to right above our location. The fighter that was bearing down on us so diligently was now in a full out scramble to pull up as three stinger missiles, shot from the ground, sought purchase.

"We've got to go!" I yelled to Brian, pulling his sleeve, he was so intent on watching the missiles he was missing our opportunity. "Dude, where do you think all those parts are going to rain down if those missiles hit!" I screamed.

He pulled his gaze away to look at me, the light of recognition dawned. "We've got to go!" he yelled like it was his idea.

Spindler was half in and half out of the shed. "We're leaving, Spindler. I'll shoot you if I have to," I yelled at him. We were three-quarters across the compound when the percussion from the missile impact threw us all to the ground. Been a long time since I ate dirt, now I remembered why it wasn't on my diet.

A large green hand wrapped around my arm and jerked me to my feet.

"Miss me?" Dee asked, smiling.

Brian was scrambling, trying to get his rifle up from under him.

"Whoa, whoa! He's with me!" I shouted to Brian. "He's the friend I was telling you about."

"Michael, I think your use of English is not as good as you presume it to be. I believe it would be more correct to say that you are with me," Drababan said.

"You should have been a New Yorker, Dee. They always tend to take their sarcasm too far. Let's get the hell out of here."

Spindler had passed out or been knocked out when he struck the ground, Dee grabbed him around the belt and hoisted him up as if he weighed no more than a gallon of milk.

Molten metal showered around us. More than one guard was crushed under the twisted metal. We were rapidly moving away from the carnage but still bits would come uncomfortably close to us.

"We must hurry, Michael!" Dee said, running in half strides. Brian was barely keeping up with him at full speed and I was hanging back a bit trying to urge an older couple on, a young woman and two boys were half way between me and Dee. "The remaining fighters are preparing to launch bombs!"

Even order-less Genogerian guards must have had the ability for self-preservation, they scattered in every direction. I heard multiple firearms begin to chatter away as the guards came into the opposing fields of fire. I had a good idea who it was and I would thank him eternally when I got back to the Hill.

"Come on!" I urged the couple for the third time.

"Can't...make...it." The man was clutching his side. "Go, Gloria," he said to his wife.

"I'd rather...die here with...you, Vern," she panted out. "Young man...go," Gloria told me.

"Alright, Mrs. Banks," Vern heaved. "It's me and you." He smiled.

Shit. I was stuck, there wasn't much I could do to urge them on, and to stay was my death too. Dee once again saved the day, he came back, threw Spindler over his shoulder like he was a sack of flour, dropped his rifle and reached down to grab the couple. They shrank away at first, but I told them that I was with him and it would be alright. Dee nodded at me.

He wrapped his powerful arms around their midsections, somehow tenderly enough to not making pudding out of their innards, and turned and began to run again. The added weight slowed him down a bit, but I still was struggling to keep up. The unmistakable sound of a massive projectile falling through the sky helped me to find a faster gear. I grabbed the running woman's arm and we moved as fast as we could.

Dee had caught up to the two boys and Brian, who was busy using the barrel of his rifle to pry open a storm drain. Dee quickly put Spindler down and stuck a claw into an opening and ripped the heavy metal circle from its resting place. My fillings were beginning to vibrate from the humming of the bomb. Brian went down the hole first. Dee unceremoniously dropped Spindler in and then gently eased the older woman and man down. His rapid come-hither movements with his arm were an unnecessary incentive for me and the girl to get moving. We were close to salvation when the ground bounced. We were sent a good two feet into the air from the impact of the alien detonation, the only thing that saved us was the vibration propelling us forward. Dee grabbed us mid-flight and like he was dunking a basketball, threw us into the hole.

I had the presence of mind to wonder what the good of this maneuver was; as soon as his giant ass came down he would crush us. Dee's huge arms came within inches of the side of my face as he fell through the hole. He was snout to nose with me and I couldn't even begin to describe how uncomfortable of a feeling that was.

I would have made some quip, but the explosion sucked all the air from my lungs. So much so that I thought perhaps Dee had landed on me after all. Dee was being pulled up from the back blast, I anchored myself and grabbed his arm, although I didn't know what my weight was going to do to help. Brian dove from the far wall and jumped onto Dee's back, I didn't know if it would help or not. In the end it seemed that the accumulated weight had the desired effect, however, it still left his massive jaw directly in front of me.

A small fact I had not known up until that time—without air, there is no sound. I was aware that the woman next to me was in a full throated scream when we headed down the shaft, but that was cut off the moment Dee landed. Who knew—it was probably me screaming, but it's much easier to write it this way after I've had some time to look at it subjectively.

As air rushed back in to fill the void, the woman next to me once again had fuel for her lungs.

"Are you hurt?" I yelled, trying to get through her shock.

She kept going for a few seconds more before she began to shake her head from side to side. "I don't…th-think so," she said hesitantly as she sat up.

"Everybody else?" I asked a general question.

"Thank you," Dee told Brian as he half stood up in the small enclosure.

Spindler was still out cold. The old man was rubbing a growing knot on the top of his head, but seemed no worse for wear; his wife was looking over him cautiously. One of the two boys just kept touching Dee's legs.

"He doesn't feel fishy," the one with darker hair told his friend.

"His arm is bent funny," the other said, looking down at Spindler.

"Aw crap, it's broken, he's going to blame me for this," I said, standing up.

"I tried to catch him," Brian said, "but the bomb knocked me off my feet. Missed him by about a foot."

"Are you a dragon?" the first boy asked Dee, still rubbing his leg. "You feel like you got scales."

"We need to splint his arm before we get moving again," I said, looking in some of the debris in the drain that would be straight and strong enough.

"Where exactly are we going?" Gloria asked.

"The only place we can," I answered her vaguely. I found a piece of wood that suspiciously looked like in a previous life it had been part of a cane.

Brian took his shirt off and was ripping it into strips so I would have something to tie the splint with.

"Would you rather I set it?" Dee asked. "Or wait until we get back and your surgeons can do it?"

"There are no such things as dragon doctors," the first boy said.

"You look tasty," Dee said to the small boy. The kid was not deterred.

"Please don't eat my brother, mister," the older boy said to Drababan. "He's all the family I have left." A small tear formed in his eye.

"He was kidding," I said to the boy. "Tell him you were kidding, Dee."

Dee was still looking down at the small boy who was now trying to pinch Dee's calf.

"Can you fly?" the small boy asked.

"No, but I chew real well," Dee said, making sure to flash all his teeth. I thought the old woman was going to swoon.

"Kid, what's your name?" I asked the older brother.

"Blake," he responded, never taking his eyes off of Dee.

"Blake, could you please get your brother away from my friend?" I asked.

"He's...he's your friend?" Blake asked, shuffling slowly forward to get his brother.

"It really gets old trying to explain this, but yes, he saved my life. Of course, just before that he was trying to kill me, but then he saved me."

"That doesn't make much sense, mister," Blake said, finally grabbing his brother by the arm.

"None of it really does."

The boy looked at me like grown-ups were just about the weirdest thing on the planet. Besides the Genogerians and the Progerians, I guess we were.

"What's your brother's name?" I asked Blake, his impish brother was pinching Dee's calf.

"Jeffrey," Blake answered.

No sound could be heard topside and except for the occasional heavy breathing and moans from Spindler not much was happening down here, either. Dee and I were busy hastily fixing Spindler's broken wing before he came to. Brian had ascended the stairs to check out what was going on topside.

"Holy shit, everything's gone."

I paused to look up at him. He was a shadow framed by a blazing sun.

"Not as bad as the city devastations. About five hundred yards across has been leveled," he continued.

"I hope Dennis is alright," I added.

"He shot the missiles?" Dee asked as he carefully

realigned the bones in Spindler's arm.

"Yes. You're pretty good at that," I told him.

"I practiced on myself," he answered, never stopping what he was doing.

I didn't ask for elaboration, I didn't want to know.

"I see movement on the far side. Can't tell who or what it is," Brian said as he prudently came back down the ladder a few rungs.

"How far past our hiding spot do we need to get before we get back under cover?" I asked Brian.

There were still two fighters out there and my guess was that they had nothing better to do than to look for survivors and eradicate that problem.

"At least a hundred yards," Brian stated, realizing how difficult a journey that was going to be.

I looked to the pipes that led away from this collection point. I had no idea where they went and the biggest wasn't much more than sixteen inches in diameter. The boys would fit if they crawled. Even if I thought I could fit, I would have not gone, because Dee would not be able to get in. At least that's what I told myself—you can add claustrophobia to my list of idiosyncrasies.

"He's waking," Dee said. There was some bone on bone grinding as Dee moved Spindler's arm about, and then the best way I can describe it is there was a 'click' like two Lego's being snapped into place. "Apply the splint, Michael," Dee said, making sure to keep Spindler's arm still.

Spindler's head was moving slightly from side to side. I could tell he was struggling to come up from the depths of unconsciousness.

I had no sooner tied the last knot holding the splint in place when Spindler's eyes fluttered open. I'm not sure who he was more chagrined to have staring over him, me or Dee. I could see the scream forming on his lips.

"Your arm is broken. My big friend here has set it and we've splinted it. You're fine for now."

He saved us all a lot of trouble by passing out again.

"That was fortuitous," Dee said, looking over at me.

"You're really getting good at this," I told him.

Brian was staring straight up. "Those fighters are still lurking around."

"Dammit, Dee, any idea how long they'll stay?"

"Not long, they are arrogant enough to think nothing could have survived."

"Probably because nothing usually does," the old man said.

I could only nod in agreement.

CHAPTER SIXTY-THREE – Mike Journal Entry 20

The fighters were out of sight within a half an hour. We waited a solid hour before emerging from the ground like reborn mole men. Dirty and bruised, we made our way across what was once considered the center of Dedham and which had now been reduced to something akin to a 1920s Kansas Dust Bowl scene.

Jeffrey rode atop Dee's broad shoulders, barely able to spread his legs far enough apart to get them around his neck. "I can see everything up here!" Jeffrey exclaimed excitedly.

"Shush." I said to Jeffrey, he paid me absolutely no attention as he figured correctly that I couldn't reach him from where I stood.

His brother looked slightly jealous, but his fear of Dee would not allow him to ask for the ride his brother had begged for.

"Hey, Dee, looks like there is plenty of room up there," I said.

"Michael, I have already told you that I am not carrying you on my shoulders," Dee replied.

Spindler had finally awakened and screamed until Dee put him down. Can't say I blame him, either. Dee had been carrying him like a football, tucked up under his arm.

Spindler was pale with pain, but surprisingly he never complained. I guess he figured if he bitched, Dee would just start carrying him again whether he wanted to be held or not.

"How many people died here today because of you, Mr. Talbot?" Spindler asked snidely.

"What the hell do you mean by that?" I shot back.

"Those aliens only dropped that bomb because their position was overrun," Spindler replied.

"I don't think you get it. For being an educated man, you certainly are kind of a stupid shit."

"Enlighten me then," he replied.

"It's our position that's been overrun. The aliens own everything now. We are desperately trying to regain what was once ours."

"By having it destroyed?"

"I'd rather the scorched earth method then have them take everything!" I yelled quietly. I knew it made no sense, but the force behind the words spoke volumes itself.

"Relax, this is merely a debate," Spindler said, condescendingly.

"This is no fucking debate! Does this look like a fucking debate? This is an all-out war, you dipshit. Man has raced to the top of the endangered species list and you were willingly putting yourself in position to take out one of the last strongholds. I should have just put a bullet in your head when I had the chance." I brought my rifle up, the barrel was mere inches from his eye, it would have been so easy to just pull that trigger and be done with it and him. Blake's brother was shying away from the whole episode. Everyone was still. The only thing that moved was the sweat free-flowing down Spindler's face.

"I'm sorry," Spindler said softly.

"Damn right, you're sorry!" I said, still shouting, driving the barrel into his cheek.

"He said he was sorry, Michael," Dee said. "Isn't that sufficient verbiage in your culture to allow you to stand down from your present course of action?"

I wasn't expecting him to be the voice of reason. I pushed Spindler away with the gun. He would have a circle imprint in his face for a few more hours. I strode ahead to get away from Spindler, afraid that I was still close to murdering him.

"You alright?" Brian asked, coming up on my side.

"I will be." And I said no more.

***

It was getting dark rapidly and I still didn't think we had covered half the distance back to The Hill. Between Spindler and the old man, we were just about crawling. We stopped for at least the twentieth time and not a moment too soon as an alien troop carrier screamed by.

"Dee?" I asked.

"Looks like they're prepping for another landing," he said, shielding his eyes from the setting sun and the glint of light off of the multitude of ships lining up in the sky.

"It looks like this is a full-scale invasion." Brian whistled.

"It is a large percentage," Dee answered.

The ground rumbled as ship after ship made land contact.

"We need to press on," I said, standing up.

"My...my husband can't go on," Gloria said.

"Well, he doesn't really have many other options. Hey, Brian, will you help me?" Brian and I each got under a shoulder to help the man to his feet.

"Michael, I can carry him," Dee said.

"You've done enough, let me do this," I said, Dee nodded in understanding. "You ready, old timer?" I asked.

"I was in the Greatest World War," Vern replied.

I thought that an understatement, I was thinking the one we were mired in now might have usurped it.

"Why don't you tell us a story to help the time go by?" Brian asked and that was the only window the man needed. "We were on Tarawa, I was in the 6th Marine regiment. I watched as our ships bombed that island into the Stone Age. We didn't think anything much bigger than a cockroach was going to be able survive that barrage...or so we hoped."

***

"What do you think, Vern?" Private Killinger asked, coming up to his friend PFC Banks.

Vern was leaning against the railing, smoking his second straight pack of Pall Malls, watching as shell after shell left the battleships and crashed into the tiny island beyond. "I think we're going to sink that island before we ever get a chance to land," Vern said, tossing the remains of his filterless cigarette into the ocean, almost swearing that he could hear it sizzle out as it hit the water below. His senses were so dialed up for the oncoming invasion, he thought maybe it wasn't so much his imagination. He pondered that even as he lit another cigarette.

"Wouldn't that be something!" Killinger replied. "I wish it would. I'd be happy if I never had to look at those yellow devils again."

Vern nodded in agreement. They had been briefed on how savage the Japanese were but words meant nothing when you were actually confronted by an enemy that seemed completely unconcerned with life, their own or his. He had watched in horror as wave after wave of attacking Japanese had come at their machine gun nest on the Philippines with nothing more than swords and bayonets. It was all he could do to run enough ammunition through his gunner's weapon to keep them at bay. The Japanese seemed all too willing to sacrifice their bodies to the American bullets.

And that was even before the Americans had started to turn the tides of the war and go on the offensive. Vern was in no rush to see what a desperate Japanese soldier was capable of.

"Nothing can survive that, right?" Killinger asked as another barrage lit up the night sky.

"We'll find out tomorrow," Vern said, finishing another cigarette. He could swear that he saw his friend shake with tremors, but it could have been the vibrations of a new volley. "You should get some sleep," Vern told him.

"You gonna hit the rack?"

"Yeah, I'll be there soon," he lied. Vern stayed there long enough to watch the sun come up and still the bombs arced over him. "What's left to destroy?" he asked himself, looking through a pair of field binoculars. And then there was blissful, peaceful, terrifying quiet. Because the quiet now meant that men, flesh and blood men, would be getting into their troop transports and heading to that desolate black lump of coagulated lava. Vern could not discern the importance of the target other than to tell the Japanese, 'Hey, we're coming, this one's for the Arizona!'

Vern shuffled into one of the first troop transports. They were stuffed in so tight he could not even check to make sure that his rifle was packed correctly in the plastic to keep the sea water out of its inner workings. He nodded to Killinger who was among one of the last into the small boat. Vern figured he would hook up with his friend once they got ashore. None of the men spoke as the boats traveled across the choppy water, the drone of multiple motors masked some of the vomiting as scared old boys and, young men prepared for battle. Nothing could have prepared those doomed souls for the next few minutes as they headed ashore. Heavy machinegun fire laced with tracers blew through the ranks of the men as the transporters opened their heavy metal doors. Marines were blown apart as rounds usually reserved for armored vehicles ripped through them.

Vern watched as death advanced row upon row over his fellow Marines. He quickly scrambled up the side of boat and plunged into the ocean. Bullets tore through the water leaving white trails as they passed by. The clear liquid quickly became cloudy with the blood of his fellow warriors.

More and more of the Marines in the boat had followed Vern's lead and were plunging into the water to escape the projectiles only to be dragged to their deaths in the water as the their heavy gear weighed them down. Vern shrugged his pack off as quickly as he could, trying to gain buoyancy. He had always been a strong swimmer, but even he was having great difficulty treading water in combat boots.

Men screamed for their mothers as Japanese lead answered instead. Vern had finally rid himself of enough gear, to come up and get his first breath of air in nearly a minute. Dead bodies floated all around him like a macabre game of bobbing for apples. He made sure to stay away from the transports boats that were garnering the lion's share of rounds. He made his way to shore as quickly as he could without attracting any fire from the opposition.

He was finally able to pull himself up against a small outcropping of rock in about a foot of water but it shielded him completely from the Japanese entrenchment. Boat after boat was getting hammered until some much needed air support came in and started firing directly on the Japanese. Within a few more minutes his secluded spot on the beach was actually becoming the beachhead.

"Someone's going to pay for this!" an eager corporal said to the burgeoning crowd.

Vern knew the words for what they were; bravado, trying to cover over abject fear. He saw nothing wrong with whatever would get any of them through the day, though. It was ten minutes later when a gunnery sergeant finally made it to shore that the Marines could go on the offensive again.

"We stay here like cowards or we go out there like

heroes!" the gunny shouted.

Vern was scared to his core at the thought of dying, but to live without honor was worse. The Gunny's words had struck a chord, inch by blood-soaked inch; those Marines had taken the beach from the Japanese. It was late into that first night when the last of the machinegun nests were silenced. The ensuing quiet had been damn near blissful until Vern began to think of Killinger. He was certain his friend had fallen in those first few moments, but he spent a good amount of time going from encampment to encampment, hoping to come across his buddy. All he saw was ghost images overlaid on vacant faces. None of them would ever be the same after that day, some would deal with it better than others, but all would remember it.

***

"It was that second day that I got wounded. Got a Purple Heart and discharged from the service," Vern continued.

"Wow," I said, mesmerized. Vern's recounting of the story had been so visceral, so authentic, I swore I could smell the smoke from the spent shells.

"How'd you get injured?" Brian asked, hefting Vern up as we continued forward.

"Well, you know the Japanese had dug themselves deep into that rock. That was why our shells didn't do as much damage as we thought they would. Damn, they were as much as twenty to thirty feet underground, probably playing cards and drinking saké while we dropped bombs all over them. So as soon as the shelling stopped, they knew what was coming, they grabbed all their gear and they made our landing a vision of hell on earth."

"I don't think I could have done it," I told him in all honesty.

"Oh, I think you could have," he said, giving me a

wink. "I know who you are."

"This sounds much like our rebellion," Dee added. He had been listening as intently as any of us.

Vern craned his neck to look up. "Well, um…"

"Continue, worthy hu-man," Dee said.

"That's a compliment," I told Vern.

"So that next day, after not sleeping again, I knew I wasn't going to find my friend."

"My brother," Gloria added.

"I went to Jack's house, Gloria's brother, when I got out, just to tell his parents that Jack had died honorably. But that's not what they wanted to hear, it does not matter in which way you die, they are all a finality. They wanted to know how he had lived, so I spent three days with Jack's family. He had two younger sisters and a younger brother not much older than that little squirt up there." He pointed to the boy on Dee's shoulders.

"My sister Connie was very smitten with him," Gloria said, rubbing Vern's shoulder. "She didn't talk to me for almost a year after we got married. It was among some of the most peaceful moments in my life." Gloria laughed, as did Vern.

I could tell it was an old inside joke amongst them and they enjoyed it immensely.

"I wanted to be around the man who had been with my brother," Gloria said with a faraway look in her eyes.

"And she helped me to heal both physically and mentally, maybe even spiritually," Vern added that last part and looked at us all quickly to see if we were going to judge him for potentially having feelings.

He was barking up the wrong tree if he thought I was going to give him any grief. I struggle with my feelings between each heartbeat.

When he was content that nobody was going to call him out on it he continued his narrative.

"The goal that day had been to completely cross the

island. It was only three miles across—how fucking bad could it be?"

"Vern, there's children, and you know I don't appreciate that language."

Vern shrugged.

"Good thing she's not around me much," I whispered in his ear, conspiratorially.

Vern grunted a laugh, I could tell the old timer was hurting, but he was soldiering on.

"We were about a half hour in. My job was to keep an eye on the men with the flamethrowers. It was the only weapon effective in getting the Japanese out of their holes or kill them where they lay. The problem was that nobody was watching my back. We had just passed a hole I didn't think a skinny badger would be able to fit in, so I told the flamethrower to keep going forward. This goo—"

"Vern!" Gloria chided.

"So this *Japanese* fella wriggled himself out and stuck his bayonet straight through the back of my knee. I wished he had just shot me the pain was so intense. The Marine on the other side of the flamethrower saw what was happening and was able to kill the soldier before he was able to pull that bayonet free and finish the job."

I was cringing at the pain he must have been in.

"They stuck me on a stretcher with that damn rifle still sticking out of my knee, nobody wanted to touch it. Every jostle was worse than the previous. I thought I was going to go insane with the pain. It was when I finally got back to the beach that a sergeant there plunged a morphine shot into my arm.

"What, are you idiots stupid or something? The sergeant had yelled at the men for not having given it to me earlier." Vern laughed. "I would have kissed him if I didn't think the other guys would have thought me fruity or something. Even then I think I would have done it if I could have gotten up. So they put me back on one of those Godforsaken transport boats and shipped me over to the medical ship. I was mostly unconscious, but I remember one of the doctors saying what a fine souvenir I had brought back with me. I didn't see it that way. When I finally awoke from the surgery, I gave it to the doctor that had taken it out of me. He couldn't have been more pleased, I never wanted to see the damn thing again anyway."

"That's a hell of a story, Vern," I told him.

"Not near as exciting as yours, so I heard," he said, limping along.

"If we have enough time, maybe I'll tell you," I told him.

"I'd like that," he said, grimacing. I think he was more enamored with the thought of having enough time rather than listening to my story, but that was fine with me.

"I smell hu-mans," Dee said. "We are close."

"Dee, get behind me," I told him. Dee looked at me funny like what the hell was that going to accomplish. "I know, I know, but I don't want any trigger happy sentries putting a bullet in you."

He shrugged, but did as I asked.

"Captain Talbot?" a voice came from beyond a small copse of trees.

"One and the same," I answered.

"But you're dead," the same voice said.

"I beg to differ," I told him.

Three armed Hillians came out of the foliage. I remembered seeing their squad leader around the base a few times. The corporal looked over to Dee. I could see his hands tense on his weapon but he made no threatening move.

"Corporal, could you're men please help with my new friend Vern, here?" I asked. I was definitely beginning to fatigue.

The corporal made some arm movements into the bushes and two more men came out, carrying a stretcher. I thought that was pretty fortuitous and my expression must have given me away.

"The general sent a bunch of patrols out in the hopes that there would be some survivors."

"I'd really hoped I'd never get in one of these things again," Vern said with some dismay. "But right now it looks like a Sealy Posturepedic."

"What about him?" the corporal asked pointing to Spindler.

Dee seemed to forget he was even carrying the slight man. "I would like to stretch my arms. Thank you," Dee said, holding Spindler out like a loaf of bread.

"I know the going is tougher," the corporal said once Spindler was situated on a stretcher. "But we have to stay within the tree line. There have been enemy fighters patrolling the entire region. Seems that something got them pretty upset," he said, smiling at me.

"I had nothing to do with it." I gave him my standard answer usually reserved for the police. "Who else is out here?" I asked the corporal as we got underway again.

"Sir?" he asked.

"Someone saved our ass back there—who else are you looking for?"

"Major Wagner, sir. He's still unaccounted for," the corporal answered. My face fell with worry for my friend. "But that could have changed, sir, we've been out here for hours and we are under strict radio silence."

"Corporal, do you mind if me and my large friend here go on ahead?"

"Not at all, sir."

"Vern, Gloria—I'll see you both. Boys, you be good. If this man tries to escape," I said, pointing to Spindler. "Shoot him."

I thought the corporal thought I was kidding at first but there was no mirth on my face.

"Yes, sir."

"You ready to make some time?" I asked Drababan.

Dee snorted. "What makes you think you could keep up?"

I started running before he finished his sentence. I was young and in the best shape of my life, so the running came easily enough but what spurred me on even faster was the sound of giant branches snapping as Dee cut a path behind me. They impeded his progress enough that he was not able to overtake me.

"If I catch you, I will eat you," Dee yelled from a few steps behind.

That's some scary shit any way you cut it. Growing up, I'd had dreams of being chased by zombies, but they weren't fast, green, and huge and they sure didn't talk.

As we approached the Hill, I held up one hand behind me to let Dee know I was coming to a stop and that he shouldn't run over me like a semi over a VW Bug. I was winded, but I used the excuse that if a sentry saw a Genogerian chasing a human, he was likely to end up with a bullet in his hide.

Dee knew it for the ruse it was. "Admit you're tired," he demanded.

"Hey, I see how wide your mouth is," I said, implying that he was cooling himself off; although I was hunched over, hands on knees, taking in large chunks of air, my chest heaving.

"Fair enough. How close are we to this entrance? I am wounded and will need some medical attention."

"What?"

Dee pulled his chest armor to the side to reveal a fist-sized hole in his side. Blood flowed from the wound.

"When the hell did that happen, Dee?" I asked in alarm.

"I believe it to be part of the Progerian fighter that was blown up."

"Shit, Dee, why didn't you say something?"

"Have you suddenly become a doctor?"

"No."

"Would you be able to carry me?"

"No."

"Then what was the purpose, other than to waste time like we are now?"

"Okay, let's go. We're almost there," I said, now worrying for another friend. Although I was pretty sure he'd be alright, we'd just run at a decent pace for the last three miles and he had been on my heels the whole time. I did not want to think what would have happened had he been completely healthy, he probably would have run me over and not even known it.

***

Another ten minutes and we found ourselves inside one of the outer Hill tunnels. We had become the center of attention once it was discovered that we still lived.

Dee was shuttled off to the medical section.

"I'll come see you later. Don't eat anyone you're not supposed to," I told him

"I'll try, but the fat one looks good," Dee said, looking at a now shivering orderly.

"He's kidding...I think," I told the man who looked like he was going to bolt "Is the general in his office?" I asked one of the men trying to take Dee's vitals but unable to get the blood pressure cuff to fit.

"I believe so, sir."

I had to gently push through the throng of folks gawking at Dee and congratulating me on our successful mission.

Tracy was just outside the major part of the crowd. "You had me worried, Talbot," she said, fully embracing me in her arms which I thankfully returned. She buried her face in my shoulder. "They said you were dead."

"I get that a lot," I told her.

"Dennis is still missing," she said, pushing back from me.

I wiped a hand across my face. "He saved us out there. We would have been dead if he hadn't shot down an enemy fighter."

"He left here with a squad of four men...against the general's orders. Paul was pissed, I thought he was going to send out another squad to hunt him down and bring him back. So is it true? Do you have Spindler? We've been preparing for a rapid evac."

"We got him and he didn't have enough time to give us up. Come on, I've got to talk to Paul." My heart slipped a beat as I saw Beth standing against the wall, watching. I didn't say anything to her as Tracy and I headed toward Paul's office.

Paul looked haggard, there was no other way to describe it. "It's good to see you, Mike," Paul said, standing and grasping my hand. "I thought I'd lost you both."

"Dennis?" I asked.

"Sit, please." Paul sat down heavily. "He's dead, Mike."

I felt like each word was hammered into my stomach with a baseball bat. I had to ask. "Are you sure?"

"I sent scouts out to see how this whole thing played out. They lost sight of you, but they were able to witness Dennis' position overrun by the retreating Genogerians. It was an intense firefight, but even if he had survived that, the bombs that came down next obliterated the entire region, even killing the Genogerians who had advanced past his position."

I buried my face in my hands and sobbed. My head and stomach ached, now my soul was stretched thin, it too ached.

"I can't even wrap my mind around how much I'm going to miss him," I told Paul, finally extracting my face from my hands.

Tracy grabbed my hand closest to her and squeezed gently. I looked over to her with red-rimmed eyes.

"I knew he was going to follow you. I almost put him under house arrest to stop him."

"He saved my life, Paul. We wouldn't have made it if not for him and his men," I said. Paul nodded at all the right times, I knew he already knew, but I still had to say it.

"We'll mourn his passing, Mike, but we've got other things going on now. The Progerians are amassing a huge landing party. My long range patrols had to get out of there before they were discovered, but we're talking upwards of ten thousand Genogerians now afoot within twenty miles of here."

I was never good at math, but I didn't have to be to realize how bad the odds were becoming. At that moment and in the depths of my grief, I just wanted to go running straight into their landing with my rifle blazing. Even as I write this, I see the contradiction for what it is, how ungrateful would I be to go and needlessly get myself killed and negate Dennis' surrendering of his life?

"Oh!" Tracy exclaimed.

"What?" I asked, half standing, thinking some other emergency was also playing out.

"I would have sworn I felt the baby kick."

That thought alone brought a smile to my face, there was hope for the continuation of human life. I needed to fight to preserve it, not to die in martyrdom.

I would grieve for Dennis for a long time, I thought, but I would honor his death with a victory over the insurgents that the gods themselves would be proud of. Grandiose, I know, but that's what I felt.

I touched Tracy's flat belly. I didn't feel anything and I didn't know if it was even too early for her to feel anything. But if she was lying, she picked the right time and the right thing to lie about.

"I know we need to talk, Paul, and soon, but I need to

see how Drababan is doing, and I need to be alone for a little while. Is that alright?"

"We'll meet back here in five hours," Paul said, coming from behind his desk to give me a hug.

"I'll see you then," I told him. "You coming?" I asked Tracy.

"I need to talk to her about our evacuation plan. She'll catch up with you later."

I gave Tracy a small kiss and with a heavy heart, lightened somewhat by the thoughts of the baby, I headed toward the hospital area.

I almost passed Beth by I was so deep in my despair. "I heard," she said reaching out with her hand.

I almost broke down in that hallway; sincerity was etched in her face. She couldn't be this cunning, could she?

"Do you want to go talk about it?" she asked.

I never wanted to talk about it or even think about it again. I knew I would never be so lucky as for either of those things to happen. "I don't, Beth. I'm going to check on Dee and then I think I'll find out how many shots it takes to get to the bottom of a vodka bottle."

"I don't know how to say this so I'm just going to blurt it out," Beth stated.

I waited, Beth seemed to be weighing whether or not this was a prudent course of action.

"Do you really think Tracy is pregnant?" she asked.

It took me a moment to process the information. Why would I even doubt Tracy's words?

"I mean," Beth continued, I think trying to make sure that I never got back on to firm ground, "it's rather fortunate she is all of a sudden pregnant when I arrive."

"I'm not sure if you're arrival would have sparked a pregnancy," I said, thinking more along the lines of the act itself as opposed to a lie created to thwart the attentions of another.

"I think she's threatened by me, Mike."

"She doesn't need to be," I said harshly, wishing to extract myself from this situation as quickly as possible.

Great, now I'd have one more thing to think about while I tried to drown my memories in fermented potatoes.

Beth looked visibly hurt at my words. I simultaneously wanted to tell her I was sorry and hold her close and to tell her to leave me alone.

"I know you're lying to yourself," she said defiantly. "And I'm pretty sure so is she. That seems like a pretty bad way for a relationship to get started," Beth said heatedly.

"Beth, I don't think either of us needs to explain ourselves to you. Why are you not getting it? You told me 'no', I moved on. I don't think it gets any simpler than that."

"Not everything is black and white, Mike!" she was near to shouting. "I am the gray area and I am standing right here in front of you. I am telling you that I made a mistake and that I am willing to do anything to get you back!"

"Fuck!" I yelled. I was exhausted, I was grief stricken, and I was concerned for my friend. Her badgering was relentless. I didn't know how much more I could take. "I can't take this shit right now, Beth. I just lost my best friend, I have another friend in the hospital, and I'm about holding on by about this fucking much," I yelled, my thumb and forefinger actually touching. She stepped back from the force of my words.

"Let's leave this place, Mike," she forged ahead. "It's like we're waiting for death to find us here. We can start over somewhere new."

"What's wrong with you, Beth? Beauty can sometimes shield you from some of the worst things in life, but it shouldn't make you ignorant. Where do you think *we* could go? Where would we be able to get this new mythical fresh start? You'd be so willing to leave these people behind? Some of these people that are 'waiting for death' are my family and friends."

"You're upset. I'll talk with you later," she said,

turning to leave.

"I wish you wouldn't," I said, heading to where I had originally intended to go.

Dee was sitting up in a bed especially designed for him. "Ahhh, Michael, how are you doing?" Dee asked lightly before he got a closer look at my face. "You have not received good news about your friend then?"

"He didn't make it," I told Dee, pulling up a chair.

"I would like to say that he died valiantly in the salvation of others, but your tone and set tell me that any consolatory words I utter will be misconstrued and thrown back at me with anger."

"Dee, if we get through this, I really think you should go into psychiatry."

"It would almost be too easy with your species," Dee replied.

"Was that a joke?" I had to ask.

"Not at all. I am sorry for the loss of your friend, he was a brave man. There is nothing in those words that can be used against me in an argument, yet I feel the truth of them has lifted your heart a bit."

"How you doing?" I asked, changing the subject. Dee's uncanny ability to read me or any human for that matter was unsettling and I didn't feel like letting him read chapter two of what I was feeling.

"I will allow the conversation to be steered away from what ails you, Michael. Perhaps we will revisit it when you're ready. Your doctors don't understand my physiology as well as I would like them to, but they are all in agreement that I should be fine as long as I do not get an infection."

"Our antibiotics won't work on you?" I asked.

"No, but they are checking your storeroom for any pet medications they feel might help."

"Makes sense," I said. "I'd hate for you to be my pet. Man, can you imagine the size of the mess you'd leave behind at a park?"

"I don't see the humor," Dee said flatly.

"No, but I do," I told him. "How long until you're up and about?"

"This is the most comfortable bed I've had in over a month. I think that I would like to lie in it for a few more hours."

"No, rush Dee. Enjoy yourself, you've earned it."

I left Dee and thought to seek out my brother. Instead I found myself inexplicably drawn to Dennis' quarters. As an officer, he was afforded one of the few rooms that actually had a door. It was locked, but that was more of a challenge than an obstacle. I rifled through my pockets until I came across something I thought might work. It was a library card from the Walpole Library System that I had carried with me almost always after the fiasco with Spindler's car. I considered it a lucky charm. I wished I had let Dennis borrow it.

The door opened and I got a sideways glance from a few people walking down the hallway, but no one stopped me or called me on it. I slid in and quickly shut the door as if I were doing something illegal. Technically, I was, but I didn't think anyone would really care. I still didn't know what I was doing there. A small envelope was lying on Dennis' pillows. A chill rippled up my spine. It had my name on it.

"Is this a fucking joke?" I asked, looking around, expecting someone to jump out from some hidden partition.

Nobody did, and I moved hesitantly over to the white rectangle. I reached out, convinced I was going to get shocked as soon as my hand made contact. I felt an electricity as I grasped the cool paper but I thought that had more to do with an overactive imagination. I ripped the seal, it sounded loud in my ears. I wanted to leave, something did not feel right. Instead, I read the small note:

I'm glad you made it, Mike. I knew you fucking
would. It's always been about you, buddy. Even when Paul

and me were building this place it was always about you. When you disappeared, I never doubted that I would see you again. There's always been something about you, my friend. I wasn't jealous, but somehow your light always burned brighter than those around you. I often wondered how someone could glow so intensely and not burn out. You draw people to you, they can sense something too.

I followed you out today because I had to. Something higher told me to. I know, I know, you think I'm crazy, but I found out about your baby and I had to make sure that baby's father came home. My friend you saved my life once, consider this a returning of the favor, I've loved you like a brother for years. I will hold a spot for you on the other side. I had a premonition I wasn't going to make it and that I should write this note. So I guess, buddy, if you're reading this, the premonition was right. And I'd do whatever I did again man, because from day one you were my friend. There I was a Yankee fan deep in Red Sox territory and you didn't give a shit.

Don't grieve too much for me. I knew what I was getting into and I did so willingly, however all this shit turns out, you are the cog on which this whole thing turns. I'll be watching, so don't let me down and I'll save a spot wherever the hell I end up. I should probably scratch 'hell' out.

Good luck, Mike, I love you, bro.

"I love you too, Dennis," I said through tear-blurred eyes.

I carefully folded the note back up and put it back in the envelope and then into my back pants pocket. My heart was simultaneously lifted and dragged down, it was a strange sensation. My goal had been to get absolutely blitzed on some cheap homemade booze. That feeling had passed.

"If I was supposed to live, then for some eff'd-up reason, so was Spindler," I said as I gently closed Dennis' door behind me. I did not then realize the finality of the act, but I would never again enter that room. Within ten minutes,

I found myself outside the detention area. Paul had seen the need to lock Spindler up, not that he was going anywhere, but Paul wanted to make sure that he wasn't going anywhere while he was here. It sounds strange as I write that, but it makes perfect sense.

"Hello, sir," The prison guard stated.

"I'd like to see Spindler," I told him.

"The general thought you might."

"I'm not really keen on everyone guessing my next moves and then being right."

"Sir?" the guard questioned.

"Nothing. Can you just point me in the right direction?"

"Third door on the left." He pointed down the hallway. "Here you go, sir." The guard handed me a door key.

I had no sooner slid the key into the lock when Spindler cried out.

"Come to beat a confession from me!" he yelled, maybe trying to instill some nerve into himself.

"Hello, Spindler," I said as I walked in.

He did not look happy to see me.

"My name is Yerdly."

"You're kidding, right?"

He flashed me some very angry eyes. "I'm just going to stick with Spindler."

"What do you want?"

"I think you know something," I said, pulling up a folding chair and sitting near him. He did not seem comfortable with the distance between us, apparently I was invading his personal space.

"I am not some master spy in whatever drama is unfolding in your head. I am a scared, middle-aged man trying to survive."

I almost yelled at him that he was trying to survive on the deaths of his fellow man, but I restrained. Nothing would be accomplished if we became confrontational.

"There's a reason we're here. You and me, Spindler."

"Are you getting existential on me, Mr. Talbot?"

"I might be. But I have reason to believe there is a higher authority working here."

"Please," Spindler answered sardonically. "I would think you too intelligent to fall for the opiate of the masses."

"Why, Mr. Spindler, are you a Leninist?" I laughed.

"I have also not seen a reason in my life to believe in the Easter Bunny."

"Maybe that's why you're such a bitter man," I shot back, my mouth working much faster than my mind. *Dammit!* I yelled in my head. I was witnessing Spindler in real time withdrawing from our conversation. "Sorry," I said sincerely. "That's not what I meant to say."

"Oh, I think it's exactly what you wanted to say, but your apology seemed real enough. Why are you here, Mr. Talbot? Certainly not to taunt me."

"There's a reason I lived today. There's a reason you lived today." My right hand absent-mindedly felt the pocket where Dennis's letter was.

Spindler looked long and hard at me, weighing what reaction his words might illicit from me. He sighed heavily before he spoke. "I did not tell the aliens about this place." He looked me in the eye directly as he spoke his next words. "But I would have. I was scared, Mr. Talbot. I have never been more scared in my life. I would have given them my mother's address if I thought it would have given me another day." He was having difficulty forcing the words out. "It is not an easy feat to admit your weaknesses, especially with a witness."

"Why don't they know about this place then?" I asked.

"Because as soon as I gave this place up, my bargaining chip, such as it was, would have been gone. I gave them the armory first, figured it would buy me a day or two. I watched them eat a person, Michael, right in front of me! One moment she was alive and the next she was screaming these blood-curdling shrieks as those damn things tore her apart! It was horrible!" He sobbed into his hands.

"It is," I said, trying to offer solace.

"They ate her because the officer told them too, but I don't think they really wanted to," Spindler said. He was still crying and sort of ranting. I did not know it in the moment, but my interest was beginning to pique.

"They were fearful if they didn't do as the officer said that they would suffer the same fate. They hate it here, they hate their officers, they hate humans. We are dangerous little monkeys to them. They just want to go home."

"Wait, how did you get all this information?" I asked, stopping Spindler.

"What?" Spindler said, looking up from his tear-soaked hands.

"How did you get this information?" I asked.

"It's what all military men do when they have free time, they complain."

"And how would you know?" I asked, truly curious.

"I did two years of ROTC in college."

"And they said all of this in English?"

"Some, not all, the rest was pretty easy to figure out." He answered.

I shrugged, it was something. "What else did they say?"

"We...we used to bitch about our C.O. and about drills and training, but it was a camaraderie, the complaining. Those beasts truly hate their lot in life. I wanted to ask them why they had enlisted in the first place, but I didn't want to be noticed...not at all."

I stood up. "They didn't enlist, they're slaves," I told Spindler. I hurriedly walked out the room.

"Wait, where are you going?" Spindler asked. But I had already flipped the key back to the guard and was heading back to see Dee.

CHAPTER SIXTY-FOUR – Mike Journal Entry 21

"We have always despised our overlords," Dee said, sitting up. "Is this why you disturbed my sleep? I am well enough that I could get up from here and show you my displeasure."

"Sorry, sorry. But what of your revolution?"

"It failed miserably. We had the numbers, but we did not possess the skill to use their technology. Once the element of surprise was gone, we became a very ineffectual fighting force. I'm not sure what we would have accomplished anyway."

"Huh?" I asked, tilting my head.

"Even if we had won, we had no desire to enslave the Progerians. We just wanted to be free. To live out our lives as our God had intended."

"Not seeing the problem, Dee."

"Even in defeat the Progerians would never have left us alone. They would have regrouped, rearmed and then come after us again. There would have been no place to find peace. They are not an honorable derivative of our species. It saddens me that our evolutionary paths once shared the same roadway.

"What about now, Dee?"

"What about it, Michael? Are you saying we should

have another revolution?"

"Why not, Dee? You still have the numbers, and if you win you now have a new home. You went from a Genogerian hell-bent on destroying me to saving me and freeing yourself within an instant once you saw the possibility of that happening. You forsook your entire race to potentially spend the rest of your days with us humans."

"In hindsight, Michael, I did not completely reason out what my actions would entail."

"Are you saying you acted irrationally?"

"In my defense, there was a lot going on."

"Dee, what's to say that your brethren would not react in the same 'irrational' way? If we can somehow dangle the carrot of freedom in front of them, won't they try to grab it?"

"It's possible, Michael, but I would not have done what I had if I had not gotten to know you first. I do not believe you will be able to instill enough confidence in the Genogerians to follow you or believe you, even if you could somehow communicate with them."

"What about you?"

Dee thought about it for a moment. "Yes, my words would carry much more weight than yours. Damn you, Michael Talbot, I was thoroughly enjoying this bed," Dee said as he arose. "What do you have in mind?"

"I don't really have a plan yet, but I think we should go see Paul."

Dee's feet had no sooner hit the floor when a klaxon blazed.

"Shit," I mumbled, my rifle was at the armory. I had a pistol, but that was like bringing a pebble to a catapult fight.

"BREECH," came over the loud speaker. "SOUTHEAST ENTRANCE."

Dee looked at me.

"That's at the end of this hallway," I told him. We were already on the move when more instructions came over the speaker.

"UNIT 17, SECTOR 12, IMMEDIATELY! FULL DETACHMENT! USE OF DEADLY FORCE AUTHORIZED!"

"It might be wiser to not get in the middle of this, Dee. I don't want anyone mistaking you for the enemy."

We were quickly making our way down the hallway as civilians wisely streamed passed us, most in near panic mode.

"Where you go, I go," Dee said, his rifle at the ready. "I had it next to me in the bed," he answered when I looked again at it.

"Don't blame you." We raced when we heard the first shots fired.

Blue streaks whistled off the top of the ceiling.

"I was really hoping it wasn't aliens," I said. "Spindler lied, the piece of shit. I should have shot him."

"Get down!" boomed an alien voice. "I will kill you if I have to!" More blue streaks flew harmlessly past our heads. Well, at least past my head, Dee had to duck as they were a lot closer to his noggin.

A couple of gate guards nearly ran into us in their haste to get away.

"Captain, we need reinforcements," one of them said frantically.

"How many of them are there?" I asked, holding tight to his shirt. I was afraid he would bolt before I had a chance to get the answer I was looking for.

"A dozen, maybe more," the guard said.

"That makes no sense," Dee said. "There would be more rifle fire and Genogerians' only sound during combat is that of a war cry, not a plea to surrender."

"I could hear the footfalls of the detachment that had been sent rapidly approaching.

"Go!" I told the guard. "Tell them Captain Talbot has told them to hold their position. Do you understand?"

The scared private nodded and headed off to intercept

the defenders.

For the moment there was a détente, no shots were being fired. All I could smell was the residue of spent ammunition and burnt ozone from the alien rifles.

"Genogerian, my name is Michael Talbot. I am going to come around this corner with my weapon raised. I would appreciate you not shooting me."

"Is this wise?" Dee asked.

"I doubt it."

Dee made a series of guttural sounds punctuated with some hisses and snarls, it was terrifying. I waited a few moments as the intruder followed with his own series of noises.

"What the hell was that?" I asked Dee.

"Native tongue," Dee said.

"Any chance you could clue me in?"

"I told him that, if he harmed you, I would rip his teeth from his face one by one so that he could not chew his way through the Bahktran and into Heaven."

"Did it work?"

"He laughed and said you would be fine."

"That was a laugh?" I asked, pointing over my shoulder.

"Come forth, Mi-chael Talbot," the alien said, having difficulty pronouncing my name.

"How do I end up in these situations?" I asked aloud. Dee shrugged. "That's the best you've got?"

I turned the corner, my pistol raised. Like I had promised. There were two entrance guards prostrate on the ground, hanging over them was a very large alien. He wasn't a Geno or a Prog, he looked to be a mix of both.

"My name is Urlack," the big beast said with a slight bow. "It is an honor to meet the mighty Earth champion, Michael Talbot. I had thought you would be bigger."

"Hello, Urlack. Any chance you could put that big blue ray gun down? Or at least stop pointing it at me."

"They have shot me, Michael Talbot."

And when I looked closer I could see at least two bullet wounds, one in his forearm and one in his shoulder. It appeared that his chest plate might have stopped at least another three.

"Did you expect anything less?"

Urlack appeared to think about it for a moment. "I do not know what I was expecting. I am still unsure as to why I have come here."

"Let's have them go on their way, and you and I will discuss it like the males of our species should."

"Up!" Urlack shouted.

The guards looked up at Urlack and then over toward me.

"Go," I told them. They didn't need any more prompting. "Do not, I repeat do *not* have anyone come down here unless you hear more gunfire. Do you both understand?" They nodded and ran past.

"I would very much like to meet the one that talked to me in our home world language."

Dee rounded the corner, his weapon secured on his back.

"Drababan Truchnel! It is truly an honor!" Urlack said. "They told us that you had been killed during the escape of Michael Talbot."

"I have not been," Dee answered.

I really had a witty sarcastic comment until I realized I was a minority at the moment.

"I have heard of you, Urlack. I thought you more of a myth than a reality," Dee said.

I could not tell if that was a veiled insult or Dee merely stating a fact, although both could be the same thing given the right circumstances.

"Most of what you heard I'm sure is truth. My sire is a high-ranking Cabinet member who rutted with a Genogerian. As you know this is a common practice especially in the slave colonies, but the chances of an off-spring are extremely rare, I think I am more the product of an experiment in hybrid vigor than a successful union."

"We are close enough relatives that we can procreate," Dee said to me. "But usually the womb of a Genogerian is hostile to Progerian insemination. That is why our females are used as vessels for the Progerians."

"Little chance of a baby coming back to bite them in the ass for their transgression," I said.

Dee took a moment to realize the meaning of my words. "Exactly," he said. "And those that do survive are usually twisted beyond recognition from their environment and die soon afterward. I have never heard of an offspring making it into adulthood."

"Those few that are not deformed are usually killed at birth by the mother, fearing that some retribution will be brought down on her head for her misbehavior," Urlack stated.

They both spoke very nonchalantly about what we would consider high crimes on Earth, but were also practices that had been committed for millennia amongst various cultures and races; who was I to judge?

"Do you mean these humans harm?" Dee questioned Urlack.

"Not anymore. I am now an outlaw among our people. I have openly protested our involvement in this world and the subjugation of Genogerians as they are being ruthlessly slaughtered by the hairless monkeys."

"Umm, hairless monkey here," I said, raising my hand.

"Yes, you are," Urlack said, acknowledging my words.

Dee snorted. "The earthling feels you have slighted him with the reference."

"But that is what they are—why would he feel insulted if I merely called him what he is?" Urlack asked.

"Their feelings are almost as soft as their skin." Dee snorted again.

"How is it that we are having such a difficult time enslaving them then?" Urlack asked.

"These feelings running deep in them…drive everything they do. When they are threatened, they are capable of just about anything and what the Progerians did not take into account is that they will fight even harder when nearly all hope has been extinguished or the fate of a loved one is in jeopardy."

"That makes no sense," Urlack said, his face taking on a classic quizzical stare. "To dismantle hope has always been a first priority; much mightier civilizations have fallen once that has happened. And love is a chemical attraction that should be weakened under threat instead of increased. If a loved one should die, it is the perpetuation of the original subject that should be increased. These hairless…humans are strange creatures. How have you found your time with them?" Urlack asked.

"They have been hospitable, but mostly out of fear from me or from my human friend."

"You consider him a friend then?" Urlack asked.

"Yes, but he is horrible at games."

"Wonderful. This is about as bad as Tracy and Beth comparing notes. This is all really fascinating stuff," I told them. "But I'm not sure how long that detachment is going to stay at bay with or without my orders. Urlack, you look like you could use some medical attention."

He nodded in response. "Are the medical facilities adequate?"

"They lack the knowledge of our surgeons, but they know enough to be helpful."

"Urlack, you are going to have to surrender your weapon," I told him. "My superiors will not feel comfortable with you having it on you."

Urlack seemed hesitant and I could not blame him.

He was in the enemy camp. Recently he had been on the side bent on the destruction of us. That he was here now had more to do with his own species' preservation than with ours.

"I will stay by you," Dee told Urlack as he approached with his hand out to take the weapon.

"That ought to make everyone comfortable," I said.

"Sarcasm?" Dee asked, looking back at me.

I nodded. Urlack took a long look at his rifle and the door behind him before handing the weapon to Dee, who immediately slung it over his shoulder.

"How did you get in?" I asked curiously.

"I knocked, following the same pattern as the humans that entered previously," Urlack replied matter-of-factly.

"I'm going to have to tell Paul to put a camera there," I said to no one in particular.

"We're coming back around. Everything is fine!" I shouted. "I'm taking our new guest to the medical facility—am I clear?"

"Very clear, Captain. The general has ordered an armed escort."

"Tell the general that I will take care of the escort—is that clear?" I said, coming around the corner.

"General...captain," the lieutenant of the detachment said, weighing his hands like a scale. "Can't do it, sir. I spent too much time earning these bars," he said, pointing to his collar.

"Alright, why is everyone a smartass? Grab two or three of your least trigger-happy men, along with yourself, and we'll get this done," I said.

The lieutenant turned and called, "Ouster, Hendricks, and Clantry—you're with me."

"Weapons holstered," I said, putting my hand up like a traffic cop.

"Sir."

"Listen, Lieutenant, you'll still be armed and behind us, should the need arise I'm sure you will be able to make ready in sufficient time."

"You're stretching the general's orders, sir," the lieutenant replied.

"It's what I do. Urlack has been injured and is already feeling the ill effects from his wounds. The longer we wait here increases the odds that he might die."

"I feel fine," Urlack shouted to me.

"Dee, could you help me out?" I asked.

"He says that he feels fine, what more could I add?" Dee asked.

"This is brutal. Lieutenant, I take personal responsibility from this moment forward. Let me just get him to sick bay."

"Alright, squad, everybody besides the three I called out, return to secondary positions. Do not move until you are ordered to do so."

"Aye-aye, sir." The remaining men and women melted down the hallways.

The walk down to medical was not quite as tense as I expected, but it also wasn't a walk in the park. That probably had more to do with my nerves than anybody else's.

Paul was waiting by the entrance to the hospital. "That the prisoner?" he asked me.

Urlack scoffed at the assumption.

"He's more of a guest," I told him hastily, hoping to head off any confrontation.

"Mike, you really need to stop usurping my authority," Paul said in no uncertain terms.

"We need to talk. Can I get Urlack some medical attention and then I promise no more usurping today," I told him.

He stepped off to the side to allow Urlack and Dee in and then looked over my shoulder to motion the lieutenant and the three guards in. "Problem with that, Mike?" Paul asked me.

"Sort of, but I'll let it slide," I told him.

"Appreciate that. Come on, let's go to my quarters."

"Dee, I'll be back. Please tell Urlack the doctors mean well," I told him. The doctor looked none too pleased at my words.

"I don't like this, Mike," Paul said, coming right at me once the door to his room was closed.

"Whoa! Hey buddy, I didn't invite him here."

"Are you sure? The big green things seem to follow you around!" He was shouting now. "How do we know he's not wired somehow?"

"Because we're still here."

"Maybe he's doing reconnaissance."

"Maybe, Paul, but that's not really their tactic. It's usually more along the lines of seek and destroy. Do you really think what we've got here could hold out against any sort of sustained attack? Shit, Paul, he knocked and your guards let him in."

"What?! Who was on duty!" Paul shouted. He looked like he was about to go head hunting.

"Paul, my point is that, if they had truly discovered us, we'd be under a full-fledged attack."

Paul sat heavily at his desk, his chair groaning from all the times he had done so. "What is he doing here, then?" he asked, a little more subdued but not by much.

"He's a deserter."

"He told you that? And you believe him?"

"They don't lie much, Paul…if at all."

"So he deserted and just so happened to stumble upon our little home then? He figured holing up with his enemies was a good idea? You cannot be so fucking naïve, can you?"

"Can you be so jaded, Paul!" My voice was raising now. "I've yet to get a complete answer out of him, even he is unsure as to why he is here, but he is as sick of the killing and the destruction as we are."

"A beast with a soul—how quaint."

"Don't underestimate their spirituality."

"Don't you underestimate what damage they could bring here!"

"Are you not listening to what I'm saying, Paul? I think he's here to help."

"I don't believe it, Mike, not for a second. And I'd much rather put a bullet in his head. Let the doctors do a little dissection and figure out how to kill them more effectively."

"Should we start with Dee?" I asked hotly.

Paul was glaring at me, but he chose not to speak.

"You'd shoot him, too, wouldn't you?"

"In a fucking heartbeat," he answered.

"They might hold the key to this whole fuck-fest and you'd rather add them to the growing pile of dead. You kill them and it's really over. We're hiding in a hole like rats. What has landed so far is nothing more than an expeditionary force. As soon as the big guns get here, we're gone. Oh, a few of us might be saved for food and games, some might even luck out and get into a zoo, but other than that, man becomes an extinct animal."

"All I think you've done by having them here is to hasten our departure."

"They're here now, Paul. I think we find a way to utilize them."

"I had to tell Dennis' mother about her son today," Paul said, abruptly changing the conversation.

I pulled up a chair and matched his heavy seat fall, my gusted sails having completely gone windless. "I'm sorry, Paul. How'd that go?"

"As well as you'd expect. Do you think these aliens can really help us?" Paul asked, looking for a glimmer of hope in an otherwise gloomy day.

"Paul, I do. By ourselves we're merely marking time and I know you know that. Oh, we'll go out guns blazing, but focus on the 'go out' part. I think we could have something here. The Genogerians are slaves, plain and simple, and I think if we can somehow get the message across to them that they can be free here, they might bite."

Paul looked up at me at my last word.

"Okay, bad choice of words, but you know what I mean. They don't want to be here, especially now that they are dying at an unprecedented rate."

"And then what, Mike, we all go strolling down the road like nothing happened?"

"Paul, the Genos make up somewhere in the neighborhood of eighty percent of the population on that ship and on the ground. They become our allies, and this war is over. I don't know what happens after that, but it would be nice to have the time to think about that, don't you think?"

"What do you propose? Drop flyers on them like the Germans did to the African-Americans fighting in World War Two?"

"You sure are young to be a cynical old bastard."

"I'm serious, Mike. They might despise the Progerians, but they downright hate us.

"But they don't hate Dee or Urlack."

"Emissaries? How would we even get their words across to the Genogerians?"

"I don't know any of that yet."

"I think you should find out soon," Paul said as he grabbed a stack of paperwork on his desk.

I was a little taken aback. My old friend was summarily dismissing me from his quarters without speaking a word. I wanted to tell him to kiss my ass, but I was afraid he'd throw me in the brig. I saw no reason to push my luck. I wanted to get back to medical as quickly as possible, mostly for selfish reasons. I knew if I stayed out in the open long enough, Beth would track me down. She was not a fan of Dee, and I could guarantee she would not want to be anywhere near Urlack either. I found myself peering down hallways before I entered, much like I had in high school while I was keeping an eye out for Spindler. I needed to remember to check in on him later.

"How's he doing, Doc?" I asked as I came in, grateful I had somehow eluded my stalker.

"He'll be fine. The bullets barely got through his hide, and he's marginally nicer than your other friend, although that isn't saying a whole bunch."

"I very much enjoy this beverage," Urlack was saying as he looked at the container he was drinking from. "Does it have medicinal properties?" he asked Dee.

"What's he drinking?" I asked. coming over, happy that Urlack was lying down and Dee was sitting. I almost felt big enough.

"Something called Moxie," Dee said.

I choked. "You like that?" I asked Urlack.

"I do not think I have ever had anything as refreshing. This must be a prized drink on your planet, perhaps reserved primarily for dignitaries. I am honored to drink it."

I didn't have the heart to tell him the last time I used Moxie was to remove rust off my bike chain when I was nine. I would no sooner drink that concoction than walk through a briar patch buck naked.

"I'm glad you like it," was all I could muster with a straight face. I thought to tell him that he might want to drink it fast before it ate through the plastic glass he was holding.

"Is Paul angry?" Dee asked, his normal intuitive self.

"You could say that. We need to come up with a plan for Operation Genogerian Freedom."

"That has a nice sound to it," Urlack said. "Not as nice as this drink, but nice nonetheless."

"I still have a hard time with you guys speaking English."

"*Würden sie eher ich deutsch sprechen?*" Urlack said, the harsh words made me pause.

"What?" I asked.

"I asked, would you rather I speak German," Urlack said.

"No, just English," I answered. "It's just weird to hear

human language come out of your mouths."

"It is a means that we use to have cultures lose their hope. If we can learn and take your language—"

"Yeah, I know—if you can do that so easily, what else could you take over as quickly. I get it. I'm just saying it's weird."

"I watched more than a few of your bouts. I always thought that you tended more toward luck than prowess," Urlack said.

"I bet you're fun at parties," I said.

"Do they serve this Moxie at parties?" Urlack asked seriously.

"God, I hope not."

"You humans can be brilliant when it comes to devising ways in which to preserve your lives. Your species' survival instinct is strong, that is why our fight has not gone as easy as the High Command thought it would. I fear for the lives of my enslaved brethren; they die while the officers sit back and plot their next move."

"It's been the same on our planet for eons," I rued.

"What will be gained if an alliance can be formed?" Urlack asked.

"Another chance. That's all I can promise, Urlack. Maybe we've learned something. I hope that's the case. If we haven't, at the very least, your kind will be able to make their own decisions."

"That will have to be enough," Urlack said, apparently some thought was weighed on an internal scale and had finally tipped into humanity's favor.

"Any idea how we'll be able to do this?" I asked.

"We have been talking in your absence, Michael," Dee said. "There has been a growing movement among the Genogerians, a discontent at our treatment. We have been waiting decades for an opportunity such as the one that is presenting itself here. Urlack has Genogerians on the inside that will risk everything to spread the word that the appropriate time has come."

I looked around conspiratorially. "Please do not let anyone know you can have communication outside of these walls," I told Urlack.

"I will agree to that," Urlack said.

"And what about that ship circling over us?" I asked. "Even if every ground troop you have defects, that ship could easily undo everything. I can't imagine there are too many Progerians sympathetic to the plight of their cousins."

"You are correct in that assumption," Urlack said. "There are certain measures that will be taken in that regard also."

"This sounds promising," I said, hope creeping its way back into my heart.

"For this to work, you will need to come with me back to the ship," Urlack said.

My throat threatened to jump out of my mouth along with my stomach and a good chunk of my liver. Dee's chair went hurtling through space as he quickly stood up.

"I will not allow it!" he shouted.

The three guards and the lieutenant quickly came into the room to see what was the matter.

"Everything alright?" the lieutenant asked me.

I doubt I looked alright. I felt like I had just swallowed a live eel and it was sending bolts of electricity through my innards. "I'm fine," I managed to say without spraying stomach juice around the room. They departed almost as quickly as they had entered.

"For this to work, they will have to see you speak the words of this new peace and a promise that they will be able to live out their lives untethered to another's will and on land they can call their own."

"Why me? I'm a lowly captain."

"You're the Earth Champion. They would not be able to think of anyone more in a position of power than yourself."

"Dee, I can't go back to that ship," I said haltingly. I wasn't proud of my response, but just the thought of going back was making staying in the standing position a difficult proposition.

"I will support you with any decision you make, Michael," Dee said.

Dee's statement hung there. It was only a fragment of what I thought he wanted to say.

"Dee, please finish the rest of your thought," I told him, even though I had no desire to know what he felt because it really didn't bode well for me.

"Please do not let my conflicting words mislead you, I do not want you to go that ship either, and I will fight alongside you down here until the end, but the end is what it will be. Your kind has fought admirably, but this is not a fight they can win. This is merely the vanguard of a much bigger occupation force. Once they get here, nothing we have done these last few months will matter. If we are to truly win, we must have a superior position from which to defend ourselves."

"Dee, say all of this works—we're able to convince the Genogerians down here and up in the ship that now is the time for their freedom. What then? I'm still not sure I see the gain if the Progerians still have a fleet on the way. I can't imagine a scout ship would be any match for what's coming and even if it was, who's going to operate it? Will the Progerians see the folly of their ways and then join up with us?"

"Valid question," Urlack said. "But a scout ship probes the depths of unknown space for years at a time. It is a battle fortress in its own right, never knowing what it may encounter along its voyages. It would hold up quite well in battle. And I will be there to teach the Genogerians how to operate the controls. Besides that, there are ways we could communicate with the Genogerians on the other ships to make them understand what is happening here."

"This is a lot of 'ifs'," I said, looking for some sort of way out of the nightmare.

"What choices are there?" Dee asked pragmatically.

"We stay, we fight, we die."

"Very inspirational," I told him.

"Really, Michael, I am not sure sarcasm is appropriate right now," Dee answered back.

"Sarcasm?" Urlack asked.

"I think you two will have plenty of time for him to teach you all about it," Dee said to Urlack.

CHAPTER SIXTY-FIVE – Mike Journal Entry 22

"Absolutely not," Tracy and Paul said in unison. Although if I remember correctly, Tracy's words were also infused with a few choice expletives.

"I smell trap all over this," Paul said.

"Normally, I'd think the same thing, Paul, but why bother? They would now know this location and could crush us within an hour or two at the most. I mean, maybe it could be an elaborate scheme to flush me out and parade me around, but they just don't operate like that. They don't see the need for deception. They are all about crush and acquire."

Paul stopped his arguing. "You can't possibly be thinking about this?" Tracy asked Paul.

"Unless we had our own spaceships, we all know we're merely biding our time until the end comes," Paul said to Tracy.

"Are you insane?" Tracy shouted. Whether it was meant for me or Paul I wasn't sure.

"Don't forget your place, Lieutenant," Paul said.

"Sir, yes, sir, General," Tracy said, snapping to attention.

"Now I understand your feelings in this matter, but we have to look at this as the sacrifice of the one for the many."

"The sacrifice?" I whispered.

"Figure of speech," Paul said.

"I've always hated that figure," I mumbled.

"Sir, I understand," Tracy said. "But can't we just make a videotape or something and send it with Urlack?"

"Genogerians are very impressed with displays of courage and valor," I said. "Being on that ship without Progerian knowledge would satisfy both of those requirements."

"Mike, I don't know if I'll ever get over Dennis' death. I cannot add you to that list," Paul said, contemplating what the plan would entail and the dangers that were inherent in it. "When?"

"Couple of days at the most," someone that sounded and looked like me answered. I was having an out-of-body experience. I was looking down on that dipshit and was busy trying to figure out what 'he' had against me.

"That soon?" Tracy nearly shrieked.

"Lieutenant, you're dismissed," Paul said coolly.

Tracy leveled a hard stare at him that I thought would cause his camouflage blouse to burst into flame.

"You have something more to add?" Paul asked her.

"No, sir," she answered, turning to leave. Her gaze swept past my face and gave second degree burns everywhere it made contact.

The door shut a fraction harder than it needed to.

"You alright?" Paul asked with a small grin.

"You mind if I sleep here?" I asked him.

"Might as well. This is where I sleep...when I get any, that is. Mike, what the fuck are you thinking?" Paul asked seriously.

"I'm thinking about the baby Tracy is carrying, Paul. Any chance I have, no matter how remote, to give him or her a chance to grow up, to laugh, to love, I have to try."

"How come you never took drama in school?" Paul asked as he fished a bottle of some smoky colored liquor out of his desk.

"Smoked too much weed, could never remember my lines," I told him as I took the full glass from him.

"It's been a good run," Paul said, holding up his glass. I clinked mine against his, downing the booze, the familiar burning sensation cascading down my throat.

"I've never liked this shit," I told him. "Pour me another one." We toasted again.

"What do you give your odds?" Paul asked, pouring a third.

"One in ten," I told him, waiting impatiently for the liquid courage to be poured.

"That high? Impressive."

"You should make this one a double."

"How is this Urlack planning on getting a hold of a ship?"

"He says he's got it all figured out."

"You sure do have a lot of faith in them, Mike."

"All Germans weren't monsters in World War Two, Paul."

"Yeah, but at least they were human," Paul said as he quaffed down his drink.

"Well, yeah there's that," I said, matching his motion. The fire in my belly spread as the liquid did it's magic. My eyes felt a little heavier as I became buzzed. "What is this shit?" I said pushing my glass over for another pour.

"It's Camus Cognac. Twenty-five hundred bucks a bottle."

"Holy shit, you got more?"

"No."

"You really don't think I'm going to make it back," I said.

Paul kept pouring.

"I don't know," I said taking another swig, "I really wouldn't pay much over two thousand for this."

Paul stopped to look at me, his gaze softened just as

he began to laugh. I joined in heartily.

***

I staggered out of Paul's office a few hours later.
Paul's head was resting on his desk and he was snoring
lightly. I wrote him a small note to tell him how much I loved
and valued him as a friend. I hoped it was legible. I'd felt like
a kindergartner tightly gripping a crayon and trying
desperately to copy the funny characters the teacher had
written on the board.

Tracy was leaning against the wall, I nearly fell into
her. "Smooth, huh?" I asked.

"You're drunk," she said, probably with a small
measure of disgust.

"That would be an understatement."

"Let's go home."

"Sounds wonderful," I told her. "You should
probably lead the way, because I don't have a clue which
way to go."

I don't remember how long it took or how many lefts
and rights, but as we finally approached my quarters I heard
Tracy mutter a sarcastic 'wonderful'.

"What's the matter—am I drooling again?" I asked
her, looking up. Somebody who had some sort of new
technology to blur themselves was standing approximately
by my doorway.

"It's Beth."

"Beth? I loved her once," I said, not even thinking.
All I can say is I'm thankful that I used the past tense or
Tracy would have dropped me where I stood, both literally
and figuratively.

"And now?" she prodded.

"Now what?" I asked, having no clue what she was
referring too.

"What are your feelings about Beth now?"

"Why are we talking about this?" I asked, confused.

"Because she's standing at your door."

I tried to focus as best I could down the hallway, but I could still only make out a blurred image. "You can see past her cloaking device?"

"How drunk are you?"

"I could probably sit in a chair without falling over for at least seven minutes."

"Seven whole minutes?" Tracy asked.

"At the least."

"I'll keep that in mind," she said.

"What in mind? I miss my bed," I told her.

"Almost there. What do you want me to tell Beth?"

"Why—does she miss my bed, too?" I asked, not realizing the innuendo I had just made, but Tracy caught it.

"I'm sure she does."

As we got closer, Beth began to come into focus. I was a hand span away from saying how beautiful I thought she was, and I might have had she not taken my breath away. She was wearing the same dress or a reasonable facsimile of it that she had worn the first time we met.

"Is he alright?" Beth asked, coming up to offer aid.

"He's fine," Tracy said frostily. "Just drunk."

Beth got under my other arm and helped to keep me propped up. Tracy fished my keys out of my pocket and got my door open. The two women shuffled me to my bed and unceremoniously deposited me on the mattress. Now, if I could have made the room stop spinning, this would almost have been a magical moment.

"I'm going to miss you, Tracy," I said as I plopped one foot onto the floor, the room came to a lurching stop as I rooted myself to something that wasn't spinning, although it seemed to be undulating quite a bit.

"Why?" Beth asked.

"Don't get your hopes up. It isn't because he's leaving me to be with you," Tracy said.

"Good one," I mumbled from the bed.

"What's going on, Mike?" Beth asked, approaching the side of the bed.

"He's decided to kill himself," Tracy answered.

"That one wasn't nearly as good," I said.

"Mike?" Beth asked again, trying to do an end-run past Tracy.

"Going to space again," I told her. "Third time's a charm."

"Are you insane?" Beth nearly screamed.

"Well, we finally agree on something," Tracy answered.

"You can't be serious? And you're letting him?" Beth turned her fury toward Tracy.

"I don't own him, and he's doing what he feels he must. Just because I don't agree with it doesn't mean I don't think it's a valid idea."

"Wait—what?" I said, trying to keep track of the conversation. Was Tracy now agreeing with me just to make sure she wasn't on the same side as Beth or did she truly feel what she had spoken?

"He could end it all," Tracy said, sitting on the corner of the bed. "Or end it all for me," she added much quieter.

"Mike?" Beth asked again.

I feigned sleep, even if my eyes were closed and I was snoring softly.

***

"Tracy, I know we're not the best of friends," Beth started.

"That's an understatement," Tracy responded. "Sorry, he's got me pretty upset."

"Why would he possibly go back?" Beth said, not acknowledging the apology or the slight for that matter.

Tracy spent the next few minutes retelling Beth the

entire plan, without the slightest hint of exaggeration it sounded insane.

"And so his egotistical self believes he is the only one capable of pulling this off?" Beth asked.

"That's the thing," Tracy said. "I don't really think he believes that, but he believes in the necessity to take the chance no matter how slight the probability of success."

"I won't stand for this!" Beth chided, nearly stomping her foot in protest.

"Come on, Ma, just a half hour more" Mike murmured in his sleep.

"Ha," Tracy laughed, not meaning to. "You let me know how that goes," she said, speaking to Beth. "I've yet to see the man do anything anybody has told him to."

"He has a problem with authority," Beth said, looking down at Michael's face.

A heavy knocking came at the door, only one or now two beings possessed the strength to make the hinges bulge with each hammer blow.

"Hello, Drababan," Tracy said, opening the door before the brute could continue his rapping.

"He has drunk again," Dee said as a statement of fact. "I could smell it from the hallway. I had hoped it was someone else."

"Is there something I can help you with?" Tracy asked.

Beth was trying her best to shrink into the far wall.

"Your fear of me is unfounded," Dee said, looking right at her. Beth looked like she wanted to cry.

"You're wrong. You're kind have destroyed my planet, killed my friends, and probably my family. I think I have every right to be afraid of you. And now when I might finally have one thing left to hold onto, you threaten his life, too," Beth said defiantly.

Dee bowed his head slightly. "Very well," he said to Beth. "Small military woman, will you please tell Michael to come and see me in my quarters when he arises?"

Tracy nodded. "I'd appreciate you calling me by my name or rank."

"Thank you," Dee said, turning and leaving.

"Is he always so gruff?" Beth asked.

"To everyone but Mike," Tracy said, holding the door open and looking at Beth. Beth understood the hint of the gesture, but took a moment longer to look down upon Mike's sleeping countenance.

"Would you mind if I say goodbye before he goes?" Beth asked Tracy.

"I'd like to say no, Beth, I really would, but I will tell him you asked. If he comes to see you, then it was by his decision, not mine."

"Thank you for that."

"I have no desire to be your friend, Beth, and I'd appreciate it if you would stop showing up unannounced. Good night." Tracy shut the door before Beth could respond.

"I thought she'd never leave," Mike said in his sleep, rolling over onto his side.

***

I woke up six hours later, not because I wanted to, but because my bladder deigned it. The room was dark and for a moment I had a start, not realizing where I was. There was a warm body next to me, the first thought that came to mind was Deb, which meant I was on the ship. The thrusting of adrenaline hammering through my system was making clear thinking difficult, my thoughts were processing the cloudiness in my head as concussion based and not alcohol related. My fight with Durgan was soon!

"Deb, what day is it?" I think I yelled.

A light next to my bed snapped on. Tracy was reaching for her weapon. "What's the matter?" she said, scanning the room for the threat.

My mind was addled, I could not piece together the juxtaposition of the woman I thought I was sharing my bed with to the one that was actually there. "Who are—" I almost completed the sentence before my mind was able to put tab 'A' in slot 'B'.

"Tracy…sorry. I had a bad dream," I said, putting my hand up to my head. Normally, I'd say it was for dramatic effect but I had been 'lost' for nearly fifteen seconds. If that was what Alzheimer's was like, I was hoping I died young.

"At least you didn't say 'Beth'. I might have had to use this," Tracy said, flashing her nine millimeter as she put it back in the holster that hung from the bed.

I smiled weakly because she wasn't kidding.

"Do you need some water?" she asked, unscrewing the top and handing me a bottle.

"Actually, the opposite. I'll be right back," I said going out the door to the head at the end of the hallway. I stopped to look at myself in the mirror. My eyes were red-rimmed and heavy with black underneath. I looked like I had come out of the wrong end of a fight. "You look like shit," I told my reflection."

"Yeah, you don't look so good either," I replied.

"Touché. I'll be back in a sec, I gotta take care of some business." I headed to one of the stalls. Some of you women may or may not know this and your man may or may not admit to it, but if a guy is tired we are not above sitting on the john to take care of our liquid disposal. I had just sat down when I heard someone else enter. Maybe more than one someones.

"I know I saw him come in here," one of the people said. I had never heard the man's voice before.

"The stall," came another male voice.

"Be out in a sec." Dammit, I was breaking man-code if they knew I was in there taking a leak. I stayed in a little longer than necessary.

"No need to hurry," the first man said.

I heard his footfalls coming closer. Something was up, I was glad I hadn't needed to take care of a more solid problem or I would have been caught with my pants down, literally. I pulled my pants up and stood on the stall seat just as the door crashed in. The man had fully expected me to still be on the john and was surprised when his face met my foot head on.

My foot blazed in pain as I struck his face with my heel, I wished I had remembered to put my boots on before I came. His head snapped back and he was going to be hurting, but he wasn't out of commission. His buddy was behind him, I could hear the crackle of the stun gun in his hand.

"Bastard kicked me," the first man said, dressed in khaki pants and a short sleeved button down shirt, he almost looked governmental—like CIA in a foreign country. His buddy, by contrast, looked like he just rolled in from Philly. He had a beer gut and baseball hat.

"Move out of the way, one zap with this and he won't be kicking anyone."

I was scared. What the hell was going on here? I doubted the company that held my car note had sent these goons to rough me up for lack of payment.

I was wary, I was preparing to make the man with the stun gun pay dearly for his lack of judgment. He passed his buddy by and approached slowly. From my crouch I stood up and visibly relaxed, I may have even smiled.

"What's he doing?" the first man said as he rubbed his cheek.

"They said he might be a little crazy after his time on the ship. This'll fix him," he said, running a blue arc across the leads.

"You're fucked," I said, smiling. This was punctuated by a large 'Ooomph' and then clatter as skull met ceramic sink.

"What the hell?" Philly asked as he was thrust violently off the ground; his head making bone jarring contact with the ceiling. He was out cold before his body landed.

"I see you have made new friends," Dee said, I think with some amusement.

"I could have taken care of them," I told him.

"I see that now," Dee said.

"Are you smiling?"

"Possibly—what is this about?"

"I don't know. I came in here and then these two followed. But they were looking for me and they're working with someone else."

I started rifling through their pockets, not sure what I was going to find. Both had knives, the first guy had pepper spray and then a bunch of change. That was it.

"Did anyone see you come in here?" I asked Dee.

"I did not smell anyone."

"How did you know I was here?"

Dee pointed to his nose.

"Were you looking for me for a reason?"

"Your time grows short. I had wished to spend some of your last few hours here together."

"I understand the gesture, bad phrasing, though," I said. Dee was looking at me quizzically. "You make it sound final."

"No, the phrasing was correct," Dee said for clarification.

The door to the bathroom opened, Tracy looked in surveying the room quickly.

"What's wrong with you that you can't even go to the bathroom without causing a scene?"

I shrugged.

"What happened here?" she asked.

"Michael would not share his roll of toilet paper," Dee said with a straight face.

My face dropped before I started laughing. My gut hurt so bad, I thought I was going to pull a muscle. Dee started a heavy snorting. I don't think I had ever heard a Genogerian in a full out hearty laugh.

"Great, Michael, as an emissary to the entire planet Earth you have taught our guests bathroom humor." Tracy turned to leave. "I'll get some guards."

I stopped long enough to tell her to get men she trusted.

After another full five minutes of laughing and the removal of my attackers. I headed to Paul's office where my would-be way-layers were being taken.

"You coming?" I asked Dee.

Dee composed himself quickly as if the matter had never happened. "Indeed."

The two men were sitting in front of Paul's desk. Smelling salts had just been administered, but both looked a bit groggy and blood was still flowing freely from the head of the one that had met the sink intimately.

"Who do you two work for?" Paul asked when he was reasonably confident that they were aware enough.

"When do we get our lawyer?" Philly, the man who had crashed into the ceiling asked.

"No, lawyer, but I'll promise a priest," Paul answered the message clearly. They talked now or they would be killed as traitors.

"You've got nothing on us. We just wanted to see how tough he was. Would have kicked his ass, too, if his big green friend hadn't of interrupted."

"So you're just a couple of regular guys looking to have an honest fight, with a stun gun, mace and knives against a guy in a bathroom? Seems like a little bit of overkill to me," Paul asked.

Philly shrugged.

Paul pulled out his pistol and placed a round in the man's knee. His screams far outdid the echo of the round being fired in the small room.

"Oh shit, oh geez, oh shit!" CIA said, coming to full

awakening. He was struggling against his handcuffs to get free. "You can't do that, we have rights!"

"That's where you're wrong. You don't have shit anymore" Paul said, putting his pistol back in its holster.

The screams of the second man subsided, but he was turning a deathly pale from pain and shock.

"Do you want medical attention?" Paul asked him calmly.

I could tell the man wanted to pull that stoic shit and give Paul a last act of defiance, but the pain and the fear of death were too great. He nodded quickly. "Please," he whispered.

"Information first," Paul said, sitting on the corner of his desk.

"Come on, man, he said he would talk. Just get him some help," CIA said. "I'll tell you whatever you want to know!"

Paul quickly pulled his pistol from his holster and leveled it on the man's forehead. "Shut up. One more word from you and I will splatter your brains on the wall behind you."

I moved to the side. I didn't think the people doing laundry would be able to get brain out of my clothes. CIA just about swallowed his lips. Philly was close to fainting.

"Better hurry up before you pass out," Paul said. "You fall asleep now and there will be no waking up."

"Alright, alright," the man said with great difficulty. "There was a man...he said he'd get us out of here and set up in a safe place if we got him the man that killed his brother." Man Two passed out.

"Get him help," his friend begged.

Paul waved to one of the guards to get a doctor.

"Where's this man reside?" Paul asked the first man, who was still busy looking at his friend for signs of life. Paul pressed the warm barrel of the pistol against his forehead. That got his attention quick.

"Hous-housing quarters seventeen, section eleven, room fourteen."

"Take a couple more men with you," Paul told the remaining guard.

I did an involuntary shudder, I killed at least a dozen or so men—any one of them could have had a brother, but odds were on one and one alone.

"Mike?" Paul asked with concern, looking over at me.

"It can't be. I mean the odds would be astronomical, but I can feel it. I know it…it has to be Durgan's brother."

"Fates are funny this way, Michael. They have a tendency to throw related events together no matter how improbable," Dee said.

"He's a philosopher," I told Paul. "I feel it and yet I still doubt it. To think that Durgan's brother was even in the same city as me seems absurd, much less that he is here now in this secured location. It can't be but it is, there's something way more insidious going on here."

"No, hold on, Mike. It's not really as far-fetched as you might be thinking," Paul said, thankfully reaching for reason. "So Durgan is at that concert, odds are he was from Colorado."

"Fair enough," I said, seeing his thread.

"So if he lived there, then there's no reason to think that his family didn't also."

"Except he was an asshole and I'd think they'd want to get as far away from him as possible."

"Can I finish?" Paul asked.

"Go ahead," I told him. I had made a valid point, however.

"We were not covert in our recruiting. There's a good chance his brother wanted answers as bad as any one of us."

"Why now and why send two henchmen?"

"Don't know about the 'why now' part; maybe he caught wind of you leaving and wanted to get his chance while he could.

"Great, kill me before I die. Wonderful."

"You know what I mean," Paul said. "And maybe he sent a couple of goons because you would have recognized him."

"You think *crazy* runs in the family?" I asked.

"He did send two men to kidnap you," Dee said.

"Maybe he just wanted to thank me for ending that bat-shit crazy brother's life," I said.

"Doubtful," Dee said.

"You're probably right," I answered.

The doctor pushed past me to get to the bleeding man. I had completely forgotten about him. The doctor looked scornfully at Paul.

"Accidental discharge, Doc. Fix him up as best you can. Don't spend too much time on him. Cut the leg off if you have to."

Man One passed out.

"If this man survives and is out of immediate danger I want him in the brig," Paul told the returning guard.

The doctor had a medical team and a gurney and was extracting his patient when the radio on Paul's desk came to life.

"Sir, we have a situation down here in general housing."

Paul grabbed the walkie off his desk. "Elaborate."

"Sir, the man you sent us to pick up says he has a bomb. He says it's big enough to take out a fair portion of the Hill and make a big enough tremor that the aliens would notice."

"Can anyone put a bullet in his brain?" Paul asked.

"Sir, we do not have a visual on him."

"Shit. I'll be right down."

"Sir, one more thing. He says he will come out peacefully if Michael Talbot comes here personally."

"Of course he did," I said in the background.

"Tell him to go fuck—" Paul started.

I put my hand up. "Don't do that, Paul. If he's got the bomb he'll use it."

"Belay that, Sergeant," Paul said in the radio. "We'll be right down. Can you evacuate the area?"

"No, sir, he said if heard anything like that he would detonate," the sergeant said.

"Sergeant, what's your gut say? Does he have an IED?" Paul asked.

"I know the man, sir. He's in munitions, my educated guess would say 'yes'."

"We're on our way. Out." Paul opened the cylinder of his revolver and replaced the spent cartridge with a new one.

"What about him?" I asked Paul, pointing to the passed out man.

Paul pulled back the hammer on his pistol and put it up against the man's eye. The man did not stir.

I could tell Paul was contemplating putting a bullet in him, I had never seen Paul so cold in my life. I thought I had spread my humanity thin, Paul's was hardly present.

"He's out, I'll deal with him later," Paul said.

I relaxed. There's not much I won't do for the preservation of the lives of those I loved, including myself, but killing a passed out handcuffed man was not on that list, I hoped.

"Corporal," Paul said as we headed into the anteroom, speaking to his attaché.

"Yes, sir."

"Make sure that piece of shit is out of my office and in the brig when I get back."

"Yes, sir."

***

The hallway was cramped with armed personnel, guns all trained on absolutely nothing. It was quiet but it was tense all the same. The thought of death by explosion was weighing heavily on every man and woman present.

"What's his name?" Paul asked the Sergeant as we came up.

"Dunner, sir," the sergeant answered, never taking his eyes off the closed door. I guess he figured if he kept a visual, the unthinkable wouldn't be able to happen.

"Really, Dunner and Durgan?" I said aloud. "Their parents couldn't get any more original than that?"

The sergeant looked back at me, he seemed a little perturbed.

"Dunner, this is General Ginson. I'd like to have a word with you," Paul stated loudly.

"Hello, General, nice of you to join my party. But I only invited one person and if he doesn't show I will be so distraught I'll just have to destroy everything."

"Sure sounds like his brother," I said softly to Dee.

Dee nodded in reply.

"Michael Talbot is here," Paul said. "Why don't you come out and say what you have to say?"

"The little fuckwad is here? I didn't think he'd have the balls!"

"I get that a lot."

"Not now, Mike," Paul said to me tensely.

"Sorry, I'm a little nervous right now."

"We all are," he said.

"I am not," Dee added for good measure.

"Send him up here!" Dunner yelled.

"I don't think that's how this is going to happen," Paul answered.

"I'm making the rules around here now, General!" Dunner screamed.

"Blow the place up, then. Because if you're in charge, it's already over," Paul answered calmly.

I wanted to ask Paul why he was egging the crazy man on.

"I'll do it!" Dunner screamed.

I truly believed he would too. I think he was squeezing up enough crazy juice.

"Your brother was an asshole!" I yelled.

"Talbot?" Dunner asked.

"Dickwad present and accounted for," I answered back.

"I didn't think you'd show. I couldn't imagine you'd risk your precious hide now that you walk on water," Dunner said.

"When did you learn how to do that?" Dee asked in earnest.

"What do you want, Dunner?" I asked.

"I want you to pay for what you did to my brother."

"He was a psychotic madman who needed to be put down like a rabid dog!" I yelled.

Paul looked at me like he wanted to know why I was egging the crazy man on now.

"I miss him," Dunner said. "And now we can all join him."

"Whoa—wait!" I yelled stepping forward. Dunner was planning on detonating the bomb when I was in range. "What kind of satisfaction is that gonna be for you?"

"What are you talking about?" he asked.

"I mean, if I walk on water, it's safe to assume where I'll be going and we all know that suicide is a mortal sin so we know where you'll be headed. How are you two planning on kicking my eternal ass if you're nowhere around?" I asked.

"Huh?" he asked. "I didn't mean you walk on water like Jesus Christ, asshole!"

"Are you a believer, Dunner?" I asked.

"Baptist, through and through!" he yelled proudly.

"Of course you are," I said calmly. "Even dumbass Baptists like yourself know if you kill yourself, you get a one-way pass to damnation."

Dunner paused, I think we could all hear the cogs in

his brain meshing together, trying to reason out what he should do now. "I would really like to kill you," he finally said.

"Get in line," I told him.

I moved a step closer to his room, if he blasted the damn thing, I wanted to be as close as possible, I could hear movement in the room and then I heard his door handle turn. Thirty rifles came to bear.

"I'm coming out, but before any of you pansies gets the wrong idea, I have the bomb on a fifteen minute timer and I can guarantee nobody in this base is qualified to disarm it in that amount of time. I am going to have a little one-on-one time with my new friend. If he bests me, I will give him the code. If he doesn't, then all of your deaths will be on his head and my God will absolve me of any wrongdoing."

"I don't think that's really how it works," I said.

His door swung inwards, my face flushed, and I involuntarily took a couple of steps backward, Durgan stepped through the door.

"You're dead," I said, softly pointing at him.

"We're twins—who's the dumbass now?"

I wanted to tell him that it was still him, but I was having great difficulty forming words with my mouth hanging open. As my mind raced to catch up, I began to notice subtle differences between the two; Dunner was maybe twenty to twenty-five pounds lighter and although he was crazy, the torch of insanity didn't burn quite as bright within him.

"Mike, I can kill him, we'll take our chances with the bomb," Paul said.

That sounded like an incredibly awesome plan at the moment.

Dunner ignored it completely. "I was supposed to go to that concert with him. Ended up in jail for a domestic dispute."

"Imagine that," I said, still backing up warily.

"We would have been unbeatable in those games together."

Games? Funny, I never thought of them as games. I didn't have the heart or enough moisture in my mouth to tell him the aliens probably would have squared them off against each other for the mere sport of it. And something tells me they both would have tried to do the other in.

"I've watched you since you've come back, and I still can't figure out how a spindly little fuck like yourself took my brother down. Best I can figure is that you drugged him."

"Yeah, we were in the sauna together and I slipped him a mickey," I said as my back came in contact with the wall behind me. My survival instinct kept me from turning and looking. Whiplash fast, Dunner struck.

I deflected his right-hand roundhouse with my left arm. The force of it still sent me to the ground.

"You ain't shit!" he screamed. "My brother was five times the man you are, there's no reason he shouldn't have killed you!" Rage-fueled spittle flew everywhere. "And I'm twice the man he was, so this oughtta be pretty easy!" he said as he advanced on me.

"Mike?" Paul shouted.

"Not yet, Paul," I said, standing back up. "Get some people in there though and see if there is a bomb, because if there isn't I would rather you just shoot him."

Dunner smiled. "Bet you'd like that, because you're chicken shit. That's the only way you could have beat him."

Dunner rushed me again, I slammed a fist into his cheek. It was pretty much like hitting a rhino with a fly swatter. He grabbed me around the waist and had me suspended in the air. I knew this was going to hurt badly as he drove me to the floor. The thin commercial carpeting did little to shield me from the brunt of the concrete underneath. All of the breath had been knocked out of me and I was paralyzed for a moment with pain.

Dunner stood up to admire his handiwork. "Shit, my

woman used to put up more of a fight than you, you fucking pussy."

I noticed he had a rug burn on his knuckles from our encounter so far; at least I had caused some damage. I was wincing with pain, but still able to get the understanding that yes indeed there was a bomb attached to a timer in Dunner's room as Paul nodded sternly in my direction a scowl lining his features. I slowly stood, taking in small breaths, each one sending electrifying shocks of pain down my spine.

"Didn't think you'd get back up," Dunner said, looking over to me.

"Glutton…for…punishment," I whispered.

He started coming toward me again.

"Wait, one second," I begged. "Just in the off-chance I win, how will I get the code?"

"Not that I think there's a chance but…" Dunner walked over to me quickly, I'm ashamed to say I flinched badly. He laughed as he got close to my head and whispered, "Five-two-zero," in my right ear. "Now before you go getting all smart and thinking you can run away and tell them the code, that's only the first three numbers out of four and you only get two chances to get it right before the failsafe kicks in."

One-in-five still sounded like better odds than me beating this guy in a fight.

"You ready?" he asked, stepping back a pace.

"No," I told him honestly.

He smirked before he bull-rushed me again. I was more prepared this time as I moved slightly to my left, his head missed my gut, but his right arm wrapped around me as I brought my left knee up into his nose. He immediately let go and went a few steps past. He whipped his head up, blood flowing freely from his damaged sniffer. His eyes were watering like lawn sprinklers.

"Fucker!" he shouted.

I wasn't Dunner; I saw no need to talk when an

opportunity presented itself. I turned to deliver a hard punch to his now tender spot. He saw it coming and turned just enough that it hit his cheek. Something snapped, either my hand or his cheekbone. My hand was throbbing, but he was howling in pain and rage.

I was about to move in for a more decisive blow, but he lashed out with a roundhouse kick that would have taken my head off if I hadn't ducked. He still caught the top of my dome, sending me off target. I wouldn't have thought he had the room for that maneuver. I would've thought wrong. And more importantly for the last time.

"Like that?" he asked as blood ran across his snarling teeth. "My brother never saw the benefit in it, but I'm a black belt in karate."

"My lucky day," I told him, looking for an opening.

He got into a classic Bruce Lee pose; he even did the finger 'come hither' move. I'd seen the movie, I didn't 'come hither'. I'd seen what had happened to Chuck Norris.

He did the gesture again. I did my own and gave him the finger. He charged me again, he might have known martial arts, but anger was clouding his judgment. I moved faster this time, getting my foot out as fast as I could, he nearly tripped over my extended appendage, his head mere inches from crashing into the cement wall in the hallway. He put his hands up just in time to keep from crushing his skull. I turned and kicked the back of his knee, collapsing his leg so he was halfway down. My next kick hit his exposed rib cage. I laid every ounce of my body weight into that and was rewarded with a sound more akin to dry branches snapping on a cold winter day.

Before I could revel in my win, Dunner righted his ship and was once again standing and facing me. A glimmer of a grimace crossed his face, but otherwise he looked fairly intact.

"I didn't think you had it in you," he said much more warily and with much less swagger in his voice. "My brother was an asshole." He coughed, the grimace came back with a vengeance. "But he was my brother." Dunner had been playing possum, he launched at me, his fist caught the side of my neck as I twisted away. I felt like someone had taken a baseball bat to me. If he had hit my Adam's apple, I was pretty sure he would have killed me.

I punched him hard in his already damaged side, my fist sunk much deeper than it should have. Dunner dropped to his knees.

"It's over," I said, making sure I was out of range of his arms.

"For all of us."

"You promised the rest of the code if I beat you," I told him.

"I never promised, and I'm as big an asshole as my brother. You've got no chance of getting that last digit from me."

"How much time on the counter?" I asked out loud to the sergeant who had gone into Dunner's room to verify its existence.

"Four minutes, thirty seconds," was his reply.

"Evac everyone as far from here as possible," I said

Paul issued a couple of commands and residents began to scurry for their lives. Paul came up to me. "He won't give the code?"

I shook my head. Paul didn't hesitate as he put a bullet through the man's forehead.

"Holy shit, Paul!" I said.

"I didn't think you had it in you," Paul said to me. "The fight, I mean. I really thought he was going to tear you apart."

"I've had a lot of practice," I told him, still staring at the body that had been Dunner. A spreading pool of blood was blossoming around his head. "And I could say the same about you."

"This man threatens our very existence. I feel nothing

for him. I feel worse for the personnel that will have to clean this mess up."

"Sir, there's a keypad for entering a stop code, should I try it?" the sergeant asked. "We're down to three minutes."

"Whoa, hold on," I told him, "He gave me the first three digits."

"You sure about that?" Paul asked. "Because if this place goes up, I would rather you weren't anywhere near. No matter what happens here, you could still stop the invasion."

"Let me try, Paul."

"Mike, you have to look at the bigger picture."

"Paul, I've got three out of four digits, just let me try. We get two tries."

"And then?"

"We run like hell," I told him.

I quickly went into the room. The bomb was ticking down just like you've seen on a hundred different shows and movies, but it's much more intimidating when it's your body parts about to be dispersed.

"Alright, so he told me five-two-six. I'm thinking he won't have any repeating numbers, that leaves zero-one-three-four-seven-eight-nine, that's a two in seven shot of not blowing up."

"Are you talking to me?" Paul asked.

"Just trying to reason this out."

"We're down to two minutes, maybe you should reason quicker."

"That oughtta help," I told him.

"Just punch in a number," Paul said.

"It is true, Michael. Inaction is as bad as a bad action in this scenario," Dee said.

"Dee, don't you maybe want to find safer ground?" I asked him with my hand hovering over the pad.

"I am confident you will figure this out," Dee said, picking up some of Dunner's possessions and looking at them as if he were at an estate sale.

I punched in five-two-six-zero. We were immediately rewarded with an ear piercing buzzing sound and thirty seconds wound off the clock. "Well, at least now it's a one in six shot," I said as sweat poured off my body. Maybe I could short it out with the salt water coming off of me. I had a good minute and fifteen seconds for that to happen.

"Mike, leave," Paul said.

"I didn't leave you in that car and I'm not leaving now," I said as I punched in five, two, six and my finger was hovering over the nine. I had made contact with the plastic when Dee turned calmly toward me and told me to stop. If a fly had landed on my finger it would have tipped the scale and the button would have been plunged.

"Got an idea?" I asked him, gingerly pulling my finger back.

Dee handed me Dunner's dog tags.

I grabbed them, not knowing what to think.

"Read them," he prodded.

"I'll be damned."

Thirty eight seconds left, I quickly but very, very precisely typed in a seven. The mechanism flashed red once, then green twice, and the timer shut down.

I'd seen closer times in the movies, but when you're living it, let's just say that it was entirely too close.

"What the hell happened?" Paul asked.

I handed him the dog tags.

"I'll be damned, it was his birthday."

"More likely, he was paying homage to his brother. Let's just be happy they shared the same date." I patted Paul on the back. "I'm going back to my room. Come on, Dee, we'll talk as we go."

"I would enjoy that," he said.

Dee and I ended up at the cafeteria. I got a coffee and Dee drank a V-8. It was his absolute favorite drink on the planet.

"I wish I was going with you, Michael," Dee said

after he downed a family-sized bottle of the liquid. I couldn't stand the stuff, there was just something about drinking something that thick that made me get queasy.

"It's not because you miss home, right?" I asked, sipping my coffee, angry that they did not have any of the iced variety.

"I never wish to be among Progerians again unless they were to have some great epiphany and wish to rejoin in the harmonies of all life. It would be for your safety alone that I would go."

"My safety? What makes you think I need any help?" I asked, not looking up from my coffee. I knew the folly of my question, plus I wanted to make sure I didn't burn my lip on the scalding brew.

"Michael, you cannot even go to relieve yourself without some form of problem arising. Trouble follows you around like children to an ice cream truck."

"Okay, how the hell would you even know what an ice cream truck is?"

"Your methods of deflection are immature. You try to steer the conversation away from what troubles you most."

"It's a defense mechanism, but I still don't know how you would know anything about that. So are you comparing me to the ice cream truck?"

Dee sighed heavily, it seemed a very human thing to do at the moment.

"Michael, the fate of three species rests on what happens tomorrow. I wish you would not be so cavalier about it."

"Dee, I'm so scared I can't even think about it for more than a few seconds. I can literally feel my mind doing all in its limited power to avoid the subject at all costs. I have wrapped those thoughts up and every time I try to wrap my mind around them they squirt right out and away. I don't want to think about it—what's the point? I have to do it. I have to try no matter the potential for disaster."

"That is a fair assessment. I did not think you were concerned at all. Do you think they have more of these?" Dee said holding his empty bottle up.

"I'm sure they can find one somewhere. I've got to go back to my room, it's been close to an hour and Tracy has got to be wondering where I've been off to.

"I'm going to stay here and meditate," Dee told me.

"Alright, my friend. Will I see you later?" I asked, but Dee was already in the early stages of his trance. "I'll take that as a maybe."

"You should get me another V-8 before you go."

"Nice," I told him sarcastically, although I did get him his drink.

I headed back to my room, thankful Beth hadn't somehow pulled another appearing act and was waiting for me somewhere along my path. I swear she had a tracer on me, probably residually attached to my heart strings.

I quietly opened the door to my room, a sleepy-eyed Tracy looked over at me. "That was quick, did you find out what those men wanted?" she asked before she rolled onto her side and back asleep.

CHAPTER SIXTY-SIX – Mike Journal Entry 23

After all the commotion of the previous evening, the following day had been calmer than I could have hoped for. Tracy and I spent the majority of the morning in bed. To say we made bliss that morning would not give what happened between us justice.

I fell asleep for what seemed moments. I had no sooner closed my eyes when Tracy was shaking me awake. She was already in her BDUs.

"Any chance I missed the bus?" I asked her.

"Get up," she said, pursing her lips. She was less than enthusiastic about my latest endeavor.

I got out of bed slowly, my body ached and for a moment I had forgotten why.

"You're getting old," Tracy said as she strapped on her belt and pistol.

"I feel it today," I told her as the memories flooded back.

I'd let her have her barb. I saw no reason to clue her in on the events of the previous evening, although she'd find out soon enough. Paul had dismissed her after she and the guards had deposited my bathroom waylayers at Paul's office. If she knew, she'd probably just knock me out, stick me under the bed, and tell the general I had gone AWOL.

Paul was coming up the hallway just as Tracy and I

exited. His face looked hardened, it softened a bit when he saw me. I think I had caught him unawares and he had not enough time to put his true game face on.

"How you doing, buddy?" he asked me.

My initial response was to tell him I felt like I was walking the Green Mile, but none of the three of us would see the humor. "Fine," was all I could muster without lying or making some bad analogy.

"No problems from last night?" he asked.

Tracy had been lost in her own thoughts, but not so deep she didn't pick up on Paul's words. "What happened last night?"

"You didn't tell her?"

"No, and I wasn't planning on it," I told Paul more than a little bit angry.

"What happened last night?" Tracy asked.

"Nothing really," I told her, knowing full well that approach wasn't going to work.

"More than what happened after the bathroom incident?" she asked with alarm.

"Mike almost blew up the entire installation." Paul said evenly.

"Paul! You're not helping," I said. He was merely smiling. I turned to Tracy, she had the look that said she was waiting for a more lengthy explanation.

"Fine."

As we walked to the eastern exit, I related the events of the entire evening. Tracy looked appalled and relieved. She could not believe she had missed it. "How would you have known?" I asked her.

"Still."

I had just finished up when we finally came to our destination. Besides the two guards there were only Dee and Urlack. The absence of Dennis was an acute pain I would not soon get over.

"I will see you soon, my friend," Dee said, grasping

my hands in his.

"Do you truly believe that?" I asked him.

"I want to," he said honestly.

"That's good enough for me," I told him.

"I will see you soon, my love, and I believe it completely," Tracy said as she kissed me.

Paul grabbed my hand. "To another adventure, my friend."

"I'll be happy when I can retire," I told him. He laughed.

"Time grows short," Urlack said, all business.

The door swung open, the fresh air helping to sweep away my anxieties. "Lead on," I told him. In hindsight, probably a poor choice of words. Urlack took off at a pace I think was challenging the current land speed record.

I was exhausted when we came to the outskirts of the new alien encampment in Roslindale, my previous night's smack-down and subsequent lack of sleep were taking their toll. Urlack on the other hand, even with his healing injuries, looked like he was ready to take on the world.

He turned to face me. "You ready?" he asked.

For a long, lingering moment, a crevice of doubt formed in my gut, replaced by a fissure of fear. What the fuck was I doing? I was willingly delivering myself and my people's location into the hands of the enemy. I cannot even convey how close I was to pulling my service revolver from its hidden location and putting a bullet in Urlack's eye.

"As ready as I'll ever be," I told him instead. He looked at me, confused. He did not understand what I had told him. "Yes," I said, answering the question less circumspectly.

"You will need to stay as close behind me as possible so as to shield your silhouette from any Progerians," Urlack told me.

"Any chance of a piggyback ride?" I asked him, my feet where killing me.

Even though I'm about ninety-eight percent sure Urlack had no idea what a 'piggyback' ride was, he scoffed at me. I really think that he did not appreciate my lackadaisical demeanor. Or at least what he supposed was lackadaisical, my guts felt like they were hopped up on espresso and I had shot-gunned a couple cans of Mountain Dew for good measure and marinated it in Jolt.

I stayed as close as possible to Urlack without tripping him up, I generally kept my head down, figuring wrongly that if I didn't look around, no one else would look at me. That was an incorrect assumption, as I dared to gaze around my eyes met more and more stares from the Genogerians. To say I was unnerved would be as big an understatement as saying that World War Two was just a misunderstanding.

Urlack walked up and into a fighter as if he owned the thing, the Genogerians guarding the area made sure to look like they were busy doing anything but watching the machine. I looked up at Urlack as he got into his seat. *This is too easy*, I was thinking. There was no way we could just walk up to a ship and steal it. Alarms began to go off in my head, I felt like a rabbit as the snare snapped on my leg.

"Where am I going to sit?" I asked, looking at the single-seated cockpit. What else could I do now?

"On my lap," he said without a hint of merriment.

"Are you kidding me? I'm not six and you sure don't look like Santa."

"We have approximately sixty seconds to get off the ground before the Progerians know something is amiss."

I looked around wildly trying to find the best avenue of escape. I was deep in the enemy trenches. If I sprinted for it now, someone would shoot me. My only chance now was to go up with Urlack. I felt hopelessly, helplessly trapped. I couldn't have put myself in a bigger bind if I had tried.

"We must leave now, hu-man," Urlack hissed.

His reverting back to the derogatory did little to appease me, but up I went. "Don't go getting any ideas," I told him.

"Sit back so I can see properly."

"This is a lousy first date," I told him as the fighter took off straight up.

For a moment, I thought the gravitational forces were going to meld myself and Urlack into some new species of mammal and amphibian. I could feel the fillings in my teeth shifting as we gained more speed and more velocity.

"I am sorry for the discomfort that your delicate frame must be experiencing but this is the only way I can keep the targeting system in the base from getting a fix on our location and destroying us."

Right now that seemed like a reasonable alternative rather than having my internal organs compressed into wafer thin versions of themselves.

And then, blessedly, it was over. I went from feeling like a cartoon character being steamrolled to my face sticking against Urlack's window. A big meaty paw dragged me back down.

"Hold on to my seat belt," he said.

"What about the ship? Won't they be targeting us?" I asked, not fully taking into account all of the variables in this mission. But that's usually my problem anyway, go charging in first, guns a blazing and try to figure a way out second.

"That will be taken care of," Urlack said cryptically.

"Comforting," I told him.

He didn't say anything for hours as we came closer to the massive ship even the syllable or two he spoke had dried up, but I'd been around Dee long enough to know that Urlack was stressed out. His large maw was partially opened and his residual (vestigial) second eyelid was closed.

"You sure about the guns?" I asked again.

"I told you it should be taken care of," he said tersely.

"No, you never said 'should be' you said 'will be'.

Big difference."

"What does Drababan see in you?" Urlack asked.

"It's my winning personality."

"Stop chattering like a *Fraterdsnip!*"

I didn't know what a 'fraterdsnip' was, but I figured easily enough that wasn't a flattering term. I did shut up, but it did little to put me at ease.

"Fighter 312, this is Home Base. Identify yourself and your intentions or we will be forced to destroy you," came over the monitor in Urlack's ship.

We watched as a squadron of fighters were dispatched from the mother ship.

"Look, an escort," I told Urlack. "You going to answer? They seem serious."

The intercepting fighters were getting closer.

"I had not expected them to send fighters. They will see you."

"You come millions of light years to come and destroy our planet and you guys can't tint your windows?"

"Tint? Color the windows? We do have sun shields."

"I'm thinking now might be a good time to use those shields."

"That should be adequate," Urlack answered.

"You can thank me later," I told him. I was wondering if there was enough room down by his feet to hide. The fighters were approaching like a hive of angry hornets and we had just tweaked the Queen's ass. "You might want to respond to the ship, too," I said, prodding him further.

"I think you are right again," Urlack simply stated. "*Julipion* this is fighter 312. This is traitor Urlack Evertrek and I am surrendering so that I may restore my honor."

"I'm not sure I would have gone with the whole honesty part," I told him.

And then my blood froze solid. Urlack flipped the switch so he could talk to the ship again. "I have captured the human Michael Talbot."

"You motherfucker!" I spat.

I moved away so I could put some leverage behind a punch. A powerful arm of Urkack's trapped me against the windshield. I was stuck like a pinned butterfly. I swung uselessly against an arm that could have been hewed from oak.

"Calm down," Urlack said. "I am doing what is right."

"You piece of shit, you come promising peace and deliver disaster."

I was subdued as our escorts circled us and guided us through the large bay doors. It appeared as if half of the entire Genogerian guard force was there along with some high-ranking Progerians.

All the fight drained out of me. Urlack might as well have been holding a wet sock. All I had to look forward to now was life in the arena until I died, maybe I'd make a mad dash for the Supreme Commander and just get cut to ribbons by rifle fire. It would be less painful and much quicker.

We landed without incident. I had hoped Urlack would skid into a structural support beam so we could burst into flames and I could push his traitorous eyes into the back of his head while we both burned.

"When we get out, you will stand on the wing and I know it will be difficult for you, but project as much strength as you can," Urlack told me.

"Why, so you can say how hard it was to capture me? You did nothing except lie. I walked into your trap. It couldn't have been any easier."

"Do as I say," Urlack demanded. His maw was open even farther, which indicated his hyper level of stress.

Urlack pushed me up and over as his canopy pulled back. I walked onto the wing and nearly into the waiting arms of a Genogerian as my heart was tripping over itself. My extremities, now leaden and dead.

Urlack stood on his pilot's seat. "My fellow Genogerians!" he yelled. "I bring you the Earth Champion, Michael Talbot."

A pin dropping would have been welcome to the ensuing silence. I watched as the confused heads of some of the Progerians swung back and forth, trying to figure out what was going on.

"The hu-man that has bested all of his kind in the games. The hu-man that launched the first successful escape from any Progerian vessel."

I didn't know if that was the right approach, a lot of Genogerian guards had died during our escape and I had a hell of a lot of help from a nuclear bomb.

"The hu-man that has befriended our great Genogerian champion Drababan."

Now there was an increased murmuring among the throng.

"Yes Drababan is not dead, he has seen something in this one hu-man that made him leave his former life behind so that he could stay on earth and become a freedom fighter."

The murmuring increased.

The Progerians were no dummies, they knew something was up. "Guards seize them!" one of them shouted from his perch a level up on a catwalk.

I saw some of the Genogerians advance, most were held back by their peers.

"This hu-man Michael Talbot has promised us peace and a place on his planet to foster our own beliefs and to live a life unhindered by cruel masters."

Any and all murmuring ceased completely.

I didn't think it was really 'my planet' to be making those kind of decisions, but I wasn't going to correct him now.

"Shoot them!" the same Progerian said. He knew what was happening, even if those around him were a little slow in the realization that this was the dawning of a revolution.

"You have been slaves long enough!" Urlack shouted forcibly.

A blue shot streaked by my face; the shooter was clubbed down by those around him. If it was possible, I now felt even more exposed. There would always be those who were comfortable with their lot in life and would fear change with every beat of their hearts, I could sympathize with the Geno that had tried to kill me, up to a point.

I didn't say a word as Urlack surveyed his brethren. I was fairly certain anything I said would not be the right thing. I watched in amazement as about a dozen or so Genogerians ran up to the catwalk and rounded up the five Progerians staged there.

"Is that it?" I asked Urlack. "That sure seemed easy." And as if my words had shattered the illusion, all hell broke loose as klaxons raged.

"What's happening?" I screamed, placing my hands over my ears.

"Someone is preparing to open the airlocks!" Urlack shouted as he dropped from the fighter and headed for the doors. I followed him; no way was I staying up there by myself. Any one of the Genos could have been hungry.

Urlack finally got to his destination, an oversized keypad. He typed in a series of commands and then came blissful silence as the alarms stopped.

"Manual override," Urlack said to me. If I hadn't known better, I would have sworn I saw sweat on his brow. The Genogerians were milling around, they didn't know what to do. Their entire lives had been dictated by a master. One minute of freedom would not be able to undo all of that.

"*Go!*" Urlack shouted. "Demand your freedom and take it from those that will not give it to you willingly! Spread the word to your clansmen, you all know who your opposition will be. If they will not surrender you must kill them!"

"Will the Progerians fight? I didn't think they liked to get their hands dirty."

"This fight is far from finished, Michael Talbot. The innermost portion of this ship is heavily guarded...first by a ring of Genogerians that have been genetically altered to be the biggest and fiercest of our kind."

I did not want to think of a bigger, meaner version of the brutes. They were already fodder enough for nightmares. "Won't they want to join the revolution?" I asked naïvely.

"No," he answered without even pondering the question. "They were bred specifically for the purpose of guarding their 'superior' masters. They can achieve no higher honor than to die in their defense. They have training, superior fire power and position."

"We have the numbers right?"

"We have the numbers, but even then I do not know if it is enough. Because even if we get past them we come to the last and most lethal defense."

"You're kidding, right?"

"Kidding? Does that mean to procreate? I do not see how the reference fits."

"Sorry, what does this next circle of hell entail?"

"Hell?"

"What's after the mutant Genogerians?"

Urlack still looked confused, but he seemed to understand what I was asking. "The elite Progerian Guard. They have studied the art of fighting since they were yearlings. They used to be allowed to fight in the games but they dominated to the point where no one would bet against them."

"They volunteered? For the games?"

"They were bored," he answered.

I looked back at the fighter and a ride back to Earth. "Today's as good a day as any other to die," I told Urlack.

"That's the spirit, hu-man," Urlack said as we descended farther into the ship and deeper into the pits of hell.

"Why all the defenses, Urlack? I would think your Progerian masters would believe to have the Genogerians completely subdued."

"We have many enemies among the stars, hu-man."

"Yeah, that's what happens when you take stuff that doesn't belong to you."

"Your anger is misdirected. I am of the same mind as you, remember?"

"Sorry," I told him.

There was the sound of sporadic shots being fired, but it could have been celebratory. Even though Genogerians really didn't seem the festive kind, I couldn't really imagine a band of them festooned in beads at *Mardi Gras*.

"It is good to see you smile in the face of death," Urlack said. "It is the true sign of a warrior."

I was in no way going to let him know what had brought the grin to my face, he might retract his statement. As we swept deeper into the ship, we began to come across casualties.

"Any chance these are the Genogerian guards you spoke of?" I asked.

"No, these are the poor souls that do not believe we can ever be set free, and fight blindly to preserve their present life no matter how dismal it is."

"Kind of like Yankees fans," I replied, and my insane grin grew wider.

"Perhaps. Although I do not know what Yankees fans are."

"You're better off," I told him, and left it at that. I grabbed the downed Geno's rifle and felt immediately better.

Now it was beginning to sound like a battle as we approached the chow hall. Screams of rebuke, betrayal, and pain emanated from the open doors.

Urlack put out his arm, barring my way. "I think it would be best if you did not go in there. You would most likely die."

"Can the rifles kill you, Urlack?" I asked.

"Most assuredly," he answered.

"Then what advantage do you have over me in there?" I asked.

"If you fall, the Genogerians might not be so willing to die," he stated.

"I think you overplay my importance, Urlack. I think they are fighting for their freedom. And if what you say is so true, how much would the Genogerians rally if they realized I was fighting alongside them?"

Urlack thought about it for a moment. "Your words are valid, but I will go in first and you will do your best to stay behind me."

"Sure. Whatever," I said it with sarcasm, but since Urlack really had no clue what that was, I would plead ignorance later, if there were to be a later.

Blue tracers arced across the room amidst all the fighting I was having a hard time distinguishing one set of Genos from the other. As I began to control my breathing, I took well-aimed shots. I began to discern that not only were the uniforms of the mutant Genos different, they were much bigger, and nowhere was this more evident when a standard Genogerian got too close and now found himself in hand-to-hand combat with the mutant. It wasn't quite the size disparity from Geno to human, it was more like a teen Geno to a fully matured adult. The regular Geno put up a good fight, but it was clear he was outmatched. My shot hit the mutant high along its skull plating, peeling back the thick hide and exposing the bone-white skull before it was flooded over with blood.

The Geno I had saved looked over to me and perhaps nodded his appreciation and immediately thrust his long knife into the throat of the mutant before it could recover from the damage I had inflicted. The fighting was fierce, and the Genogerians took some serious casualties, but within twenty minutes, all of the mutants had been killed. To a being, each had stayed and fought until its death. Not one ran or surrendered.

"Well, that is the opening salvo," Urlack said, standing tall.

"Apparently, that's not all of them?" I asked dismayed.

"No, they rotate by platoon to the feeding hall."

"This was a platoon?" I asked.

I looked over the carnage, a full twenty mutant Genos were dead, but close to fifty regular Genos were dead or dying and another thirty or so injured and we had a huge element of surprise. Next time we wouldn't be so lucky.

"We cannot sustain these types of losses," Urlack said, summing up everything I was wondering. "They will dig in now."

"Does the ship itself employ any type of defensive measures, Urlack?" I asked. "Can they electrocute hallways or shut off life support systems or anything along those lines?"

"If they felt all was lost, they have at their disposal a self-destruct mode."

"Great. Another bomb. Not a big fan of bombs, Urlack."

"Not a bomb. They would pilot the ship to the nearest atmosphere, so it would destroy itself."

"Don't see how that's much better."

"It is not. They would both lead to our deaths."

I thought for a moment how long it was before Dee began to catch on to how I communicated and then I wondered if Urlack and I would have that kind of time together.

"Should we get some Genogerians together who can act as leaders and begin to formulate some plans as to how we can take this ship over? Are all the Genogerians even aware that a rebellion is happening?" It was amazing how quickly that second question was solved for me. I would have liked to thank the Progerians for their thoughtfulness in that matter.

Over the speakers that permeated the ship came the voice of a Progerian officer. "Genogerian soldiers, you are in direct violation of the Gesteindt Dictum that states all Genogerians will bow in deference to all Progerian commands. You will return to your barracks where you will await your deaths for your treasonous acts. Drop your weapons and honor the accord which your ancestors bowed to many millennia before."

Astounded, I watched as a fair number of Genogerians did just that. The clatter as multiple weapons fell to the floor was unnerving. Urlack's shoulders slumped as he realized that perhaps he had underestimated his allies. The rest that had not dropped their weapons now looked around confused; for something, for some sort of direction. They had been led for so long they knew no other way.

I jumped on a table and plowed three shots into the ceiling, never really thinking how incredibly stupid that was and hoping they didn't ricochet.

"Until now I had absolutely no idea how stupid you Genogerians are." I was not sure all of them understood my words, but it would have been impossible to not hear the derision in my tone. "Your freedom is within your grasp, yet you yield and meekly head back…to await your deaths, no less. I don't know why I ever feared you or your kind. You are among some of the most pathetic creatures we have ever encountered. *Go!* Go to your fucking bunks, maybe they'll let you live so you can fight on Earth! I hope so, because I can't wait to tell my fellow man how you really are big losers! It'll be my pleasure to shoot each one of you because, while my kind and I will be fighting for *our* freedom, you and your kind will be fighting because you were afraid to fight for your own!"

I was enflamed, my throat was hoarse with rage,

spittle arced from my mouth as I screamed. I could not believe the temerity of the beings!

Some stopped their progress back to their barracks; some openly growled and hissed at me. Some began to advance—they were mad—and now I was the focus of their attention.

"The next motherfucker that takes a step I will blast him into Geno Heaven, if there even is such a thing, and you can grovel at the feet of Gropytheon for your worthless souls!"

They stopped. I could see them asking among themselves how this outsider knew about the Heaven of their forbidden religion. More than a few pressed their palms to their foreheads. "If you fight and possibly die for what you believe in, those of you that survive will be able to believe in and pray to whomever you wish down on Earth. You will be able to raise your off-spring without the yolk of oppression."

"You speak the truth?" one of the closer Genogerians asked.

"I do," I told him.

"My name is Tantor. I wish to be part of this new world," he told me.

"You will have to fight for what you want, Tantor. Nobody, especially the Progerians, is going to give it to you."

Tantor snarled some harsh words that would make a German blush, the Genogerians came back and picked up their weapons.

"What'd he say?" I asked Urlack.

"He basically echoed your same words, with two added parts."

"I'm waiting."

"He told them to gather all the idiots that went back to their bunks and to make sure that no one eats you."

"Well, I feel worlds better."

"I would think so," Urlack said.

***

It was an hour later when we were all in one of the massive barracks that housed the Genogerians. It was immense. It was so vast, it curved out of sight. I sat on one of the large racks going over the paw drawn outline of the ship, not at all happy with what I was looking at. Attacking a medieval castle with nothing more than a slingshot would have been easier. There were layers upon layers of defenses set up.

"Urlack, Michael," Tantor said, damn near shredding my name. "There are ten thousand, two hundred forty-seven Genogerians aboard this ship that are in fighting ability. Although one thousand, two hundred twenty-six will not fight with us, they have given their word that they will not impede us, either."

"That's insane, they await their deaths if we lose and reap the benefits if we win with no bloodshed on their part," I said angrily.

"They will not leave here if we are victorious," Tantor said.

"They would rather die like sheep?" I asked him.

"I do not know what sheep are, but yes, they would rather die by the hands of their masters than do their masters any harm."

"Their funeral. That gives us around nine thousand Genogerians." The vast numbers of the Genogerians were already on earth most likely wreaking havoc. It was going to be difficult to convince the surviving humans down there that we were now allies, should we get to that point.

One thing at a time, I thought, trying to refocus on the task before me.

"How many mutants are there?" I asked Urlack.

"Easily seven thousand," he said.

I moaned softly. If we had the proportionate losses like we did in the feeding hall, we were done for.

"And the Progerian Elite?" I asked, heaping bad news on top of bad news.

"I do not think it is more than a thousand."

"Well, there's something! We have advantage in numbers!"

"There are still the two to three thousand Progerian pilots on board to deal with," Tantor added.

"Will they fight?" I asked Urlack.

"Perhaps, if they feel pushed to the wall. They do not know much of fighting beyond what their ship can do, though."

"What if we give them an out?"

Urlack waited for further clarification.

"Would they surrender over death?"

"I think perhaps they may be too haughty to surrender to Genogerians."

"Okay, let's suppose it wasn't Genos?"

"It would not be unheard of. They have surrendered before with the hopes that they will be freed later on by their superiors."

"And how does that go?"

"The Progerians are very protective of their own."

I sat and discussed my plan with Urlack and Tantor for a few more minutes. Even they seemed dubious with my thoughts, but unlike their counterparts on Earth they didn't completely rip them apart.

I stood outside the door leading to the officer's quarters. I still amazed myself each and every time I got into one of these predicaments, it was like I was playing Russian roulette with myself and the revolver was fully loaded. "Who does this shit?" I said aloud.

Tantor looked at me. "You are going in?" he asked.

"Want to trade places?" I asked. He started to move. "Just kidding, sorry," I said, placing my hand on his chest.

Urlack came over to the pad and entered the appropriate code. The door slid quietly open. I walked in alone—*like a lamb to the slaughter*—flashed across my mind. Progerian officers were milling about, they appeared to be trying to relax, but I could see traces of stress in their mannerisms. Besides being in a war with a planet of savages, they now had an open rebellion aboard their own ship.

"Hu-man, you cannot be here!" one of the Progerians said, rushing at me.

I leveled my rifle on him, my heart thudding in my chest. I felt like I was pointing a bb gun at a rhino.

"Hold on a moment," I told him, hoping my voice didn't crack.

He pulled up short. "What is the meaning of this?" he screamed in rage.

"Well, I would have thought it was pretty self-explanatory. I'm pointing a rifle at your midsection, and I can either blow a hole in you, or you can surrender."

"Surrender to a filthy hu-man?" he asked.

Now some of his pilot jockey friends were flanking him in a show of solidarity. I noted that none of them were armed, which made me feel only slightly better.

"Die then, it doesn't really make all that much difference to me," I said as I brought the rifle up to my shoulder.

"You cannot kill all of us before we overpower you," he said haughtily.

"No, but we can," Urlack said as I was forced forward from the influx of Genogerians.

"Urlack? You have truly betrayed your people? I thought it was lies from higher command because they did not like your heritage. I should have known that your weaker Genogerian traits would pull you down with them," the pilot spat.

Urlack did not rise to the barb, but I could tell he wanted to. "You are wrong, Betar, I do what I do for all of us. Genogerian, Progerian, and hu-mans—even if they are filthy."

"Hey," I said.

He continued. "For far too long we have enslaved the Genogerians to do all the work we have deemed menial or dangerous for the Progerian class. We have suppressed their beliefs, forced them to fight for our causes and entertainment. They grow weary of the burden we make them carry."

"They are meant to carry our burden. We are their masters," Betar spat.

I thought Tantor was going to blow a hole in him. "Hold on," I told him, "you do that and we'll probably have to kill them all and then we won't have a bargaining chip."

Somewhere deep inside, the words registered with Tantor, but he wasn't happy about it.

Another pilot spoke out. "They cannot fend for themselves. They need us to lead them. That is the way it is, the way it has always been."

"Only because you have forced us!" one of the Genogerians in the back spoke.

"Stop!" I yelled, blasting another hole in the ceiling. "Listen, we know the Progerians are not going to get over the biases they have built up their entire lives at this moment. If we stay here and debate, I know how this is going to end up—a lot of blood. I will ask again, Betar, as a representative of the planet Earth. My name is Michael Talbot." *Good, that got a murmuring of surprise from them.* "Will you surrender?" I asked, and at that moment, at least fifty Genogerian weapons came to bear.

I would have loved to have been able to turn around and see the impressive Geno display, but it was echoed in the shocked looks of the Progerians to my front. Betar was shaking with rage. I could see him rapidly weighing his diminishing options.

"Betar, your death will accomplish nothing," I said softly. I did not need to speak loudly to be heard, tension was the only thing filling the room and of course aliens.

"When my superiors crush this rebellion, you will be

the first one that I hunt down and kill," Betar said attempting to salvage some of his pride.

"You'll probably have to get in line," I told him.

"What…what does that mean?" he asked, angry and confused.

"He is saying there are plenty that want him dead, Betar, and if you want to accomplish that you will have to find your place among them," Urlack said.

"I will then!" he yelled.

"How have you conquered the stars without humor?" I asked. Nobody answered. "So I take it your surrendering?" I asked Betar.

***

I'll say this, the Genogerians were efficient. Within an hour, all of the pilots were housed in the gladiator cells.

"What now?" Urlack asked as we leaned against the far wall. A Progerian was glaring back at me through the force shield. I had made sure to move away from Betar's cell. His glares were beginning to burn holes in my insides.

"Are the men—I mean, Genos—in place?" I asked.

"They are," he answered.

"You know this is going to get messy, right?" I asked him.

"I did not know from watching the games that your kind were so squeamish," Urlack said. "There is no such thing as a clean rebellion. True change requires a steep price paid in blood."

"Wisely said, but there's something different about killing in the heat of battle and cold assassination."

"Death is death, Michael."

"I know that, too. I know what we need to do. The Mutes are buried in deep as a fat tick. To attack them head on would be our folly, but that only makes what we need to do next only marginally easier to swallow. Have your men linked into the ship's surveillance system yet?"

Urlack looked down at me with his head cocked to one side. I might have thought he looked somewhat cute; like a puppy if he was maybe one-eighth his present size.

"You must know, Michael, that it is not I that leads the Genogerians. It is you," he stated without a hint of malice. It was sort of a shock, I had never really thought about it. I guess it made some sort of weird sense, but it still left me a little bit dumbfounded. "And yes, we have tapped into the cameras. We have blocked their ability to watch us. Unless we want them to," he added at the end.

And we did want them to. That was the key to our plan.

"Well, let's get this show on the road then," I told Urlack, I wanted to hold my head high, but right then it seemed to weigh a thousand pounds. "Will this be two-way communication?" I asked.

"They will be able to reply over the ship's intercom system."

Urlack pointed a device at me that looked suspiciously like a toaster oven, but I guessed was their version of a handheld camcorder. Made sense. If theirs were as small as the ones we were using, they wouldn't be able to operate them.

"You are on," Urlack said.

"It would be nice if you had given me a countdown or something," I told him angrily.

"You are on," he repeated.

"Shit. Hello, Supreme Commander." I tried my best to not sneer. "My name is Michael Talbot."

"I am aware of who you are," blared over the speakers.

"Can we get that lowered?" I asked Urlack as I rubbed my left ear.

"Why are you not deceased?" the voice asked again, but at a much more pleasant volume.

"You could always come out and give it a go," I taunted.

I heard a hiss on the other side. Good, I was pissing him off, my specialty!

"We have your pilots locked up," I told the commander.

"I am well aware of that."

So he was not going to be forthcoming. "We demand the surrender of those that are resistant to the freedom of the Genogerians and the humans alike."

"Savages aligning with savages. I wouldn't have thought it possible. But your small victory in the feeding hall, at a high price I might add, has done little to alter the course of this vessel or its mission."

"Oh, I'm not so sure," I told him. "These pilots will not be able to fly anymore, and right about…" I waited for Urlack's signal which was taking longer than it should and ruining my dramatic build-up effect. He finally gave me a small bob of his head as he received some communication through his earpiece. "…now, you've lost communication with the planet."

"It is so," I heard someone telling the Supreme Commander.

"So, right now, you're probably thinking, worst case scenario, that you cannot be the first ship in your history to fall into the hands of the Genogerians. Sure, maybe a half hour ago you could have flown this ship right into the Earth, but since we have disengaged your drive, you are really kind of limping along in space right now."

"That is also so," came the bearer of bad news to the Supreme Commander again.

"This is not possible!" the Supreme Commander bellowed.

"Don't let your arrogance get the better of you. It *has* happened," I emphasized. "We are demanding your surrender."

The power on our deck flickered for a moment and then came back on.

"Life support," Urlack said. "They can shut down wherever they want."

"We can't get a hold of that?"

Urlack shook his head.

"Your pilots will die if you do that," I told the commander.

The commander eerily echoed my earlier words. "It would be the sacrifice of the few for the many."

"You cannot!" came another forceful voice. "The senate will hang us all!"

"And what will they do if we hand the ship over!" the commander said. There was some rustling, but I think it was more of a posturing than a scuffle.

This was not turning out exactly as I had planned. "Captured pilots, you have heard the words of your leader. He has deemed you as expendable. One of your own kind has left you to fend for yourselves while he has threatened to shut off the very air you breathe." I could hear some grumbling, but I thought the Progerians were probably in a bit of shock as they tried to assimilate the new information. "I will release any of you that decide to take your chances with us and fight." It was truly a long shot, and nobody had quite bitten, but my guess was that I'd get a few converts when the air began to thin.

Urlack let the toaster oven drop down. "They are coming," he said with as much inflection as if he were talking about the mailman. Urlack and I ran for the far end of the corridor where the Mutes would most likely hit first.

"We will be free soon, hu-man!" Betar shouted as we ran past his cell. "You will be in my stew for dinner."

I flipped him the bird as I went by. I didn't know if he understood the gesture, but he howled in anger all the same.

The firefight had begun, I could hear muffled explosions all around.

"Grenades?" I asked Urlack.

"They are actually your flash-bangs. One of our first reconnaissance patrols grabbed a box when they overran a police station. The Mutes have been making their own version and playing with them ever since."

"Playing?"

"They made them stronger and now see how many they can detonate at their feet before they are overwhelmed."

"Sounds like fun."

"It is not," Urlack said. "The concussion is strong enough to kill a man."

"Urlack, I think that you have a low estimate of just how strong we are."

"I am telling you, Michael, the concussion is strong enough to rearrange a man's internal organs. They die a terribly painful death."

Urlack wasn't speculating, he had witnessed it. I didn't want to know if it was a test or Mutes merely playing. Either way, I hated them and they would have to pay.

Intense fighting was concentrated to our front. We were still a good two hundred yards when a door to my left opened up. Not sure which of us was more surprised, the huge Mute who nearly fell over me or myself. Urlack put a round in its shoulder. I don't even think it noticed as it saw me tangled up in its legs.

My rifle was not going to be effective. I let it go, the sling kept it from dropping to the ground. I reached into my holster and pulled out the Colt. Urlack was hesitant to shoot as the Mute bent over to get at me. I twisted away from his hand as I placed the cold blue steel of the .45 against the exposed back of his knee. *No padding there*, I thought as I pulled the trigger.

Urlack jarringly extracted me from the Mute as he collapsed; a three-inch around hole blown into its knee pad. *Bet that fucking hurts*, I was thinking. But even with that crippling wound, it was still seeking to aim its weapon at me.

Urlack put a shot in its forehead. If it didn't die now, I was thinking of maybe joining their side. I was saved from that decision as it slumped to the floor.

"He sure is ugly," Urlack said.

He looked bigger sure, but they all looked ugly to me. Except Dee. And I was wishing he was with me right about now.

"Has the barracks been breached?" I asked Urlack.

The Genogerians were housed across the hallway from the Progerians combatants in the arena, that more than anything should have let the Genos know their station in life.

"Perhaps not. It is a large area to defend with not enough troops."

"Well, we can't let them get behind our guys," I said, heading into the barracks.

"Agreed," Urlack said as he waved a few Genos to come with us.

I didn't think it was enough, but I didn't voice my concerns. We ran into the barracks. This end was far quieter than it should have been. It had that air of expectation. Our troops were already stretched thin, so we had the foresight to cripple a bunch of the doors forcing the Mutes into a choke point.

A few Geno guards had been posted at every few doors just as back up, but I didn't see them. My guess was that they had abandoned their posts when they had realized all the action was happening elsewhere.

"Something is not right here," Urlack said.

The air smelled of ozone from all the blue shots arcing throughout the ship. We moved slowly forward. Right at the edges of my hearing, I thought I could hear muted whispering. I motioned for our small band to hunch down. You really don't get the desired effect when an eight foot Geno stoops, still looking at about a six and a half foot silhouette. That would have to do.

"What is it?" Urlack asked softly.

"You don't hear that?" I asked.

"From our studies of your species we have deduced that one of the few attributes that you possess better than us is hearing. But our scientists attribute that to the fact that you were hunted for the majority of your evolution, whereas we have been at the top of our food chain for untold millennia."

"Yet you still have absolutely no tact or humor. Go figure. Anyway, there is some low talking up ahead and I don't think it's our side."

"Then the one we killed was a scout," Urlack stated.

"It would appear that way. Any thoughts?"

"Attack," he said.

"Well, I guess we're in agreement. Let's get in as close as we can, though. Make our shots count."

"I hear them now," Urlack said after another fifteen feet of slow moving.

I slowly peaked my head around an upturned bunk. One of the heavy doors had somehow been pried open slightly. By 'slightly' I meant I could walk straight through and have room at both shoulders to spare, the Mutes were having difficulty getting through. The ones already on our side were pulling the others in.

"Twelve and counting," I told Urlack, coming back around to him. "They have two keeping a lookout and the rest are starting to get themselves ready for battle."

"I will ask because I must. I told Drababan I would look out for you. Will you stay behind?"

"Not a chance," I told him.

"I have fulfilled my obligation," Urlack said.

Our shots had to count. Even with the element of surprise, we were clearly out matched in numbers, training, weaponry, size and demeanor. But the one thing we did have on our side was a cause. We were fighting for something and that had to trump all else or we were in a world of shit.

I thought Urlack was gonna go with the whole stealthy thing, so I was wholly unprepared for his battle cry as he rushed past me and leapt over the bed, immediately followed by the four other Genogerians. I had time enough to see Tantor and about a squadron of Genos heading our way but this fight would be decided one way or the other, before they had time to get there.

We caught them unawares, but they recovered quickly. Return fire was already heading our way. Had I been any taller I would have been decapitated as I made my way across the bunks.

Four Mutes lay dead or dying as the first of our band took a round. His body armor was ineffectual against the heavier rifles the Mutes were using. The bolt it shot looked to have a greenish hue to it and was thicker in appearance. Didn't matter much to me, either one would cut me in half. And I wasn't overly concerned about them not being able to identify my remains, considering I was the only human around.

The greater numbers and greater firepower were beginning to sway the tide of the battle, but still Urlack pressed on, overturning furniture as he encountered it, trying to make himself less of a target.

Another Geno dropped. We had to stop but there was no cover. Ahead was certain death and we couldn't move back, we were being pinned down. The cavalry was on the way, we just had to hold on for a few more seconds.

"We cannot stay here," Urlack bellowed.

I was going to have to make up a nickname for him. Maybe General? Colonel? Major? Captain? Yeah, that worked, he was Captain Obvious! The Mutes' fire was ripping through the overturned furniture Urlack had spread around. It was only a matter of time until they got lucky.

The corner of the bed I was hiding behind had landed on a small table and was propped up maybe a foot at best. I ducked down and could see what appeared to be some type of leather-clad feet coming toward us. It wasn't much of a target but I was going to make the most out of it.

My first shot sheared off the foot of the approaching Mute. His face landed less than ten feet from mine as he hit the ground heavily. His face contorted in pain and still he made no discernible noise of his agony. He turned up to look at me just as I drilled him in the skull with another shot, the hiss as the blue round cooked his brain was a little too visceral for my liking. The Mutes had not yet learned where the shots were coming from and another one immediately stepped into my field of fire. I didn't get as clean a shot off this time, but the effect was the same as he landed on top of the one I had already killed.

Hands reached down and were pulling their injured comrade up and away. I had halted their advance for the moment. I was just about to pat myself on the back when my table burst under a couple of rounds, the only thing saving my life was the bed crashing down to fill in the void.

Urlack gave me a thumbs-up and pointed behind us. Tantor was fast approaching with what looked like a full platoon. I saw a few green shots come over our position but those were immediately drowned out by a high volume of our fire.

Tantor stopped as he got up to our position. "They have gone back to rethink their strategy, I believe," he said.

"Fortuitous for us," Urlack said.

"Understatement," I said, finally feeling safe enough to stand. "Thank you, Tantor," I said as I reached out to clasp his forearm like Dee had shown me. He seemed hesitant at first, maybe he thought he would break me, or he had not yet fully come to approve our alliance. In the end he accepted my thanks.

We had lost three Genogerians in the brief but intense fighting. The Mutes lost seven and had at least one injured and out of action. Those were better odds, but this was going to be a costly battle.

The next hour was a stand-off. The Mutes attacked at every point available to them, but were thwarted. We tried to reason with them when we could, but they seemed extremely happy with their lives especially now that they were actually doing some fighting. Didn't matter in the least to them that they were in a battle with their own people—killing was killing.

The only good thing I could say about the whole affair was we were blooding them. It was close to a near even exchange and should have been much better considering we were in the defensive position, but one-for-one right now was still sustainable numbers. I knew the Genogerians were now my allies except for a select few, however, I still carried a great deal of animosity toward them, maybe if I got real lucky they would all take each other out.

I was safely away from the action, pouring over the diagrams of the ship, looking for a way to get around our adversary when Tantor came over with a periodic report.

"The 'Mutes' as you call them are not attacking with as much vigor as they once were. I believe it to mean we are winning," he said.

"Possibly, but I'm thinking they are trying to find a way around us much like we are. I don't think they were expecting so many casualties. My concern is if they stop attacking completely that the high command will stop all life support in these sections."

"They cannot," Urlack said as if he knew this for fact. "That would mean the death of their pilots."

"At any time in the history of your race, Urlack, have not some been sacrificed for the many?" I asked.

He did not answer, he didn't seem too thrilled that I had painted him in a corner.

"What do you propose we do?" he said indignantly.

"I think we have to do exactly what the Mutes and the Supreme Commander are thinking we won't do. We need to go on the offensive. They will not be expecting us to do that and if we can overrun them we have a straight shot for the bridge and this whole thing could be over."

"It is a solid plan," Tantor said. "Many families will be honored with a war widow today."

Urlack looked at me and snorted. "That is a compliment in our culture," he said with merriment. "Humans are very sensitive," he said to Tantor who still hadn't seemed to grasp Urlack's words.

"Dying as a compliment. I'll keep that in mind— don't be offended if I have no desire to be counted as one of the 'lucky' ones. Let's figure out the best place to launch an attack," I said, changing the subject. But I guess I really hadn't.

***

Within the hour we had formulated a plan. It was high risk with a high reward factor. It's easy to distance yourself from the action (and terror) when you are making lines on paper, but when you are standing at the ready point waiting for the order the terror becomes a tangible entity threatening to overrun every other sensation. Why we never made politicians fight on Earth, I'll never know. I would bet everything I had that wars would have been outlawed. Lesson learned, I supposed.

Tantor must have rummaged deep to find some armor that almost fit me. Maybe one of the Genos made some and was planning to give it as a gift to an infant Geno. I know the stuff was pretty effective against bullets, at least the non-steel-jacketed kind. It could deflect some of the Genos' blue rays, but it might as well have been a coating of powder for all it did against the Mutes weaponry.

Some of the Genos were now carrying the heavier rifles, I envied them. I had been offered one, thing must have weighed around forty-five pounds. I could carry it, but it was entirely too unwieldy in a combat situation, I stuck with the twenty pound Geno rifle, still heavy for a human, but at least I didn't struggle to keep it on target.

"Michael?" Urlack asked for at least the seventh time.

"I'm short, Urlack, they won't even see me," I told him.

This was where he usually scowled at me and said I was not being smart in my decision making. He didn't let me down.

The only place our ambush had any chance of success was on the far side of the cafeteria. It had so far been no-man's land (misnomer I know since I'm the only man, but you get the point). The Mutes had tried three times to come this most direct route and had been driven back with their worst casualties of the night. They would not try a fourth.

We had not explored that avenue because, first, we weren't on the offensive and, secondly, it would be their most heavily guarded access point. Yet I had placed myself high up on the front lines. I was glad I was nowhere near the backhand Tracy would dole out if she knew.

There were somewhere in the neighborhood of five hundred of us making this assault. It was really about the maximum amount that would fit in the staging area. There was another five hundred waiting at our rear should we break through with the initial thrust. Timing was going to be crucial, though. The doors that led out were about as wide as a two car garage, that wasn't nearly as big as would have been desired given the size of the Genos and the number.

If we broke through, we needed the reserves to be almost behind us so we didn't get encircled and cut off. If we didn't make it through and needed to retreat and they had already followed us we would be caught in a quagmire of stuck Genos. Now I fully knew why politicians didn't fight; because they weren't stupid. My bowels wanted to liquefy, I was thankful I hadn't eaten much in the last few hours although I far from doubted I'd be the first person who had ever made a hot mess in his pants before getting shot at.

I acquiesced a little to Urlack's desires when he said I should not be in the very front of the charge. I'd seen enough movies in my day to know the first men in a charge usually only had cameos. I won't lie, I felt I was sacrificing some honor for position, but Urlack kept telling me I shouldn't be in this charge at all. There were still all the Genos on the ground that were going to need convincing, and I was the man who needed to be the face of that campaign.

Tantor was at the head of the pack. Even from the middle, I could see his large hand up in the air as he counted down from four. A typical Geno charge involved a lung emptying war cry that I had a very difficult time telling them was not in their best interest this time. They had seen the wisdom of my decision even if they weren't enamored with it.

Tantor finished his countdown. The large doors swung out; from there he would have a short corridor that led directly into the housing for the Mutes. I already heard shooting before we even had the opportunity to move. At first it was slow, small furtive shuffles forward, then we moved to a slow trot, and then we were at a full-on sprint. Or at least I was. If I went any slower I would be crushed. Fuck Pamplona, this was way worse than running with the bulls. Urlack, who had situated himself directly in front of me, realized just how much danger I was in from the rear and with some effort was able to get behind me. Awesome, I'd much rather get crushed by someone I knew.

We were still moving forward but our push was slowing, we had made it through the doors to the Mutes' barracks. It was bedlam, an epileptic's nightmare. Streaks of high intensity flashes were everywhere, I didn't have enough room to bring my rifle to bear and even if I did, I'd only succeed in shooting the legs of the Geno in front of me. There was a fair amount of hand-to-hand combat going on; bones snapping was even louder than the percussions the rifles made. I moved over to the left and the wall closest to me. I let the rifle drop down on its tactical sling and grabbed my revolver.

A Mute must have been sleeping when the whole thing started. It approached me without a weapon. I would have reached down to re-grab my rifle if I thought I had enough time. I planted a .357 round straight into his eye. Genetically altered or not, there was no recovering from that. My view became obstructed as more and more Genos made their way in and fanned out. The maneuver had worked, at least at first; initial contact had caught them with only a small guard presence which had been easily overrun. The Mutes ran to the defense, a fair portion not even taking the time to get their weapons.

Our forward thrust began to stall as more and more Mutes came to the defense. It was touch and go for a moment, but as if on cue our reinforcements began to stream in. We were gaining precious feet at the expense of Mute blood. The floor ran thick with it. Even with a thousand Genos (and one man) spearheading the endeavor, we were still in great jeopardy of being stopped and pushed back or worse trapped. Once the Mutes regrouped and attacked we would be at a serious disadvantage.

This would begin phase three of our plan and the most vital of them all. As the Mutes around the ship collapsed and came to the rescue of their peers, it would be imperative that the Genos who had been in fighting contact with them, move also and pursue them. It was going to be risky to say the least and the body count per square foot would rival anything ever seen on Earth.

I kept my back against the wall, fearful I would get lost in the din I kept moving farther and farther along the side as more beings poured into the cavernous room. I couldn't see the doors I had entered through anymore but I figured to have gone about a hundred feet along the wall before I once again found myself in combat. I had my rifle up and was rapidly engaging the enemy. A couple of shots floated nearby, but I was mostly going unseen, not that I was complaining. I got down on one knee to keep the rifle steady as I repeatedly acquired a target and shot.

I'm not delusional to think I was swaying the battle, but in this small neck of the woods, I think it was safe to say I was a contributing factor. Genos locked in mortal combat with their bigger brethren thanked me as I took Mutes out one by one. I don't know if it was derision on the part of the Mutes or if they did not perceive me as a true threat, but I was really left alone. Maybe that was a downfall of the Mutes they had never been in combat with humans and maybe had little to fear from them. I was doing my part to make them regret that decision. That was, if any of them made it through the day. They didn't really seem like the type to throw in the towel.

"I've been looking for you!" Urlack shouted.

"Well, you found me," I told him after taking another shot.

"We have received word the Mutes are coming en masse."

"Well, that's good, right?" I asked, my shoulder rocking back as I blew off the snout of a Mute.

"Yes, it is according to plan, but until our forces arrive, this will be a very lethal place to be for a while."

I saw his point as the Mute numbers began to overwhelm our small thrust. We would absorb some casualties, where I now fired from would be deep within enemy hands again and soon.

"You should come back with me," Urlack said.

The deck plating was bouncing. I could feel it vibrating through my knees. Oh yeah, they were definitely coming. My aim was being compromised as the vibrations became more intense, and like a stampede of elephants, I watched a huge line of Mutes heading our way. I had never seen anything as frightening in my entire life. The twisted, contorted displays of rage on their faces as they barreled down on us was beyond anything I could explain.

I turned to face the new threat and just began to pull

the trigger as fast as my finger could move. I shot indiscriminately, sheets of Mutes hit the floor as the shots tore into them. I noted that some took notice of me, to stop shooting now would mean I would die by trampling. More than a few of the Mutes went down, tangled in the feet of their fallen predecessors, the newly deceased and dying.

My finger was cramping and still they were coming and I was no longer 'unnoticed'. Murderous intent was branded on at least ten of the Mutes heading for me.

Although this was war so murder didn't really factor in.

I kept firing, I would never be able to get up quickly enough and run for it.

"I am not sorry for this!" Urlack yelled as he snatched me into the air. He had the presence of mind to throw me over his back so I could cover our retreat. Mutes were screaming in rage.

"You are a valiant warrior," Urlack said as we made our way back to the relative safety of the doorway.

I don't know how I felt about those words. Not too many 'valiant warriors' got piggyback rides.

"Thanks," I told him.

Genos were being compressed tightly as they absorbed more of the influx of the Mutes. We only had moments before the bubble would burst and our forces would collapse in on themselves.

"Hold!"

I somehow heard this voice over the clang of metal on metal and the reports of the rifles. "Tantor?" I asked aloud.

"It very much sounded like him," Urlack said, I noticed he had difficulty getting the words out. It was then I felt the wetness on my left arm, blood and it wasn't mine.

"Urlack?" I asked, showing him, my blood-soaked hand.

"It is nothing," he said, as he finally pulled up and put me down.

I walked behind him because there was not anyway I was going to be able to turn him myself. Roughly where I had been was a wound the size of which I suspected would have severed me in half had it got to me.

"Oh, shit. Let's go!"

Urlack seemed to hesitate.

"Oh, come on, I've been through this with Drababan. If you pass out, I'll never be able to carry you!"

Urlack obliged.

We had set up some first aid stations, but they were about as advanced as anything from the Civil War. Anything more serious than a flesh wound was almost a death sentence.

"Stop the bleeding!" I yelled to two previously injured Genos who were back at the aid station so they could do something. To their credit, they grabbed some heavy material and pressed it with maybe a little too much vigor into Urlack's wounds.

I had an idea. I wasn't sure if it would pan out, but I had to try something. The only thing the Genos working on Urlack would accomplish would be to keep his blood from spilling all over the floor as he bled out.

I ran to where we were holding the pilots captive. The two Geno guards here were also wounded and were not combat ready, but guard duty was a different matter.

"Show me the highest ranking pilot" I shouted to them.

They looked confused for a moment, but the less injured one, Jraco, I think was his name, got up and shuffled over to a cell nearby.

"What's your name?" I demanded.

"Tyrendlen," he sneered.

"Are any among you qualified for field surgery?"

"All of us have received basic aid in the event we are on our own," he said lazily, not even sitting up from his rack.

"Could you fix a rifle blast from one of your

weapons?"

"I could," he said. "But unless it's on a Progerian, I won't."

"Open the door," I told Jraco evenly.

Jraco did not know what I was asking.

"Let the field down so I can get in, please." This he understood.

The small hum of the door dissipated and I walked in. Tyrendlen still had not stirred, he was busy staring at the ceiling as if it were the Sistine Chapel.

"I have an injured friend who has suffered a wound at the hands of your mutated Genogerians. I am going to ask you once and only once. Will you help him?"

"I hope he is sent to your hell for what he has done," Tyrendlen responded. "He does not even deserve to go through the gates of 'zrevklet.'"

The report of a .357 round in such a small enclosed space should have been deafening, I barely heard it. At least Tyrendlen did not have to fall far, blood oozed off the cot and onto the floor. Jraco was at my side as soon as he was able.

"Accident," I told him, even though he hadn't asked.

That got some of the closer prisoners' attentions. Some were either right up by the door, trying to figure out what was going on, or as far back as possible, already having a good idea and not wanting to be part of it.

"I asked your leader Tyrendlen for some help!" I shouted. "He was not very willing to do so. I have a friend that has been shot with one of your weapons. He will die unless someone knows how to treat the wound. Tyrendlen said you all have been trained in this type of aid. Until I get some help, I am going to walk up this hallway and kill every one of you worthless pieces of shit! You mean absolutely nothing to me. No, that's wrong, I actually hate and despise each and every one of you for what you are and what you have done to my world. I care more for the bullet I will put in your brain than you. I'm waiting!"

I still had no takers.

"Jraco open the door," I said as I walked to the next cell. The Progerian was staring back at me from about halfway across his room. "Will you help?"

He stood silently. The top of his head erupted into a blossom of red and gray. He fell heavily to the floor, a loud resounding crack as what remained of his head hit the toilet.

The next Progerian was right up by the bars. "I will help," he said softly.

He actually stepped half a step back from the wicked grin on my face. I was killing in cold blood. I had stepped over another line from which there was no way back.

"What do you need?" I asked him.

"We have what you would call a medical kit back at our barracks."

I nodded to Jraco to open the door. Some part of me expected this Progerian to rush me when he realized he was safe but for better or worse deception was not part of their genetic make-up, I would imagine it made for awkward social circumstances when the female would ask if her new tunic made her look fat.

Within ten minutes we were back at Urlack's side, he looked pale, if such a thing were even possible for them. His breathing had become shallow and his eyes were half closed.

"How you doing?" I asked him as I grabbed his giant hand.

"I am prepared to greet the afterlife," he told me.

"I have to turn him over," my prisoner/medic said.

"Got some help, Urlack," I told him.

"I welcome the attempt, Mi-chael, but I fear it may be too late," he said as I helped the medic get Urlack onto his stomach.

The medic pulled the towels off and inspected the wound closely, I couldn't gauge any reaction as he began to dig around in his bag. He pulled out a foil pack that looked suspiciously like a Pop-Tart, but was filled with a silver sand he poured liberally into Urlack's wound. The stench it produced almost made me swoon.

"Infection," the medic said.

I didn't know if he meant what was causing the stink or was just going over an internal dialogue.

Although I think it was the latter as a yellowy, green, bubbling ooze began to spill out of the wound. I thought the initial contact stunk. Even the medic backed away as the medicine did its magic.

The medic went back into his bag and pulled out a hypodermic needle that looked big for a horse. "He needs to sleep," the medic told me as he saw the look on my face.

"Yeah, I know. Most of my time on this damn ship involved sleeping while I was healing."

"Right," the medic answered.

Urlack was asleep before the medic removed the needle. He looked so peaceful. I wanted to join him, maybe when I awoke this whole nightmare would be over.

"What now?"

"I will wait until the wound starts running clear and then I will sew him up."

"That's it?" I asked incredulously.

"You of all people should know how advanced our medicine is," the medic said, not with derision he was merely relating facts. "Will you kill me when I am done?" he asked. There might have been a tremor in his voice, but it was next to impossible to tell and it may have just been my own slant on the conversation.

"Honestly, I would like to kill each and every one of you. You are nothing more than a plague that has descended on my world. You and your kind have wiped billions of us off the planet. I'm not sure what answer besides that you'd be expecting."

"We do not generally run into sentient beings on our missions," the medic said.

"It's not like that stopped you this time. I said I wanted to kill you, I did not say I would. I will let your fate rest in the hands of those you consider your inferiors."

This seemed to affect the medic more than anything else I had said thus far.

"The Genogerians? Surely, you cannot mean this, they are savages barely able to function without our help."

"That's rich," I laughed. "Is that what you tell yourself when you try to sleep at night?"

The irony of the question was lost on him.

"I hope, for your sake, these 'savages' take pity on you." As I spoke the words, the lights flickered and went off, dim red lights came on a few moments later.

"What happened?" the medic asked.

"We beat the Mutes," I told him. "And now your commander has shut off life support to every part of the ship in Genogerian hands."

"But that includes the holding cells," the medic said as if he couldn't believe he was being sacrificed along with the Genogerians.

"How much time do we have?" I asked him.

"Three…four hours at the most," he said, staring at the red light as if it was the answer to the universe.

Who the hell knew, maybe it was.

"This cannot be," the medic said, looking around wildly.

"What's so hard to believe? That your superiors value their existence more than yours? I can assure you that leaders always believe themselves superior to those below them. Just think how you feel about the Genogerians."

"That's different," the medic said angrily.

"Not as much as you would lie to yourself to believe that," I said. Again I thought that was lost on him. "The question now is what are you going to do about it?"

"Do about it?" he asked.

"You're as good as dead. They are not going to turn

the air or heat back on until we are dead or close to death so they can collect us up and make us pay."

What I knew for a small sign of approval flitted across the medic's face.

"Don't go getting yourself all excited, I will make sure each of you prisoners is dead long before we are."

"I have a family," he said.

"So do I—what's your point? You and the other pilots help or we're all dead. Simple as that."

The medic poured another bag of 'sand' on Urlack's wound, when it came back clear he rooted around in his bag and pulled out what I would learn was an electronic needle and thread. He quickly stitched Urlack's wound, leaving a small inch long opening for the wound to keep seeping out any toxins.

He stuffed the equipment back into his bag and then spoke. "I need to speak to some of the other pilots."

"He's alright?" I asked.

"He will be if the life support comes back on."

"Makes sense. Let's go."

I could hear the thunderous cheering of Genogerians who had just defeated their enemy. They cared little for this newest tactic by their former captors, at least not yet. Maybe when the euphoria of the victory wore off but not now.

Tantor came running down the hallway before we had a chance to leave. "We have defeated the Mutes!" he yelled loudly. "I would not have thought such a thing possible, Michael Talbot!"

"It is good to see you, Tantor," I said, meaning it. The warrior had a half dozen minor bleeding wounds but noticed none of them.

"Urlack has fallen?" he asked with alarm, looking on Urlack's prone body.

"He should be fine as long as we can get the lights back on."

"It is not the lights being off that is of a major

concern," Tantor said, as if he were talking to a child.

"Not sure if I will ever get over the differences of how we look at the world, Tantor. I understand about the life support system. This Progerian is going to talk to his fellow pilots to discuss the matter."

Tantor finally looked over and recognized the medic. I saw an internal battle waging in him. For his entire life, he had been taught that the Progerians were superior to him in every way and that he was supposed to, without question, defer to everything he was told to do. And now he was celebrating a major victory over the power that had kept him down for so long.

"You are now equals," I told them both. Neither believed my words.

"I must check on my wounded," Tantor said, extracting himself from the situation.

I walked quickly with the medic to the holding cells.

"I will need to talk as a group with some of the senior pilots. Will this be possible?" the medic turned to me asking.

"No funny stuff?" I asked.

The medic was staring at me blankly.

"Why do I ask?" I said. I motioned for a few guards to come over. "Allow him to grab five of the senior Progerians to have some time together.

"Five isn't enough," the medic said.

"It will have to be," I told him. I wasn't expecting any subterfuge, but I felt it safer to err on the side of caution. "I'm going to check on the troops," I told the Genogerians. "Please send someone to get me when they are done with their meeting."

With a slight bow, the nearest guard answered. "Yes, sir."

Weird, how this is turning out, was all I could think as I headed down the long hallway.

Genogerians were all over the place, drunk with celebration. More than one would stop what they were doing to give me a slight bow. At first, I kept thinking they were just bending down to get a better look and see if I was something worth eating. None seemed concerned at all with their lives now hanging precariously to the viciousness of space.

Tantor was now surrounded by at least a couple dozen Genogerians who were talking animatedly. He immediately got up and looked around. Someone must have told him I was approaching.

"Hello, Michael," he said, rushing to meet me. He clapped my shoulder and almost sent me sprawling. "Come, we have much to discuss." He escorted me to the middle of the circle. "This is the hu-man that has delivered us into freedom!"

Shouts, snarls and hisses ensued. It was actually their method of expressing pleasure, but to be surrounded by it, you would have thought I was in New York City after the Yankees lost a series to the Red Sox.

"I know your species well enough, Michael, to understand the contortions of muscles on your face do not equate to a smile," Tantor said.

"I'm afraid, Tantor, that I have not quite given you the freedom you and your soldiers are envisioning. We only have about four hours."

Tantor laughed. "You do not understand us, Michael. We are all of us here, happy to die in the next few hours if it means we are no longer harnessed to the whims of the Progerians. Of course, we would rather live out our lives in a more natural way, but I will take four hours of freedom to forty years of slavery. And you have given that to us." The cheering started up again.

"Tantor, I *gave* you nothing. You and your men *took* it. You fought for what you believed in. I just gave you the chance to start over, to have a place you could call your own."

"For that we will always be in your debt," Tantor said

with an exaggerated bow, which was immediately followed by the rest of his men.

I could see over all the bowed heads, a Genogerian came running into the room looking frantically around. When he caught sight of me he came at a full tilt.

"Commander!" he shouted. I had no idea who he was talking to. All I could think was this wasn't good.

"Sir, the pilots have finished talking," the guard said. He was still looking at me.

Tantor had turned to look. "He speaks to you, Michael."

"When the hell did I become the commander?"

"With Urlack down for now, the assignment falls to you," he said.

"Oh, hell no. Why not you?" I asked Tantor.

"Perhaps in time, Michael, but I do not yet have the experience to lead."

I wanted to tell him he was wrong. He had already proved he was a leader. But with the whole life and death clock clicking loudly over our heads, I figured maybe today wasn't the best time to discuss the matter.

"You're coming with me, then," I told him.

"I would be honored."

Within a few minutes, I was at the door of the meeting room with the medic and I supposed five of the most senior pilots.

I had about as much desire to enter that room as I did having my balls crushed under a rubber mallet. They looked extremely hostile, but I was to learn they were far angrier their leaders had subjected them to the same fate as the Genogerians than the fact that myself and the Genogerians had put them in that place to begin with. Don't misunderstand me, they were pissed off that the Genogerians *dared* to rebel against their rule, but it wasn't completely without precedent. And being as they considered them inferior beings, they would be wrought with inferiority. But their leaders! That was inexcusable.

"We have come to a decision," the medic told me, stone-faced.

His tone and stance did not leave me with any promise of help from this unlikely alliance. *Well, shit, everything that happened today was an unlikely alliance*, I thought.

"I'm listening," I prodded when they weren't forthcoming with any more information.

It wasn't the medic that spoke this time. "My name is Iserwan," the Progerian said, standing up. It was all I could do to not back up a step or dozen. "We have come to an agreement that the Interim Supreme Commander is not acting in accordance with the laws and regulations that rule the Progerian society, and as such, he must be removed from power."

"We're in agreement there," I told him. "Does your acknowledgement of your leader's miscues mean you will do something to actively remove him from power?"

I think Iserwan was sneering down at me or he was just under an extreme amount of stress. Here he was, plotting with slaves and a representative from a near conquered planet to dethrone his leader. I can't imagine what the sentence on his home planet would be for that high act of treason.

"We can force the commander to yield to our demands," Iserwan stated.

"And by 'our' do you mean everyone in this room?" I asked, pointing to myself and the Genogerian guard next to me.

"I do," he said with some hesitation. "And after we are successful, what happens to myself and the rest of the officers?"

I knew why he was asking. The conquered from his perspective did not have very good lives to look forward to. There were the feeding troughs, slavery, or the games—none were great choices.

"I'd be lying if I told you I had all the answers. And even if I did, I would not unilaterally be able to make those decisions. I would imagine, at least for a while, you would be considered prisoners of war. You would be treated far better than the reception I got. And in time I would think there would be some part of my world that would be carved out for you to start over."

"We would not be allowed to return to our homes?" he asked.

"No," I stated flatly.

"That is a death sentence, Michael."

"It's better than the one you gave me."

"I will have to confer with my officers again."

"You've got half an hour."

"And then?" Iserwan asked.

"I'm going to see how dirty your Supreme Commander wants to get his hands."

Iserwan looked at me for further explanation.

"At that time I will begin to execute your officers," I told him as I walked out of the room.

There must have been something in the set of my eyes because it wasn't five minutes later when I was summoned back to Iserwan's cell.

"Your terms are acceptable," he told me.

'*Of course they are*,' I wanted to tell him. Nobody wants a bullet in the brain.

Iserwan laid out his plan. "Is it getting hot in here?" I asked.

"It has actually dropped fifteen of your Earth degrees," my guard told me.

"Fahrenheit or Celsius?" I asked, not that it mattered; I just wanted to know which standard they were using.

"We do not have much time, Michael," Iserwan told me. "If it gets too cold, our internal systems will begin to shut down."

"Sorry, man, I'm burning up and the temperature is

falling. It's got to be stress. How can I trust you enough to take five fighters?" I asked. The amount of sweat pouring off my body was in direct proportion to the feelings of dread washing over me.

"Because I have told you so," Iserwan said as if this were the most normal thing in the world.

"This is hard for me, Iserwan. Words on my planet do not carry as much weight as they do with your kind. People have a habit of saying one thing and doing another."

"Perhaps that is why we were able to take you over as swiftly as we did." He was not boasting when he said it.

"Perhaps."

"Do you agree to our terms?" he asked.

In exchange for his help, he wanted the immediate pardon of all of the officers in the holding cells. The rest of the crew would be on their own for their allegiance to the Interim Supreme Commander or to me.

I didn't think I had the power to authorize it, but he thought I did and my options were few. "I agree to your terms."

"Are your words as light in integrity as the rest of your species?" he asked as he extended his huge paw.

"No." I hoped I spoke the truth as I reached out and shook his hand. Of all the strikes against my soul, what was one more?

Ten minutes later, Tantor and I were behind the heavy glass partitions that separated us from the launch bay. Iserwan and four pilots were suited up and getting into their fighters. Trepidation was wriggling around in my stomach like a live worm.

"I have dreamed about this, day Michael Talbot," Tantor said as we watched the large doors open up to the vast emptiness of space.

"At any point did it turn into a nightmare?" I asked him in all seriousness.

"The nightmare has been while I was awake," he said

as the fighters jetted out into the inky blackness.

I had made sure Iserwan's communications would be patched through to the entire ship. I could not afford for him to contact the commander directly and somehow undo what we had come to terms on. I was feeling like the idiot that had opened Pandora's box.

Within a minute, the speakers crackled to life. "Interim Supreme Commander, this is Flight Wing Omega leader Iserwan Durenge. I have conferred with my officers and we feel you are in violation of executive order 227.4, willingly placing your troops into harm's way. If you do not immediately restore life support systems to the ship, we will be forced to fire upon the bridge."

It was a full minute without any response from the ISC. A heavy vibration passed under my feet as a blast rocked into the ship.

A startled angry voice screamed through the speakers, I had to cover my ears. "Omega leader Iserwan, your acts of cowardice and treason will bring shame to your family for generations!"

Two more vibrations rippled through the ship. I could hear whatever material this thing was made of popping and groaning as it tried to accommodate for the stresses.

"We can argue all you want, Commander," Iserwan said coolly. "Yet it is you that had initially threatened the lives of your officer core. Turn the life support back on and we will discuss terms accordingly, like the civilized beings we are."

"Civilized, my ass," I said. Tantor looked at me sidelong.

"*Never!*" the ISC screamed.

I gripped the railing next to me as the ship rocked back and forth from the barrage, I wasn't sure it would be able to withstand the onslaught it was under. Tantor began to chant a prayer that was far from comforting. And then as quickly as it started, it stopped.

"Sir, we have a breach on deck 17," an alarmed Progerian said from the bridge.

"We will never yield!" the ISC shouted.

And then there were sounds of a struggle; some grunts, groans, possibly a punch or two and then another voice came over the speaker. "This is Sub-Commander Tuvok, under article 13.8, I have assumed command of this ship."

I had to shield my eyes as the lights blazed on.

"I have restored life support to the rest of the ship. What are your demands, Omega Leader Iserwan?"

Again the ripples erupted under my feet. I thought Iserwan had either not heard the last communiqué or he had rethought his strategy and decided the ship should not fall into enemy hands. And then I realized it was the Genogerians stomping their feet and shouting for victory. I think I would rather take the fighters firing. It was less disruptive.

"Michael Talbot, he is speaking to you," Iserwan said over the speakers.

Tantor handed me a giant walkie-talkie—giant in my hand at least.

"Michael Talbot is still alive?" the sub-commander asked.

"Yes," I told him. I could hear his sharp intake of air.

"You have turned Genogerians against their Progerian masters and somehow even managed to fracture Progerians," he said heatedly.

"You have sowed the seeds of discord among the Genogerians for millennia. I merely watered what you had planted." I hoped I hadn't added a layer of fertilizer too. I wanted to think that everything I had promised Tantor and the others would come to fruition. "As for your officers wanting to help us—what choice did they have when all you offered them was death?"

"And what do you offer?" he asked.

"A chance."

"And what of us? That you now ask to forfeit our positions?"

"I can offer nothing more than you will be treated much better than my kind were."

"No games?"

"No games," I answered truthfully.

It was two hours and five or six minor scuffles later that all of the Royal Guard and all the personnel on the other end of the lifeline, so to speak, were in captivity. True to my word, I let the Progerian pilots free.

"What now, Urlack?" I asked, sitting at the helm.

Urlack snorted. I think it was his attempt at a laugh, but he was much more out of practice than Dee.

"I have never seen anyone but a supreme commander sit in that chair. It is funny to see one as small as yourself with your legs dangling like a child sitting there."

"Don't make me have you beamed off the deck," I told him.

"Beamed off?" he asked.

"Old show, don't worry about. Do we land this thing now?" I asked.

"We cannot. This ship is not designed for atmospheric travel, it will crush under the stresses. It was built in space and is meant to always reside there."

"Have you contacted all the landings?" I asked.

"We have. Most have acquiesced, some will need a stronger show of force."

"Iserwan is on board with that?" I asked.

"As long as he doesn't need to fire upon his own kind, yes."

"Are this ship's defenses restored and manned?"

"The Genogerians are learning quickly. I am unsure if they could repel a determined attack quite yet, though. You have Iserwan's word. He is not human, you have nothing to fear."

"Old habits die hard. I'm glad you are up and about."

"As am I."

"Are you going to run this ship?" I asked him.

"It is yours, Michael."

"I don't want it. I could never afford the payments, the gas alone must be monstrous, and who the hell is going to insure this thing?"

"I know not what you speak of, Michael," Urlack said with unease.

"Relax, my friend. I'm telling you, you would be much better suited to running this contraption than I would."

"What would you have me do with it?"

"I'd rather you put it on autopilot and crash it into the moon."

"We could do that."

I stopped to look at him, I was completely unsure as to his true intention.

"My people are going to want to go over this thing. Will you have a problem with that?"

"Again, Michael, this ship is yours to do with as you please. I will merely monitor it for you if that is what you desire."

"What else, Urlack? I really feel like you're holding out on me."

"I do not think crashing this ship to be a good idea."

"I was mostly kidding about the crashing part."

"There are more to fear in the universe than the Progerians. Only your remoteness in space has allowed you to stay relatively undiscovered."

"Relatively?"

"We had conquered a species that had been monitoring your planet for centuries. They were more interested in your evolutionary development than the Progerians were. At first, it had to be decided if we would spend the resources to send a ship this far out. It was quite possible the aliens we had captured were trying to send us off on a fruitless endeavor. We are not the only ones that know of your existence in addition to that. Conquering ships will be dispatched here."

That sounded far from good. "Ships?" I asked holding up my fingers.

"It is usually two, but early reports had you as a highly intelligent, war capable species. They will send three."

"Lucky us."

"That is not fortuitous."

"Sorry, I forget that it's Dee who understands the sarcasm. Can this ship stop them?"

"I will try my best at one of your Earth analogies. This ship would be equal to an aircraft carrier, and the conquering ships would be equal to your heavy destroyers."

"So head-to-head...not a chance. But the fighters give us an edge."

"Any destroyer is more than a match for a thousand fighters."

I was wondering with the infrastructure of the world below in shambles would we be able to rebound quickly enough to manufacture more fighters and possibly our own heavy destroyer. People have a tendency to do the miraculous with their lives on the line.

"How much time do we have?"

"If we are able to hold off the initial Battle Fleet, they will surely send reinforcement, three to five years, depending on what else is happening in the Regime."

"That sounds like a lot, but I know it's not," I answered.

"There is one more thing you should know, Michael," Urlack said solemnly.

"Urlack, I'm going to need some antacid soon."

"As we were going through the cells we came upon Supreme Commander Valletz."

"He was the original Supreme Commander? Why would he be in a cell?"

"It appears that Kuvlar was going to use him for his

own purposes. Would you like me to have him brought to you?"

"How does your kind feel about public execution? Forget it, sorry. No…let him rot where he lay. On second thought, why not stick Kuvlar in with him, I'm sure they will get along fabulously."

CHAPTER SIXTY-SEVEN

While the rest of the Hill stayed glued to their monitors for early news of the Genogerian rebellion, Beth was busy rifling through medical files.

"Shit, I thought the bitch was lying," Beth sighed as she held up a sonogram of Tracy's baby. She felt her grip on Mike slipping with every developmental cell split of the unborn fetus.

"Dammit," she uttered as she hastily tossed the file back into the cabinet at the sound of footsteps coming back down the hallway.

"What are you doing?" a nurse asked as Beth stepped out of the medical room and quickly departed down the hallway.

"Lost," was all she uttered before she turned the corner and was out of sight.

She headed toward the cafeteria, where a large gathering had assembled to listen for news. Nobody said anything as they waited but there was a calming affect being around so many others.

The majority of her hoped for Mike's victory, but there was a darker part that hoped for his defeat. If he were to die or be defeated she could be done with him. It hurt her more than she could ever have imagined to want something so bad and not be able to have it. She knew her weakness for what it was and even laughed at herself. When he was falling all over himself for her, her interest hadn't been a tenth of what it was now.

When Mike's voice had boomed across the speakers from aboard the helm of the *Julipion*, the Hill had gone ecstatic, it was not something Beth felt that she could share in. Victory did not bring back her loved ones, she was to be alone in this new world and pretty would only get you so far. She purposefully strode out of the cafeteria and towards the only destination she could think of that did not stop in a dead end.

"What can I do for you, Beth?" Paul asked jubilantly as he sat at his desk a large decanter of brown liquid being poured liberally amongst his senior officers.

"Is there any chance we could talk privately?" She nearly had to yell to be heard on top of the cacophony.

"Absolutely," he said, getting up and grabbing her in friendly way to steer her back out to the empty waiting area. "Glorious day," Paul said, beaming as he looked at a picture that was mimicking a window.

Beth only shared some of his enthusiasm. "I'm going to leave here, Paul."

"What?" he asked coming back from his reverie.

"There's nothing for me here anymore."

Paul almost said 'What about Mike?' But he knew that wasn't what she was looking for.

"I can tell by your face, Paul, you're wondering what I'm doing here."

"It's that obvious?"

"Yes, as friends I just wanted to say goodbye."

Paul stared long and hard. "Beth, just because Mike won today, the war is far from over, and you know as well as I do that it will be years before there is law and order established outside these walls."

"I know that," she answered. But in reality, she hadn't even thought about it. She figured as soon as Mike was victorious everything would revert back to the way it had been, why wouldn't people want that?

"I could have you detained."

"For what reason?" she asked haughtily.

"Personal safety. This facility is still a closely guarded secret."

"And?"

"And what else?" Paul asked. "What more do I need?"

"I know once…long ago, Paul, you wanted something more."

"Hold on, Beth, we were kids. A lot has happened since then. And since you've gone out with my best friend, you are pretty much off limits anyway."

"Oh don't pull that man-code bullshit on me. If you think there's a chance between you and me, I'll stay for a while. If not, I'm grabbing my stuff and heading out…no matter the consequences."

Paul was stuck. He didn't know what to say.

Beth waited a moment longer before she walked past him heading towards her room.

"Beth…" Paul began.

A smile spread across her lips as she kept walking, she was careful to not let him see.

"Beth, wait, give me a chance to talk to Mike."

"I'll wait for a little while," she answered as she kept on walking.

CHAPTER SIXTY-EIGHT

Within a week, the fighting on the planet was over. Almost to a being, the Genogerians desired freedom; there were a few hold outs. Some that had never known freedom and did not yet know how to wield it, but they were of the vast minority.

The Progerians were another matter completely. Very few took the offer of peace. Most were still in shock from the rapid turn of events. They had gone from colonizing a planet, to prisoners in their own holds. Some would come around, but I wasn't holding hope out for most of them.

A small colony of Genogerians set up homesteads right outside what was once Atlanta. A militia had to be hastily put together to keep them safe. For a very long time, there would be people that wanted to exact some measure of revenge against the invaders. It was going to take time and knowledge to let people know Genogerians were as much a victim as they were.

Most of the Genogerians understood the importance of learning the technology of their 'masters' so they could better defend themselves against the inevitability of a strike back. They had now tasted freedom and had no desire to give it back.

***

"Welcome aboard!" I shouted to Paul as I came into

the hangar.

His jaw was about scraping the floor as he took in the sights. "Nice ride!" he yelled, with a huge grin on his face. "Bet you wouldn't have to worry about a telephone pole in this thing," he said, referring to his accident a few years back.

A small (growing by the moment) pool of men and women poured out of the shuttle. They looked like they had the pocket protector market cornered. "Did you bring enough?"

"Scientists, theorists, engineers—everyone we could scrounge up. All of them said two years wouldn't be enough time."

"Not really a choice. This deadline is a true *dead*line."

"Oh, buddy, horrible pun. I think you've been hanging with the enemy too long. Speaking of which, I brought a few more folks I'm sure you'd like to see."

Dee appeared in the hatchway and began to descend the steps. He did not look too entirely pleased to be back on the vessel; and why would he? His entire time aboard had been one of death and survival. I moved quickly to meet him.

"Hello, friend." I waved as I approached.

Dee snarled. "It is good to see you hale of health, Michael Talbot," Dee said, coming quickly to close the distance between us. He picked me up like I was a discarded rag doll. I was slightly embarrassed, but it felt good to be swept up in the moment, so to speak.

"Is there something you need to tell me?" Tracy asked from the doorway to the shuttle.

"Tracy?" I asked as I went twirling by. My heart leapt even as my stomach lurched from Dee's ministrations. "You should probably put me down, Dee," I told him.

"I was very overtaken with emotions, having seen you again without injury," Dee said, gently placing me on solid ground.

"It is always good to see you, my friend, and we will

talk, but…" I said, pointing to Tracy.

He turned. "Oh, yes…your mate is here. Have I emasculated you in front of her?"

"It'll be alright" I said, reaching up to smack his arm. I ran up the stairs to twirl Tracy around much like Dee had to me.

"Don't you dare!" she smiled. "I'm not your plaything!!"

"It's good to see you," I told her, placing my forehead against hers.

***

Three billion people died as a direct result of the Progerian attack. Most were killed in the initial attacks, but a good number came from the riots, starvation and lack of an infrastructure afterward. There was nothing much left in terms of government or military. That was also by design of the invasion.

And from the ashes, we had at most a two year reprieve before the battle fleet arrived. Earth, at present, resembled something more along the lines of the 1850s, with the help of the Genogerians and some Progerians, communications would be up and running to the entire planet in a month or so. And then the real work of rebuilding and preparing for the worst would take place.

A team of over a thousand of the finest minds the world still had left to offer worked around the clock to reverse engineer everything on the Progerian vessel. It was believed that factories could be built and have the first human-sized Progerian fighters roll off the assembly line in eighteen months. Paul demanded it happen in nine.

Paul talked to me regarding him and Beth starting up a relationship. I was happy for him on one hand…and a little hurt. It felt a little like a betrayal, but with Tracy getting ready to have our child, I had other concerns on my mind.

And as long as she had him to keep her busy, that meant she would be out of my hair, at least that was how I hoped it was going to happen.

Nobody knows what the future holds. The planet is both a safer and a more hostile place at the same time. Within the new cities that are being built, there is a sense of hope, of camaraderie, of man striving to come out on top against all odds. Outside, lawlessness is the dominant force. It is still very much every man or woman for themselves.

For some, having tasted the freedom to do *whatever* they pleased was too great a treat to give up…even if it were to save themselves or their eternal soul.

I hope you enjoyed the book. If you did please consider leaving a review.

For more in The Zombie Fallout Series by Mark Tufo:

Zombie Fallout 1

Zombie Fallout 2 A Plague Upon Your Family

Zombie Fallout 3 The End....

Zombie Fallout 3.5 Dr. Hugh Mann

Zombie Fallout 4 The End Has Come And Gone

Zombie Fallout 5 Alive In A Dead World

Zombie Fallout 6 Til Death Do Us Part

Zombie Fallout 7 For The Fallen

The newest Post Apocalyptic Horror by Mark Tufo:

Lycan Fallout Rise of the Werewolf

Fun with zombies in The Book of Riley Series by Mark Tufo

The Book Of Riley A Zombie Tale pt 1

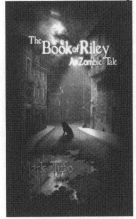

The Book Of Riley A Zombie Tale pt 2

The Book Of Riley A Zombie Tale pt 3

The Book Of Riley A Zombie Tale pt 4

Or all in one neat package:

The Book Of Riley A Zombie Tale Boxed set plus a bonus short

Dark Zombie Fiction can be found in The Timothy Series by Mark Tufo

Timothy

Tim2

Michael Talbot is at it again in this Post Apocalyptic Alternative History series Indian Hill by Mark Tufo

Indian Hill 1 Encounters:

Indian Hill 2 Reckoning

Indian Hill 3 Conquest

Indian Hill 4 From The Ashes

Writing as M.R. Tufo

Dystance Winter's Rising

The Spirit Clearing

Callis Rose

I love hearing from readers, you can reach me at:

email
mark@marktufo.com

website
www.marktufo.com

Facebook
https://www.facebook.com/pages/Mark-Tufo/133954330009843?ref=hl

Twitter
@zombiefallout

All books are available in audio version at Audible.com or itunes.
All books are available in print at Amazon.com or Barnes and Noble.com